Music Notes

by
Lacey Black

Music Notes

Copyright © 2016 Lacey Black

Photograph & Cover design by Sara Eirew

Website: www.saraeirew.com

Editing by Kara Hildebrand

Format by Brenda Wright, Formatting Done Wright

This book is a work of fiction. Any reference to historical events, real people, or real places are used fictitiously. Other names, characters, places and events are products of the author's imagination, and any resemblance to actual events or places or persons, living or dead, is entirely coincidental.

No part of this publication may be reproduced by any means without the prior written permission of the author.

All rights reserved.

Index

Dedication 5
Chapter One 7
Chapter Two 22
Chapter Three 39
Chapter Four 46
Chapter Five 55
Chapter Six 64
Chapter Seven 81
Chapter Eight 91
Chapter Nine 109
Chapter Ten 126
Chapter Eleven 139
Chapter Twelve 149
Chapter Thirteen 158
Chapter Fourteen 181
Chapter Fifteen 192
Chapter Sixteen 209
Chapter Seventeen 218
Chapter Eighteen 242
Chapter Nineteen 250
The Safe Door 269
Chapter Twenty 272
Chapter Twenty-One 281
Chapter Twenty-Two 300
Chapter Twenty-Three 310
Chapter Twenty-Four 319
The Dangerous Door 329
Chapter Twenty 336
Chapter Twenty-One 345

Epilogue 349
Also by Lacey Black 365
Acknowledgements 367
About the Author 368

Dedication

For my parents – all of them.

Thank you for your constant encouragement and support through the journey of life. This means that much more to me to have you by my side!

Lacey Black

Music Notes

Note to self: When your mom hands you a new dress, a bus pass, and a bikini wax certificate, be afraid. Very afraid.

"What can I get ya, sugar?" I ask the young twenty-one year old college student across the bar. He's been staring at my girls for the past fifteen seconds solid. Like tongue dangling out on your chin and drooling all over yourself kind of staring. At this point, I don't even think he knows I have eyes, let alone what color they may be.

"Corona with lime and your phone number, baby," he says with a huge grin. Great. Just what I need tonight. Another winner with a stellar pick-up line. It's not like I haven't heard that one before. Shit, I've already heard it more times tonight than I can count on one hand.

"All out of phone numbers, but I'd be happy to grab that beer for ya," I say as I reach down into the chest cooler under the bar. "Three seventy-five," I tell him with a friendly smile as I pop the top and slide it in front of him with a napkin. As much as I want to accidentally drop the beer in his lap, I have to be nice to the customers. It's guys like him who make bartending so lucrative.

Show just a little skin and flash a pearly white smile and the tips are usually pretty decent.

The pick-up lines? Not so much.

"Keep the change, baby doll," the awkward college kid says as he slides four bucks across the bar at me.

Instead of throwing the smart-assed comment that is hanging dangerously close to the tip of my tongue, I give him a forced smile and drop my shiny quarter in the tip jar. Tight ass.

Saturday Nights are always hopping, but throw in karaoke on the first Saturday of the month, and the bar is packed. I've worked at Chaser's Bar on Madison Street on the lower South side of Chicago for almost three years. There's a ton of regulars that tip well, and a crap-ton of college kids that don't. Chaser's is a great place to relax, watch a game on one of the big screen televisions, and have a good drink. The burly bouncers rarely have to get in the middle of a scuffle, but when they do? It's always on karaoke night.

"The crowd is thickening early tonight," Tiffany says as she sets a case of Bud Light down on the floor.

"It's the first nice weekend of spring. I think everyone's been a little stir crazy after the frigid winter," I tell my boss. Winter in Chicago can be very unforgiving, and this past one wasn't any different. You know, Windy City and all. It definitely holds up to its name. As much as I love Chicago, I'm just thankful that I'm not along Lake Michigan.

"That just means they'll be starting crap early and causing trouble. Watch yourself," she says over her shoulder as she continues to stock the chest cooler with popular bottles of beer.

Tiffany opened Chaser's seven years ago after her ex-husband left her for a younger model. And I mean that–a model. Tiffany is only thirty-five now which made her twenty-eight when the jerkwad took off. Nikki (AKA Slutbag Model) wasn't the only dirty little secret he kept, either. After a little digging, Tiffany discovered that Gordo had a nice little nest egg worth half a million dollars tucked away in an off-shore account in the Caymans. I guess if you want to hide your extra cash from your soon-to-be-ex-wife, then you better make sure you take all of the bank paperwork with you when you leave.

And don't have your password be: Tiffany.

Note to self: Stay away from guys who go by Gordo.

After her lawyer annihilated the assbag in court, Tiffany was awarded a quarter of a million dollars and their small colonial home in a decent suburban subdivision. The first thing she did with her half of the divorce? Tiff purchased this old, rundown bar for a steal, along with a nice pair of Double D's, and she has been content and happy ever since. It's amazing what fake boobs do for a girl's trashed confidence.

"Keep your eyes open tonight. I've already had enough crap-tastic pick-up lines to keep me warm for a long time," Tiffany says sarcastically as she tears down the empty boxes.

It's kind of our thing. We share those incredibly annoying pick-ups at the end of each shift. You wouldn't believe some of the things young guys say when they think they can get a free beer and a piece of ass. Of course, it never happens. Tiffany has been anti-men since her divorce. That doesn't mean she doesn't engage in extracurricular bedroom activities, she just doesn't take home anyone from her bar. And I don't need to get into my past drama. We don't have enough time for that right now.

"I hear ya. I've had the same phone number line already six times," I say as a group of guys saddle up to the bar in front of me. Their laughing and carrying on reminds me more of high school boys at a pep rally than of college and young twenty-year-olds. Tonight's going to be interesting to say the least.

"What can I get you guys?" I ask, dropping napkins on the bar.

"How about a Miller Light draft," the first one says with a huge grin. The other three throw their orders at me as I pour drinks.

"Fourteen dollars," I say as they each throw a few bucks onto the smooth, refinished wood top. I watch as they grab their respective drinks before the taller blond turns around.

And here we go…

"So, I'm new in town," he says with a sideways grin. "I was wondering if you could give me directions to your place."

I refrain from the dramatic eye roll that I'm so close to doing. Really? Do they teach Lame Pick-Up Lines 101 in school now?

"Wow, that's a new one for me. Sorry, but I don't think that's going to happen," I tell him with a wink and smile.

"I could be the love of your life, you know," he adds with another huge smile.

That makes me laugh out loud. "It's a risk I'm just going to have to take," I say before turning towards the next customer. Out of the corner of my eye, I watch as he rejoins his friends a few feet away from the bar. He actually isn't a bad looking guy. Okay, fine. He's hot. His blond hair is a little on the shaggy side, but styled to perfection. Combine that with his high cheekbones, blue eyes, and his handsome smile, he's a pretty hot specimen of the male species.

Unfortunately, I'm just not interested. Not now. Not ever.

"How's your mom, Layne?" I hear over my shoulder. Lee Shore sits down at his usual stool at the very end of the bar. Lee has been a regular for two years, and I frequently find myself chatting it up with him during slow times.

Lee is in his late forties and recently divorced. He started coming in here when they separated as a way to avoid the solitude of his quiet house. Since the divorce, he's turned into one of the regulars at Chaser's. His stool is always left open for him by other frequent patrons, and he never makes a scene. Furthermore, he's probably the only person who knows my story outside of Tiffany and my mom. Lee is easy to talk to and offers sound advice without leaving you feeling like he's imposing.

"She's good. Working like crazy still," I tell the man before me. I've watched the lines around his eyes become more defined and his caramel brown hair slowly fade to gray over the recent months. Even then, aging is graceful on Lee. He's definitely what I'd classify a handsome man.

"Tell her I said hello," he says before taking a sip of the Heineken I just deposited automatically in front of him. Lee and my mom have only met once, probably more than a year ago, but it was enough to leave an impression on him. He asks about her every time he's here. Mom on the other hand isn't looking for love and has avoided my encouragements at giving the divorcee a call.

"You gonna sing tonight?" Lee asks as I mix a Jack and Coke for a young male with a preppy button down shirt and khaki pants. Even his haircut screams country club.

"I don't know." It's my standard response to his regular karaoke night question. The fact is, I need to sing. I need it like I

11

need air. Singing calms me and allows me to take a breath for what feels like the first time in days. It's my solace. My drug.

"You know she will, Lee. If she doesn't kick off karaoke night, you know we'll have a revolt on our hands. And since I'm running low on martini glasses, we can't have that," Tiffany says as she pulls bottles out of the cooler.

And she's right. I will sing. I sing the first song every karaoke night. It's great PR for the bar and has the customers lined up three deep when I'm done, or so Tiffany says. It also gets the natives all primed for the night's singing. Everyone thinks they can sing better than the person before them, right? Plus, no one really likes going first. So, Tiffany and I agreed that I'd start it off every night.

"Do you know what you're singing tonight?" she asks with a knowing look.

Tiffany is one of only two people who know my dreams. My aspirations and desires. She also knows that those dreams aren't obtainable anymore. I walked away from them years ago, so she encourages me by singing karaoke the first Saturday of the month as the only way I can still quench that thirst that still pulls from within.

"I thought I'd do Bob Seger tonight," I say as I blend a margarita.

"'Turn the Page'?" she asks, eyes sparkling with excitement.

"No, I thought I'd do 'Still the Same,'" I tell her with a knowing look. "Turn the Page" became her anthem after her divorce, and I sing it for her regularly. But tonight, I'm feeling like drowning in my own sorrows and misery. So I choose one of my favorites that remind me that people don't change, as much as you want, pray, and beg them to. A person is who they are; good or bad, take it or leave it.

"Good choice," she says before we both turn back to the bar, which is already two deep.

My phone vibrates in my pocket and I grab it quickly to check the message that I've been expecting. It's from my mom.

Mom: *And he's out for the night. Be safe coming home.*

I smile a soft grin as I look at the message. My fingers fly over the keypad and I send a quick reply. When my message is sent, I grab the washcloth and wash down the bar just as the next round of customers takes the few available seats. Yep, it's going to be a busy night.

At nine o'clock, our resident DJ, Doc MZ, cues up the selection that I already shared with him earlier in the night. "Ladies and gentlemen, welcome to Chaser's Karaoke Night," he says into the microphone attached to his earpiece. A huge round of applause erupts from the audience. "Let's give it up for our first singer of the night, Layne."

The crowd explodes again into cheers and catcalls. Tiffany says that half the people here come to hear me sing, but I'm pretty sure it's because her perky breasts are always on display for the masses to fawn over. That and the mean mixed drinks we offer at cheaper rates than the sports bar down the block.

I weave through the standing crowd towards the stage. The lights have warmed the inside of the bar several degrees in the past half hour as Doc played upbeat dance hits to get them pumped up and energized. Tonight, I'm wearing our standard Chaser's logo tee, which is form fitting and accentuates all of the female assets you want accentuated. Plus, it hits right at the top of the pants and occasionally will give a shot of fleshy belly. Add my favorite pair of skinny jeans and comfy black knee-high riding boots, and you have a stylish, yet comfortable outfit for a night on your feet.

"Hey, everyone. Are you ready to have a good time tonight?" I ask the masses and throw them a dazzling smile. Tips. It's for the tips. More cheers and catcalls erupt, ensuring that the alcohol is doing what it's supposed to do.

I pull the mic out of the stand as the familiar intro is piped through the speakers. I give Doc a wink before I start singing the lines I know by heart. I haven't needed to look at the words on the television monitors in years. Calm washes over me as I belt each line out by memory. The faces in the crowd may change, but the music never does. It centers me and brings me more peace than I've ever experienced. It washes over me like a spring rain, cleansing my soul and rejuvenating my spirit.

The song is over just a few short minutes later. I open my eyes when the applause pulls me back from being lost in the melody and notice that I'm on the opposite end of the stage. When the music takes hold, I lose myself so completely that sometimes I don't even realize I'm moving. The music moves me.

I replace the microphone on the stand, throw a wave at the crowd, and start to make my way back to the bar. As I push through the thrones of bodies, Mr. New In Town steps in front of me, blocking my path with broad shoulders. The smile he throws is sinful, and it's hard for my body not to react.

"So, about that address," he says with another award-winning smile. I laugh despite myself. He's determined; I'll give him that.

"Sorry," I say with a firm shake of my head as I steer myself around him and head back to the bar. Tiffany is slinging beer bottles and grabbing crumpled bills when I finally make my way up front. It's time to work.

Four hours pass in a blur of mixed drinks, spilled beer, and decent renditions of popular karaoke hits. Jay and Zane start to clear out the crowd as Doc begins to play some classic Aerosmith. It is part of our nightly ritual that we play and sing along with some of our favorite classic hits as we close up the bar.

We were lucky that only two fights broke out tonight. The first was a couple of guys both vying for the same woman's attention. Typical. Fists started to fly just as Jay arrived to break-up the scuffle before it escalated into a brawl. Of course, it doesn't help when everyone has liquid courage flowing through their veins and you have the encouragements of your friends in your ears, making you feel invincible and bulletproof. Both were kicked out of the bar for the night, along with their friends, and their beloved woman went home with the next guy in line. How's that for a kicker?

The second fight was a chick fight, and those are actually worse. Women are vicious, catty creatures who pull hair and claw with their long, fake nails. Zane was the unfortunate one who was closer to this catfight, and had to pull the women apart while they kicked and screamed at each other in ear-piercing levels. I'm pretty sure only dogs could hear them. A few deep scratches that drew blood and a throbbing headache later, Zane was able to break apart the fight and escort the ladies each to the door. The cause? Someone said the other's best friend's butt was Kardashian sized. Apparently, a Kardashian sized rump isn't a compliment anymore. Figures.

When the last of the patrons are ushered out, Zane throws the lock on the front door and we get to work disassembling the bar. The guys lift the chairs and place them on the tabletops, while the bar stools stand tall on the top of the bar. I move my body to the beat of the music when Aerosmith quickly turns to AC/DC. As I fill the deep tub with sudsy, hot water, Tiffany delivers trays of dirty glasses, stacking them on the counter around me.

"We made decent tips tonight," she says with a hip-bump that moves me out of her way so she can dip her fresh towel in the hot water.

"That's good," I reply noting that my checking account could us an influx of cash.

When the glasses are all washed, dried, and put away on the shelves for tomorrow, I turn to find Tiffany dumping out the tip jar on the countertop. Tips are split three ways. The two bartenders each get an equal third, and then the remaining third is split between the guys. Since it is karaoke night, the tips are generally higher and it's only fitting that Doc gets a cut, too.

After helping Doc load up his van with equipment, Jay and Zane walk Tiffany and me out to our cars. The early March night is still brisk and damp as we make our way to the small parking lot between our bar and the drycleaner next door.

"Drive safely, sweetie," Tiffany says with a hug before slipping into her new Chevy Tahoe.

I follow at a very close distance behind Jay as he leads me to my ten-year-old Honda Civic. It's rusty and sometimes doesn't start right away, but it has been dependable at getting me to where I need to go. As long as I keep my fingers crossed, hold my tongue just right, and do a "please start" chant as you crank over the engine.

"Thanks, guys," I holler as I get inside and turn up the heat. Jay and Zane slide into Zane's black Silverado and patiently wait for me to pull out of the parking lot. Always the gentlemen.

It takes me fifteen minutes to get to the small apartment I've shared for many years with my mom. Parking in the wee early hours isn't usually an easy feat in our neighborhood, and tonight, I'm fortunate to find a spot only half a block down. Afternoons are the worst. Our apartment only comes with one designated spot, which we use for Mom's car, so I'm left to find whatever, wherever I can.

Making my way up the sidewalk, I revel in the quiet and stillness of the early morning hours. Most of Chicago is winding down for the night and traffic is as usual–light. Few lights are on inside of the buildings around me, and I thankfully don't pass anyone as I approach the front of our building.

After a quick shower to scrub the stale beer from my skin, lime from my fingertips, and my face free of make-up, I slip into warm flannel lounge pants and an old concert tee. I'm exhausted and rung out and am instantly lulled to sleep by the soft, gentle snores of Eli. He sleeps peacefully in the toddler bed on the opposite wall of the twin bed I've had since I was a teenager.

As I close my eyes, I slowly relax into my pillow and can't help but to run through the night's events. Singing on stage. The corny pick-up lines. The good looking, blue eyed stranger looking for my address. Dividing up the tip jars so that I could replenish my checking account for food, heat, and other necessities.

Just a typical night in the life of Layne Carter.

*****

"So, I have something for you," my mom says as she places a large garment box on the kitchen table in front of me.

17

Grace Carter is the spitting image of the woman I look at in the mirror every day. Though she stands a few inches shorter than me, her caramel colored hair that she keeps cut at shoulder length and deep green eyes are identical. She's been accused on more than one occasion of being my sister. She was only nineteen when I was born twenty-four years ago and doesn't look anywhere near her forty-three years of age. In fact, she could easily pass for mid-thirties. She always shocks people when she mentions that she's a grandma.

"Why does that scare me just a little when you say that?" I ask as I take a sip of my sugary coffee.

"Don't be mad," she says with bright, consuming eyes. I can already tell that I'm not going to like whatever is in that box.

Eli eats a pancake from his booster seat next to me as I rip open the lid to the white box. Inside is a beautiful black and gold dress. It looks like a vintage as I pull it out, revealing a deep scoop neck and high waist. The dress is sleeveless and hits at the knees. It's retro, gorgeous and just my style.

"Ummm?" I ask, stumped as to why my mom is giving me this beautiful dress. It's not my birthday and I don't recall having any upcoming engagements that would require such a lovely dress.

"There's more." She gathers up her to-go coffee mug and purse from the counter, refusing to make eye contact.

Mom works as a personal assistant at a large accounting firm a few miles away. She's been there for thirteen years, working her way up from a fill-in secretary to being the woman solely responsible for one man's schedule and office. She loves her job, and they love her. Plus, she's fortunate enough that they've been flexible with her schedule where Eli and I are concerned.

I reach into the box and pull out two envelopes. The first one contains a certificate for the salon Mom uses. It's not the amount on the certificate that draws my attention, but the item listed. Bikini wax? Is she serious?

But as I glance over at her as she stands in the kitchen doorway, ready to go to work, I can tell by the way she still won't make eye contact that she is, in fact, dead serious.

"Uh, Mom, I know we're close, but I don't think the state of my bikini line is anything for us to be concerned about right now," I tell her, shocked that she has chosen this moment to give such a personal and private gift.

Mom says nothing as I pull out the other envelope. Dread starts to set in as the quiet of the room takes hold. Hell, even Eli isn't saying anything right now which makes the walls feel like they're closing in on me. Mom remains mum as I remove the eight and a half by eleven sheet of copy paper revealing the date and time for an upcoming flight to Los Angeles.

My eyebrows shoot straight towards the heavens as I look up at her. "What's this?" I finally ask.

Mom clears her throat before answering, "That's your ticket to your audition to *Rising Star*."

I peel my eyes off the sheet of paper that is suddenly shaking in my hand and stare at the woman in front of me. I wait for her to yell, "Gotcha!" but it never comes. She appears nervous, yet excited as she stares down at me. I, on the other hand, am ready to pee down my leg, and it isn't from excitement.

"What did you do?" I whisper hoarsely as I look back down at the piece of paper. According to the document that I'm trying to strangle in my hands, I'm boarding a flight in less than one week and heading to The Golden State to audition for the hit new singing competition, *Rising Star*.

"I'm giving you the little nudge you need–and deserve. This is your chance, Layne. I sent in an audition video of you singing last month at Chaser's and they called. They want you to be on their audition show in California next week. I've already booked your flight, and with the network's help, your hotel room and a car are arranged for you."

I stare up at the woman who has been my sole provider since I was six years old. "I can't do this," I mumble, my mind swarming with dread and fear. "I have Eli," I state matter-of-factly.

"Yes, you do have Eli and I've already talked to Jane next door who is going to help me for a few days. Tiffany has already arranged for Callie and Kyle to handle your shifts at the bar."

I blink up at my mom because it's the only thing I can do. My mind is running a million miles a second in every direction imaginable as I try to process what she's saying–and what it means for me.

"This is your time, Layne. I won't let you sit here and dwell on the crap-hand that life dealt you. Eli and I will be fine for a few days. Go. Give this a try. If you are invited to the show, then we'll cross that bridge when we get to it. But, at least try. At least go and sing the way I know you can. Go and show the world that Layne Carter is as good as all those other guys and girls. Show them you've got it," she says with a motherly smile and a hug.

But that's the thing. I don't know if I've got it. I used to think I could do anything, sing any song and perform in front of a few hundred. But, now? Confidence has long ago been replaced with fear and self-doubt. Performing at Chaser's is one thing. This? This is something completely different. This is terrifying.

"Why the bikini wax? I don't think the judges are going to be looking that closely," I say with a sassy smile.

Mom laughs. "Nothing helps improve your mood and self-confidence like smooth lady parts," Mom says with a wink.

I'll have to take her word for it. Self-grooming in the lady part region hasn't exactly been high on my to-do list for quite some time. You know, with working full time at the bar and raising a toddler. I haven't found the time to add regular visits to the salon to my to-do list.

Note to self: Check into regular self-grooming waxing.

"You've got this, Layne. I don't want you to worry about anything at home. I've got Eli. Besides, a record contract and one hundred grand? Can you imagine what that grand prize can do for you and Eli? What kind of life it will give you both?" she asks as we both look over at my three-year-old son sitting at the table next to me. His green eyes are the same as mine, but his hair is lighter, almost blond. Like his father's was.

I look back down at the paper in my hand. Trepidation and uncertainty still churn in my stomach like bad eggs, but so does exhilaration. Excitement.

Am I really going to do this?

Apparently, the answer is yes.

Chapter Two

Note to self: When the going gets tough, the tough just try not to hyperventilate or vomit on the shoes of the person next to you.

The flight to Los Angeles was eventful, to say the least. Since this was my first time flying, I was filled with excitement at the unknown. The takeoff wasn't as scary as I anticipated, and the ear popping wasn't as bad as I was warned. Then the turbulence started. The constant dropping and shaking of the plane at thirty thousand feet was enough to send even the calmest passenger into drinking-mode. Me? I'd kill for a nice alcohol induced buzz right now. The only thing that kept me from downing five-dollar bottles of vodka was the fact that I'd probably throw up all over the guy in thirty-two B.

And that's not the impression I'm looking to make on the residents of LA.

LAX is huge. Overwhelming. Scary. Other flyers push and move their way through the masses, barely saying excuse me or looking up from their electronic devices. Chicago has its fair share of rude people, but LA seems to be in a category entirely on its own. I've been stepped on, tripped over, and moved out of the way five times. And I haven't even made it to the luggage carousel yet.

With Mom's ancient suitcase in hand, I finally make my way towards the arrivals doors. The sun is shining somewhat brightly through a thick cloud of haze as I scan the crowd looking for my ride. Mom said a car from the show would pick me up, but didn't give me any more details. A scan of the crowd reveals my name in big thick marker on a piece of cardboard, held up by a tall, older man in a hat.

"I'm Layne," I say as I approach the gentleman. He doesn't say anything as he grabs the suitcase out of my hand, turns, and walks out the sliding glass doors.

Well, then…

I follow at a quick pace to catch up with his long legs. He's already throwing my suitcase in the trunk of a black town car when I reach the slick automobile.

"I'm Bill. I'll be your driver today. We are waiting for one more passenger and then we'll head to the hotel," he says as he opens the rear passenger door for me.

I slide onto the soft, buttery leather seats and barely have my feet inside before the door is shut, engulfing me in silence and cool air conditioning; all before I can even say thank you. Twenty-two agonizing minutes later–and yes, I kept track–I see Bill approach the car pulling a large suitcase on wheels. Behind him stands an impossibly tall, hairy man with a shaggy long beard and dreads. Dreads.

The door next to me flies open as Bill waits for the newest arrival to take a seat. I slide over to the driver's side, since I'm apparently in the way, and watch out of the corner of my eye as Lurch slides in. I try my hardest not to stare, but my need to gawk is powerful.

"Hey, I'm Troy," he says with a big, friendly smile.

I'm thrown against the rear driver's side door with a thump as Bill pulls out his best high-speed chase maneuvers and we file in line to leave LAX. "Layne," I say, sticking out my hand as I offer a friendly shake.

His hand is warm and his blue eyes sparkle as he smiles a dazzling grin. For a hairy man, he has an incredibly attractive smile. I do feel a little bad for him as he attempts to curl his large frame comfortably inside the town car. The man is tall.

"Nice to meet you. Are you nervous?" he asks, not taking his eyes off of me.

"A little, I guess," I say.

"Me, too," he confesses, blowing out a large exhale of air.

Troy and I continue to make small talk the entire ride. Sixty long, traffic-crawling minutes pass before we pull up in front of a large hotel. BLVD Hotel is nestled on Highland Avenue in Hollywood and has a sleek, modern feel with deep rich earth tone colors. And apparently, it's going to be my home away from home for the next few days.

"After you," Troy says as he steps away from the car to allow me room to exit.

Together, we walk into the lobby of the hotel and approach the front counter.

"Welcome to BLVD Hotel," the slim, attractive brunette says behind the counter. "You must be here for *Rising Star*," she adds with a smile.

"Yes," we both say.

Ten minutes later, and with plastic room keycards in hand, we're handed a stack of papers. "Everything you need is here. Your audition schedule is right here and the departure times for each group here," she says, pointing to one of the sheets in the stack. "You each have a roommate that should already be here since you are some of the last to arrive," she adds.

"Thank you," we each reply as we head towards the bank of elevators.

It turns out that Troy's room isn't too far away from mine. With the promise to meet downstairs where the contestants are all gathering around dinnertime, I slip into my hotel room. My need to take a nap before heading down to meet the rest of the hopefuls is overwhelming. Who knew traveling halfway across the country was so exhausting?

Before I even have the door completely open, a thick southern accent heckles the hairs on the back of my neck. She sounds annoyed. Okay, she sounds pissed.

"I told you to get me my own room, Richard. I can't share a room with some stranger," she demands into the slim cell phone in her hand. The slam of the hotel door forces her to turn around and face me for the first time. Excitement isn't exactly the term I would use to describe the look on her face. Actually, the *opposite* of excitement is closer. Definitely not excitement.

"Uh, hi," I say with a forced smile as I walk towards the bed that has the least amount of clothes on it.

"That's my bed," she practically growls at me before turning her attention back towards the phone in her hand. "I thought we had a deal, Richard. I would do this show–win this show–and get the record contract. You are supposed to help make sure that no one stands in my way. That includes making sure I don't share a room with trash," she spits into the phone as if it were evil.

I instantly become offended, as any sane person would. Not necessarily because she called me trash but because I realize this is the woman I'm going to be trapped in sleeping quarters with for the next three days. I'd rather be wearing a paper gown with my feet in the stirrups showing my hooch to everyone and their brother at the gynie's office right now. Awesome.

Note to self: Never again complain about your yearly female exam. Ever.

After a few terse words with whoever Richard is, Country Diva Barbie finally hangs up and slams the phone down on the bed. On the other bed–the one that I assume is supposed to be mine–I start to push some of her clothes over so I have room to unpack.

"You can hang those in the closet," she says as she goes about unpacking her cosmetic bag on top of the only dresser.

"Um, I think we might have gotten off on the wrong foot, here. I'm Layne. Your roommate. Not the maid," I tell her directly.

Suddenly, I feel completely inadequate with my appearance. I'm wearing my favorite red skinny jeans and kitten heeled black ankle boots. My retro, faded black tee is loose and hanging over my left shoulder, displaying the strap of my black tank underneath. My face is practically make-up free and my hair pulled back in a no-mess pony. Simple. Travel-easy. Comfy. And has completely left me feeling lacking as I stare up at the tall model-perfect woman in front of me.

"Shawna Reece," she says without shaking my proffered hand. In fact, the way she rolls her eyes at the gesture leaves me feeling like she's afraid to touch me for fear of getting cooties.

Barbie–or Shawna, if you prefer to address her a bit more formally–is wearing a classy pink tea-length dress with a deep scoop back. It flows freely and displays her curves perfectly. Of course, her shoes are tall and strappy and probably designer. Her entire outfit looks expensive as hell and worth well more than the twenty or thirty I spent on mine at the resale, vintage store back at home.

After hanging up my meager belongings in the closet and placing my other clothes in the two available drawers on the very bottom of the dresser–apparently, Shawna doesn't like to bend over–I notice that my roommate has made no effort at removing her clothes from my bed. If I plan to catch a nap before dinner downstairs, I'm going to have to suck it up and move her shit.

I wish I was the type of person to not care about others–you know, like Shawna. I wish I could just pick up her pile and dispose of them on the taupe lounger in the corner. I wish I could just drop them on the floor in front of her fancy designer shoes. I wish I could toss them over my shoulder like some scorn lover tossing her ex's clothing out the window. But, I'm not that person. Not that I don't *think* it. I just can't *do* it.

Instead of throwing a diva fit like High Maintenance Barbie, I decide to be the bigger person and hang up her clothes. Not because I want to, but because it's probably the only way I'll get to lie down on my bed. Lord knows she isn't about to do it.

Shawna's phone rings three times before I have the last of her belongs hung up in the closet. After glancing through her wardrobe, I realize that I am severely underdressed for this whole shebang. I brought comfy, trendy clothes. Not stylish and expensive.

When I finally have a clear bed, I plop down very un-lady like and pull out my cell phone. I had texted Mom when I arrived at LAX, but I want to call before I have to go downstairs. I know it's only been about eight hours, but I miss them already. I've never been away from Eli before, and the only time I was away from Mom was when I was staying with Colton.

Four years ago. And sometimes it barely feels like four days.

I decide to step out into the hall to place my call to Mom. I don't need Judgmental Barbie overhearing my entire phone conversation. As soon as I find a little alcove vending machine area, I dial the familiar number. It rings twice before my mom answers.

"Are you there?" she asks, voice laced with excitement.

"Yes. I'm already checked into the hotel."

"Oh? Is it a nice one?" she asks.

"Yeah, it's pretty cool. You'd like it. Though, my roommate is completely impossible," I say as I fill her in on our first meeting.

"Well, don't let the Country Bimbo get to you," Mom says. She always has a way with words.

"I'm not. How's Eli?" I ask, excited to hear just a sliver of information about my son.

"He did just fine after you left this morning. I called Jane at noon and checked in with her. She said he's fine and was getting ready to take a nap," Mom says.

I smile absently at the thought of my son. "I'll call you later tonight after dinner, okay?"

"Sounds good. Try to relax and have a little fun. We'll be fine so don't worry about us. Oh, and kick ass tomorrow," Mom says with a laugh.

"Thanks, Mom. I love you," I tell her before signing off.

As I walk back towards my room, Troy walks out of his, followed closely behind by another tall, muscular man. He has blond hair and dark blue eyes the color of sapphires. Throw in his walk and the way he carries himself, and he reminds me of Colton. Already I don't like him.

"Hey," Troy says with a friendly smile. "Watcha doing in the hallway?"

"Oh, I called home," I tell him as I linger outside of my door.

"This is my roommate, Ben Atwood. Ben, Layne Carter." I give the newcomer a small smile as Ben continues to stare at me.

"Hey, Ben. Nice to meet you," I say as I shake his hand. His touch is warm and lingers a few seconds too long. You know, one of those handshakes that boarder on creepy.

"We're going down to check out the hotel. Wanna come?" he asks with twinkling eyes. It takes me a few moments to extract my hand from within his without seeming too obvious.

"Sure. Let me grab my bag," I say as I slip back inside my room. Shawna is still there, talking rudely on the phone to whoever is less than fortunate enough to receive that phone call. I feel instant pity for whoever it is.

"So, where are you from?" Troy asks as we hop on the elevator and head down to the first floor.

"Chicago. You guys?"

"I'm from St. Louis," Troy says.

"Nashville," Ben adds.

We find ourselves in a quaint little bar on the first floor. Over a few house brand beers, I find out that Troy is twenty-nine, married to his high school sweetheart, and has four kids. A chorus and band teacher by trade, his wife encouraged him to finally follow his musical aspirations and try out for the show. He loves everything from Bob Marley to Billy Joel and sings an equally eclectic variety. Though he won't tell me which song he plans to sing, he did tell me he's going with one of my personal favorites from Fleetwood Mac.

Ben is as country as country gets. With a deep southern drawl and worn, dusty cowboy hat, he was raised in the heart of Nashville, singing everything from Johnny Cash to Waylon Jennings. Though he grew up singing the classics, he says that his music choices today steer more towards Jason Aldean and Beau Tanner.

"If you get the chance to pick which team you're on, who are you going with?" Troy asks as I take a sip of the brew.

"Well, my first choice is going to be Felix Booker. He's an amazing record producer and I really think I could learn a lot from him. He's produced some huge hits from some award-winning rockers," I say. Felix has this look about him that demands respect. Always dressed in all black, the man's name is attached to some of the biggest artists and albums from all over the country.

"So, you sing more rock music?" Ben asks.

"Yeah, I love Heart and Journey. Bob Seger is another of my favorites. Anything with beat and soul," I tell them. "Just no country."

Ben's right eyebrow reaches skyward. "You don't like country?"

"It's just not my thing. It's so twangy and sad. It's all broken hearts and crying over lost dogs. I'll take an acoustic guitar or a big bass over anything."

"It's not all like that. You find plenty of bass and acoustics in country, too. Look at Beau Tanner," Ben says with the shrug of his broad shoulders.

Ah, yes. Beau Tanner. Tall. Dark. Handsome. Tight Wranglers. Stetson cowboy hat. Anyone with a pulse knows Beau Tanner and it isn't exactly because of his music. In fact, I barely know his music. But I know those dark steel gray eyes and that devilishly handsome smile. You know the type of smile. The one that creeps up oh so slowly on just one side. The type of smile that promises dirty, dirty things to come. The one that gives your battery operated boyfriend a workout late at night. *That* smile.

"Beau has really made a name for himself this past year," Troy adds.

"That's because of his position on the show," I throw out there. "He's only as big as he is because of being a coach on *Rising Star*. Otherwise, he'd be another name on the marquee sign trying to sell tickets."

"Well, however he did it, he definitely doesn't need to try to sell tickets anymore. I heard his last set of shows sold out in under three minutes flat. Fifteen thousand seats. Gone," Troy adds with the snap of his fingers.

"True. I'm going with Beau if I get a choice. I have a country background and it just seems right, you know?" Ben asks with a smile.

"How about you?" I ask Troy.

"I think I'm going with JoJo. She's a little more Joss Stone and her music is great," Troy says. JoJo Warner has a deep, soulful voice. Her range is amazing and every song she writes lately is certified Platinum. Plus, she's as smart as they come, utilizing her business degree from Harvard to manage her own management company. And she's only Twenty-Eight.

"She's my second choice," I tell them.

Sophia is the fourth and final coach. At the ripe ol' age of twenty-two, Sophia is huge with the tweens and teens. Her debut pop hit shot up the charts so fast that they almost had to create a category just for her. And she hasn't looked back since. Three Double Platinum albums and millions of downloads later, Sophia seems to be at the top of her game. Even a recent hotel "incident" can't seem to tarnish the good girl's name. She's practically untouchable.

Dozens of other men and women start to file into the lounge. Ages range from the eighteen to the thirty-year-old cap for the show. People of every race, musical genre, and background. All walks of life, all convening together with one common goal: to be the next *Rising Star*.

"Everyone, we're going to walk down the block and have dinner. You'll be introduced to the producers of the show, *Rising Star*, and we'll run through what to expect over the next three days. Are you ready?" a man in a suit and tie says from the doorway.

I follow Troy and Ben as we head outside. The streets are busy and lined with fast moving cars. Horns honk and birds fly– and I'm not talking about the ones in the sky–as we make our way down Highland Avenue.

The restaurant is your basic family style restaurant. Dark tables and padded chairs with paper place settings fill the open room. High class, it is not. But, that doesn't bother me any. I prefer small and quaint to overpriced and fancy, any day. Our group is led back to a banquet room in the rear of the restaurant. Banquet style tables span the entire length of the room as everyone scurries to find a seat. Troy, Ben, and I grab some seats at the end of one of the rows.

"Is this seat taken?" a petite redhead asks, indicating the seat next to me.

"No, it's all yours," I tell her as she pulls out the available seat.

"Thank you so much. I was just praying I wouldn't get stuck sitting next to that blond viper over there," she says, shaking her head. Further down the row, people scramble to make way for Bitchy Barbie. Of course. Shawna.

"I don't know who she is, but she sure is a snarky thing," the woman next to me says. "Corie Brooks," she adds as she extends her manicured hand.

"Layne Carter."

She shakes hands with Troy seated across from me and Ben on my other side.

"Seriously, I was walking close to that woman and she bitched at everyone within a two block radius. Apparently, she's going to win the whole thing and us peons are just for show," she says with a friendly smile.

"Be lucky you were only close to her for a few minutes. I have to share a room with the woman," I mumble. Eyes practically pop out of the heads of everyone around me.

"Really? You poor thing," Corie says with pity. "I hope she doesn't slaughter you and sharpen her claws on your carcass in the night."

I laugh hard and turn to the woman next to me. I can tell instantly that I like her and we're going to be friends. She appears to have just enough sass inside of that polite, pleasant persona.

"Ladies and Gentlemen, can I have your attention?" The entire room quiets down until you can hear a pin drop. "Thank you. Welcome to *Rising Star*. Each of you was hand chosen from your audition videos by our panel of experts and invited here to tryout. Auditions will take place over the next two days. There are one hundred and twenty-four singers here from all walks of life vying for forty-eight positions on the show. Tomorrow, we start our recorded auditions with the four show coaches. Each coach is looking to fill twelve spots on their team. If a single coach chooses you, they will drop a red flag in front of their designated seat, and you will be on that coach's team. If more than one coach chooses you, you get the final say over which team you are on.

"From there, you will be whittled down until there are four singers on each coach's team who will compete for votes in front of our live studio audience. Each elimination week will be conducted with a live performance show on Wednesday and the live elimination show on Thursday. If you are chosen this week as a team member for one of our four coaches, you will be asked to return in two months when we begin our live shows. From there, you will have a potential eight to ten week show commitment. Those chosen to fill the twelve vacant positions on each coach's team are required to attend a meeting on day three of this week to go over more details of the show. Does everyone understand?"

We all nod our heads, knowing that the contract we signed before we even boarded the plane spelled out the rules. If I'm chosen to come back for the live shows, I'm theirs for a minimum of eight weeks. Don't ask me how I'm going to pay my bills because I don't know. Mom convinced me that she could handle everything at home and had been saving for a while for this moment. I couldn't say no. And believe me, I tried.

The hardest part is being away from Eli for any length of time. How am I going to sustain a separation of two to three months? Will he forget me? Will he even notice I'm gone? Again, Mom sensed my internal struggle and promised nightly FaceTime chats if we get to that point. My son won't forget me, and win or lose, will be waiting for me when I get home.

But that's a bridge I'll cross if I make it to the live show. *If.*

"What group are you guys in?" Corie asks between bites of her salad.

"We're in the last group of day one," Troy says about him and Ben.

"I'm in the first group of day two," I confirm.

"I'm in the first group of day one," Corie says. "I think they're going by room number. My roommate and neighbors are in the same group I am."

After we walk back to the hotel, we all decide to head up to our rooms for the evening. Nerves are coursing through the entire hotel so thick you can practically see them bouncing off the walls like a little rubber ball. Throw in the fact that everyone seems to be sizing up the competition. Everywhere you look, someone is checking you out; gauging your strengths and weaknesses just by appearance alone.

While Troy and Ben are right down the hall, Corie's room appears to be on the opposite side of the hotel. Before we part ways, we arrange to meet for breakfast in the morning. Well, if our nervous stomachs will allow us to eat anything. I'm not sure how much food my stomach will handle tomorrow.

Shawna makes her grand entrance into the room just as I'm exiting the bathroom. Donning my favorite pair of flannel boxers and vintage Kiss concert shirt, I scramble into bed and grab my phone. I dial that familiar number through FaceTime and wait for the answer.

"Hi, honey," my mom says as soon as her happy face fills the screen.

"Hi, Mom," I reply with an equally joyful smile.

"How was the first day? Did you make any new friends?" she asks eagerly.

"Uh," Shawna says loudly as she grabs something silky from the top drawer.

Ignoring Snooty Barbie as she gathers up her belongs and steps into the bathroom, I fill Mom in on the dinner. I tell her about the conversations I've had with Ben, Troy, and Corie, avoiding mentioning the extent of my anxieties.

"Is your roommate still foul?" she whispers into the screen.

I award her with a small chuckle before answering. "Rabid dogs won't even go near her," I whisper as I tune out the singing coming from the bathroom.

"Do you want to say hello to Eli? He's getting ready for bed," Mom says.

The face of my greatest joy fills the small screen. I blink back tears as he tells me in great detail about playing with Jane this afternoon. "And then we sorted all of the balls by colors. The blue ones were my favorite. There were six of them. I had some grapes with lunch. But not the green ones cause I don't like the green ones. We watched some cartoons too. Did you know Tom is a cat and Jerry is a mouse? Jerry is my favorite because he's fast. I like to run. Did you see Tom and Jerry on TV?" Eli says practically in one long, breathless sentence. You couldn't scrape the smile off my face with a putty knife.

After thirty of the fastest minutes known to man, Shawna finally emerges from the bathroom, a cloud of steam billowing behind her. She looks fresh, clean, and fashionable as she struts towards her queen sized bed in a long, satin nightgown. Hairbrush in hand, I watch as she begins to count to one hundred, each number representing a stroke of the brush through her golden locks.

"I should probably head to bed," I tell my mom as longing starts to settle deep within my chest.

"Don't you worry about me and Eli. We are just fine. I want you to do your thing and sing for those judges like I know you can. I love you and am so proud of you," Mom says as I struggle to rein in my tears.

"I love you, too," I croak over the lump in my throat.

When I hang up the phone, I just start to reach for the remote. "It's about time you finished that phone call. Some of us require beauty sleep. Though, it looks like you could use a few day's worth of sleep to catch up," Shawna snipes.

Bitch.

Note to self: Accidentally drop her toothbrush in the toilet tomorrow morning.

"Yes, well we can't all be as fortunate as you," I reply with as much sarcasm as I can muster.

I decide to forgo the television. There's probably not anything good on anyway, but I don't really want to listen to

Shawna complain and moan all night about the sound or the show I pick. So I settle for Facebooking and Internet browsing.

An hour later, my eyes are finally droopy and my hands are numb from blood loss. Shawna fell asleep with her iPod securely in her diamond-studded ears about thirty minutes ago, so I roll over and try to get comfy. My mind automatically goes to images of Eli's bright eyes and big, toothy grin. He's my other solace. He brings me inner peace like no one person ever has before. He has no clue that he saved my life before he was even born. No clue of the power he holds over me. In his three short years of life, he is everything to me.

I hold on tightly to the images of my little boy as I slowly succumb to sleep.

Chapter Three

Note to self: Take up knitting. Basket weaving. Sudoku. Anything is better than staring at four walls with a raging prima donna and listening to country music all day.

Just when my tolerance of shitty music has hit its limit, a knock sounds at the door. I practically throw myself at the solid wooden gateway, fumbling with the doorknob in my excitement to get it open. It has been three hours since we returned to our room after lunch. Three long hours while Shawna plays every female country song known to man. And if I don't get out of this room quick, I will slowly bleed out every ounce of blood my body contains through my ears. I. Can't. Take. It. Anymore.

Corie is all smiles as I open the door.

"How did it go?" I ask with an equally bright smile.

Corie looks over my shoulder and sees Shawna lounging in the chaise while flipping through a fashion magazine looking completely bored and uninterested in our guest. "Can we go somewhere else?" she whispers.

"Abso-freaking-lutely!" I exclaim. Grabbing my bag and keycard, I follow her out the door and towards the bank of elevators.

As soon as we're enclosed in the privacy of the elevator, I turn to see her huge smile. It's infectious and you can't help but smile right back at her. Corie is practically glowing as we make our way to the lounge on the first floor.

"Spill," I tell her as we find two empty seats at the bar.

"Oh my God, it was so exciting and so scary all at the same time. I can't believe I just sang in front of those four people," she says in one quick breath. "I thought I was going to die from nerves."

"So, did you make it?" I ask as the bartender places to draft beers in front of us.

"Well, let me start at the beginning. That room is pure intimidation. When you walk in, all four coaches are sitting at a long table. Felix, JoJo, and Sophia each smiled at me while Beau kept his head down and didn't make eye contact. It was like he was waiting to hear me sing to form his first impression. The very first thing you do is introduce yourself. They asked me about where I was from, my musical inspirations, and my song selection. Then, your chosen music starts. It was the longest two minutes of my life. They all sat there, straight faced, without giving up any inclination as to what they were thinking or whether they liked you, until the very end. I was just starting to think that I wasn't going to make it when JoJo flipped her flag! JoJo freakin' flipped her flag! I practically started jumping up and down and was barely able to finish the song. She even got up and hugged me when I was finished. Then, I was out the door."

I absorb what she said and return her huge, flashy smile. The excitement and energy is radiating off her in tidal waves of delight. "Congratulations, honey," I tell her with a big hug. I'm happy to know that I honestly mean it. Even if I don't make it on the show, I'm happy that Corie is getting her shot.

"Have you heard from the guys yet? Are they back?" she asks as she wipes tears from her eyes.

"They're not back yet. They left at two o'clock. Since they're the last group to go, I can't imagine them getting back before six, right?"

"Yeah, you're probably right. At least I don't have to head home tomorrow," Corie says. "I get to stay until Thursday."

True. Now that Corie was chosen for a team, she gets to attend the big meeting on Thursday. I only hope that I'll be attending that meeting with her. Otherwise, this has all been for nothing.

At six-thirty, everyone is gathering on the ground floor when the final van returns to the hotel. I notice the group waiting is slightly smaller than it was the night before. Eliminations have been made and those hopefuls are now disappointed, returning home to their everyday lives. Corie and I watch as Troy and Ben each make their way out of the van. Their smiles aren't mistaken. There's no camouflaging their excitement. They're in.

"I can tell by the way you're smiling that you both have good news," Corie says with an equally bright smile.

"You first. Did you get in?" Troy asks Corie.

"Yes!" she exclaims, throwing her arms around his large chest. She doesn't quite get her arms wrapped around him, but that's okay. Troy picks her up and swings her around like a rag doll. "I'm on JoJo's team!"

"Congratulations, darlin'," Ben adds with his own hug.

"So, now you two," she says.

"We're both in," Ben exclaims.

"What teams did you get?" I ask as others around us eavesdrop on our conversation.

We slowly start to make our way towards the restaurant as Troy says, "I'm on Beau's team. Both he and Sophia flipped their flags. Even though Sophia has a lot to offer as a coach, I just felt like Beau was the better fit for me." I nod in agreement.

"And I'm also on Beau's team. He flipped his flag after I got into the chorus of the song. As soon as he flipped, Felix and JoJo both flipped, too. It was a no-brainer for me being that he has the country background, and he was the one I wanted."

"So you're both on Beau's team. That's awesome," I tell them as we make our way to the back room of the restaurant. Many empty seats are now scattered around the room, and after tomorrow's round of eliminations, there will be even more. I just hope I'm not one of them. Especially with all three of my new friends each making it to the live show.

"Are you ready for tomorrow?" Corie asks me while we enjoy our dinner.

"As ready as I'll ever be. I wanted to practice a bit this afternoon, but Superstar Barbie was always in the room. I guess I'll just have to wait until I get there tomorrow morning," I say.

"Come down to my room. My roommate got the boot, so I'm sleeping solo tonight. You can come down and practice a bit," Corie offers.

"I may just take you up on it," I reply, though the thought of leaving Shawna alone in our room for any length of time doesn't sit well. You never know what she may have planned.

Note to self: Buy a new toothbrush before you go to bed tonight. Just in case...

Dinner is pleasant as we listen to those around us recount their auditions. I'm sitting near three people on Felix's team, one on JoJo's team, two on Sophia's team, and one other on Beau's team. I wish we could have watched their auditions–you know, check out the competition, and all.

Later that night, after a twenty-minute phone call to Mom and Eli, I head over to Corie's room. She has her stuff spread out everywhere since her roommate is gone, but makes a little room for me on the other bed. I feel like a girl at a sleepover suddenly, which is a crazy feeling because I was never one for girl-talk and sleepovers. I was more of the sneaking out and cuddling with your boyfriend in the backseat of his dad's old Chevy kind of girl.

"So, what are you singing?" she asks.

I haven't told anyone about my song selection yet. In fact, the week prior to coming to Los Angeles, I changed my mind probably ten times. Every song was too happy or too sad. I have so many that I love to sing that it was hard to decide.

"I'm singing 'Lovin', Touchin', Squeezin' by Journey."

"Really? I love that song. Let's hear it," Corie says from her post, cross-legged and wide-eyed on the other bed.

I jump straight in, not afraid to sing in front of my new friend. The lyrics roll off my tongue so naturally it's as if the song was made for me. And, in a way, it was.

"Wow, you're a Shoo-in! That was amazing," Corie says when I finish the song.

"Thanks. I really connect with that song and it's easy to sing the words when you feel them so deeply, you know?" I ask without really thinking about what I'm saying.

"So, you were cheated on?" she asks in response to my off-the-wall comment.

I look at her for several heartbeats before I finally answer. "Yeah. I was cheated on."

"Oh, I'm sorry. That sucks," she says. The silence between us is louder than the song I just sang.

"So, do you have a favorite movie?" she asks, breaking the ice and steering the conversation to safer territory.

And just like that, we're talking like old friends. I learn all about her life outside of the audition, and I find myself easily sharing some of the details of my life that I usually guard intently. Of course, I steer clear of the Colton saga, which includes Eli.

An hour later, I'm heading back to my hotel room. Just before I press the button for my floor in the elevator, I remember my toothbrush fear and decide to detour down to the lobby and snatch a new, complementary one. A girl can never be too careful when she has a crazy, diva roommate from hell.

When I make it back to my room, the alarm clock on the nightstand between the beds says ten-thirty. Shawna is softly snoring in her bed; satin eye mask covering her freshly scrubbed face. She looks beautiful, even in her sleep. She's the kind of woman who wakes up with perfect hair, glowing skin, and as fresh as spring rain. And then she opens her mouth and talks, and it's like the devil reincarnated as a blond with big boobs.

I bet her manicurist cringes every time she walks through the door.

It takes me longer than usual to fall asleep. I'm edgy and fidgety and know exactly what is causing it. I tried a shower to relieve some of the tension, but I ended up running out of hot water halfway through. Apparently, Conceited Barbie took an extra-long shower this evening.

After flipping through all of the channels three times, I end up turning off the television. Even if I actually found something worth seeing, trying to watch it on mute doesn't exactly do it for me. Even if I found *Friends,* which I've seen every episode at least forty times, I'd still be hard-pressed to enjoy the show. Reading is out and the Internet proves to be useless.

As I toss and turn for the better part of another hour, my mind continues to wander to the judges and my audition tomorrow. What if no one throws a flag? What if they laugh me off the stage? And that shit will probably be broadcasted front and center on the first show they televise in a few months. Hell, they'll probably use it in all of their promotional coverage leading up to the show! Shit, people will YouTube it. I'll be the laughing stock of Chicago. Of the Midwest. Of the United States. I'm going to be the next Justin Beiber or Miley Cyrus. Christ! I'm going to be that Justin guy from the first season of American Idol. No one remembers his name.

Sleep doesn't come until the early morning hours, and even then it's sporadic and light.

Welcome to the longest night of my life.

Chapter Four

Note to self: Sing like no one is listening. And in case they really aren't listening, chase your dreams with a shot of tequila.

Would you believe that I overslept this morning? Shocker, right?

I was lost in a fitful dream where Sophia and JoJo were demonstrating the proper ways to give bikini waxes when a distant door slamming pulls me out of my nightmare. I shudder as I recall the great detail of the dream–or nightmare, as I prefer to call it– and it took me several minutes to rouse myself out of my coma.

The door slamming turned out to be my hotel room door. The door leading to the hallway. The same hallway Shawna just entered to go meet up with our group for the audition.

The audition!

I jump out of bed and take quick stock of my appearance. I have to be downstairs and in the departing van in fifteen minutes. I grab the vintage dress that my mom purchased for me and throw it on my body with way less finesse than normal. Thank God I took a shower last night.

My hair doesn't look too bad considering I washed it last night as well, so I quickly brush it out and pull it back in a sleek ponytail at the nape of my neck. The dress fits like second skin and, with my vintage black ankle boots, I appear sheik and retro. Stylish. With a quick sweep of dark eye shadow, a few swipes of black mascara, and a quick–yet thorough–brush of my teeth with my new toothbrush, I'm out the door. No time to spare.

I'm the last one in the bus so I squeeze into the only available seat left. Shawna sits in the row behind me and smirks as she plays on her smartphone, all while I'm trying to settle my racing heart.

Note to self: There is no such thing as an "accident" anymore. Her toothbrush is getting dipped in toilet water.

The ride to the studio is fairly quick by Los Angeles traffic standards. The buzz inside the vehicle bounces between excitement and vomit-inducing nerves. I've flip-flopped between the two emotions so many times myself that I might actually feel both–simultaneously. Nervous chitchat fills the time as we pull up in front of the large building. Then, silence ascends the now motionless vehicle.

And I forget how to breathe.

We're filed inside and led to a large vestibule. Since we're the first group of the day, the room is empty and lifeless. The ceilings are huge and echo as we all settle into the chairs provided. Women immediately begin digging out compacts and hair products while the men try to relax and warm up. Groups form as warm-up runs begin around the room. While the person standing next to you may be your biggest competition, everyone seems to be helpful and friendly towards his or her neighbor.

Everyone except Shawna.

The vibe around her is fearful. Her appearance can only be described as perfection in her stylish dress with a country feel. Her black leather cowboy boots are obviously brand new and expensive. Her blond hair flows gracefully down her back, towards a stunning black dress. Even as beautiful as she is, everyone avoids her like the plague as she runs through a few warm-up solo exercises. She has a loud and powerful voice, hitting all the notes with precision and ease. It's evident that she's going to be a frontrunner in the race for the final positions. Dammit.

As names are called, I run through some warm-ups with a girl named Beth. She's friendly and sings well, yet you can clearly hear the nerves in each note she sings. Unless Beth can pull it together quickly and calm her shaky voice, I don't think she's going to be happy with her audition today.

Smiles actually return to the crowd as Shawna is called back. Even those that have already been cut from our group wear smiles now that she's out of the room. I've watched alongside of everyone else as five of the twenty in our group have come out smiling. I am one of the last to go, though, and I hope and pray that they haven't hit some sort of quota already for this group. Especially when Shawna comes out of the room with a beaming smile.

Clearly she's in.

And if you had any doubt whatsoever, when she proudly announces, "Meet the newest *Rising Star*," well, that pretty much seals it.

My name is called next so I have little time to dwell on the fact that Shawna moves on to the next round. Right now, I need to focus on singing my song and impressing the coaches. Just one. That's all I need is just one to flip a flag.

When I enter the room, my lungs fail me. Their sole function in life is to provide oxygen in and out of my body. Yet, that one simple job, they can't seem to do right now. I walk into the center of the room and give the coaches my best smile, and pray they can't see the extent of my nervousness.

They all return my smile. Well, three out of four. As Corie mentioned yesterday, Beau's eyes are cast downward as he avoids looking at me. I'm not sure if I feel relief that he's not looking at me or if that makes it worse.

"Good morning," Felix says with a big smile. He's so much better looking in person. Dressed in all black, the black man's smile is infectious as his dark eyes take in my appearance from head to toe without making me feel violated.

"Hi," I respond with a nod.

"So, tell us who you are and where you hail from," JoJo says.

"My name is Layne Carter, and I'm from Chicago," I respond.

"What are you going to sing for us today?" Sophia asks as she twists her dark brown locks around her fingers.

"I'm going to sing Journey today."

"Okay, we're ready," she responds with a blinding white smile.

Just as the intro starts–low and slow–I notice Beau sit up straighter in his chair. While he appeared to be slouchy moments ago, now he appears eager and anxious. He still hasn't looked up, but he seems to be all ears all of a sudden.

"*You make me weak,*" I sing as I close my eyes and let the music wash over me. I love how this song starts seductively, sexy, before it turns into something entirely different. A lover scorned. Each note, word, line is sung with feeling and heart. My soul is pouring into the song as I give it everything I have. The song concludes with a much shorter version of the popular "Na na na na na" part since time is a major factor here. When I finish, I finally open my eyes. I didn't realize that I kept them closed the entire song, but I'm standing in a different spot than I started and I'm staring at flags.

Four flags.

"Wow," Felix says with a shocked expression on his handsome face.

"That was amazing," JoJo adds with a huge grin as Sophia shakes her head eagerly next to her.

Then my eyes finally land on the fourth coach. His steel gray eyes are fixed so intently on me that I'm afraid I might actually burst into flames from the heat of his gaze. Unexpected desire courses recklessly through my body so fast and out of control. I take a step backwards just to try to alleviate some of the sexual tension I suddenly feel from one look from this man.

Yowzers.

"Beau, I can't believe you threw your flag so fast," Sophia says. "You seriously had it thrown before she finished that first line," she adds with the shake of her head.

Beau Tanner has yet to speak. I'm trapped in the heat of his eyes and the rest of it just fades away. The other coaches. The room. The reason for my trip to LA. Gone. Now, it's just Beau and me.

"Hello! Earth to Beau! What made you throw your flag so fast?" Sophia asks with a firm voice.

"I, uh…" he starts before clearing his throat. His eyes are like missiles shooting straight at me from underneath the brim of his low cowboy hat. "I just instantly liked what I heard. I knew, in that moment, she was the one I wanted," he adds in that deep, rich, and incredibly sexy voice that almost makes my panties erupt in a blazing inferno. Throw in the fact that it didn't entirely feel like he was solely referring to my singing, and I'm practically a big pile of hormonal mush on the hardwood. Shivers of something foreign sweep through my body.

"I agree. That was amazing, Layne. You have an outstanding voice, and by the looks of it, all four of us agree. You're on to the next round. Now, you just have to tell us what team you're going to be on," Felix says with another dazzling smile.

I look over at the judges as I recall my original thought process for choosing a team. Choosing Felix's team seems like the logical way to go. He can provide me with much needed direction from the producer side of the business. Yet, when I look at Beau, his steel eyes intoxicate me like never before. I feel a connection with him that I can't explain. Sure, it's a connection that scares me a little, yet it completely leaves me yearning to find out more. Why do I feel this way about him?

"Beau," I say without even really processing the word. It's one word and it seals my fate on this show. Whether it's the right choice or not, I am on Team Beau.

I exit the room in a haze. I barely recognize the disappointed looks on the other three coaches' faces when they learn that I didn't choose them. I hardly recall the directions given by Felix right before I vacated the room. The only thing I noticed was the intensity in those hypnotic gray orbs. Eyes that I will be seeing again. Very soon.

Other contestants wait to see whether I wear a smile or a frown. I don't think the audition has completely sunk in as I'm swept up in the crowd. The next group of hopefuls have arrived, making the vestibule crowded and suffocating, as if all of the oxygen in the room is being sucked up by everyone else, leaving little to no air for me.

"Oh, she didn't get in," Shawna mocks with fake pity from behind me. "Too bad for you," she says with a snide grin.

"Actually, I got in," I tell her flatly. Saying those words out loud finally helps everything sink in. The past ten minutes finally starts to come back to me in full force, and I can't hide the smile that spreads across my face.

I got it.

Beth, while disappointed for herself since she wasn't chosen, gives me a huge hug and warm congratulations. I pay no attention to Beast Barbie behind me and instead welcome the congratulations from everyone else. It's surreal and almost feels like an out of body experience. I can clearly see the faces of those around me, but it's like I'm not actually here.

Keeping to myself, we make our way back to the hotel. My mind races as I mentally prepare for the next phase of the show. I'll fly out on Friday morning, but with the knowledge that I'll be making a return trip at the end of May. Believe it or not, I'm actually coming back to Los Angeles to perform on *Rising Star*.

The thought is so exciting and completely terrifying at the exact same time.

Troy, Ben, and Corie are waiting for the van when it pulls up. I can't contain the irrefutably thrilled smile that spreads wide as I see my three new friends. I'm barely out of the van before I'm encompassed in a tight group hug.

"We all got in! How amazing is that?" Corie says.

"Come on in to the lounge and you can tell us all about it," Ben says with a lingering, almost overfriendly glance.

I follow the group inside the hotel. Some veer off towards their respective rooms. Packing. Many are going home after today. We make our way into the lounge and order soft drinks since it's not even noon yet. Not that I couldn't use a celebratory drink or two right about now, but I refrain from indulging in alcohol to fuel our excitement.

"So?" Corie asks as she takes a sip of her ice tea.

"I was picked by all four coaches," I confess without really making eye contact with them.

"Seriously?" Ben asks.

"Yep. I can't believe it myself," I admit.

"So, you're on Felix's team then?" Troy asks.

"Actually…" I start and then stop, taking a deep breath before I continue. "I'm on Team Beau."

Three sets of shocked eyes stare back at me. I couldn't have shocked them more right now if I had actually tried.

"But…I don't…wait. Beau is country," Ben finally spits out.

"I know that. It's just when I was up there and they were all staring at me, there was something in Beau's gaze that made me stop and actually consider him. I hope I didn't just make a huge mistake," I mumble before gulping down huge swigs of cold diet cola.

"Honey, nothing about Beau Tanner is a mistake. If you chose him, then there must be some reason. Like fate or destiny," she says with a wicked grin which results in an eye roll from Ben.

"Well, I don't know about that, but I definitely felt like it was the right choice in the moment," I add.

"Besides, he's completely hot, and now you get to stare at his gorgeous face all the time," she adds with a giggle. I fight to keep the smile at bay, especially when Ben glowers at her comment as if he just ate something gross.

Eventually, everyone around me goes on to talk about the show and what he or she needs to do over the course of the next several weeks to prepare. My mind wanders back to dangerous, uncharted territory. Beau's gaze had pulled me in so deep that I could have drowned in a sea of those smoky eyes. I felt something way more than a crush or excitement when our eyes locked. I can't describe it or explain it, but one thing's certain: I know I'm never going to be the same again.

Chapter Five

Note to self: Dress for success. Or dress like yourself and pray no one notices the difference.

I've spent the past six weeks working as many extra shifts as I can and squeezing as much one-on-one time with Eli that I can possibly manage. But, the time is flying by, and before I know it, it'll be time for me to head back to LA.

Mom and I are going shopping this afternoon to grab a few new tops and pants for my looming trip. I don't need to bring anything for the show since they have their own stylists whose sole purpose for being there is to dress me. But I'll have plenty of other moments that will be recorded and broadcasted to the viewing audience. Plus, at the post-audition meeting, we found out that parts of the hotel and all practices will be streamed to their website so the audience will have twenty-four-seven access to the contestants. Awesome.

"What do you think of this?" Mom asks as she holds up a loosely knitted gray top. The deep, rich color instantly reminds me of a certain cowboy's eyes that I'm trying not to think about. Six weeks of trying not to picture his face, and six weeks of failing miserably. Beau Tanner invades my dreams almost nightly.

"I really like it. With a burgundy or purple cami underneath, it'll be great," I tell her as I grab the shirt from her hands.

"Go with the purple. When you had that streak in your hair last summer, it really looked great on you. Hey, maybe you should streak your hair again," Mom says as she digs through the rack of tops in my size.

I've never been afraid of used clothes. It's not like I had to have them when I was growing up. Mom made decent money to support both of us, and with my dad's life insurance, we were able to make ends meet. Of course, that doesn't mean we bought expensive clothes. Expensive to us was shopping at Target instead of Wal-Mart.

My love for used clothes came right after high school. I was walking past the used clothing store on my way to Colton's place where a vintage concert t-shirt hanging in the window caught my attention. Together with a pair of retro jeans with rhinestones on the ass and a jean jacket, I left with a great new outfit at the everyday low price of fifteen dollars. Plus, I like the idea that not everyone around me is going to have the same clothes.

"What about this?" I ask as I hold up a navy and cream-colored dress. It's strapless and gathered just below the breast and flows down to the knees. Pair it with the tan boots I've been breaking in and an armful of golden bangle bracelets, and I think this would make a great rehearsal outfit.

I glance down at Eli playing happily in the stroller with his Spiderman action figure. We're taking advantage of the mid-May day and doing a little shopping before my shift at Chaser's. We stopped at the deli down the street and had soup and sandwiches, played on the swings at the community park around the corner, and are now hitting my favorite store before heading home.

"That's great. Get that dress. What about these pants? I think they'll make your ass look great!" Mom is holding up a pair of black leather pants in just my size. I have another pair of leather pants that I rarely wear since they cost Mom practically a month's salary. These are worn and broken in, and I can't wait to pair them with the red lace top with the single left side sleeve that we found over in another section.

"Yes! Grab those."

"So, I was thinking that next weekend we could have a salon day before you go to work. I want you to have a fresh haircut and maybe some highlights before you go," Mom says.

"Mom, I don't need to spend all that extra money on stuff like that. I imagine that their stylist is going to do whatever they want with my hair," I tell her, remembering the discussion we had at the meeting about not making any major changes to your appearance or body.

"I guess. Oh, do you want to get your nose pierced? All great rocker chicks have their nose pierced," she adds.

"Mom. No one I know has their nose pierced anymore. And besides, I'm not supposed to make any changes, remember."

"I know. I just want to make sure you look your best, not that you don't every day. You're without a doubt the most beautiful girl there. I already know you sing better than all those other contestants, but I want to make sure you look the part. Rocker chick is in right now, and I want you to be a trendsetter."

I exhale dramatically. I've never been concerned about setting any trends or following the crowd. I've always been more of the outcast or the rebel when it comes to my appearance. I don't want to follow in anyone's fashion footsteps.

"Do you need to groom the southern region again?" Mom says, breaking me out of my daze.

"My southern region is fine. Thanks for asking," I tell her, absently squeezing my legs together a little more. The memory of my first bikini waxing still gives me uncontrollable shivers. Doesn't hurt, my ass.

Note to self: Make sure you remember your Aloe Vera and shot of Jack before your next bikini wax.

"Well, you should still get it trimmed up before you go. You don't want stragglers when you're dressing in front of those people," Mom says. She always has a way with words.

"I'll make sure to get that taken care of," I mumble as I head up to the cashier.

As we slowly make our way through the streets of Chicago, I can't help but think about the upcoming weeks. My flight leaves a week from Monday which means I have just over seven days to get everything in order. Plus, spend as much time with Eli as humanly possible. Part of me wants to be kicked out in the first round so that I can board the flight and return home. Return to my life at Chaser's. Return to my life as a single mom.

But then there's the other part of me that wants to know if I can actually make it all the way. Do I have what it takes to win the whole thing? The trophy. The prize money. The recording contract.

I guess there's only one way to find out.

Ready or not, I'm heading to Los Angeles to see if I'm the next *Rising Star*.

*****

The bar is packed which surprises me since it's not a karaoke night. Doc MZ spins high-energy dance music from his position on the stage while the patrons dance and drink the alcohol I'm serving. It's the Saturday before I leave for the show, and Tiffany has to be happy with the turnout tonight.

I'm just pouring a draft beer in a tall, frozen mug when the guy in front of me catches my eye. "Hey," he says with a smile and a head nod.

"Hi. I'll be right with you," I tell him as I finish filling up the mug of beer.

After I hand the first man his beer and collect the money, I turn back to the guy who was standing in front of me. "What can I get you?"

"How about a Bud Light bottle, sweetie," he says with wiggly eyebrows. Good lord. Every time. I was just thinking how attractive the guy is, and then he goes and does that.

"Coming right up," I tell him as I grab his brew from the cooler.

"Three-seventy-five," I tell him as I pop the top.

"So, I was wondering if after you get off work, maybe you want to come over and watch porn on my sixty-two inch flat screen mirror above my bed." Again with the eyebrow wiggle. His statement actually completely catches me off guard that I almost miss the mirror part. Full, grab your belly laughter erupts uncontrollably from deep within.

"I don't think it's that funny," he mumbles as he takes a big pull from his beer bottle.

"I'm sorry. It's just that that might be my favorite of the night," I say through fits of laughter.

"Uh, so that's a good thing?" he asks with confusion and hope mixed together.

"Not really," I tell him as I wipe the tears from my eyes. "I'm sorry. No, I'm not available to make–or watch–porn on your mirror. Thanks for the offer, though," I tell him with a wink as I collect his money.

"Some guy just asked me if I work for UPS because I've been checking out his package all night," Tiffany says next to me with a dramatic eye roll.

"Classic. Wait until you hear the one I just got," I tell her as Lee sits down on his usual barstool in the corner. "Who's that with Lee?" I ask, taking stock of the woman standing next to him with her back to us. She's short with shoulder length brown hair and reminds me of someone I know well. Moments later, the woman turns around revealing…my mother.

"Mom?" I ask as I approach the end of the bar, completely forgetting about the pick-up line I was just about to share with Tiffany.

"Oh, Layne! We have a surprise for you," she beams next to Lee.

"What's going on?" I ask moments before Doc takes the microphone in his hand.

"Hey hey, party people! On Monday, our own little Layne is going to fly out to LA and kick some major ass on *Rising Star*!

Who thinks Layne's gonna win the whole thing?" he asks the crowd who screams their approval.

"Well, Tiffany just told me that every Wednesday and Thursday night, Chaser's Bar is gonna be watching Layne perform. We're gonna expect everyone to grab their phones when she's done, though, and cast your vote for the hometown girl. Tiff'll have drink specials each night and everyone is invited to come watch our girl shine like the true star she is," he adds with a wink and point in my direction.

"So, in honor of Layne's departure, let's have her come on up here and sing a song or two for ya. How 'bout it?" he says as the bar explodes into more cheers.

My mom shouts her encouragement as Tiffany pushes me towards the end of the bar. My legs carry me towards the stage, the masses barely having enough room to make way for my progress.

"Well, I wasn't expecting this and I don't even have a song picked out, so I'll leave the song choice up to Doc," I say into the microphone.

"I got ya covered, girl," he says just before the intro to Kelly Clarkson's "Since U Been Gone" starts. I have about two seconds to think before the opening line starts.

For the next three minutes, I lose myself in the music. The lights don't bother me and the staring eyes don't matter. The music. That's the only thing that matters when I'm on stage. As if pulled deep from within my soul, the music grabs me and doesn't let go. It's like this every time.

Kelly's song flows right into Joan Jett's "I Love Rock N Roll" and the entire bar sings along with me. Every mouth in the place is singing as we croon about a woman taking a man home

61

from a bar–not unlike many of the hook-ups that'll happen at Chaser's tonight.

"Don't forget that Layne's taking off for up to eight weeks, so I better see those tip jars overflowing with cash at the end of the night," Doc says before starting another upbeat dance number.

At the end of the night, the tip jars are, indeed, overflowing and the crowd is slow to exit. Jay nurses the fat lip he received when breaking up a scuffle on the dance floor while Zane keeps the people moving out the door.

"I can't believe you guys did this," I say to Tiffany who is wrapping up what's left of the congratulations cake that my mom brought.

She took off hours ago, only staying long enough to watch me perform and cut the cake. Jane from next door stopped over to watch Eli for us, and Mom was anxious to get back home to her grandson.

"Well, we couldn't be more proud of you, honey," Tiffany says with what could be our thirtieth hug of the night. Every time someone asked me about the show, I got a hug and was told how much she's gonna miss me.

"You probably won't even notice I'm gone. I bet Kyle and Callie will do a better job than I do," I tell her as I start to clean up the empties on the bar.

"Are you kidding me? I have to have Kyle and Callie work together to replace you."

"Well, I'll be back before you know it. I probably won't even be gone the full eight weeks," I say.

Tiffany turns me firmly around so that I'm staring directly at her. "You listen to me, young lady. You have everything it takes to win that show. You are by far the best singer that has ever graced this stage. Promise me that you'll give it your all and that you won't think about this place or me for even a second." Her eyes are firm and trained directly at me.

"I promise," I whisper as tears fill my eyes.

"Good. Now get rid of the rest of the empties before you make me smear my mascara. You know I hate smearing my mascara," she says as she fights her own tears. "Besides, you still have to tell me about your favorite pick-up line of the night."

Chapter Six

Note to self: Don't forget to breathe. Because when all else fails you, breathing may be all you have left.

I have this eerie sense of Déjà vu as a black town car drives me towards the BLVD Hotel. This time around, I share the vehicle with a girl who looks to be all of fourteen, a guy who carries his guitar around like a baby, and a hipster who smells like pot. And I'm stuck riding bitch in the backseat between the young girl with a cell phone permanently molded to her fingers and the guy who reeks like he smoked a fatty in the airport bathroom. Awesome.

The only silver lining is that there's a slim chance that I'll have to share a room with Shawna again. With forty-seven other contestants, I'd say I'm good to assume that I'll be roomies with any other woman on the show. I mean, what are the odds, right?

After checking in at the front counter, we all make our way up to our respective rooms in the same section of the hotel. Since teenie bopper continues down the hallway in search of another room, it's safe to say that I won't be sharing a room with her.

Maybe I'll be rooming with Corie? We kept in touch through email and text over the past two months, and I'd definitely be happy to bunk with her.

I slide the keycard into the door and give the nob a turn. "You've got to be kidding me," I hear in an all too familiar voice as I push aside the heavy door.

Note to self: If it wasn't for bad luck, I'm pretty sure I wouldn't have any luck at all.

"Shawna. We meet again," I mumble while staring down my arch-nemesis. After a two second stand-off, I drop my luggage on the floor in front of the first bed.

"That one is yours. I'm not sleeping next to the bathroom this time since you were in and out all night long the last time. Is your bladder the size of a pea?" she asks with a huff and a flip of her perfect blond hair.

"My bladder is perfectly normal." I think.

I begin the unpacking process while doing everything within my power to ignore my roommate. I admit that it's hard, though, when a cloud of perfume and hairspray follows her wherever she goes. And it's not like the hotel room is that big or anything. The bathroom or the closet is the only place to grab peace and quiet here.

When my bags are empty and stacked within the small confines of the closet, I glance through the paperwork I received at check-in. Dinner tonight is at six o'clock and will be followed by drinks in the lounge downstairs. Then, tomorrow begins with scheduled coach's sessions.

Round one pins each contestant against another on the same team chosen by the coach. This round is more duet style as each pair sing together with only one being chosen to move on to the next round. Round two will showcase each remaining singer as an individual. However, at the end of the team performances, each coach will choose their top three performers, as well as choose one from the pool of the other castoffs from the other coaches. This gives each coach four contestants.

The third week starts the actual voting round where contestants perform for votes from the viewers. The more votes you have, the better shot you have at making it to the next round. The performer with the least score at the end of the voting period will go home.

The coaches don't actually vote. They are here as mentors and will be responsible for picking out the songs that each performer will sing. They will sit at the end of the stage as each singer performs their song, and will provide you with their thoughts and feedback at the end of the performance. At the very end of the show, each coach wants to be one standing beside the winner. It's a great honor and a battle between the coaches. Basically, it's for bragging rights.

I decide to get the hell out of dodge and head down a little early to the lounge. When I step over the threshold of the lovely room which will supply me with some much needed alcohol, I'm pleasantly surprised to find Corie, Ben, and Troy already there.

"Hey," Corie says with a big smile and a hug.

"Hi. How long have you guys been here?" I ask.

"Just a few minutes. Did you get settled in your room?" Troy asks following his hug.

"You aren't going to believe who I'm rooming with again," I mumble as I take the seat next to Ben.

"No! How is it possible you get stuck with her again?" Corie asks horrified.

"I don't know but apparently the universe is trying to tell me something," I reply before ordering a diet coke with a shot of Jack.

"Well, I busted my roommate trying to dismantle the smoke detector. I'm pretty sure he's already higher than a kite," Troy says with the shake of his hairy head.

"And my new roommate hasn't noticed me because I'm not an image on her phone screen. I'm pretty sure she keeps calling me Cary," Corie says.

"Hey, my roommate is completely normal. His name is Oakley. Not sure if that's his first or his last name, but he seems like a pretty cool guy," Ben says with a shrug.

"So, what do you think tomorrow is going to be like?" Corie asks the group at large.

"I overheard that guy, Gus, telling a group at registration that the coaches will meet with their teams tomorrow and go over the scheduling. We'll have practices on Wednesday, Thursday and Friday morning with the show's voice team, plus individually with our coach. Then, some of the teams are on their own for the weekend because Sophia and Beau have concerts," Troy says.

"And I guess we'll meet with the stylists and stuff this weekend and all get our 'image' established for the show. Can you believe the first showdown is next Wednesday night?" Ben adds.

"It's going to be a long, crazy week," Corie says.

I'm feeling a little overwhelmed so I just shake my head. I knew that this was going to be a lot of hard work, but I didn't realize the schedule would be so intense. Daily practices with the coach and a voice coach, plus sessions with a stylist. It honestly worries me a little to know that the show may change my appearance and the way I dress. As long as they don't try to make me look like Country Barbie upstairs, I guess I'll roll with anything. Though, I secretly hope they leave my hair alone.

"I wonder if we'll be able to do anything fun on the weekends," Corie states.

"I'm sure they can't keep us locked up in a hotel the entire time we're not at the studio, right?" Ben tries to reassure her. Though, I'm not one hundred percent sure. That contract we signed was pretty ironclad. The show pretty much owns our souls from this point on.

"Maybe we can go to the movies or the mall?" she says to no one in particular.

"If we're able to leave the prison, I'll go," I tell her, finally joining in on the conversation.

"Me too," Ben says with a smile. I turn away quickly when it looks like he wants to say something more.

"Then, I guess I'm in, too," Troy chimes in with a smile.

"Great! It's a date," Corie says as we all go back to our drinks.

*****

"Listen to me. Are you listening? Because I'm not going to repeat myself again. Get. Me. My. Own. Room. I can't stand to share a room with some common woman one more night. I mean, seriously! Who doesn't use Chanel exfoliates? I'm pretty sure her body wash is from Wal-Mart," Shawna says into the pink cell phone in her hand.

Seriously. Like I'm not even here.

Note to self: Check into getting your own room. ASAP.

"Fine. Do what you can and make it happen. That's why I pay you the ridiculous amount that I do. Do your job or I'll find someone else to do it for you," she says venomously before hanging up the phone.

How does a young woman without a record contract already have "people?" I've heard that people who've been in this business for years don't even have their own people. Yet, she seems to have at least one person pulling strings and making calls. She reeks of daddy's money like her expensive perfume. That's the only thing I can think of and the only reason why that poor Richard guy wouldn't have told her to stick it up her manicured ass by now. Daddy must be loaded.

Shawna storms off with a huff and slams the bathroom door, leaving me in pleasant peace. Finally. Lounging in a pair of cotton shorts and a tank top, I take the opportunity to text my mom again. The thirty-minute phone call after dinner tonight just wasn't enough. And the worst part of it is that I haven't even been here fifteen hours and I'm already homesick.

Somewhere between my Facebooking and my channel surfing, the bathroom door finally opens. Shawna looks shower fresh, yet her make-up appears flawless. For bed. She flits by me, completely ignoring my existence. If we both happen to make it to the end, I don't think I can endure eight more weeks of her ignoring and insulting me around every corner. I decide to strap on my big girl panties and try to be the bigger person.

"So, where are you from?" I ask as the easiest, safest way to break the ice.

"Savannah," she says after several heartbeats with her perfect southern drawl. The ways she says it, though, is pure annoyance. I'm bothering her.

But I'm not about to let her get away so easily. "I'm from Chicago," I tell her. I glance over and she blinks several times, but doesn't so much as look up from the fashion magazine she's holding. Whoever is on that cover must be the most fascinating person in the world.

"Have you always liked to sing?" I ask, grasping at straws here.

She thumbs through the magazine sitting on her lap and doesn't even look up. "I've always been the best at it. I have natural talent. It has nothing to do with liking it."

"That's…awesome," I reply, stumbling for the right word. Awesome isn't it, but I can't seem to put my finger on the right one. I wait several more seconds to see if she's going to pick up the thread I'm dangling, but it appears that I'm out of luck tonight. Oh well.

I roll over onto my side and stare at the taupe painted wall.

I think about Eli and my mom and the conversation we had earlier. I'd do anything to see them in person instead of through that small phone screen. It's definitely not the same as being able to physically hug them. But for now, it'll have to do.

My mind then wanders to our team meeting tomorrow. I have no idea what to expect since we aren't privy to that behind-the-scenes part of the show when it airs. Besides Beau, I have no idea who will be in attendance. My nerves are high, coursing dangerously through my taut body, as I will myself to relax and sleep. Tomorrow is going to be a big day, and I don't want to oversleep like the last time. Heaven knows Jezebel Barbie isn't going to do me any favors and make sure I'm awake.

I check the alarm set on my cell phone one more time and try to find a comfortable position. The sound of deep, dramatic sighs and pages flipping is the last thing I remember as I finally succumb to sleep.

*****

At ten a.m., I meet the rest of the contestants in the main lobby of the hotel. Shawna seems to already have secured a following as several young guys flock to her like groupies at a rock concert. Well, I guess to them, they see her perfect blond hair, her pristine make-up, and her stylish wardrobe. Throw in her killer body with just the right amount of curves, and you have what wet dreams are made of. Too bad they haven't seen the vile lurking from within. Give it time. She'll show her true colors to everyone eventually.

"Good luck today," Corie says with her arms extended.

"You, too," I reply, returning her friendly hug just before she breaks off from our group to gather with the rest of Team JoJo.

I congregate with eleven other hopefuls on Beau's team just outside of the hotel. Our van is the third one in line. As we slowly make our way towards it, I feel a warm hand on my lower back. I turn, startled, and see Ben's smiling face looking down at me. The look he sends me is…what? Interested? Adoring? I don't know, but it leaves me feeling slightly unsettled.

I take a half step forward and turn my body slightly so that his hand disconnects from my back. He doesn't say anything, and neither do I, as we make our way into the van. Of course, since he's standing right behind me, Ben takes the seat right next to me. Great. His arm casually rests of the seat behind my head. If I move it the slightest, my neck will brush against it. The problem is that it doesn't send those chills of awareness through my body. In fact, my body doesn't respond to him at all which is a shame because Ben is a good looking guy. I just feel nothing but friendship when he's around.

Note to self: Consider developing a fake boyfriend. Those always come in very handy when trying to get rid of a date seeker at the bar.

It doesn't take us long before our caravan of big white vehicles makes their way to the studio. Nervous energy buzzes around inside the vehicle much like it did on audition day. Girls chat uncontrollably, legs jump up and down to an imaginary beat, and breathing seems to be deeper and slightly labored. Yeah, nerves are definitely showing today.

Except for Shawna. She just stares at the cell phone in her hand, ignoring everyone and everything around her. She purposefully throws her long blond locks over her shoulder every chance she gets, much to the annoyance of the poor girl stuck sitting next to her.

We file out of the van like sheep and are led inside the studio by a petite woman with a clipboard. Her dark hair is pulled back in a no nonsense bun and her black, wrinkle-free skirt suit matches the glasses perched on the end of her button nose.

"This way, Team Beau," she says as she opens a heavy wooden door leading to a large studio.

I'm in awe at the magnificent room. It's not that it's flashy or glamorous, it's the fact that I've never actually seen the inside of a rehearsal studio before. The walls have white soundboard on them. A large, shiny black piano sits along one wall, and two microphone stands are positioned in the middle of the room. Stools are spread out atop the tan with brown and white patterned carpeting. This is the room I'm going to rehearse in before I go on live television.

I think I might throw up.

Ben grabs my hand and leads me towards the stools in the center of the room next to Troy. I notice instantly that Ben doesn't drop my hand as we take our seats, so I gently pull my hand free. I use it to adjust myself comfortably on the wooden stool so it doesn't appear that I'm just being rude. Troy and Ben instantly start chatting while I take in the others around me. Shawna is in the front row, dead center, of course.

"My name is Gabby Phillips. I am the production assistant assigned to your team so you will receive your instructions and directions from me. If you have any questions along the way, you would direct those to me as well. I am expecting Beau any moment, but before he gets here, let's run over a few ground rules. I'm sure you all read over the lengthy contract before you auditioned, but now that you have advanced to this stage of the competition, there are a few we should go over.

"You will always conduct yourself with professionalism and grace as you are representing this show and the network. No physical fighting amongst contestants and any such activity could result in your immediate departure from the show. Also, no part of this is off limits to our cameras with the exception of your personal hotel rooms. This season, we are offering behind the scenes streaming on the network's website so anytime you step out of your room, you should expect to be on camera. Polling has shown that viewers enjoy the behind-the-scenes drama of reality television.

"You will all have down time in which you can do whatever you want, within reason, of course. You are not chained to the hotel, but just remember that the cameras can and will follow you wherever you go. Within each of your rooms you'll find a list of approved local activities that you may consider. This studio has a gym, health classes and activities that you are all *encouraged* to participate in," she says.

"No sexual relationships are allowed amongst a coach and any contestant, on their team or any other. Inter-contestant relationships are not forbidden, however," Grace adds. As soon as she says that, Ben sets his large, warm hand down on my knee making me groan internally. I'm going to have to nip this in the bud as soon as possible.

Just then, the door at the front of the room opens and in struts a walking, talking wet dream. Beau moseys into the room like he owns it. He takes in the twelve people staring at him from our positions on the stools and offers us his trademarked smile. My panties practically evaporate into thin air. Poof. Gone. Which isn't so bad because they're practically useless at this point anyway.

Two young girls giggle in the seats behind me. Beau walks up to the front of the group wearing his standard black Stetson hat, a tight black t-shirt that shows off strong, muscular arms, and tight, dark Wranglers. The pants hug his lean hips and powerful thighs to perfection, leaving nothing underneath to the imagination. And right now, all female eyes appear to be on the bulge on the front of those tight pants. Scuffed up black cowboy boots and a silver belt buckle finish off his outfit. He's delicious. Absolutely scrumptious. Like an ice cream cone on a hot summer day, I want to lick him. Head. To. Toe.

"Mornin'," Beau says with his hands resting casually on his hips.

"Good morning," we all reply in some form or another.

"I was just going over some of the rules with them. Why don't you go ahead and start your portion," Gabby says to Beau.

"Okay. Today there are twelve of ya on my team. By the end of next week, there will be six of you left. In just a few minutes, I will pair you up with your competitor for this first stage of the competition. This is the person y'all will battle in the first round of eliminations. This round is duet style meanin' I will pick a song for each duet and you will sing it together based on my direction. I will also give you each your practice schedule for the next week. Each duet will practice with me together for an hour each of four days. Additional practicing with any of the network voice coaches is to be done outside of the schedule I give ya. Any interference with my schedule will not be tolerated," Beau says.

"And I'd like to add that transportation from the hotel to the studio is scheduled each day with regular runs between the two. You are responsible for knowing the schedule and making sure you get from one place to the next. If you miss the transport van, you can wait for the next one, walk, or take a taxi at your own expense," Gabby adds.

"Any questions?" Beau asks the group at large. "Good. Let's pair y'all up then," he says as he pulls a slip of paper from the back pocket of his jeans. Damn. What a lucky slip of paper.

"So, here we go. When I call your name, come stand up front next to your partner. Chelsea?" he says as one of the gigglers from behind me practically throws herself at the front of the room.

"You're with Ben," he says. The hand that Ben had rested on my knee gives a gentle squeeze before he saunters up to the room. What is it about cowboys and their swagger, anyway? Are they born with it or something they teach in Cowboy 101?

"Tara, you're with Josie," Beau adds as two young girls get up and walk to the front of the room. "Troy and Jackson. Jonah and Benny. Veronica, you're with Marshall," Beau adds as they all walk towards the front of the room, leaving only two people left in their seats.

"Shawna, you're up against Layne," he says, and his mesmerizing gray eyes lock on mine for the first time since his arrival.

It might sound crazy, but the room shifts. I all but stumble as I make my way up to the front, my progression being followed by those all-consuming eyes. Thank God there isn't anything in my way to trip over because I'm looking at nothing but the most amazing pair of eyes peeking out from beneath a black Stetson. I shiver uncontrollably at the depth of his stare. It's so deep he surely can see into my soul. Those eyes could melt the habit right off a nun. My body responds to him in a way it hasn't in so very long. Hell, if ever.

When I finally reach the front of the room, our gaze is broken when blond hair is flipped in my face, and more particularly, my eyes. I blink and tear up as I dig Blond Barbie's extensions out of my watering eyes.

Note to self: Check into purchasing a pair of scissors.

"Now you know who you're up against next week. You will learn your music selection at your first practice tomorrow. Here is your schedule," he says as Gabby starts to hand each of us a schedule. "If there are no questions, then I think y'all are done for the day," Beau adds before giving us all a nod.

"Thank you, Beau. If there are no more questions, then everyone is welcome to visit for a few minutes until we're ready to head back to the hotel," Gabby says and turns her attention towards Beau. They instantly drop their heads down and start to discuss something they don't want anyone to hear.

"I heard he was asked to do *Playgirl*," Chelsea says.

"Ohmygod, I would buy that issue in a heartbeat," the other adds.

"*Country Weekly* magazine is reporting that he just started dating Penelope Shaw," Chelsea says. I can't help it, but my curiosity is peeked so I turn around.

Chelsea is a tiny little thing. You can practically put her in your pocket. She's adorable with her short, curly brown hair and big green eyes. Where Chelsea is small, Tara is tall and slender. She stands a good two inches taller than my five foot seven inches, and has no curves to her whatsoever. She's like a tall, lean, beanpole. But her lack of curves doesn't detract from her natural beauty. She has long dark hair the color of midnight and striking brown eyes.

"Did you hear the same report?" Tara asks me, pulling me into their conversation.

"Uh, no, not really. I don't really follow country music," I confess, cringing at my lack of knowledge about my coach.

"Shut up! How is that possible?" Chelsea asks in horror.

"Well, I just don't listen to country music. I know who Beau is, of course, but that's the extent of it," I add, feeling the shocked stares of the two young girls in front of me.

"You are so screwed in this competition," Tara says as Chelsea shakes her head dramatically like a bobble head.

"Yeah, I might have a long road ahead of me," I say as I turn to see my roommate and duet partner pounce on Beau. He smiles that million-dollar smile directly at her and you can hear the audible gasps from the two ladies around me.

"I heard Shawna is really good. Like really, really good. She's the frontrunner on this team," Chelsea says in a whisper. "At least that's what I overheard from another production assistant."

"Ladies, I'm Ben. It's nice to meet you," Ben says just over my shoulder as he introduces himself, resulting in a collective giggle from the giggle twins. "You about ready?" he asks, directing his question at me.

Before I can answer, Tara asks with a huge smile, "Is he your boyfriend?"

"Oh, no!" I exclaim, probably a little too quickly and with too much emphasis. However, my answer still doesn't stop Ben from resting his hand on my lower back again.

"Are y'all ready for tomorrow?" I hear from behind me in that deep, rich southern drawl. Again, with the uncontrollable shiver.

"Hi, Beau!" Chelsea exclaims. "I am sooooooo excited to be on your team," she adds with a few bats of her overdone eyelashes.

"I'm glad you're here," Beau adds with a wink. Flirt. Oh, he's definitely charming and knows how to work the ladies.

"Me, too. I can't wait for tomorrow," Tara adds as she twists a long strand of her dark hair around her pointer finger.

"And you? Layne, is that correct?" he asks, turning those stunning eyes directly at me.

"Yes, Layne. I'm ready for tomorrow," I answer but without the schoolgirl crush effect.

Beau nods his head at me and continues to watch, intoxicating me as if I just downed a fifth of something hard and potent. His eyes appear so much deeper and darker up close. How that's even possible, I don't know.

"And you are Ben, correct?" Beau asks, turning his attention towards the man standing next to me.

"Yes, sir. I can't wait to get started tomorrow," Ben says as he shakes his hand.

Beau glances down and seems to notice Ben's hand return to my lower back. I try to step aside a little and create some space between Ben and myself. The last thing I want to do is encourage his advances.

"I guess I'll see y'all tomorrow," Beau says as he turns his attention to the next group of contestants. Just before he shakes hands with Troy, I catch Beau's eyes roaming my body. It's a quick once-over, but it's definitely a look, nonetheless. Tingles of excitement race through me at the idea of Beau Tanner checking me out. Me. But as quickly as the excitement races through me, it's snuffed out. There's no way Beau Tanner would want anything to do with me. He's a country superstar, dating an A-list movie star. Why in the hell would he be interested in a bartending rocker-wannabe like me?

Gabby starts to round us up and we all head towards the exit. Just before I get ready to leave the room, the hairs on the back of my neck start to prickle with awareness. I glance backwards and notice Beau. He's standing alone at the back of the room and his eyes are focused on me. My entire body goes up in flames every time he looks my way. I have no idea why I'm reacting the way I am, but I don't like it. There is no room in this competition for distractions. And Beau Tanner? Oh, he's definitely a distraction.

A tall, gorgeous distraction.

I might be in trouble.

Chapter Seven

Note to self: Every girl needs a least one fabulous pair of panties. Nothing boosts your confidence like a little scrap of lace.

Shawna and I are the last duet to meet with Beau on Wednesday afternoon. We ride in silence, with a few of the other duets for the other teams, towards the studio. It makes for the longest day ever when you're stuck in a room with someone who ignores your existence. Finally after lunch, I decided to do a little sightseeing around the exterior of the hotel. The fresh air was a welcome reprive over the stuffy perfume and high priced body lotion I'm forced to inhale in the room.

When we exit the van, I follow behind Shawna. She's dressed in a casual, yet stylish sundress with brown and pink cowboy boots. As always, she's perfectly assembled and gorgeous as she makes her way into the building. Confidence and determination roll off her in waves. I know this is going to be a huge battle for me. One I hope that I'll overcome as the victor. I glance down at my red skinny jeans and black halter top. It's nothing fancy or glamorous since I chose to go the comfortable route. My favorite pair of black ankle boots gives me the confidence boost I need as I step inside the atrium.

We wait with Gabby outside of our assigned studio. Gabby and Shawna chat animatedly about who knows what. I choose to lose myself in my own thoughts as I try to remain calm and focused. Eli. Nothing focuses and grounds me like my son. His smile has gotten me through so many hard times that he's all I need to bring me to my center of gravity.

At exactly five o'clock, the door opens and Marshall and Veronica exit the studio with smiles on their faces. I'll take it as a good sign since they're both smiling after spending their first hour with our coach.

"Ladies, you're up next," Gabby says as she motions towards the door. Shawna practically sprints to the doorway to be the first one inside. I try a few deep, calming breaths before stepping through the entryway.

Inside, Beau is seated on a stool in front of a music stand. Shawna is at his side two point three seconds later, practically salivating all over her designer duds. I wonder if her lip-gloss is drool proof? Laughter erupts from the front of the room before I'm even halfway there. At least she's not pulling any punches in this competition, right?

"Hey," Beau says, their laughter dying down as I approach them.

"Hi," I reply as I take my place next to Shawna. She instantly tries another hair flip, but I'm prepared this time and am able to duck out of the way from the flying dreads.

"So, I had a harder time choosing a song for you two to sing. Shawna, you're pure country and so just about any song choice would have fit you. Layne, you're more of a rocker and so I struggled to choose a song that still stuck to my country routes. Ultimately, I went with Miranda Lambert. She's stone cold country for Shawna but still has all the sass and attitude that I associate with Layne."

"I love Miranda Lambert," Shawna coos as she sets her perfectly manicured hand on Beau's forearm. "She's one of my favorites."

I instantly start racking my brain for Miranda Lambert. Songs…songs…songs…What songs does she sing? Wait! She was once married to some famous guy, right?

Shit. I'm so screwed.

"Well, I really think that Miranda's song "Fastest Girl in Town" will complement both of your singing styles. Here are the music sheets," he says as he hands us each a booklet, complete with music and lyrics.

"Do you know the song?" Beau asks, turning those steel eyes on me.

"Uh, no. Sorry," I reply with a sheepish grin.

"That's okay. We'll run through it a few times today and you'll have time to learn the words. I was afraid you may not know it, so I have it on my phone," he says as he digs his cell phone out of his back pocket and brings up the song.

It immediately starts with the standard country twang, but after the first few beats, I realize it's not that bad. And then Miranda starts to sing. Instantly with the opening line, *"You got the bullets, I got the gun, I got a hankerin' for gettin' into something,"* I'm immediately pulled into the song. I like it. A lot. I'm even able to ignore the fact that Shawna is singing along.

After it's over, Beau turns to me, "So, what do you think?"

"I actually really like it. The beat is super catchy and the words are edgy and brash. I think it's the perfect song," I tell him honestly. "I never would have thought I'd be so excited to sing a country song," I add with a little laugh.

Beau stares at me with a beautiful smile on his face. His smile is breathtaking. It lights up his entire face and transforms him from Country Hottie to Holy Shit, He's Smokin'!

"I think it's the perfect song," Shawna says, pulling our attention towards her.

"Yeah," Beau says as he clears his throat. "So, Layne, I have you singin' the red parts and Shawna, you're singin' the black parts."

"But Beau, I would be perfect to start off the song. I'm actually a country singer and all," Shawna quickly adds.

"True, but it's not about who sings what style of music or who sings first. I picked parts that I thought would complement each of you. I've got a few parts that y'all sing together and those are in blue," Beau says as we skim the music sheets and find the blue highlighted parts.

"So, are ya ready to give it a dry run through?" he asks.

Forty-five minutes later, our time is up and I feel like I finally have most of the lyrics down. At least my part, anyway. Tonight, I'll work on studying the music and memorizing the entire song. I want to have the entire thing down before tomorrow's practice session with Beau. Plus, he gave me plenty of suggestions to work on for tomorrow.

"I'll be honest with you both. This is the duet that I'm lookin' forward to the most. I think y'all are both dynamic behind the mic and have plenty of charisma to charm the hell out of the audience," he says with a slight lift of the corner of his lip.

"Oh, Beau. You are too sweet," Shawna coos and touches his forearm. Again, with the touching.

"I believe this is gonna to be an epic battle. I'll see ya both here tomorrow," he says before we head out of the room.

Those tiny hairs on the back of my neck stand straight up again causing me to turn around before I reach the door. Those eyes. They're mesmerizing and hypnotizing all at the same time. I'm afraid I'd be completely useless against their power. Beau smiles that half smile one more time before I'm whisked out of the room and led towards an awaiting van.

The entire trip back to the hotel, I relive the last hour. From his lingering glances to his southern drawl, I quickly determine that Beau Tanner might be my kryptonite. He might be the one thing that brings me to my knees and makes me forget all of the guy tips I've been schooling for the past four years. Four longs years. I haven't been celibate, but I haven't been what I would call sexually active either. I've gotten by. But the sight of that tall cowboy has my body humming and my blood pumping like never before. He makes me want to throw all of the rules straight out the window. And it's only the first week.

I am in so much trouble.

*****

"I need to go shopping," Corie says just after dinner.

"Okay, so go," I tell her as we make our way down the sidewalk and back to the hotel.

"No, I want you to go with me. I was checking out that schedule and the list of services available at the studio. It has a full gym, you know. There's a whole list of classes I want to take," she adds with a huge smile.

"Are you talking about exercise?" I ask, stumbling on the word like it might bite me.

"Yes, silly. That and I need to get some new underwear," she adds quietly while looking around to make sure no one heard her.

"Underwear?" I ask, both of my eyebrows sky-high.

"Yep. My grandma always said that a new pair of fancy underwear is a great way to boost your spirits or your confidence. Since I'm already practically higher than a kite on adrenaline from today's session with JoJo, I figured a good confidence booster couldn't hurt. I'm up against a girl who sang back up for JLo two years ago, so I could use a little self-assurance."

"Your grandma told you that?" I ask curiously.

"Yep. Well, that and not to sleep with a man until the second date. You don't want to appear too easy," Corie says with a decisive head nod.

"That's…weird."

"My Gram was the best. I lived with her from the time I was sixteen until about two years ago when she passed."

"Oh, I'm sorry," I tell her when I see the pain in her eyes.

"Yeah. She was hit by a car crossing the street after leaving The Pussycat Club," she tells me with melancholy.

"Wait. What? Your grandma was at a strip club?" I ask, stopping dead in my tracks on the sidewalk.

"She wasn't there to watch or anything. She worked there. Gram could sling a beer like no other," she tells me. "She had regulars of all ages. Gram had a huge following," Corie says.

"Oh. Well, okay then. So, underwear?" I ask looking to change the subject. Whoever would have thought that I would be interested in changing the topic *to* underwear?

"Yes! Let's go to that nice department store on the top of that one place on Quincy. It looks like it'll have great stuff," she says as we head into the hotel. "I'll meet you down here in fifteen, okay?" she hollers as she hops on the elevator.

"What was that about?" Troy asks beside me as I watch the elevator doors close.

"I just had the strangest conversation about underwear and strippers and her grandma. I think I could use a shot."

"Do I want to know?" he asks as he leads me into the lounge.

"I'm pretty sure you don't," I tell him, trying to shake off the images in my mind.

Note to self: Avoid future topics that involve grandparents and strippers.

Fifteen minutes later, Corie joins us in the lounge. After another shot of liquid courage in the form of Jim Beam, we head out of the lounge and towards the street. Corie tells me all about her life before the show. Growing up in Cleveland and being raised by her grandma after her parents were killed in a car accident her sophomore year of high school, Corie is determined to make her Gram proud and win the show. Apparently, Gram was a huge fan of other reality singing shows and always encouraged Corie to give it a shot. I tell Corie about living with my mom and about working at Chaser's. I even tell her about Eli, though I don't give her the backstory that I know she's itching to find out.

Together, we steer through the stacks of undergarments at the large department store. I keep thinking back to what she said about it boosting your confidence. As I hold a dainty black lace thong in my hands, I start to think there's something to what Gram preached. I can feel my spirits lifting as I contemplate which pair I'm going to buy. Not that I have a place or time to wear these panties, but the thought of having something so sexy and delicate against my skin *is* doing wonders for my self-confidence.

Maybe I should wear them every day.

Or not.

I take my selection up to the counter and let the girl who could be Shawna's Barbie twin ring me up. "$32.60," she says.

"Thirty dollars? For a scrap of lace?" I ask as I fish out my debit card.

"There's a Target down the street if you'd prefer something cheaper," she snips back to me with a snide look.

Oh, she's Shawna's twin, all right.

Note to self: Avoid bitchy blonds wearing makeup more expensive than my entire outfit. And always check the price tag before you go to pay.

"So what song are you singing?" I ask as we head down a floor to hit the athletic wear section.

"We're singing 'Escapade' by Janet Jackson," she says excitedly.

"Really?"

"Yeah, Jackie's range is a little higher than mine, but it should be a good duet. I haven't heard that song since I was really little so we spent the entire time relearning the lyrics. Heck, I'm pretty sure that song came out the year I was born. How about you? What are you and the Diva singing?"

"We're singing Miranda Lambert's 'Fastest Girl in Town'."

"And what are your thoughts on singing a country song?" she asks while pulling a pair of tight black stretchy shorts off the rack.

"I'm surprisingly okay with it. At first, I was a little bummed. I mean, I know Beau is a country singer so the chances of having to sing country was pretty good, but I was hoping he'd humor me and pull out some Stevie Nicks or something."

"Don't we wish," she mumbles as she digs through workout tank tops until she finds her size.

"Aren't you getting anything?" she asks, flicking her chin towards the breathable nylon material.

"You're really going to make me do this?" I whine before diving into the little stretchy shorts.

"Yep, I am. Get a sports bra, too, if you don't have one. We don't want your girls popping out while you're doing aerobics or spinning."

Another fifty-five dollars, a pair of tiny blue shorts, a black tank top that barely covers anything, and one sports bra later, we're heading back towards the hotel. I'm surprised that my spirits are actually pretty high. I don't know if it's the shopping, the lacy underwear, or the company, but I feel less homesick tonight than I have in the past two days.

"I don't understand why I couldn't just wear my yoga pants and a t-shirt to workout in," I mumble.

"No one wears that to workout in LA. Yoga pants are for cleaning your bathroom and drinking wine. Shorty shorts and sports bras are for showing off what your mama gave you," she counters.

"But, we're going to be all sweaty and gross. And I'm pretty sure hyperventilating isn't sexy."

"Yes, but we'll look good while trying not to die," she adds with a wink.

Only a few days in and I'm not sure I'll survive the remaining weeks. And I'm not talking about the singing competition. Corie may actually try to kill me. I just pray she doesn't sign us up for kickboxing or step aerobics for experts. Maybe I'll get lucky and they offer a relaxation with wine class.

Maybe?

Chapter Eight

Note to self: Don't mess with my cornflakes. I'm liable to cut a bitch.

Day two of practices with Beau is upon us. Shawna darts around the room like Hurricane Barbie, tearing up every drawer and cabinet in the hotel room. Even the ones that aren't hers.

"What are you looking for?" I ask, irritated that she's destroying the place. Especially because I know that I'll be the one cleaning it up.

"My Blushing Mango lip gloss. I had it yesterday and now it's gone," she hollers from the bathroom.

"You're tearing this place apart for lip gloss? Don't you have an entire bag of it?" I ask, incredulously shaking my head from my bed.

"Of course I have more," she says as she steps back into the room with an eye roll. "I wouldn't expect you to understand. This is the color I specifically wear with this dress. I can't wear it without that lip gloss," she seethes through pearly white teeth.

"I'm going down for breakfast," I mumble as I get up from the bed.

"You know, it wouldn't hurt you to skip a meal or two. The cameras are going to add at least ten pounds and you're already pushing it a little," she says with so much sugar, I practically get a sugar rush headache.

"Thanks for the advice. But if I don't get my big slab of beef for breakfast, I'm a real bear the rest of the day," I tell her as I fly out the door. Shawna's shocked expression still makes me laugh as I climb into the elevator and head down to the small dining room for breakfast.

Note to self: Order the biggest steak available next time I eat near Vegetarian Barbie.

Troy and Ben join me for breakfast. A creature of habit, I enjoy a bowl of Frosted Flakes, a few strips of bacon, and a cup of strong coffee while the guys each load up biscuits and sausage gravy, scrambled eggs, and at least four pieces of toast on their plates. The breakfast buffet really is the greatest invention since sliced bread.

"You ready for day two?" Troy asks before shoveling a huge bite into his mouth.

"I guess. Between fits of flirting with our coach yesterday, Shawna whined about my parts in the song saying that they were better suited for her," I tell them as I enjoy a bite of the sweet, sugary goodness.

"She's unbelievable. Ignore her and kick her ass in the duet," Ben says with an encouraging smile.

"That's my plan. Hey, have you guys heard from Corie this morning?"

"Not yet. She's one of the first groups out, and I heard her competition is going to be tough," Troy says. "Hey, did I tell you that my wife and kids are going to try to drive here in two weeks?" he adds, his entire face lighting up with excitement.

"No, that's wonderful!" I exclaim, knowing that it's so hard for everyone to be away from his or her family and loved ones for such an extended period of time.

"Well, if I'm still here in two weeks," he adds with a grin.

"You will be," I tell him confidently.

"Saturday night, Troy and I were talking about going out and having a drink somewhere. You'll go, right?" Ben asks.

"Yeah, I can do that. It'll be better than hanging out with Snobby Barbie and watch her brush her hair all night," I say as I finish off my cereal. "Is it okay if I ask Corie to come?"

"Absolutely," Ben says. "I've got to get goin' in a few. I'm on the next van out to practice."

Corie flies into the dining room looking completely frazzled. Her red hair is haphazardly pulled back in a loose ponytail, and her clothes appear slightly wrinkled. The petite spitfire grabs a muffin and a carton of chocolate milk before coming over to our table. "I totally overslept this morning. Chelsea, my roommate, was up half the night talking on her phone and I couldn't fall asleep. Then, my alarm didn't go off," she says before ripping the paper off her muffin.

"Sorry," I offer with condolence. "If it makes you feel better, I did the same thing on audition day."

"I guess."

"Hey, we need to get to the van," Ben says. "But we're going out Saturday night. We want you to come, too."

"Yay! I can't wait to check out the LA nightlife," she says as she stuffs almost half her muffin in her mouth. Waving over her shoulder, Corie follows Ben out of the dining room and towards the front of the hotel.

"So," Troy starts before clearing his throat. "What's the deal with you and Ben?" he asks curiously.

"There is no Ben and me."

"Is he aware of that?" he asks, his dreads pulled back in a low ponytail at the nape of his neck.

"I'm not encouraging him, Troy. Ben is sweet and charming with that southern drawl, but I'm not looking for a relationship right now. I'm not sure if I'll ever be ready for that," I say, my voice dropping down to just above a whisper.

"Sounds like a story," Troy says, encouragingly.

"Yeah, it's a story. A pretty long one," I say, hoping that he'll drop the topic, but when he gives me a pointed look, I know there's no getting out of it.

I exhale loudly before I continue, "It's not something I really talk about too much, Troy. There was a guy. He was a liar and I didn't discover it for a long time. He's not around anymore, and we have a three year old son together." Just saying those words out loud still gets my heart racing and the anxiety rushing through my body. I was a mess for several months following Colton's betrayal. Yet four years later, it still hurts almost as much as it did back then.

"I'm sorry, honey. I hate to hear you having to go through something like that. Just know that not all guys are jerks, okay? There are still plenty of good ones out there. My wife? She's got a hell of a man, I tell you," he says with a huge wolfish grin, and you can't help but laugh. And it feels good to laugh, even when talking about something as painful as Colton.

Note to self: Laugh more.

I spend the next couple of hours in the empty dining room with Troy. He shares stories of his life in St. Louis, his job as a music teacher, and plenty of stories involving his children. He talks about the love he has for his wife, all of the adventures they've had together, and the dreams they share, and while it doesn't completely restore my faith in the male race, it lightens my heart to know that goods ones do actually exist in this world. Whether or not I'll find one? Well, the jury's still out on that one.

Just before the lunch crowd starts to roll in, I share with Troy a few stories of Eli and my mom. It actually feels pretty good to talk about them. It's as if they're closer than they actually are. Sharing stories and a few laughs makes me feel relaxed for the first time since I arrived in Los Angeles.

"Promise me that if you ever find yourself in St. Louis, you'll look me up," Troy says.

"I will. As long as you promise to come and visit me in Chicago someday," I agree with a smile.

"Deal. Patti and I have always talked about going and seeing the Sears Tower, or whatever it's called now."

I leave the dining room after lunch feeling lighter than I have in days. Troy is a great man and I can tell exactly what kind of husband and father he is just by interacting and talking with him. I hope his family knows how lucky they are to have him in their lives.

And I'm lucky to have him as a friend.

*****

"She hasn't practiced at all, Beau." Shawna screeches next to me at an ear-piercing volume, and I'm about point two seconds away from shoving my size seven up her ass. "She's not taking this as seriously as I am."

I exhale in and out, deeply. "I practiced all afternoon, but I'm having a hard time with this run," I defend, looking up at our coach.

Beau is standing at his music stand directly in front of us with his arms crossed over his broad chest wearing his signature black Stetson, a tight white t-shirt, and those delicious Wranglers. He's pure sex in his dark leather cowboy boots. He makes my girly parts stand up and salute every time we're in the same room together.

"It's a challengin' run, Shawna. But I know Layne can do it. That's why I wanted her to do this part," he says in that sexy, deep southern accent. "Let's run it again. Layne, I want you to take a breath here," he says as he walks over and points down at my music sheet. "That should give ya enough juice to nail the run. Don't think about anything other than those last two notes. You got this, darlin'."

When he uses the term of endearment, my insides turn to gooey mush. Of course, I'm not the only one he calls darlin' or sugar, but when he says it to me, I feel those eyes of his piercing my body with their intensity. And don't get me started on his scent when he invades my space. Beau Tanner does things to my body that are illegal in half the states of this country.

Music Notes

We run through the troublesome part of the song several more times. Each time, I do what Beau instructed and clear my mind, concentrating on those last two notes. His tips and suggestions are welcome and definitely helpful. I've always enjoyed singing, but I have no professional education or training. It's just something I've loved to do in high school plays or in the car. So, I feel like I'm way behind everyone else that's here. It's like they all know so much more than I do. We're two days in and I'm already struggling.

"There. That's better. You're gettin' it, darlin'," he says with a smile and a wink. "Shawna, let's run through the second refrain one more time before our time's up."

Shawna sings effortlessly next to me. She actually has a very beautiful voice, light with just enough of that southern twang. Too bad what's on the inside is as ugly as dog shit. Messy too.

"I think we made great progress today, ladies. I'm flyin' out tomorrow morning for shows and won't be back until early Monday mornin'. We'll meet on Monday here, and I believe Tuesday will be inside the arena we use for live shows. Gabby will probably get you the schedules soon," he says. "Any questions?"

Hearing none, Beau indicates that he wants to speak with Shawna privately. Though I can't hear what they're saying, the sound of her teasing cackle sends an uneasy ripple through my body. It's almost…jealousy. Which is completely crazy because I have no reason to be jealous. I am nothing to Beau, and he sure is nothing to me other than my coach. Right?

After a few minutes, Beau sends Shawna out the door and meets me halfway across the room as I'm heading out. "Hey. Today was much better. Don't let Shawna stress you out. You have exactly what it takes to be here, and you deserve it. I knew it the first note I heard come from your beautiful mouth," he says, dropping that last part down to a whisper even though we are alone in the room. Well, alone except for the man holding the camera a few feet away. The fact that his eyes seem to be focused on the very mouth he was just speaking of, well that makes me all giddy. My heartbeat kicks up to a gallop and my breath gets lodged in my throat. Did he just say my mouth was beautiful? Is that a normal compliment? I've never been told my mouth was beautiful before.

"Uhh, thank you," I mumble quiet. My words must snap him out of the trance he's in because, suddenly, steely eyes are focused intensely on mine.

Beau steps in close, very close, and I can smell his soap or aftershave again. Whatever it is smells musky and wild, like sandalwood with a touch of spice. I have to physically restrain myself from leaning forward and running my nose up the enticing column of his lean neck, from his collarbone to his five o'clock shadow covered jaw. I shiver uncontrollably at the sudden need coursing through my blood. My entire being–everything I have and everything I am–was just set ablaze.

Beau stares down at my slightly agape mouth again. The strength of his eyes is so overwhelming that I'm actually very thankful that he's not staring into my eyes. Talk about knocking me off kilter. *Holy hell, this man is dangerous.* Without even realizing what I'm doing, I lick my dry lips. His eyes widen and dilate until they're practically black with desire. What I see there is unmistakable. I can see it as clearly as I see the man standing in front of me. Beau is reacting to me as powerfully as I am to him.

After several of the most erotic moments I've ever experienced, most of which have merely included our eyes transfixed on each other, movement out of the corner of my eye breaks the spell. Beau's eyes finally snap back up to my eyes, guarded by the low bill of his cowboy hat. Probably for the best, anyway. I'm sure I read this entire exchange incorrectly, and the last thing I want to do is embarrass myself. There's no way Beau Tanner was looking at me with anything other than professionalism.

Right?

I step back and throw my satchel over my shoulder. "Keep up the great work, Layne. You're doin' awesome, darlin'. I'll see ya Monday," he says, eyes burning into me once again.

"Yes. Monday." The words are shallow as I take several steps backwards until the door is at my back. Without looking at Beau, I turn around and all but run out of the practice studio.

Shawna and a handful of contestants are already in the van waiting. Looks of annoyance are sent my way as everyone waits patiently for me to get inside so we can get a move on. I'm quiet, lost in my own thoughts, as we make our way back towards the hotel. I barely even hear Shawna tell the man next to her about how unprepared I was for today's practice.

Note to self: Concentrating on Beau's lips is a great way to take your mind off Snarly Barbie.

What exactly was that in the studio? I know I feel this crazy, schoolgirl attraction to the man, but him? There's no way. I'm a twenty-four year old bartender with a three-year-old son who lives with her mother. I get excited on the months I can make my portion of the mortgage, the phone bill, and the television payment all at the same time. I drive a used car, for God's sake, and my detergent isn't even Tide because Purex is cheaper.

But then I recall the intensity of his eyes. There was so much more there, deep in that slate gaze that I can't explain. Need. Want. It was there. I know it was. And I can't deny the way my body physically responds to him whether he's across the room or standing right in front of me. I've never felt this pull, this connection before. It's exciting and terrifying all at the same time. There are so many unanswered questions, and no real way to get the answers. He's my coach. That's it. End of story.

But that still doesn't explain why I suddenly feel the need to explore this attraction, because that look he sent me will forever haunt my dreams. It isn't one-sided.

I just wish I knew what all of this meant.

*****

Saturday night brings a five-dollar cover charge at a club in Hollywood. Several of us gathered after dinner and made plans for the evening. In addition to Troy, Corie, and Ben, three other contestants are with us at Club Z; all ready to let our hair down.

Earlier today I had my first appointment with the stylist. The fact that she's leaving my outfits alone and doesn't seem to want to change them is a huge relief. I don't know what I would have done if she would have wanted to turn me into some country belle like the others on Team Beau. That's not me.

Zara is actually considering adding a strip of color to my hair before the first live show, which will probably make Mom happy. She wrote it down in her notebook with all of her other notes and measurements and will take it all into consideration before our meeting tomorrow afternoon where I'll receive the outfits I was fitted for.

"What do you want to drink?" Troy asks as he uses his large body to protect me from the mass of people all pushing their way towards the expansive bar.

"Jack and Coke," I tell him with a grin.

Even though this isn't the type of place I frequent back in Chicago, I felt at home instantly when I stepped over the threshold. It's still early enough that there wasn't a line outside. Guys and girls are shoulder to shoulder everywhere you look, though. The dance floor is half full with sweaty bodies moving to the beat of the hip-hop music. My body instantly starts to move.

"Come on," Corie yells in my ear. "There's a table over there we can grab while they get the drinks."

I follow the petite little thing as she pushes her way through the crowd. Elbows fly and toes are trampled, but we finally emerge victorious on the other side of the room and claim the small table with four chairs as our own.

Ten minutes later, the guys and a few of the others make their way to our table. Ben instantly sits next to me as he places my drink on the table. He's so close I can feel the heat radiating from his body. I try to scoot my chair backwards a few inches to keep him from completely invading my personal space, but I end up hitting the chair of the guy behind me. These tables weren't placed here with comfort in mind.

"Do you want to dance?" Ben asks, drawing my eyes away from the dance floor.

"What?" I ask, completely pretending like I didn't hear his question over the loud thumping of the music.

"Dance. Do you want to dance? You've been watching the dance floor since we got here," he yells and leans in even closer.

His breath tickles my ear as he all but rubs his nose against the shell of my ear.

"Oh, no thank you."

"Come on, Layne," he says as he stands up, takes my hand in his, and leads me towards the dance floor.

When we get there, Ben finds us a small sliver of dance floor real estate and pulls me in close. The song is upbeat with lots of bass that vibrates the entire room, and even though I try not to, I find myself completely lost in the music. I've always loved to dance, but there's something about being able to let loose after a stressful week that makes tonight so much more enjoyable.

I don't even feel Ben's hands on my hips at the end of the song when the upbeat number quickly fades into a slow number. I tense as he draws me into his arms, pulling my body flush against his. I hold my breath for several seconds as I contemplate what to do next. I could excuse myself, making up a reason to use the restroom, or I could dance one slow song with Ben. He's a great looking guy, and by the way his strong arms and hard chest are pressed against me, it's obvious that he works out and takes care of himself.

But, he's not Beau.

I mentally chastise myself for that thought. Beau has nothing to do with anything. There's no relationship–not even the hint of one. Yet, I can't seem to stop thinking about him. All last night, I laid in bed wondering where his show was until I finally got up and Googled it on my cell phone. Dallas. Beau was in Dallas. And tonight? Houston.

"Everything alright?" Ben yells as we move together on the dance floor.

"Yeah, I'm just getting hot," I lie.

"We can go get another drink," he offers, never taking his eyes off me. Everything I see there is clear. Ben has a crush. A big one.

"Can I ask you something?" I start, slightly hesitant. I have to do it. Troy's comment about wondering if Ben knew that we were only friends keeps playing over and over again in my mind like some jacked up broken record.

"Sure, honey," he says, dipping his head in so close his forehead is practically touching my neck.

"You know we're friends, right?"

He looks up at me with slight confusion before his eyes take on a wounded look. I can tell he's processing my question and doesn't really know how to answer it. The hurt is evident to me, yet he masks himself quickly to guard his heart.

"Because I value you as a friend and I want to keep it that way," I tell him honestly.

"Sure. Of course. Friends. Yeah, we're friends," he says standing up a little straighter. The moment bypasses uncomfortable and goes straight to awkward in about point two seconds. "So, how about that drink?" Ben says as he pulls back. Even though he pulls away from me on the dance floor, he still takes my hand within his and leads me back to our table.

"You guys are so cute," Corie hollers over the music.

"Who?" I ask her knowing exactly "who" she's referring to.

"Duh! You and Ben. You're like the perfect blend of country and rock. Classic and edgy. You two would make adorable babies," she adds before taking another drink of her mixed fruity concoction. If I had to guess? Daiquiri.

"We're friends," I defend.

"Friends who get frisky on the dance floor?" she throws back at me.

"What?"

"Oh come on, the cameras were zoomed in on you two like you wouldn't believe waiting for someone to make the next move. Our money was on Ben, but I was prepared for you to surprise us. You seem like the type to take what you want. Oh, you've got some killer dance moves, by the way."

"I don't want Ben," I tell her quietly so that no one around us hears. When she arches an eyebrow at the ceiling, I add, "Seriously. Ben is a friend. I think he has a crush on me, but I'm trying not to encourage it. We danced the same way I'd dance with any of the guys."

Apparently, I say that a little too loud because Hugo pulls me up out of my seat and leads me to the dance floor. He's a saucy blend of Mexican and American with dark eyes and a gorgeous smile, though his grandfather–whom he's named after–is full-blooded German. He's an interesting mix, and an even more interesting soul. He's funny and charismatic, and has a fashion sense to rival some of the leading magazines. I've gotten to know him well in the two hours we've been at the club.

After several songs, Hugo and I make our way back to the table. Eyes are starting to droop and I realize that it is somehow already after midnight. We've been here for several hours, dancing and letting loose. Everyone has danced and carried on, singing along to all the songs, even those we don't know.

This time, I don't even take my seat. Instead, I point towards the door indicating that we should go. Corie practically jumps up off her chair, leading the way towards the exit. I yawn widely as Troy takes his protective position next to me. Corie winds her arm through mine on my other side, and Ben seems to hang back with Hugo and the other two.

"Did you talk to him?" Troy asks just loud enough for me to hear.

"Yeah. I think I hurt him, though," I tell him through the slightly alcohol induced haze.

"He'll get over it. I'm just glad you said something before it got completely out of hand," he says as he hails us a cab.

Five people cram into the backseat, while two ride up front, as we make our way back to the hotel. I'm sitting on Troy's lap which considering his height and size, is a difficult feat. My head is cocked to the side and smashed against the ceiling while my legs are pinned between the seat in front of me and Troy's long limbs. It doesn't help that Ben is sitting Bitch in the middle and I'm half sitting on his lap, too. Just a few more blocks.

When we arrive back at the hotel, we all break off and head towards our respective rooms. Shawna is sleeping beautifully in her bed–yes, she's even beautiful when she sleeps–so I slip quietly into the bathroom to get ready for bed.

I can't help but wonder what Beau is doing right now. Is he done with his show? Is he hanging out backstage? Is his movie star girlfriend, Penelope Shaw, there with him?

After I Googled his tour schedule, I searched for any sign of him and her together, but the only thing I found was the story in *Country Weekly* that speculated the relationship. They didn't even have any photos to back it up. Yet.

105

I toss and turn for another half hour as I think about the two practices I've had with Beau, all of the helpful suggestions he's given me so far, how things are going to play out with Ben, what my family is doing back home in Chicago, and even what I'll say to Beau on Monday. Again, I have way more questions than I do answers, but the one thing I know for certain is that I can't wait for Monday.

Monday means seeing Beau.

*****

When his eyes lock on mine, I swear they penetrate straight to my soul. He walks towards me, stealthy as a cat, with a look of hunger on his face. A hunger I've never seen direct towards me. He stops directly in front of me, his hard breath a slight pant against my face. His eyes devour me from head to toe, causing a flood of wetness to soak my panties.

What is it about the way he looks at me? So intense, intoxicating, consuming. As if I'm the only woman he can see, and he can't wait to sink his teeth into me.

My body is alive, fully charged and ready. My panties were rendered useless the moment my eyes look upon on his steel gray ones. I'm barely able to breathe, but somehow I lack the concern or the care. Being with this man, right here, right now, is my purpose.

Goose bumps cover my body the moment he touches me. It's the slightest of touches; him grazing his pinky down my exposed arm, from my shoulder to my wrist. His touch sears my skin, branding me in a bold statement of declaration. It's as if he's claiming me as his own with just this one simple touch. A touch that I crave more than my next breath of air.

I'm on fire with desire. My brain is telling me to step forward, to touch this man. But my legs and my head aren't communicating at this point. I can't seem to move. I'm locked in a trance, pulled into an alternate universe, possessed by his dark eyes and smoldering heat.

Decisively, he steps forward, his mouth a mere whisper away from my own. I watch, helplessly, as he leans in just the tiniest bit. He's going to kiss me. Finally.

Just before his lips touch mine, he pins me with a look of pure lust and proclamation. I can see my own desire reflected in his eyes. It's a statement. A claim.

"Mine," he growls seconds before his lips slam into mine.

The sound of my own gasp startles me from the beginning of what could very possibly have been the best damn dream I've ever had. *What the hell!?*

I'm covered in sweat, the sheets are tangled around my body, and there's a dull throb between my legs. I've never had a dream so real, so erotic that I've awoken in the dead of night raring to go. And it never got past the initial kiss.

Throwing myself to the other side of my bed, I try to find a comfortable position. However, the only thing I'm successful in finding, are soaked panties. My entire body is vibrating with need. A need so deep and so strong, I wonder if it'll ever ebb.

I toss and turn for the better part of a half hour. Unfortunately, the constant replay of my dream keeps me from settling back to sleep. There's only one thing to do.

I quietly slip into the bathroom, slide my fingers into my useless panties, and picture steel gray eyes, while pretending it's his fingers and not my own. My orgasm is quick and gives me sweet relief from the ache left by the dream. The only thing that worries me is that the release will be short-lived. In a matter of hours, I'll see those eyes once more. Only this time, it won't be in my dreams. I'll be standing before him and the only thing I'll be able to picture is the look he gave me when he spoke that one word.

That one word that turns me on like never before.

Mine.

Chapter Nine

Note to self: Man invented deodorant for a reason. Use it.

These lights? Horribly hot. Like standing next to the sun and forgetting to wear your deodorant. I thought I put on deodorant this morning, but now I'm questioning that one little mundane task in my daily routine. I was in a hurry to get away from Bitchy Barbie, so what if I forgot? What if I was in such a big hurry that I forgot the one thing that would keep me from smelling like I just completed my first 5k? *Holy Hell!*

"Let's run it again," Beau says from the coach's table dead center in the massive studio. Right now, with the exception of a handful of the production staff and camera crew, the studio is empty, and surprisingly, that might be more intimidating. My words echo off the walls and the high ceiling. Hundreds of empty seats stare back at me, mocking me.

Sunday morning brought on my first hangover in I don't know how long. I didn't drink that much–or so I thought–but the headache that accompanied me pretty much everywhere I went that day, was miserable. What made it worse were the dye fumes I was forced to inhale all afternoon. I met with a stylist for the show who decided that I definitely needed a little color added to my hair. My

109

locks are a caramel brown and when the sun hits them just right, you catch a glimpse of natural highlights. Staci decided that my hair needed color. After a very brief conversation, in which I had very little input, Staci started to cut dramatic layers in my long hair and dyed the underside a deep purple. As soon as I saw the finished product, I knew it was the perfect look for me.

Sunday also brought a little solo practicing in the studio before my appointment with wardrobe. We settled on a deep purple netted top over a black tank top with black leather pants–real leather, no less–and very tall spiky heels, much taller than the ones I'm used to. Throw in tons of walking around my hotel room in the death traps and a long, grueling practice with Beau and Shawna on Monday, and I'm already exhausted come Tuesday.

"Go to your starting positions," Beau says as Shawna and I each take opposite corners of the stage.

The band starts the opening notes of Miranda's song and I slowly start my strut across the stage, belting out the words I now know by heart. Two days of wearing these shoes have me practically walking like I've been doing it for years. I don't even feel the need to constantly look down at my steps anymore. Plus, they do incredible things for my confidence.

Note to self: Buy more sexy heels.

I finish my first solo and flip my flat, limp hair out of my face. I feel like a big sweaty sausage right now. Unforgiving, bright lights are positioned from every angle on the stage front and are stationed from metal rafters throughout the large studio. If I'm this hot already, I can't image what it's going to be like when the room is filled with bodies. Of course, it doesn't help that I look over at Shawna as she sings and notice that she still looks fresh and perfect.

Again, I question my lack of deodorant.

"That was better. Remember to work the stage–don't be afraid of it. Stage presence is a huge part of what the audience will see, not just your ability to sing. Shawna, remember to hold your position until it's your turn to sing. Layne gives ya the spotlight when it's your solos, so don't crowd the stage front when she's singing," Beau says.

Shawna smiles an impish little smile that tells me exactly how she feels about giving me the spotlight. Obviously, her immature stage hogging wasn't done by accident. "Of course, Beau. Whatever you say, darling," she coos at the handsome cowboy as she runs her hands down her side to land on her thin hips.

"Our time is up. You gals are goin' to do great tomorrow. I'll meet ya backstage early, and then I'll be up at the table when ya go on. Don't be nervous," he says with the raise of the corner of his lip. It's a smile I associate with casual, yet flirty Beau.

"Thanks, Beau. I'm so honored to be on your team. I know we're going to go a long way together," Shawna coos as she runs her manicured hand up Beau's forearm. Then, before I even have time to process what's happening, she leans forward and places a gentle, lipstick kiss on his scruffy cheek. The shock on his face must mirror my own because he doesn't even pull back. I start to wonder if he enjoyed her kiss. Except the way his mouth opened and closed a few times before settling into a thin, grim line, I can tell it wasn't something he was pleased about.

Unless it's an act for the show's–and my–benefit. I mean, he's not allowed to have relationships with the contestants so it's not like he can show his pleasure at Shawna pawing him and kissing his cheek. And honestly, what man would be put off by

Shawna showing him some attention? Hell, there's a hotel full of men falling all over themselves to try to get just a little bit closer to her.

"Okay, well, I'll see ya tomorrow," Beau states matter-of-factly as he starts to straighten his papers on the table.

I quickly turn away and go to gather my bag and take off my heels. I can't wait to get out from underneath these harsh lights and into a little fresh air. Plus, stretching my tired, sore feet is pretty high up on my priority list right now. God, what I wouldn't give for a foot rub.

"There will be cooler air pumped into the room tomorrow," I hear from behind. The hair on the back of my neck prickles as I stand up and turn to face Beau. "I know it's super hot in here right now, but it'll be better when we do the shows. They just don't crank up the air until show days," he adds with that half grin.

Great. Beau notices how ungodly hot I am. I can imagine the lighting only illuminated the sweat marks on my lower back and under my arms. "Hot Mess" doesn't even come close to describing me right now.

"Yeah, it's a little warm," I reply as casually as possible.

"You'll get used to it," he says stepping in until he's invading my personal space. Instinctively, I almost step backwards. Then, I mentally smack myself across the face for even thinking of doing such a thing. Hell no, you don't step back when Beau Tanner invades your space. "Don't be surprised when Shawna completely tries to take over the performance. You're goin' to have to be ready for her monopolizing the routine and doin' everything she can to be center stage."

"It would surprise me if she *didn't* try something of those sorts," I mumble.

"She's kind of a piranha, isn't she?" he whispers with a full smile.

"You don't even know the half of it. At least you're not rooming with her," I tell him with a chuckle.

"Seriously? That has to be the roughest thing I've heard all day," he says. "I'd let ya room with me if I could." The statement forces all of the air out of my lungs in one big swoosh. Breathing suddenly seems like the biggest chore ever. My widened eyes remain locked on his, words seem completely lost. *Oh God, I can't form a sentence!*

After several seconds, he finally says, "Why are you glarin' at me?"

"Oh," I start, snapping out of my funk. "It's not you, it's just -" I say as I bring my hand up and try to rub Shawna's lipstick off of his cheek. His skin is warm and rough and the whiskers tickle my fingertips. But it's the invisible lightning strike that singes my lady parts. Sexual energy floods my body like never before.

"She left lipstick?" he asks without moving his face from my hand.

"Yeah. This shade of pink isn't exactly your color," I tease with a small smile.

He chuckles as I attempt to free him of her marking. Unfortunately, all I really do is smear it. "I think you're going to have to scrub it off. I basically just smeared it around," I say as I drop my hand. Even though I'm not touching him anymore, I can't seem to make myself move. I'm held hostage by some invisible pull towards his body.

"I'll see ya tomorrow," he says as his hand comes up, hovering next to my face. I can see so much in his eyes and face.

Question. Longing. Desire. My face burns as the deep blush takes over when Beau tucks a long stand of my hair behind my eyes.

"Okay," I finally mumble almost incoherently.

"Oh," he says as he leans forward. His breath fans across my cheek and ear. Goosebumps pepper my entire body as desire courses uncontrollably through me like a freight train. *Oh, God.* "I really like your hair this way. Totally hot," he whispers against my ear causing me to shiver before he pulls back, turns, and walks away.

I'm left standing, reeling. I'm seriously questioning my ability to walk right now. Just standing seems to take every ounce of energy I possess. I watch Beau's retreating backside as he makes his way to the table. The corded muscles of his back are evident through his thin, gray t-shirt. The way his jeans hug his ass causes warmth to flood between my legs. Those Wranglers leave nothing to the imagination, that's for sure.

I gather my stuff, my pride, and my sense and head out of the colossal room. The cool air kisses my overly heated skin as soon as I'm in the atrium. Shawna stands next to Gabby and a few other production assistants as I make my way towards the group. The look she gives me lets me know she suspects something. What? Hell, maybe when she figures it out, she'll let me know. Because I'm as confused as ever.

*****

Hair–check. Caked on make-up–check. Hooker heels and leather pants–check and check. Deodorant–double, triple, quadruple check!

I pace back and forth in the large sitting room behind the stage. Contestants range from biting their fingernails to nervously crossing and then re-crossing their legs while we wait for the live show to begin. Ben, Corie and Troy have all tried to engage me in conversation, but I can't seem to focus on their words.

I am in the group to perform tonight. Corie will perform tomorrow night so her state of nervousness isn't anywhere close to what I'm feeling right now. *Am I really here? Am I good enough to perform on National television? Can I win against someone like Shawna?*

Speaking of the devil, I glance over and see her casually running her French tips through her blond extensions as if she has not a care in the world. The fact that she's not nervous, clearly having done this sort of thing before, has my nerve ends exposed and completely frayed. *I can't do this.*

Suddenly, the four lead production assistants–one for each team–step into the large room. "Five minutes until we're live," the first man says. "Let's go, everyone."

The room clears out fast, as if no one wants to be the last one out, and we all make our way to the main studio. The assistants arrange us by team and then by height. The crowd hypnotizes me. This room is huge, but when you fill it to capacity, it seems almost titanic. Like the biggest room I've ever seen. And that doesn't help my nervousness.

"One minute," someone yells from behind the camera at center stage. The lights for the stage aren't on yet, but I imagine it'll be only a matter of moments before we're baking under the intense beams.

"Remember to smile," Gabby says to us before running off the stage.

I clasp and re-clasp my hands together behind my back. I've been in these shoes for almost four hours and my arches are starting to throb. I long to sit, even for just a few minutes, and take some of the pressure off my swollen toes.

"Five, four, three, two…" The crowd erupts on cue and the *Rising Star* jingle starts up. I paste on my best smile, not knowing which camera is pointed where. For all I know, three of the five cameras are angled on me at this exact moment, just waiting for me to pick my nose or check for lipstick by scrubbing my finger over my teeth with my finger on National television.

"Ladies and gentleman, welcome to *Rising Star*! I'm your host, Becker James, and I can't tell you how excited I am to show you the amazing group of rising talent that we have in store for you this season. Are you ready to meet our returning coaches?" Again, the crowd erupts into thunderous applause. "Help me welcome JoJo Warner, Sophia, Felix Booker, and Beau Tanner!"

Every girl screams her excitement as the gorgeous cowboy struts onto the stage. I'm mesmerized by his grace and male beauty as he throws a wave at the crowd. A full watt smile sparkles from beneath his signature hat, and I practically swoon like these young girls in the audience. The pain in my feet and my uneasiness are suddenly forgotten as Beau walks over and stands directly next to me. He accidentally–or completely on purpose, take your pick– bumps into my arm with his. Its skin on skin contact and I'm pretty sure I'm now blushing on National television. When I look at him out of the corner of my eye, I see him grinning a little smirk. Yep, definitely not an accident.

"Our first round of eliminations is tonight. Team Sophia is up first. Are you ready?"

After the applause dies down and we cut to commercial break, all of the contestants, except the two up first, head back into the waiting room. Several cameras hover nearby, documenting our every movement. I grab a bottle of water from the glass cooler, determined to give myself something to do and stay hydrated. There's no television in this room, though every once in a while, you can hear the cheers of the audience.

"The coaches are singing together now," Gabby says from the doorway just before leading the next duet out to another waiting area.

Over the next hour, we watch twosomes leave the room and not return. We're told that the winners and the losers of the duets are separated into different post-show rooms where interviews are conducted for the show's website, as well as with a few entertainment news channels. The winners will return to the stage at the end of the evening while the losers will be escorted to the hotel until their fate is decided at the end of next week's final coaches' elimination round. Done. It's that quick. As if all of your hard work and dedication didn't matter in the least.

Ben is in the first twosome to go on Team Beau. I give him a quick, friendly hug moments before he follows Gabby out the door and towards the stage. I wish I could watch their performance, or at the very least, see if Beau chooses him to advance or not. Ben was wearing standard dark jeans with his tan cowboy boots. His white and blue button down shirt is wrinkle-free and his brown cowboy hat, spotless. He looks every bit the handsome cowboy he is. Too bad I just don't feel that spark.

After several minutes, Gabby returns to gather the next duet. It continues on this path until Shawna and I are the only remaining contestants to perform tonight. At this point, my nerves are all over the place. I'm excited and so scared that I probably couldn't even tell you my name right now. I just pray that Becker waits to ask us questions until *after* we perform.

Finally, the moment is here. Gabby returns and Shawna and I follow her out. We walk down the long corridor that leads to the main studio. The closer we get, the louder the commotion around us. I can hear two contestants singing their hearts out on stage right now and the audience's applause when they're done.

This is it. I'm next.

Gabby and another guy, I think his name is Duncan, position me and Shawna at the edge of the stage. When I take the microphone she offers, there's a slight tremble in my hand. God, I hope that doesn't show up on camera.

"Welcome back to *Rising Star*. Our final duet of the evening is up next. Shawna Reece and Layne Carter have spent the past week with their coach, Beau Tanner. Let's take a look at how their rehearsals went," Becker says to the audience.

While their attention is focused on the screen above the stage, the production staff ushers us out to our marks on the stage. Part of me wants to turn and look at myself on the screen, but I don't think my nerves can handle it. The best thing to do is just to stare straight ahead and focus on getting through this performance. But when I look straight ahead, I'm staring directly into steel gray eyes.

Beau focuses all of his intensity directly at me. The crazy thing, though, is that it doesn't get me worked up. No. It does the complete opposite. As I gaze at Beau, tension seems to leave my body. Everything fades away. It's as if there's only him and me. Beau and me. Together.

"And now, the sixth and final performance for Team Beau, Shawna and Layne," Becker says as he steps off the stage.

Moments later the familiar melody that I could now sing backwards in my sleep starts. The lights are bright and warm, but it doesn't seem as bad as yesterday's run through. I smile automatically at Beau who returns the smile. My heart practically beats out of my chest as I move the mic up to my mouth and sing.

I walk towards center stage, and my eyes remain focused on Beau. While he's watching me perform, peace and reassurance radiating off of him, and any lingering restraint breaks free. This is it. My element. Even though I'm standing on a stage larger than ever before, singing before millions on live National television, I feel the calm and peace settle over me like a warm blanket.

I give everything I have into the performance. Even though Shawna steps into my path multiple times–as predicted–I don't let it get to me. No one can get to me right now. I connect with the audience as I belt out each note, singing to each one personally. Without even realizing it, I'm completely consumed by the music as it pulls me from one end of the stage to the other. My body moves in ways that would probably cause a little embarrassment if I really stopped to think about it. But I don't. I don't think. I feel.

At the end of the song, I know that win or lose, I gave it my all. Goosebumps prickle my skin as I make my way towards Becker at the center of the stage. Shawna comes over and stands next to me, and after several long seconds, we each wave at the continued cheering crowd. Her pink dress and white cowboy boots sparkle under the intense lighting and her golden hair looks like a halo. She's the complete opposite of me as I stand in my black leather pants and my black and purple top and matching hair.

"What a performance," Becker says to the audience. "This may be the showdown of the night, folks. Before we get to Beau and his incredibly hard decision, let's chat with the other coaches. Felix?"

"Wow. That was amazing. Shawna, you dazzled us all with your beautiful voice in your audition, and I could tell right away that you would be a crowd favorite. Layne, you surprise me most of all. Every time you open your mouth, beauty and soul spills forth. This was an astounding performance, ladies, and I don't envy your coach right now," Felix says.

After Sophia and JoJo each give their comments, Becker turns his attention towards Beau who has remained calm and collected the entire time, as if his decision was already made. That can't be good for me.

"I'll be honest, when I went into this, I thought I'd have an easier time makin' my decision. Shawna has been probably *the* frontrunner of the show since auditions months back. Singin' seems so effortless to her, and she has been outstandin' in every practice we've had."

Cold chills of dread slide through my body.

"And Layne," he starts and shakes his head before turning to look directly at me. "I don't know what it is about you. From the first note I heard come from your mouth, I've been entranced by you. I knew you'd have your work cut out for you when I paired you up to duet with Shawna, and even though you struggled a bit with your first country song, I think you're the Cinderella story of the hour." He turns his attention to Becker. "I don't want to make this decision," he adds with another shake of his head.

"Well, unfortunately, Beau, you do have to make a decision. Who are you taking with you to the next round for Team Beau? Shawna or Layne?"

Members of the audience scream out their choices while I hold my breath and wait for Beau's answer. This is it. End of the road or one more hurdle overcome.

"I think I have my decision. This one was by far the hardest one I've had to make tonight, but I gotta do it. The sixth member of Team Beau and the person movin' on to the next round is…" Beau takes another glance between Shawna and me. My heart is beating at stroke level and is painfully lodged in my throat. I want to jump up and down and just yell, "Pick already!" But I don't. Instead, I focus on my need to pee.

Note to self: Pee before you go on stage and stand before a live studio audience of thousands.

"Layne." I almost completely miss that single word. Even though my eyes are glued to his face, I barely process what he's saying. The audience? Shawna's audible gasp? Becker talking into the microphone on the other side of her? I hear nothing. Relief and joy replace the coiled tension in my body as I tear up and smile blindingly from the stage at the man sitting at the table.

I'm safe.

For now.

*****

Did you ever watch wrestling when you were a kid? You know where the big, burly wrestler—on camera, no less—grabs the folding chair that is always conveniently sitting along the wall and starts to smash everything in the room? That's what I walk into in my hotel room. Except the big, burly wrestler is none other than a very pissed off Irrational Barbie.

Shawna remained quiet and poised on camera, but I could feel the hatred rolling off her in huge tsunami-sized waves. She remained unaffected as she conducted a quick interview with Becker before walking off stage to the awaiting production staff.

I knew it was too good to be true.

Clothes are everywhere. Her stuff, my stuff, everything from the closet and all the drawers, all thrown haphazardly throughout the room. The bathroom floor is littered with broken glass and plastic bottles–my stuff, of course. Not hers. The flat television is sitting at a dangerous angle on the top of the dresser and the bedding is thrown on top of the upturned table and chairs. It looks like a hurricane went through this room. Hurricane Shawna.

"You!" she screamed at me in an octane that only dogs could hear. "You've ruined everything!" she yells moments before a shoe flies within inches of my face.

Survival mode kicks in, snapping me out of my daze, and I retreat as quickly as possible from the room. Just as I get the door closed, something large and breakable slams into the other side of the door spraying shards of glass all over the room. That woman is fucking crazy.

I stand there for several seconds trying to collect my thoughts and get my erratic heartbeat under control.

"Hey. You okay? I was just talking to you and it's like you completely have no idea I'm here," Troy says as he turns me to face him. Just as I get ready to speak, something else breaks loudly from within the room behind me.

"Is she?"

"Yes, she is," I state.

"Let's get out of here," he says as he pulls me towards the elevator. I follow Troy in astonishment as he steers me to the front lobby.

"She needs a new room," he says forcefully to the slim young college kid working the counter.

"Is there a problem with the room?" he asks.

"Yep. There's a crazy she-devil tearing it apart at the seams right now."

"Are you from the show?" he asks nervously.

"Yes," I finally say.

"Let me make a call," he says before excusing himself to use the phone on the opposite side of the counter. After several minutes of animated, hushed conversation, he finally returns to Troy and me.

"A producer is on his way. Please take a seat over on the couch," he says.

Fifteen minutes later, the same man from the first night we were here comes hustling into the lobby and directly towards us. "What's going on?" he asks.

"Shawna is tearing apart our room piece by piece. She threw a shoe at me and something glass. The entire room is in shambles and I'm pretty sure she's broken just about everything in there, including all of my stuff."

"I'll go up and talk to her. Can you get her another room for the night?" he asks the skinny guy not so subtly eavesdropping on the other side of the counter.

"Only a night? That girl is unstable," Troy adds.

The executive rubs the wrinkle between his eyebrows for several seconds. "She's been asking for a solo room since day one. Maybe I can get her moved to another room," he final concedes.

"Why her? She tore apart their current room. Layne should get the new room that isn't covered in glass and broken furniture," Troy says with a little force.

"Whatever. I'll go up and try to calm her down enough so you can go in and get your stuff. Or what's left of it," he says, walking towards the elevator. "New room. Now," he barks at the kid behind the counter.

"Well, I guess we should go up too and gather your stuff." We wait until we have the "all clear" sign from the producer before we head back upstairs.

By the time Troy and I gather up what's left of my stuff and move it to another room, it's almost two in the morning. As we sort and pitch all of the stuff we salvaged from the room, I'm actually kind of surprised I'm only down to half of my makeup. Some of my clothes didn't fare so well. Apparently, when I left the room, Shawna found scissors. Now my favorite jeans and three of my most expensive tops all have air conditioning.

Of course, now, all is forgotten. Shawna pulled out the fake tears and the bogus apologies and is resting comfortably in the room we used to share–after housekeeping came up to clean and straighten it back up, that is. After a few promises to the producer that she'll never behave like a two-year-old again, Shawna was left to sleep for the night.

"I'm going to bed," Troy says as I hang the last of my clothes in the closet.

"Thank you for your help," I mumble, my body exhausted from todays–or yesterdays–excitement.

"You're welcome. Call me if you need anything," he says before slipping out of my room and leaving me in silence.

I didn't even get to enjoy my victory. As soon as I was done performing and did a quick interview, they ushered the rest of the winners back on stage. That was the first glance I got at Beau's team of six. I was happy to see Troy and Ben amongst them. As soon as the live show was done, we received our next day's schedule. Fortunately, my part in tonight's show is very minimal: hair, make-up, and wardrobe. Then I'm onstage for the beginning of the show and the very end when the six contestants from each team are presented.

Then, we start all over again with a new song.

That's the last thing I think about as I succumb to the exhaustion taking over my body.

Chapter Ten

Note to self: When a hot, country superstar calls, you answer the damn phone!

"I have a surprise for you," Beau says early Friday morning. He has a concert tonight and will be flying out this afternoon to places unknown, but he scheduled a short session with each of us to prepare us for the next round.

"What kind of surprise?" I yawn before taking a sip of my French vanilla latte with a double shot of espresso and extra whip.

"Trouble sleeping?" he asks with that eyebrow and corner of his lip raised.

"You wouldn't believe me if I told you," I mumble as I recall all of the destruction and damage to my hotel room two nights ago. Last night, finding sleep wasn't much easier either. Every time I started to doze, I pictured blond hair extensions and red demonic eyes.

"You're going to tell me about it later, but first I need to tell you which song you're singing next week."

"Oh, let's hear it," I say, sitting up straight on my stool.

"What do you think of Heart?" he asks with that sexy little grin.

"Are you kidding me? They're my favorite!" I tell him, wide eyed.

"I figured. You look like you'd enjoy the Wilson sisters," he chuckles.

"I will take that as a compliment," I say. "So which song?" I encourage.

"'Crazy On You'," he says with a big grin.

"Shut up! I fucking love that song," I exclaim as I practically bounce in my seat like a toddler, unable to control my face-splitting smile. Finally, something that feels like home.

"So I made a good call?" he asks as he hands me the music sheet. "We have ten minutes before I have to head out, so let's run it once so I can hear it." Beau pushes a button the machine next to him and the start of the song fills the room. "We'll have to cut the intro down for the band, but that's not a problem."

I don't even have to look down at the music in front of me. I know these words like I know the back of my hand. *"We may still have time, we might still get by..."*

As soon as I get through the song, I burst out laughing. Images of Shawna going crazy on my stuff the other night, fill my head. Beau looks at me like I've lost my mind, and honestly, with the lack of sleep, I kind of feel like I have.

"What?"

"It's part of the story I'll tell you later," I say through my big smile. A smile that I try to contain, unsuccessfully. Something about being near Beau makes me break into a high school crush, giddy smile.

"You should do that more," Beau says as he gathers up his stuff.

"What?" Confusion mares my features as I struggle to figure out what he's talking about.

Before I know what's happening, Beau is standing directly in front of me. His captivating steel eyes are boring into me like heat-seeking missiles. "Smile." *Shudder*.

I gulp so big that I can hear it in the quiet of the room. I have to physically restrain myself from swooning which kind of ticks me off since I'm not the kind of girl to swoon over a guy. *Any guy*. "Come on, give me one little smile before I go," he whispers with encouraging eyes, trying to control his own handsome smirk.

Our eyes remain locked as we stare at each other. Crazy sexual tension crackles and sparks around us like sparklers on the Fourth of July. The smile I give him starts small until I'm awarded with one of his great smiles back. Then, my smile seems to take over my face. Can you say cheesy?

"Thank you," he whispers with a wink. "That memory should get me through my weekend."

"Beau, are you ready?" an older man asks from the doorway. I didn't even hear him come in.

"Yep, 'bout ready. Give me your phone," Beau orders as he extends his calloused hand.

"Why?" I ask, digging my phone out of the messenger bag that I use to carry my music and supplies.

"'Cause I said so," he replies with an ornery, lopsided grin.

His fingers fly over my screen before he hands it back to me. "What did you do?" I ask curiously.

"Put my phone number in there and sent myself a text so I have your number," he says with a shrug like it's no big deal. Sure, no big deal that an award winning Nashville recording superstar just put his cell phone number in my phone. "I want to know that story."

*****

"Do you want me to get on a plane and come kick her ass?" My mom's angry face fills the computer screen through Skype.

"Absolutely not. You'd probably twist your ankle fighting for a cab at the airport," I tell her and manage to contain my grin.

"Oh, don't think a little sprain is going to keep me from defending my little girl," she adds fiercely.

"I'm not in third grade anymore, Mom. I can fight my own battles."

"Yes, but it sounds like someone needs to teach that girl some manners."

"It wouldn't do any good, Mom. Shawna isn't the type of person to understand and appreciate life lessons. She's the type to use whatever means necessary to get ahead. If that means throwing me under the bus or throwing a temper tantrum that rivals Eli at the toy store, that's what she is going to do. That's what spoiled, entitled brats do."

"Don't I know it, honey. I've met dozens of her kind in my life. Oh, did you see the picture Eli is helping me paint?"

"Yeah. It made me miss him so much I couldn't sleep last night," I tell her honestly. Being away from Eli has been the hardest thing I've ever done and definitely the hardest part of this competition. Even though I talk to him every night and kiss the computer or phone screen before we sign off, it's not the same as holding my baby.

I've had to resort to sleeping with the television on every night. When I'm enclosed in the quiet of my hotel room, sleep doesn't come as easy as it did when Eli was sleeping in the toddler bed across the room. It's the little things that you take for granted. I never realized how silence could be so deafening. Maddening.

"He misses you just as much. We talk about you every night at bedtime. I think watching you on the show this past week helped, too. He was so excited to see you on the TV. I still don't think he quite understands how he's seeing you in that little box where the Bubble Guppies are," Mom says, earning a chuckle from me. The Guppies are definitely his favorite show. He could sit there and watch them for hours on end. And as a mom, I rationalize his television consumption since it's actually a really cute and very educational show. I've caught myself singing along to the "outside" bit on numerous occasions.

"Can I speak to him?" I ask as I steel my emotions for our conversation. The last thing I want is to tear up and cry before we hang up.

"Hi, Mommy!" Eli exclaims into the computer.

"Hi, baby. Are you being good for grandma?"

"Yep!" he says just before taking a bite of his cheese stick.

"Good. I miss you so much. You know that, right?" I all but choke on the last few words.

"Yep. We played with blocks today and built a fort and den blew it up with more blocks!"

"That sounds like fun. I wish I were there with you. I love you so much."

"Wove you too, Mommy," he says before kissing the computer screen. I watch helplessly as his lips smash down on the monitor leaving behind a trail of soggy cheese.

"We'll talk to you tomorrow," Mom says with a smile.

"Okay. Love you, Mom," I tell her, fighting to keep the tears at bay once more.

"Love you, too. And if you need me to come out and whoop some country diva ass, you just call your mom. I've got ways of protecting you, you know," she says with a serious expression and a firm head nod.

"I'll call you," I tell her with the shake of my head. After a few seconds of waves, I finally sign off.

Note to self: Do not, *under any circumstances, let your mom loose in LA without checking her bag for brass knuckles.*

*****

I've spent very little free time with those few people I call my friends on this show. For the past several days, we've all been busy at individual practices with one of the many show vocal coaches. Since all four of the professional coaches have busy careers that require them to perform to legions of fans, we practice from time to time with other coaches. They don't offer as much input and advice as our coaches do, but it still allows us to practice and receive feedback from someone within the industry. Even if that person is just a high school music teacher.

I personally enjoy the one-on-one time with someone other than Beau. For one, I can actually concentrate. I don't have to worry about amazing gray eyes and a killer smile distracting me to the point of insanity. Then there's the fact that my assistant coach is just an everyday, regular Joe. Like me.

Not a Grammy winning mega country star who looks amazing in a pair of tight jeans.

It's almost five and I'm just getting ready to leave the practice studio. It's Sunday night and I promised Corie that I'd join her at the studio gym tonight. I'm hoping she'll find us a nice, easy little yoga class or at least a beginner's Pilates class.

But knowing the feisty little redhead, I'll probably be suckered into a self-defense or an advanced spinning class.

Note to self: Practice your fake sick cough.

As I'm stepping outside, preparing to walk the six blocks back to the hotel, my phone pings signaling a text message. My heart skips a beat and then does the tango in my chest when I see Beau's initials on the screen. I noticed he put his initials instead of his name. I'm assuming it was for anonymity. I quickly slide my finger across the screen with a slight tremble.

BT: *Hey. Hope practices are going well. You busy?*

My fingers fly over the keypad as if completely on their own as I type back my reply.

Me: *Just leaving studio. Walking to hotel.*

I stare at my phone with bated breath as I wait for his reply, but it doesn't come; at least not in the form of a text message.

Instead, my phone starts ringing and displays Beau's initials in the middle of the screen.

Note to self: Breathe.

"Hello?" I answer, hoping that the slight tremble in my voice isn't noticeable.

"Hey," he says with that deep Southern drawl. "You're walkin' to the hotel?"

"Yeah, I haven't even crossed the street yet from the studio. What are you doing?"

"Just finished a sound check in Boise. I've got an hour to kill before I have to be ready for the Meet and Greet so I thought I'd call ya and get that story," he says, voice thick with rich tones and long syllables.

"Oh, that. It's not anything to worry about," I tell him, not really wanting to relive my crazy night with Shawna.

"I didn't think it was somethin' to worry about, Layne. I thought it was a funny story, but now I'm startin' to believe it's not really funny at all. Am I going to like this story?"

"Probably not any more than I like telling it," I respond.

"What happened?" he asks, firm and direct.

"The night after the vote off, Shawna sort of trashed our room. I walked in when she was mid-tizzy fit, and she tried taking my head off with something breakable and probably expensive. Fortunately, I own nothing of that nature so it wasn't mine. Though a good chunk of my stuff in the bathroom didn't survive the temper tantrum."

"Are you kiddin' me? Did you report it?"

"Yeah, Troy took me down and we called a producer. He came and smoothed things over and got me a new room, but she brutally stabs me with eye daggers every time I see her."

"She's still on the show?" he asks incredulous.

"Of course. She said she was sorry and didn't mean it and blah blah blah. They don't want to let her go because she's a shoo-in to get picked up by one of the other teams this week." At least that was the opinion of Ben when we discussed it Friday night.

"It's all political network bullshit, darlin'. It pisses me the fuck off that she's still potentially on the show and you have to deal with her every day. They should have packed her bags for her immediately and sent her expensive perfumed ass steppin'. I don't like the fact that she's here and could potentially hurt you again just because you beat her fair and square in a head to head competition."

This possessive side he's displaying used to always turn me off faster than a unibrow, but for some reason, possessive Beau? Well, that's hot. Damn hot. I stumble over a non-existent crack in the sidewalk as my body flushes with heat.

I clear my throat and try to clear the mental images of a half-naked Beau that my mind conjured up completely on its own. "So, you'll be back tomorrow?" I ask, steering the conversation back to a safer topic.

"In the morning. I'm takin' a very early flight from Idaho to LAX and should be back at the studio around eight."

"I don't know how you do this constant travel. Just flying from Chicago to LA was taxing for me. And I've only done it twice."

"You get used to it. Eventually your life becomes one big blur of airports, tour buses, and hotels. As crazy and drainin' as it can be at times, I wouldn't want it any other way. I couldn't picture myself doin' anything else with this life."

For the first time in so long, I get that itch. The itch to experience the lifestyle he's talking about. Singing on stage every night and not just the local sports bar karaoke. I mean to sing, really sing up on stage to a crowd of thousands who are screaming your name and singing along with all of your songs. I haven't thought much about the dream in a few years. Not since I had Eli and that dream transformed into a softer, tamer one. One with diapers and cartoons. Sleepless nights and baby strollers. That's the dream I've been living the past few years. And I wouldn't trade it for the world.

But now? This entirely different lifestyle is being dangled before me like a carrot. What will I do if I actually win this competition? Hell if I know, but it's something I'm going to have to think about in the near future. Of course, if I don't make it past the next round, then I guess I don't have to consider that future, right?

"What?" I ask into the phone, realizing that Beau was talking and I wasn't listening.

"I asked what you were doin' tonight."

"Oh, Corie is dragging me off to our first class of some sort of physical torture at the studio tonight."

"Physical torture?" he asks with a chuckle.

"You know, physical fitness. I have no clue what kind of class she has signed us up for, but I've been told to be ready at six o'clock."

"Just don't pull a muscle. I'd hate to see you waddling around stage in those sexy as sin heels while trying to sing with pulled muscles. Those hurt like a bitch without having to perform with one. Trust me."

My brain is frozen. It's sputtering, completely unable to process a thought. It's a puddle of mush that keeps replaying his comment about my sexy as sin heels. Good God, my lady parts are all but bursting into flames and singing a hallelujah chorus.

I stop, realizing that I've already walked the six blocks back to the hotel. I stand underneath the shaded large brown awning, reveling in the cool breeze of the mid-May day. "I'm back at the hotel. Thanks for keeping me company."

"You're welcome, Layne. I'll see ya tomorrow?" he asks, though it really isn't a question. Of course he'll see me tomorrow.

"Yes," I whisper, suddenly my throat too dry to speak.

"Have a great night, darlin'," Beau says before hanging up. I don't even reply because I can't seem to get past this crazy feeling I'm having. It feels like Beau was flirting with me, but I know that has to be just wishful thinking, right? Right?!

I step inside the lobby and head straight up to my room to get ready for yoga. Or pilates. Or bootcamp. I have no idea what I'm stepping into, but ever since my phone call with Beau, I'm okay with not knowing the direction we're shortly heading in. I might actually be looking forward to releasing a little stress and working out.

Almost.

*****

"Mine," he growls seconds before his lips slam into mine.

The kiss is possessive. Before I know it, I'm in his arms; the corded muscles of his arms wrapped tightly around my body.

He tastes like mint and a touch of something else. A taste that's unfamiliar, yet so very familiar all at the same time. My body recognizes it and responds to his taste instantly.

Powerful hands thread into my hair and his lips plunder and devour mine. The slide of his tongue against mine sends another wave of wetness flooding from my core. He pulls my body flush against his, and there's no mistaking the extent of his desire. It's pressed firmly against my stomach.

My body aches in a way it never has before. I long to wrap my legs around him, grinding against his body, looking for any ounce of relief I can find. He must sense my need because he thrusts his erection against me, as if looking for his own slice of respite in the form of my body.

I claw my nails into the cotton of his shirt, pulling and digging my way to the bare flesh beneath. When I finally reach smooth, hot flesh, I almost come right there. He's so hard, so hot, and so damn perfect.

Dragging my nails against his skin, he hisses against my mouth. His teeth latch onto my earlobe, the sting triggering me to emit a slight gasp. He uses his tongue to soothe the sensitive flesh, causing the ache to subside completely from my ear, and only to cause the ache between my legs to completely intensify.

He pulls away and looks into my hazy eyes.

"Mine," he growls again.

And I am. His.

I grip my eyes shut, willing myself to fall back asleep. This can't be happening again! Just when we start to get down and dirty in my dreams, I'm awakened and left so damn turned on, I'm practically a faucet beneath the sheets.

The throbbing is intense. My body craves the release that only Beau-inspired dreams can produce. Because I've been moved to my own room since my last lusty wet dream, I don't even have to get out of bed.

My fingers find my soaked core immediately as thoughts of a certain handsome cowboy parade through my mind. Beau Tanner has completely wormed his way into my head and subsequently, my panties since they seem to be disappearing faster than a joint at a Tom Petty concert.

The orgasm sweeps through me, slowly washing away all of the details of my erotic dream. I'm left spent, yet slightly unsatisfied as I come down from the high of my intense masturbation session.

There's no end in sight, is there? I'm going to keep dreaming of the one man I shouldn't want, but can't seem to let go of. He's embedded in me like sand. He's there. Maybe not on the surface, but deep down and slowly working his way to the top.

After washing my hands and cleaning up in the bathroom, I settle in for what will probably be a very long, sleepless night.

Chapter Eleven

Note to self: Never trust a redhead with a friendly smile and sparkling eyes.

"It'll be fun, she said. Fun my ass. My legs burn in places that I didn't even realize I had muscles. And don't get me started on my ass," I mumble as I chug more water in between practice runs of the song that I'll be singing this week.

Beau's face lights up with laughter at my discomfort before taking a long, perusing glance down to my butt. His eyes linger longer than I'd ever expect which makes me squirm that much more.

"I don't see anything wrong with your ass," he whispers with that half-smile that melts my defenses like butter in a frying pan.

"You can't see my aching muscles," I reply as I try to will the blush away.

"No, but I could massage them for you," he offers with the gentle raise of that right eyebrow, causing it to disappear completely beneath his hat.

Tempting. Oh, so very tempting.

"Anyway," I start as I clear my throat. "My point is that I will never trust Corie again. She said spinning class is great for beginners and that I'd love it. She lied. It was horrible and the only thing I loved was when he said it was a wrap."

Beau laughs that deep, intoxicating laugh that makes me think of honey and sex, though not together. "Can't say I've ever takin' a spinnin' class before. I'm more of a free weights kinda guy."

Don't I know it. I've had plenty of opportunities over the past two weeks to check out the way his plain t-shirt molds to his biceps and chest. If there's one thing I know, it's that Beau Tanner takes excellent care of his body.

"So, who am I up against on Wednesday?" I ask.

Beau stares at me for several heartbeats before answering. "Troy."

Shit.

"Troy? Are you serious?" I ask, my heart instantly dropping down to the toes of my black leather boots.

"Yeah, I'm serious. I know you're friends with him, but ya need to think of the competition. This isn't about friendship. Everyone here wants the half million and the record contract. You and Troy are no exclusion. Ya can't both win it at the end, right?" he asks with a pointed look, even though his eyes fill with sympathy for my uncomfortable situation.

"I know. It just sucks that we have to go against each other. I had kinda hoped we'd both still be here til the very end."

"And ya both could be. After each team picks their final three, then the coaches get to choose one contestant from the pool of cast-offs. Either one of ya will still have a chance."

Even though I understand what he's saying, doesn't mean I have to like it.

"Tomorrow we're meeting at the main studio to do run-throughs of the performances. You'll perform with the band and we'll finalize any last minute tweaks to the music, if needed. Any questions?" Beau asks as he hands me my schedule for the next few days.

Practice tomorrow, ensemble fitting, stage walk-through, and dress rehearsal.

"Nope, I'm good." I tell him as I grab my satchel.

"Don't worry about who you're going against," Beau says as he walks up and stands directly in front of me. I can smell the musk and woodiness in his cologne and the clean scent of his detergent. It takes everything I have not to run my nose up his chest and lick his neck.

I shudder at the mental images I'll be able to carry with me later tonight.

"Just give it your all like ya did with Shawna. You've got this. I have complete faith in ya," he says with that grin.

"You say that to everyone," I chastise.

Beau laughs before stepping into my personal space. The way my body responds to his invasion pretty much tells me he's welcome to occupy said space anytime. "True. But I really mean it with *you*."

I swallow hard and turn as the door opens. I barely even remember that a cameraman has been following me around for the past several days, documenting my every movement. I've become so accustomed to their voyeurism that I don't even realize they're there anymore.

"I'll see ya tomorrow on stage."

"You will. I'll be the one with the killer black leather dress and thigh-high boots."

Beau's face becomes darker and intense. His lighter demeanor and carefree features are replaced by stormy desire and lust. A raging storm brews within those gray eyes as they fill with a look I haven't seen in a man in forever. "I guess I have somethin' to look forward to then," he says in all seriousness.

"See you tomorrow," I whisper as I turn tail and head quickly towards the exit. If I hadn't witnessed the transformation first hand, I'd probably refute the thought that Beau responded to my description of tomorrow's attire. But watching his cheekbones tighten and his eyes widen with need was as plain as the nose on my face. And it definitely isn't something I'm going to forget anytime soon.

If ever.

*****

Note to self: Tuck your skirt in, Sally. You've got work to do.

I pace back and forth in that small green room. Tonight the room only contains half the bodies since the first half was thinned out last week. And after tonight's live show, we'll be down to even less.

Teams Beau and Sophia will go tonight, followed by Teams Felix and JoJo tomorrow night. At the very end of tomorrow night's show, the four coaches will have one final pick from the exiting contestants to round out their team of four. Next week starts the eliminations by viewer votes.

I've been running through my song all day, which isn't exactly a hardship when it's one of your favorites. Plus, it has one of those melodies that get stuck in your head for days at a time. Troy was bummed when I told him Monday night about going head to head, but his response was more humbling than anything I've ever experienced.

He said, "If I have to be eliminated, I want it to be against you. Because then I know I was eliminated by the best."

"You ready?" Ben asks, pulling me out of my melancholy moment.

"As I'll ever be. It just sucks having to go against Troy, you know?"

"Yeah, I know. But that's the nature of the beast. Eventually, we'll all have to square off against each other. Even if it's just in the next few rounds for votes."

"True. I just wish it didn't have to be this way tonight."

"Well, if you lose, then you still have a great chance of getting picked up by another coach. And if you win, same goes for Troy." Ben turns me so I'm squarely facing him. "Don't worry about all that right now. Don't think about who you're up against or what Beau might think. Just go out there and sing. Give it everything you've got, and if at the end of it, Beau doesn't pick you? Then, you go home with your head held high cause you gave it everything you had. You've got this tonight."

"Thanks, Ben," I tell him with a small smile as he pulls me in for a hug. It lasts several heartbeats longer than your typical friendship hug, which tells me that Ben's feelings for me still haven't gone anywhere. He continues to hold me tight in his warm embrace.

I wish I felt something for Ben. Even though he lives a couple of states away, he's a great looking guy. He's funny and sweet, and he seems to really like me. That alone seems like a major feat in itself because it's been awhile since a guy has seemed interested in me. Not the bartender with a sliver of belly showing or the great voice, but the girl underneath all of that. The girl who guards her heart like Fort Knox, but loves fiercely when she finally lets you in.

Of course, it has been years since I've let anyone in. Not since Colton. And thinking about him is a trip down to Sadville that I don't need to take right now. Right now, I need to concentrate on singing.

I gently pull back and let Ben's arms fall from around my back. The brief look on his face confirms that he's saddened by my lack of interest, but in true Ben fashion, he smiles that sexy cowboy grin and turns back on the teasing charm.

"We're on in about five minutes," he says as he steers me towards the table of bottled water. "Drink up a little and let's get ready to go."

Ten minutes later, we'll all standing with our designated teams waiting for the live show to begin. I'm standing next to Troy at the end of our group. I can't help but tap my heel against the stage, dreading that moment when they fire up the lights. I'm still as nervous as a prostitute in church, but not nearly as terrified as I was last week.

I've got this.

*****

"Ready?" Beau's deep southern timber draws me out of my meditation behind the stage. I'm next. Troy and I will walk onto the stage with Beau, who will proceed to his seat along side of the other coaches at the table, leaving Troy and I on stage to perform.

"Yes," I tell him confidently.

"I wish I could take ya both to the next round, but I can't. Do your best and have fun. That's the most important part, right?" he asks with that half smile that I've come to love.

When we get the countdown, Troy and I are escorted to the entrance to the stage. On cue, we walk through the entrance and out into the blinding lights. The cheers of the audience naturally bring out a big smile as we both give waves to the masses.

We walk up to stand next to Becker at center stage. "Layne. Troy. Are you ready to square-off tonight?"

We both nod our heads in confirmation. "Then, let's get this competition underway. Troy, you're first."

I stand back as Troy confidently holds his microphone and waits for the music to start. The band starts up the recognizable music, and I hold my breath waiting for Troy to start singing the incredibly popular lyrics of Rod Stewart's "Maggie May." It doesn't take long before he's singing and letting the music carry him. He's confident and concentrating fiercely, all while performing outstandingly for the audience. And more importantly, for Beau. Beau's expression isn't giving anything away, though, even when Troy wraps up the song and receives huge applause from the crowd.

"Great job on a great song, Troy." Becker asks a couple of questions to Troy before he turns his attention to me. "And now, Layne Carter."

When the applause dies down and all of the lights are pointed at me like lasers, I patiently wait for the familiar melody. The guitar starts and the symbols chime. The faint beat of the drum beats low and firm as I let the music take over. Time to perform.

I stand still as I start that familiar first line of Heart's "Crazy On You."

"If we still have time, we might still get by…"

I move, I sing, I perform as if my life depends on it. And frankly, my life on this show does. I feel these lyrics, this melody straight to my core. I feel it deep down in my bones, my heart singing along with each word that comes from my mouth. That's what singing does to me. My heart beats wildly in my chest and I feel the music so profoundly, it becomes me.

Before I know it, the song is done. The audience is going crazy just as I did a few moments ago in the song. The coaches all clap and offer smiles as I take a quick little bow. However, the one face that isn't smiling is the one of my handsome coach. Beau.

Dread and a little bit of fear tingles all the way down to my toes. My smile falters as I try to compose the raging emotions that are trying to break free from my body. As much as I try to calm myself, the feeling that this is it takes root in my body and won't let go. I know. He won't pick me. He looks so intense, almost angry.

"Layne Carter, everyone," Becker says. "Layne, how do you feel after your second week on *Rising Star*?"

"I feel great. I'm having an amazing time and have a great coach."

"Now, if you are chosen in this round to advance, next week starts the viewer voting. How confident are you that you have what it takes to be the next *Rising Star*?"

"Well, I hope I have what it takes. I have my own struggles just like everyone else, so I am confident that I'll give it my best. That's all I can ask for."

"Thank you, Layne. Troy. Layne. Are you ready to hear from your coach, Beau Tanner?" The crowd erupts into screams just from saying his name.

"Well, y'all did a great job this week. I knew that this was going to be a hard decision for me." Troy reaches over and takes my hand within his. Comfort washes over me as I cling to this one last thread. Troy has become my friend. From day one, he was supportive. He's funny and passionate. He's a phenomenal singer and could easily be the next *Rising Star*.

"Troy, I knew you'd nail that song. Rod Stewart is an icon in this industry and your rendition of "Maggie May" was spot on. Layne, I realized that I needed a rock song to truly get ya comfortable on that stage, and you proved that ya belong here. Ya rocked it," he says which surprises me since he looked so mad after I was done singing earlier.

Becker turns to Beau. "So, Beau, who are you taking to the next round? Layne or Troy?"

Beau stares hard at the ground in front of our feet. You can practically see him weighing the odds in his mind. I still have no idea which way he's leaning as his face gives nothing away. I hope that he says my name, but I'm prepared from him to say Troy's. And that's okay.

"Tonight, I'm goin' to pick…" he gazes from Troy to me and back again several times. "My heart is leadin' me to pick Layne."

The audience explodes in eardrum piercing cheers. Troy pulls me into his big arms and hugs me fiercely. I have no idea what to do or say because as happy as I am to move on to the next round, the thought of not having Troy beside me breaks my heart.

"Win this damn thing," he whispers in my ear before placing a hard kiss on my forehead.

The rest of the show is a blur. I answer more questions on stage before I'm ushered back to the room with other contestants who are advancing. The others are whisked away to another room before tomorrow night's final appeal to the coaches. They'll have one last chance at becoming the next *Rising Star*. For everyone else, it's a plane ticket home and empty dreams.

And for at least another week, I am safe.

Chapter Twelve

Note to self: When they say the camera adds ten pounds, it's a lie. It adds twenty.

"What the hell is going on with you and Beau?" Tiffany yells into the phone after I return to the hotel. It's late. Damn late.

"Well, hello to you too, Tiff."

"Don't be cute. You. Beau. What's the scoop?"

"I don't know what you're talking about," I tell my boss slash friend. I plop down on my bed, stretching out as the tension and the excitement of the evening starts to ebb from my body.

"Uh, hello!? Are you for real? I saw how ablaze his eyes were when he watched you perform! You couldn't miss it. The cameraman kept zooming in on him while you sang, and he was practically stripping you naked and eye-fucking you to Sunday!"

"Oh. My. God. Did you just say eye-fucking?"

"Yes. Don't try to change the direction of this conversation. He was totally giving you the bedroom eyes while you were up there. I wouldn't be surprised if you didn't just get pregnant tonight. And on National television, you hussy."

"Tiff, get real. There's no way…" I start before she completely cuts me off.

"So, then after the show was over, I went to the website they've been promoting as a way to catch up with the behind the scenes drama. Layne, that man wants you. Like wants to do dirty things to your body for days on end, wants you. I'm not even going to get upset at the fact that you didn't call me the minute you left the studio after he was touching you. Okay, so maybe I'll hold just a little tinge of annoyance, and probably a little bit of jealousy, but -"

"Wait. What?"

"You heard me. Touching. You. Your face, your hair, your arm. It was all there on camera."

Oh. My. God. On freaking camera? How could I have forgotten that our entire lives are being filmed as a big voyeurism behind the scenes campaign?! I know instantly what she's talking about. It's a moment I haven't been able to erase from the forefront of my mind. It's imbedded like a tattoo.

"And not just one time, Layne. I'm a little pissed that you haven't told me about these moments you've shared with Mr. Hot Country Megastar before. By the way, did you know that he watches you when you're studying your music?" she asks in a hushed tone as if harboring a huge secret.

"What?" I ask as all of the oxygen is sucked out of the room.

"Yeah. He watches you all the time. It's actually really hot. It's like watching the building sexual tension in a porno. Well, if pornos had building sexual tension. And a storyline. Pornos definitely don't have a storyline. Unless you consider that cheese dialog where the guy comes into the office and finds his 'secretary' conveniently bent over his…"

"Tiff! Focus, please?"

"Oh. Right."

"What am I going to do?" I ask.

"What do you mean? If you want to kiss him, just kiss him."

"I can't. Contractual obligations, yada yada yada. He could lose his coaching job with the network and be sued. I would be kicked off the show."

"Oh. So, you let the sexual tension build and as soon as the show's over, you find a hall closet and unleash the tension. I bet that man has a huge piece of sexual tension in those tight pants. Have you seen the size of his hands?"

I actually laugh at her matter-of-fact tone. To her, it's just that simple. Get through the show, sneak off backstage and have a quickie in the first janitor's closet we come across. Piece of cake.

"Listen, sweetie. Obviously it won't be that easy. You both have commitments and obligations with the show. That doesn't mean you can't flirt, does it? Surely they don't have a freaking flirting clause in that phonebook of a contract you signed, right?"

"No. Relationships between contestants are fine. Something about ratings gold. Everyone likes a little drama, right? But the coaches are off limits."

"That's too bad because Beau Tanner should definitely *not* be off limits."

Right? There's no way in hell I can tell her about his starring roll in my dirty dreams lately. Lord knows what she'd do with that TMI. "So, tell me more about this behind-the-scenes garbage," I say, looking for a subtle subject change, and for the next fifteen minutes, she recalls all the behind-the-scenes drama that I've been missing including a few catfights and an affair between a young male contestant and an older female. She asked about the Shawna situation since she caught a few minutes of the "after." After agreeing to talk again soon, I signed off and jumped in the shower.

Very early in the morning as the sun threatens to peek over the mountaintops, I still can't sleep or stop thinking about what Tiff said about Beau. Does he really watch me when he thinks no one is looking? There are other women here who are much better looking than I am. Take Shawna for instance. You know that someday she's going to grace the pages of Country Weekly, wrapped in the arms of some gorgeous actor, model, or professional football player. She's stunning. Hell, even the young Bobbsey Twins are gorgeous. Sure they're barely legal, but when has that stopped a man with money, power, and influence?

Finally, I can't take it any longer and I fire up my laptop. With the few clicks of the mouse, I'm bringing up the *Rising Star* website and clicking the Behind the Scenes link. There are tons of daily videos posted, all right there for any Tom, Dick, or Harry to watch. I try not to dwell on the creepy thought as I click on a link titled, "Rehearsals." I pay no attention to the ones that don't mention my name. At the first one mentioning me, I click the link.

The video loads quickly and I instantly hear the sound of my voice filling my hotel room. The position of the camera is at the far wall smack in the middle between where I am standing and where Beau is sitting on his stool. It's the latest rehearsal. I'm singing the last series of lines. My eyes are closed and my hands move as if punctuating each note, each word of the song.

That's when I finally look over to Beau. He sits statue-still and his gray eyes look almost black from the distance of the camera. They appear dark and stormy as he watches me sing. But it's the unspoken emotions that flint across his face and those eyes that are the most startling. Lust. Desire. Want.

Holy shit, Tiffany might have been right.

I click on each video with my name above it and am drawn into our rehearsals, reliving them as if it were the first time, watching with fresh, new eyes. Each one is much of the same. Beau smiles at me so naturally and so easily. We talk and discuss music like old friends, practicing new ways to liven up whatever song I'm singing. After I watch every single one with my name on it, including the one Tiffany referred to about his touch, I click on the first video with Shawna. I watch for several seconds, waiting for those same emotions to cross Beau's face. But they never come.

Video after video, I watch, waiting for a reaction to those other girls. Younger girls, skinnier girls, girls with bigger boobs. Girls who practically offer themselves up on a platter like a Thanksgiving Day turkey. But I never see it. I never see him give them a second glance, and believe me, I look. The smiles are friendly, but not open. The gazes are assessing, but not all-consuming. The words are helpful, but not personal. Beau is completely different with everyone else.

Everyone but me.

*****

"This is our week for team performances, so in addition to your individual practices, we'll have a few scheduled team practices," Beau says at large to his final team of four. Me, Ben, Chelsea, and Maxwell, who was Beau's pick from the cast offs last night.

After Team Felix and JoJo performed, the four coaches each picked one contestant from the sea of cast offs to fill their final spot. They drew numbers to determine their picking order. I was pleasantly surprised to see Troy picked up on Team Felix and cheered harder than anyone else when Felix called his name. What I was least surprised about, but even less excited for, was that Shawna, AKA Dramatic Barbie, was picked up on Team Sophia. Girl power or something like that.

"We'll have a quick practice this mornin' before I have to catch a flight, but I'll be back on Sunday mid-afternoon. I want to have a lengthy practice on Sunday and Monday night to nail down our team performance. We'll be singin' 'Love Shack' by the B-52's."

We all give a little cheer, unable to control our excitement of singing the iconic B-52's song.

"Here are the music sheets for everyone. I've made indications so everyone can start to learn their parts. I picked a fun song because I want y'all to just have fun with it. There's no votes, no comments on this one. It's just us all havin' a good time together," Beau stresses with a warm smile.

Over the next hour, we run through the song several times. This rendition is totally different from the version you hear on the radio because so much of our team is predominantly country. There's a hint of twang in each line. Well, each line but mine.

Beau is going to sing with us, but he'll be perched at the top of a ramp playing the drums. I didn't know he could play which doesn't seem to surprise everyone else in the room. Apparently, I'm the only one who really didn't follow Beau Tanner prior to arriving on the show. At the very end of practice, Beau runs through our stage positioning for this performance. Since this is a non-judged routine, the stage set-up is a little more elaborate. Risers and stage props are used to give a different feel to the show. Chelsea and I will be singing from a set of risers for the first half of the performance before we all start to work the stage and move around in strategic, pre-determined positions.

"Ready to go?" Ben asks as he places his hand on my lower back and gently steers me towards the door at the end of our group practice. My practice time isn't until late morning so I have a couple of hours before I have to be back here to learn what song I'm going to be singing next week.

"Yeah, let's go grab some breakfast before we have to be back here," I say as we get ready to walk through the door.

Suddenly, the hairs on the back of my neck stand up and I feel his gaze following me. I turn just before walking through the open door and find Beau intently watching me. His eyes peruse down my body, stopping at my lower back. It's when they return to mine a moment later, full of fire, that I realize that Ben is still touching me. Stepping to the left, I dislodge myself from Ben's hand and turn to walk out the door. As I go, I feel the force of those eyes following me the entire way. It's moments like this that stir my body to life. I feel wanted, but in a greater way than I feel while working at the bar. Yeah, guys there want me and hit on me left and right. But the way Beau watches me? That's an entirely different sensation. One that I'm unfamiliar with. One that I wouldn't mind finding out a little bit more about.

*****

Talking with Mom and Eli tonight is excruciating. I can't control the tears that gather in my eyes as I see his perfect little face on the computer monitor. If Skype could somehow figure out how to transport my son to my hotel room, I would give my soul.

It's been over two weeks since I held him in my arms. Seeing his face every night is one thing, but not holding him is an entirely different animal. I feel loss like I've never really experienced before–even after Colton. I crave those little moments that I took for granted when we had so much free time together. Now, I have nothing but a few kisses and touches against the hard computer screen.

I knew this was coming, sure. But that doesn't make this distance any easier. You can prepare yourself for the loss as much as possible, but until you're living it, day in and day out, your preparations are futile.

Eli presses his sticky lips against the computer screen. "I wove you, Mommy," he says with a big grin.

I don't even try to stop the tears as I blow a kiss to the camera, giving him the biggest smile I can fake. My heart breaks wide open as I gear up for another goodbye. "Good night, buddy. Mommy loves you so, so, so, so much. Be a good boy for Grandma, okay?"

"Tay!" he yells before hopping down off my mom's lap and heading off to play.

"This is getting so hard," I confess to my mom.

"I know, sweetie. He struggles in the mornings when he wakes up. He always looks over at your empty bed and starts to whine. I know you don't want to hear it, but he misses you just as much as you are missing him. He's just easier to distract with cartoons and toys." The tears fall unchecked as I think about his perfect little face marred with little tears and distress. I'm rarely ever there when he goes to bed at night, but I'm always there when he wakes in the morning. Or at least I used to be.

"There's still up to six weeks left, Mom. I don't know if I can make it."

"You can, and you will. We did not go through rearranging our entire lives for you to quit now. You've got this, sweetie. You are the strongest woman I know. You are brave and fearless and deserve this shot more than anyone there. I promise it won't be too much longer, okay?" she offers with a small smile.

"I love you, Mom. I promise to give it my all."

"I love you, too, baby girl. Just focus on your practices and singing. We'll all be here for you when you get back."

"I know. I will."

After signing off, I cry for several minutes as the loneliness washes over me like the first cold rain in March. I'd do anything to hold Eli in my arms and fall asleep with him snuggled against my body.

But as much as I want to walk away from all of this and just go home–home to Eli–I want the future that this show could provide for him more. I want to not have to worry about the balance in my checkbook. I want to be able to buy him a toy and not worry if I'll be able to pay the phone bill because of it. I want to provide him with a solid education, stable home and background, and as much love as I could possibly offer. If I can't do all of the above, at least I know I can do the last. Because at the end of the day, I love that little boy more than life itself. I would do anything in my power to give him the life he deserves.

And today, that includes finishing this competition.

Chapter Thirteen

Note to self: Not all surprises are good surprises!

"I thought you were supposed to have practice tonight," Corie says as she gathers up her workout bag.

"I thought so too. I don't know what happened. We had our individual practice earlier today and Beau never mentioned anything about a cancellation. In fact, he told me he'd see me tonight. Maybe he's sick?" I say as I walk with Corie towards the door. We're supposed to have our last group practice for our team performance tonight for this week's performance. We're supposed to practice at the studio one more time before we do the run through on the stage Wednesday morning.

"Maybe. I don't know, but I do know this: you now have the night off. So come with me!"

"And where would you be going? Last time I trusted you and went along with your shenanigans, my ass hurt for a week," I remind my pint-sized friend.

"That's because you're out of shape. All the more reason for you to join me in tonight's class," Corie says as we leave her hotel room and head down to mine.

"What kind of class is it?" I ask as I insert the plastic keycard.

"One that every woman should do at least once."

"I don't like the sound of that," I mumble as I step inside and grab my workout clothes.

"No t-shirt. You need to wear tight stuff. Just grab your sports bra and a pair of stretchy shorts. Oh, grab those tiny purple ones," she says with a saucy grin.

I don't like the feel of this. Not one bit.

"Corie -" I start before she cuts me off.

"Don't question. Just grab the clothes, change, and let's go! Class starts in thirty minutes," she says with twinkling eyes.

I gather my belongings and step inside my bathroom. Something tells me I'm going to regret the day I met Corie Brooks.

We decide to walk to the studio since it'll be a great warm-up, or so Corie says. Me? I just want to stretch out on the bed and take a nap. There are so many more things I'd rather be doing other than working out on my night off. Namely sleeping. I haven't slept well since my phone conversation with Tiffany last week. I analyze everything from the length of time Beau glances at me to the way he brushes my fingers casually when he's pointing to the music sheets we're discussing.

Corie tells me all about the drama surrounding her team. Apparently the older woman and younger man contestants have been flaunting their tryst on and off the camera. After a few blocks of discussing who's sleeping with who, she tries to pick my brain about Beau, but I've become a pro at the art of deflection. Even Corie isn't going to get more out of me right now. Besides, I can't exactly talk openly about what–if anything–is happening with Beau when you're being trailed by a camera crew everywhere you go. Plus, there's the fact that I, myself, don't even really understand what is happening with the man. I do know this: there is chemistry and enough sexual tension to slice it with a dull knife. But that's the end of it. Beau has never made an advance or a proposition for anything more than subtle flirting. It's almost like I'm imagining the whole thing. But then I'll catch him watching me from beneath the brim of his cowboy hat, and the fire is evident in his eyes. I know there's more there. I feel it.

We walk into the front of the studio and head back towards the gym. I follow along as Corie leads me down a long hallway towards the back room. The sign outside of the door catches my eye instantly sending little shivers of dread, and maybe a little bit of excitement, coursing through my body.

Introduction to Pole Dancing.

I stop dead in my tracks as Corie opens the big wooden door. "Please tell me you're kidding, Corie," I mumble, searching her eyes as I wait for the moment she yells 'Gotcha!'

"Why would I joke about something like this? I've heard these are the best workouts out there! They're supposed to do amazing things to your Abdominals and Gluteus Maximus," she says with a little bit of a smirk.

"My abs and glutes are just fine," I tell her.

"Fine. They're great, but this is going to be fun! You never know when the things you learn here will come in handy. Come on," she says as she pulls me into the classroom.

Inside, a dozen poles are bolted from the ceiling to the floor, strategically placed around the room so that each girl has enough room to maneuver. I drudge along behind my little spitfire friend until we find an empty spot along the back wall for our bags. Now I see why she told me not to wear loose clothing.

"Come on, let's grab a spot," she says as she pulls me towards two open poles in the back of the room. They might be right by the entrance, but at least they're as far away from those floor-to-ceiling mirrors that line the walls around the room.

"Good evening, good evening," an older petite woman says as she steps out from a hidden door at the front of the room. "I am Eleanor and I will be your instructor for Introduction to Pole Dancing," she adds dramatically as she does a little curtsy.

"We're going to get a great workout tonight. Let's begin with a little stretching, shall we?" she asks before pressing a button on the sound system on the floor by her pole. Instantly, Bruno Mars "Uptown Funk" is piped through the ceiling. It's a catchy tune that I've heard several times and instantaneously pulls you into the beat and soul of the music.

"Grab your bar with your right hand and reach down to your foot, stretching and extending for a count of five, four, three, two, and one. And now switch. Stretch and reach. Feel the pull as you reach and hold it. Five, four, three, two, and one."

After Eleanor takes us through a series of stretches and warm ups, all involving our metal pole, she begins to teach us the basics of the routine we are apparently learning this evening.

"Ok, ladies, we're going to start with three basic maneuvers for pole dancing. The first is the Fireman. You're going to stand on the tips of your toes like so and use your dominant arm to grip the pole as high as possible without feeling uncomfortable."

The eleven other ladies all follow the instructions, watching Eleanor as she extends gracefully up on the balls of her feet and grabs the pole.

"Grip the pole tightly in what is called a baseball hold, similar to how you would grip a baseball bat. Keeping your shoulders back, you're going to take three steps around your pole, like so," she says as she demonstrates the move. "Give yourself a little push off of your outside leg and use that momentum to swing around the pole and spin. Make sure you keep your inside arm in a firm position so that you don't kiss the pole," she adds with a smile.

It takes me several attempts to feel comfortable enough to actually try this move on the pole, but once I let go and actually do it, I find it easier than I thought. Fun, actually. Freeing.

"Excellent, ladies, excellent. Our next move we're going to learn is the Pinwheel. This maneuver has the same technique as the Fireman, but instead of both legs wrapping around the pole like this," she says as she demonstrates a perfect Fireman twirl, "you're going to extend a leg out, low and back, like this," she continues as she shows us the move.

It doesn't take us long to catch on to the slight variation of the move we've already learned, so Eleanor moves us along to our third maneuver, the V Spin.

"This one is going to showcase your strength, ladies. You are going to extend your dominant hand up to the top, but instead of your other hand being chest level, you're going to extend it downward like this," she says, showing us the arm positioning.

"Keep your pelvis forward and your grip wide as your extend your legs," she says, showing us a damn good V Spin. My arms are already throbbing and just the thought of having to use them in this twirl scares me a little.

"Very slowly slide down the pole as you twirl, keeping your arms extended and your legs straight."

After we practice our three basic moves, Eleanor teaches us some seductive dancing moves. I should probably die of embarrassment at this point, but to be honest, it's actually kind of fun. I'm probably going to be feeling it tomorrow in my arms and legs, but to be able to let loose and dance somewhat provocatively is freeing. It makes me feel like a woman. Sexy. Alluring.

"Excellent work. We're going to take a quick water break and then start to piece it all together into the small routine," Eleanor says as we all venture over to our water bottles.

"Well?" Corie asks as she takes a big pull from her pink bottle.

"It's actually kinda fun," I confess before taking another drink of my own water.

"You have moves, girl," she says with a big smile and a wink.

"Well, I don't know about that, but it's fun to try." I take the hand towel and wipe off as much sweat as I can from my face and arms. This is definitely a workout.

"Okay, let's get back to our poles. The last half of class is going to be putting the routine together and executing. I'm going to teach you the dance piece by piece. If you have any questions at any point, just holler," Eleanor instructs as we all take our places at our poles.

After another thirty minutes of learning the routine, we're finally running through it with music. "Lady Marmalade" by Christina Aguilera, P!nk, Lil' Kim, and Mya pipes through the speakers, loud and proud. It's the perfect song for seduction. It's tantalizing and provocative, and makes me want to put a little extra shake in my hips.

"We've only got five minutes left, ladies. Let's take it from the top one last time. Give it your all. Put your hips and your ass into the dance. Feel the music and let it move you," Eleanor tutors from the front of the room.

We all take our places around the outside of the room as the music starts one final time. The walk towards the pole is key to setting the tempo and the mood for the dance. I crisscross my legs over each other as I walk, putting as much hip action into the act until I reach my pole. I touch it, caressing it, as I take my position for our first spin. I close my eyes and let the music wash over me, absently singing along. I move my hips, running my hand seductively down my side, and roll my neck backwards as I dance the moves I now know by heart. Another twirl and hip thrust later and I'm almost to my favorite part of the routine. The V Spin.

I gather myself and get ready for the spin. I open my eyes, placing my hands in the proper position on the pole when my eyes collide with a set of dark ones full of smoldering embers…and anger. I stumble momentarily at the realization that Beau is standing in the open doorway right behind me. He's watching me through the mirror, shock written all over his gorgeous features.

I keep my eyes locked on his through the mirror as I start the V Spin. I take my eyes off of him just long enough to spin completely around the pole, dropping down to a squatting position before I roll my body back up from my knees all the way up to my chest, rolling against the cold hard metal. When I hit the final pose, I'm panting from exertion and probably a little from the sparks of desire my own body is suddenly producing.

"Oh my God, that's Beau," Corie gasps next to me.

No shit. And he looks pissed.

"I didn't realize we had a guest," Eleanor says from the front of the room, drawing the attention from everyone in the room.

Loud giggles and gasps of shock bounce off the mirror-covered walls as Beau Tanner's dark eyes remain locked on mine.

"Ladies, y'all did great. I was hopin' I could speak to Layne for a moment. In private," he says through gritted teeth, the intensity in his eyes never wavering from mine.

"Oh, Beau Tanner. You can borrow her for as long as you'd like," Eleanor purrs like a cat as she fans her suddenly flush face.

"Layne," Beau says as more of a statement than a question.

My legs are Jell-O as I follow him through the doorway and into the narrow hall; though I'm not one hundred percent sure my shaky legs are from the workout. He walks with purpose straight across the hall and opens a closet marked "Janitor." Without even looking at me, he holds the door open and waits.

Once inside, Beau doesn't flip on the light as the heavy door shuts with finality, encompassing us in nothing. It takes my eyes several seconds to adjust to the darkness. The only light is what little bit is filtering through the cracks in the mini blinds on the windows. The only sound is the deep pants coming from Beau. Or coming from me. Take your pick.

Before I can even question what I'm doing in the janitor's closet, I hear the heavy steps of Beau's cowboy boots as he takes three large steps towards me. He spins me around and slams his mouth down onto mine so fast and with so much dominance that all thought evaporates from my mind. Poof. Gone into thin air.

Beau sweeps his tongue along the seam of my lips causing my mouth to open instantaneously as I moan my approval. The feel of his hot, wet tongue against mine sends shockwaves of lust spiraling out of control throughout my body. He wraps his strong, muscular arms around my sweaty body, plastering me against unforgiving muscles and hot flesh. I can feel his body heat burning me through his tight black t-shirt, but I don't mind. Hell no, I don't mind at all. Beau nips at my lips, sucking my lower lip ever so gently into his mouth. I practically melt into a pile of hormonal mush right then and there.

"God, you drive me crazy," Beau mumbles through gritted teeth. "Watchin' you work that pole may have been the sexiest fuckin' thing I've ever witnessed. I will forever picture your body wrapped around that damn piece of metal. The way your hips swayed in rhythm to the music. The way your body moved. It reminded me of sex, Layne. Pure, unadulterated, rough sex that I want to have with you so fuckin' bad my entire body is throbbin'." And to prove his point, Beau presses his rock hard groin against the slickness of my spandex shorts. The friction alone practically causes me to orgasm.

"Where were ya tonight?" he whispers harshly as he pulls away from me, causing me to stumble from the sudden vacancy. Tension fills the space where his body once was.

"What?" I ask, trying to shake lose any ounce of dignity and common sense I can muster.

"Tonight. Ya skipped rehearsal to pole dance? Do you even understand what you've done and what message you've sent to the network by skippin' our final rehearsal before Wednesday mornin's run-through? I can't believe -" he says as I cut him off.

"Wait. What? I didn't skip rehearsal, you cancelled."

"I did not. Why would you even think that?" he asks as those gray eyes blaze a trail straight to my soul. Even through the darkness, I can see those hungry eyes.

"I got a note," I whisper. "There was a note left for me at the front counter. It said you were cancelling team practice tonight."

"Darlin', I didn't send any note. Everyone else was there. Everyone but you."

"But…that doesn't make any sense," I whisper, dumbfounded. Why did I get that note?

"Shawna stopped by the rehearsal on her way out and mentioned that she saw you goin' into that dance studio."

Of course. Shawna.

Well played, Conniving Bitch Barbie. Well played.

"Shawna," I mumble, dropping my head and giving it a little shake. I can't control the bubble of laughter that erupts from my mouth. Lord knows this situation isn't funny. Not once tiny bit. "I can't believe she did this. No wait. I can believe it."

"You're sayin' Shawna did this?" Beau asks, his anger subsiding dramatically as he takes two steps forward and right back into my personal space.

"Who else? You said it yourself that I was the only one who wasn't at practice. Then she 'conveniently' stopped by and ratted me out on where I was? She totally set me up," I defend, making air quotes when I say conveniently to better accentuate my point.

"You didn't intentionally skip practice to prepare yourself for your new career as a pole dancer?" he asks, wrapping those large, defined arms around me once more.

"Is that what she said?" I laugh.

"She said you couldn't handle the pressure of performin'. She said she heard you were quittin'."

"I'm not quitting, not even a little. I will fight until I'm voted off, Beau. I want to be here," I tell him a little breathlessly since his arms are wrapped around me again.

"What about here?" he asks as he pulls me taut against his body. "Do ya want to be right here?"

"Yes," I whisper, knowing that it's probably the wrong answer. I try to latch onto the tiny voice in my head screaming that this is a mistake. I grab onto that little sliver speaking on behalf of my conscious with so much force, that I practically stumble backwards. Fortunately, if I'm thinking with my heart, Beau is still holding onto me and keeps me from faltering. Or unfortunately if I let my head do the talking. "We can't do this," I finally get out between my desert-dry lips.

"I know," Beau answers as his lips hover momentarily above mine. "But I don't know how much longer I can fight this."

His confession is like a punch to the esophagus. Swallowing becomes harder and breathing non-existent. The air between us sizzles and crackles as he moves a fraction of an inch forward and places his warm, wet lips against mine. I respond instantly...again. But this time, the kiss doesn't deepen. It doesn't last longer than a few seconds, yet it's long enough to scramble any remaining brain cells.

Beau is panting and his eyes remain closed as he leans forward, placing his forehead against mine. "I'm goin' to do everything in my power to not do that again, but I need ya to understand somethin'. I need ya to know that, while I'm not physically kissin' ya, I'm imaginin' that I am. While I'm not touching your soft skin, my fingers are twitching to caress you. And while my arms aren't wrapped around ya, my body aches to have you against me. Being in your presence isn't near enough. I need to touch you, and now that I've had a little taste, this is goin' to be the greatest struggle of my life."

God, those words. Like words to a song, they're deep and meaningful and have me so completely spellbound with him that I don't know which way is up. And I'm starting to think that's okay.

"Practice tomorrow mornin' at nine. We'll run through your parts of the group song first and then do your individual practice afterwards. I'll see you tomorrow, right?" Beau finally opens those dark, soulful eyes, stealing my breath once more.

"Yes," I whisper.

"Good. I'll be lookin' forward to it," he says as he places one more kiss on my swollen lips. "And I'll be thinkin' of you tonight." His confession is like a lightning strike straight to my tingling lady parts.

I can't even respond. The words I try to say come out a mumbled grunt. I feel cool air against my body as Beau steps away, putting great distance between us. We both take several minutes to get our breathing under control before Beau grabs the doorknob.

"Ready?" he asks and I can feel his eyes on me even through the darkness.

"Yes."

Suddenly we're bathed in florescent lighting from the hallway. I blink rapidly as my eyes adjust to the sudden onslaught of brightness, and as soon as my eyes adjust, I'm staring straight into the lens of a large black camera.

Beau stands between me and the device recording my every move as Corie approaches from my left. "Oh my God, girl!" she whispers harshly into my ear. "I thought you were supposed to wait until after that final show before you maul the man in the closet." Her eyes twinkle and her smile is mischievous.

"It's not like that," I defend even though my face colors the same shade as a fuchsia crayon. It's a good thing a liar's pants don't *actually* catch on fire.

"It's never like that," she replies with a wink before throwing my workout bag into my chest and dragging me down the hallway, leaving Beau and the nosey camera in our wake. I don't turn around, fearful of what the camera would see on my face. Fearful of what I'll see on Beau's face.

We head straight towards a waiting van, ready to take the last few contestants back to the hotel. The hotel. Where I'm expected to not let the images of Beau and the memories of that kiss consume my thoughts. Where I'm not supposed to lie in bed and imagine that I'm not alone. Where I'm supposed to find sleep and rest for tomorrow's practice.

I have a feeling sleep won't be my friend at all tonight.

Note to self: Grab some sleeping pills. Maybe some Jack Daniels. Yeah, go with the Jack.

*****

"Layne and Chelsea are going to be right here," Mallory says at the base of the riser. Mallory is the resident choreographer who dictates our placement during the routines. Usually when we work with her on our individual performances, it's not nearly as time consuming and detailed. But, this is a group performance and there's a lot to take in.

"Ben, you're going to be over here," she says as she leads Ben to the opposite side of the stage. "And finally, Maxwell, over here," she says situating him to center stage.

Beau is sitting at the top of back risers, a hard metal staircase leading up from the stage. Halfway through the song, Chelsea and I will split up and work the crowd as we try to get them into the song–as if someone needs help getting into "Love Shack." However, while Chelsea goes out and into the audience, I will go up the stairs and towards our team leader.

He's perched up at the top of the center stage riser, casually sitting behind a drum set wearing his trademark tight jeans and a black t-shirt. His legs are extended and his arms are crossed over his chest. Each hand holds a drumstick and he looks as carefree as humanly possible. Until you get to his eyes. His eyes are always intense. Constantly.

In addition to our team performance, tonight is our first performance where the fan votes determine our future. For my individual number, Beau picked a song I haven't heard in years. Years. When he said Nancy Sinatra, I just prayed that I could do his song choice justice because it's a classic. The video is iconic. And tonight, I'll be wearing a tasteful black leather bustier with red satin ribbons laced up the front, matching black leather shorty-shorts and boots. Thigh high black leather boots with red satin laced up the fronts. My hair will be teased high in a true Nancy do, and my makeup dark and dramatic.

"Let's run through it again," Mallory says as we get back in our starting places as instructed.

Our outfits for tonight are something straight out of the seventies, which works well for me with my big, teased Nancy hair. My dress is white with big pink and blue flowers. How they found matching heels, I'll never know. And I probably don't want to know. Chelsea's dress is a pink number with silver and gold sequins in a psychedelic pattern. The guys sport some crazy, brightly colored shirts with tall collars and black dress pants.

We all spend the rest of the day doing run-throughs with Mallory, vocal run-throughs with network vocal assistants, and hair and makeup. On live show days, you don't have time to pee, let alone think. These are the days that give me a sense of purpose. They remind me of why I'm here. They leave no room for wallowing in self-pity.

At 6:45, Gabby gathers us all up from the back green room, which couldn't have come at a better time. I've caught stares and glares from some of the other contestants tonight, especially Shawna. An uneasy feeling settles in, as I get ready to go on stage.

"Hey, is it just me or is everyone staring at me?" I whisper to Corie before she goes to stand with her teammates.

"Um, well…" she starts but stops.

"What, Corie?"

"So rumor has it that you're sleeping with Beau, and that's why you were chosen over Shawna and Troy," she says quietly.

"You've got to be kidding me," I mumble, taking several calming breaths in and out. "Why would they think that?"

"Well, everyone seems to be listening to whatever garbage Shawna is spewing. Throw in that video that went live last night with you and Beau coming out of that janitor's closet, and she has just enough leverage to make it look like her lies are true."

"I don't believe this," I mumble.

"Listen, honey. I know that you're not sleeping with him and that you have what it takes to win this whole thing. Use that and show these skinny, catty bitches who's the boss!"

I can't help but laugh as I throw my arms around my friend. She hugs me back fiercely which is just what I need since I can't hug my loved ones right now.

"Five minutes," Gabby yells from the front of the backstage area.

"Tonight, you're going to sing for votes so it doesn't matter what everyone says. It's not Beau's choice whether you stay or go tonight. Got it?" I nod at my friend and get into position for the start of the live show.

"Welcome to *Rising Star*," Becker says as he flashes that bright white smile to the camera. "Tonight, each of these sixteen contestants will perform for your votes. If you want a contestant to stay, then you need to vote because every vote counts." I smile as the camera pans across the stage giving each contestant camera time.

"Let's bring out the coaches, shall we?" When Beau, Felix, Sophia, and JoJo step onto the stage, Becker throws us the biggest shock of the evening. "Tonight, each contestant will perform. Tomorrow night, someone will go home. And not just one person. Tomorrow night, live, the contestant with the lowest votes from *each* team will go home! That's right. Tomorrow night, we will go from sixteen contestants to twelve. Are you ready?"

And just like that, the competition is officially on.

When it's finally time for me to perform, I give myself one last look in the tall mirror behind the stage. My hair is big and poofy and my lips are blood red. The bustier classily pushes a little cleavage heavenward, and I'm thankful for the extra time I've put in at the gym recently with Corie because these shorts leave nothing to the imagination. But my favorite part is these boots. I've been trying to figure out how to smuggle them out of here when I'm done.

Note to self: Bring large tote bag tomorrow to the reveal.

Because if I'm going home, I'd prefer to be going home with fabulous boots.

I walk out onto the stage, positioning myself in the spot Mallory indicated for me, and I wait for the audience cheers to die down before I hear the familiar start of the song.

"You keep saying, you've got something for me. Something you call love but confess."

I look out at the audience as I make my way to the front of the stage where the coaches are sitting and watching. They all wear big smiles as I sing the classic tune, but it's Beau's eyes that all but steal my breath. I have to look away quickly to keep myself from fumbling the song. Knowing that he's watching is equally intoxicating and nerve-wracking. It makes me put a little more swing in my hips, a little more sass in my walk. I channel my inner pole dancer as I use some of the hip moves to my advantage. I put everything I have into this routine, giving it every ounce of energy and feistiness I possess. I'm a woman scorn, but hell bent on proving that I don't need a man. Just like the song.

When I finish, the audience is on their feet and cheering for me. The smile on my red lips is genuine as I take in the accolades before making my way over to where Becker is standing. I have yet to look over at Beau or the rest of the coaches for fear that I'll lose my bearings and do something incredibly stupid like trip.

"Layne Carter," Becker says to the crowd. "Layne, how are you feeling tonight?"

"Great, Becker. How can you not after a song like that?" I ask with a sassy smile.

"Your coach, Beau Tanner, seems to have a way of bringing your natural attitude and charisma out with each performance."

"He picks great songs for me that fit my personality," I say.

"That he does, Layne. Let's hear from some of the coaches about your performance tonight. JoJo?"

JoJo flips her coal black hair over her shoulder before speaking. "I agree. Beau seems to have this knack for picking awesome songs that fit your style. Tonight's performance was entertaining and energetic. I loved it."

"Sophia?" Becker cues.

"First off, great performance tonight. But what I really want to know is if I can borrow those boots when we're done here," she says with a huge smile while the audience erupts into cheers. "Seriously! I love them and would figure out how to work them into my wardrobe on the road."

"Felix?"

"Layne, Layne, Layne. That was amazing. You worked that stage like you've been doing this for years. Each time you come out here, I kick myself for not pleading harder to get you on my team," Felix says.

"Beau? What did you think of tonight performance?" Becker asks the cowboy in front of us. My heart rate kicks up a few hundred beats per minute while I wait for him to critique me.

Clearing his throat before he speaks, Beau finally says, "After hearin' ya sing that song, I feel like it was written just for you. Like you were meant to perform that song live on this stage.

You have this natural ability to make any song your own without changing much. Your version was probably better than Nancy's and way better than Jessica Simpson's."

"Well, there you have it. If you want to see Layne Carter next week, she needs your votes. Call 1-800-555-7006 or log on to rising star dot com and cast your votes there. Up next, Corie Brooks."

And with that, my performance for tonight is complete.

*****

"Hey, Layne, great performance," Ben says as we gather up our personal belongs after the show. The audience has finally cleared out and the stage crew is busy prepping the studio for tomorrow night's vote off.

"Oh, thanks. You did great, too."

"Layne, can I have a word, please?" I hear from behind. I don't need to turn to see exactly who is standing behind me. If the deep twangy timbers of his voice didn't give it away, the invisible electricity coursing through the air and shooting straight at me would do it.

"Sure," I reply as I follow Beau towards a door at the end of the hallway.

I know instantly where we're going. I've never been this far down the hallway, but everyone knows that the end of the hall is reserved for the coaches. Beau opens a door with his name on it, politely ushering me through. The door closes with a definitive latch, sealing us off from the rest of the contestants and production crew. Suddenly, I'm apprehensive about how it's going to look to everyone else that I'm alone with this man…again.

"There are no cameras in here," Beau states as if sensing my anxiety.

"Oh," I reply, the word hitching in my dry throat.

"Are ya okay?" he asks, removing that trademark black Stetson and running his hand through his midnight hair.

"Yeah, why?" I ask as I shuffle from foot to foot, trying to figure out something to do with my hands. Something that *doesn't* involve running my own fingers through those dark, dark locks.

"Well, I was informed of a rumor runnin' around amongst the contestants."

"Oh, that. Yeah, it's fine. I imagine they just need something to talk about. It'll blow over soon enough."

Beau takes a step forward, so very close to invading the personal space that I want him to enter. *Oh, no you don't!* "For your sake, I hope you're right. I'm used to this shit, but you aren't. Just don't listen to the crap. They'll say and do just about anything to get ahead in this game. That includes sabotagin' your game to better their own," he adds while giving me a pointed look as if to remind me of Monday night's FUBAR.

"I'll keep my eyes open," I reply, willing my legs to stay planted and not step closer to Beau.

As if reading my mind, he steps forward once more until I'm consumed by his body heat. If it was anyone else, I would have stepped back and put some distance between us, but with Beau, I only want to greedily step closer yet.

"You did great tonight," he whispers as he tucks a piece of my teased, hairsprayed-to-heaven hair behind my ear.

"Thank you," I respond, feeling a slight blush creep in at the compliment.

Another slight step forward.

"I really, really want to kiss you right now," he confesses as he runs his hand up my bare arm and lets it rest at my neck. His warm fingers kneed and flex as his thumb gently strokes my pulse point.

"I wouldn't mind that…if we weren't in the middle of this competition," I state, hypnotized by those damn eyes of his.

"I know." Beau rests his head against my forehead in the same manner he did the other night in the closet. We're close, so close, but not quite close enough.

"Can I ask you something?" I ask, knowing that I need to know the answer to the burning question that has been nagging me since I heard the rumor before tonight's show.

"Of course, darlin'."

It's now or never. "Last week, did you vote for me to advance to the next round because you're attracted to me?"

Beau's eyes darken instantly. I don't know how it's possible, but they do. His nostrils also flare out in a way that I would associate with anger or annoyance. "No," he says decisively. "I voted ya to the next round because you were better. Having you here with me every day is just an added bonus because I'm attracted to ya."

And then his lips are on mine. The kiss is hesitant at first, but as soon as I open my mouth, granting him the access he's seeking, all bets are off. My tongue duels with his, sliding back and forth in the most delicious way possible. I thread my fingers into that black hair, tugging ever so gently, while he pulls me flush against his hard body. When he moans into my mouth, my knees buckle. Fortunately, Beau holds me with such intensity that I know I'm not going anywhere.

A knock sounds at the door breaking the spell of the kiss. "Shit," Beau mumbles, yet not letting me go.

"I should go," I whimper, trying to pull away.

"I don't want you to go," he declares, locking his arms securely around my waist.

"I have to."

Beau leans forward one more time, placing his forehead against mine. The action has a calming response from me, and it appears to have the same effect on him. Our breathing starts to even out, but my heart rate is nowhere near normal.

"I'll see ya in the mornin'," he whispers before stepping back and away from me. The void of his body heat is felt instantaneously. I crave his touch, his kisses, his presence.

"I'll be there," I reply as he goes to open the door.

Gabby stands on the other side giving each of us a pointed, direct look. "Jackson is looking for you," she says to Beau while bouncing her eyes from him to me. You can practically see the wheels in her head spinning.

"I'll be right there. I was just discussin' tomorrow's performance with Layne," Beau says casually. You'd have no idea he had his tongue down my throat thirty seconds ago. I just pray that my lips aren't as swollen as I fear they are.

"Don't be long. The other coaches are already there." Gabby glances my way one last time before turning and heading back down the hall.

"I need to go and catch up with the others. I don't need to give them anymore reason to question me," I say.

"Tomorrow."

"Tomorrow," I confirm, taking in his heated gaze one more time before turning and walking out the door.

Damn. It's been two days since the closet incident and I'm already failing. And, miserably, at that. I'm never going to make it another five weeks. I'm not going to be able to resist him.

But I have to.

My life on this show–my career–depends on it.

Chapter Fourteen

Note to self: Stick that in your pipe and smoke it.

We all gather on stage for the big reveal. I'm wearing yesterday's ensemble like the other fifteen contestants on stage, huge smile plastered on my stiff face. Stiff because I'm wearing a quarter of an inch of putty–also known as makeup.

"Tonight, we'll have team performances for two of our four teams, plus a special performance from our musical guest, Carrie Underwood. We'll also reveal the fate of our sixteen contestants. Four will go home this evening, but right now, I'll reveal the first two saved contestants who will return next week." Becker pauses for dramatic effect before reading the card in his hand. "Our first contestant who is safe another week is…Shawna Reece! Our second contestant who is safe is…Ben Atwood!"

The audience cheers for both Shawna and Ben, while I reserve my accolades for only Ben. Getting rid of Shawna would have been a dream come true! Especially since the whispers after last night's performances about Beau and I only grew louder and more predominant.

Up next is our team performance, and I'm super nervous to perform with Beau and the rest of my group. Add in the fact that my fate on this show still hasn't been decided, and I'm jittery like a bouncy ball let loose in a confined space.

Chelsea and I head into a small dressing room and throw on our next outfits. After a quick spin in the chair to refresh hair and makeup, we're meeting up with the guys at stage right. When a member of the production crew gives us the sign, we all head out to our places on the darkened stage. We only have to wait a few moments before the commercial break ends and Becker starts to speak.

"Ladies and gentlemen, Team Beau performing 'Love Shack.'"

Beau counts down the beat with his drumsticks, and starts us off. *"If you see a faded sign at the side of the road that says fifteen miles to the..."*

"Love shack! Love shack, yeah." I belt out.

"I'm heading down the Atlanta highway," Chelsea sings.

There's something about this song that makes you want to stand up and sing. You can't sing it without picturing the B-52's video: the big hair, the big car, and the party atmosphere, and the crowd gets into the performance right along with us. By the time I make my way up the stairs towards Beau, I'm practically pulsating with excitement. Or maybe I'm actually pulsating because the closer I get to Beau, the more aware I am of his presence. He watches me from underneath his hat as I approach, never missing a beat as he plays his drums. I sing my next line from my position next to him, vibrating from the electricity coursing through the metal risers. The smirk he gives me almost melts me like an ice cube on a hot July afternoon. Those lips should come with a warning label.

Warning: Deadly weapons with the intent to render any woman speechless, immobile, and ready to drop her panties.

My body moves in rhythm to the song. I sing my part for the crowd and the millions of people watching through the television. I sing for my three-year-old son who is watching me from his position on the floor in our living room. I sing for the man playing the drums next to me. Why? I don't know. I've never been concerned about what a man thinks of my singing, nor have I ever really sung for anyone. I sing for me. But tonight, I find myself singing for the man who intrigues me, intoxicates me, and consumes me. Tonight, I sing for Beau.

When the song is over, we all take our bows. Beau stands and waves his hands at each of us, giving us as much credit as he can. I'll admit we have a solid team. Ben has that strong country voice that reminds me of Jason Aldean. Yes, I might not be a country fan, but every woman in America knows who Jason Aldean is. Same with Beau Tanner.

Chelsea is a cute little sprite of a girl, barely the legal age. She's adorable in that overly endearing and peppy way that makes me want to vomit half the time. She's tiny enough to fit in my back pocket. But what endears me the most to Chelsea is that she's surprisingly *not* one of the people I hear constantly talking about the rumors. If she's talking, she hides it well.

And then there's Maxwell who I haven't really had much of an opportunity to chat with too much. He has a country vibe to him with a hint of classic rock, which might be why Beau gravitated towards him as his final pick for his team.

Either way, our team will suffer a loss tonight.

I just pray it isn't me.

*****

As I stand up on stage with seven other contestants, Chelsea directly to my right, I hold my breath as I patiently await the verdict of my future on the show. We're down to the final two for each team, and I've never been so nervous in my entire life.

"Ladies and gentlemen, it's time to reveal which contestant is saved from each team and which one will be saying goodbye tonight." Becker grabs the envelope and rips it open in a dramatic fashion.

"Team Sophia. The contestant who is safe and will return next week is…Kristie Maloney! That means Brock McMillan will be leaving us tonight."

After departing hugs are given to Brock, and Kristie joins the saved contestants on the opposite side of the stage, Becker returns his attention to his envelope. "Team JoJo. The contestant who is safe and returning to the competition next week is…Philippe Consuela! Jess Johansson, I'm sorry but your time on *Rising Star* is over tonight."

Again, more hugs and tears are shed at center stage. I glance over and see Troy with his big grin plastered on his face. He looks cool, calm, and way more collected than I'm sure I do right now.

"Team Felix. The contestant who is safe another week is…Marcus Hogan! Unfortunately, that means Troy Cartwright's time on *Rising Star* has come to an end."

I think Becker says something else, but I don't hear it. As soon as Marcus's name is read as the safe contestant, my entire body sinks down into a pool of sadness and loss. I knew that Troy and I couldn't both be here until the end, but it was a beautiful pipe dream that I would have loved to continue. Tonight, I say goodbye to the first person I met on this show. The first person I connected with. My friend.

I wrap my much smaller arms around Troy's chest. His dreads hang down, tickling my face and neck as he returns my fierce embrace. "Win this damn thing, will you?" he mumbles against my ear.

A single tear slides down my face as I chuckle. "I'll try." It's all I've got.

He pulls me back, looking down at me with a happy smile. "This experience was amazing because of you. Thank you for your friendship. Patti wants to meet you after the show, okay? She's here and wants a hug," he tells me quickly before being urged to move on down the line.

I feel Chelsea's tiny hand as she threads it into mine. We're the last ones. Our fate is about to be decided. It's her or me. I hold my breath and try to contain the urge to bounce around like Tigger.

"Just so you know, I didn't think there was ever anything going on between you and Beau," Chelsea whispers.

"Really?" I whisper back, my relief filled eyes meeting her crystal blue ones.

"Of course not. I mean, come on. Beau Tanner is a freaking God and absolutely gorgeous. What would he see in you, really?" she asks so casually that I almost completely miss the slam. She's so sincere and nice when she says it; I really don't think she realizes what she really said.

I barely have time to react to her comment when Becker steps back up front. "And now for our final elimination for the evening. Team Beau."

"Good luck," she whispers again with a bright white smile.

"Uh, yeah. You too," I mumble, still completely dumbfounded.

"The contestant who is safe and will return to compete next week is...Layne Carter! That means Chelsea Gordon will be departing this evening."

I'm swept up in more hugs–first with Chelsea and then by the other safe contestants. As I join the other remaining eleven hopefuls on the opposite side of the stage, I finally take my first deep breath. It's like my lungs feel oxygen for the first time in minutes. Hours. Days.

The crazy thing is, this is how I feel when I'm around Beau. Breathless. Excited. Nervous. There's electricity in the air, but this time from the vote-off, not from the mere presence of the man on the opposite side of the stage wearing his trademark Stetson and scuffed up cowboy boots.

As Becker wraps up the broadcast, I chance a quick glance over at the coaches. My eyes instantly connect with those deep gray ones that I think about 24/7. Beau doesn't make any movement except a quick wink before returning his eyes to the front of the stage.

When the red light finally goes off, we all take off to gather our belongings and to wait for our rides back to the hotel. Before I get much further from the stage, though, big arms pull me into an even bigger body. I'd know it anywhere.

"Hey, doll. This is Patti."

"It's so wonderful to finally meet you face to face, Layne. Troy has told me so much about you. He feels like you're a little sister to him," she says with a warm, friendly smile. I instantly like her. If we lived closer, I could even picture her as a friend.

"You, too, Patti. I'm sorry that Troy was voted off tonight," I tell her honestly. "He deserves to be here til the end."

"Yes, he does, but that's okay. I'm still proud of him for coming out here and trying. Even if he didn't win, he's still a winner to me," she says as she wraps her arms around his waist. "I love him just as much today as I did the day I met him in high school," she adds with smile.

"You better get in back and get your stuff gathered up. I know we'll all need to catch the vans back shortly," Troy says before disentangling himself from his wife. He wraps himself around me one more time. "You got this, Layne. You've got what it takes to make it to the end and win it. Don't listen to what everyone is saying," he says with the raise of his eyebrow.

I blush slightly as I reply without making eye contact. "I don't know what you're talking about."

"You know. Don't play coy with me. Beau. Them jealous girls are gonna run their mouths. Just ignore them and sing your heart out. I better come back at this finale and see you standing on that stage."

"I'll try my hardest," I tell him, giving him one final hug.

"Do it for Eli," he whispers before kissing the top of my head.

And that's all it takes. The tears I've felt hovering at the tip of the levee burst through. I smile as I think about my son back at home in Chicago with my mom. It doesn't take me long to realize that once the tears start, it's impossible to get them to stop. I wipe and wipe, to no avail, they continue to fall.

"Look at what you did," Patti chastises her husband as she pushes him out of the way.

"I'm sorry, doll. I didn't mean to make you cry," he says as Patti wraps me in another fierce hug.

"It's okay. It's not you. I've been emotional the last few days. I just miss him so much," I mumble as the hiccups start, and the true mortification starts to set in.

When I glance around, I realize we're still standing in the middle of the stage. I'm wearing thigh high boots, a bustier, and can feel my makeup deteriorating underneath the weight and wetness of my tears. The crew, contestants, and a handful of family and fans linger…all watching me have my mini-emotional breakdown.

Awesome.

Note to self: Wait to have emotional breakdown until you're behind closed doors. Preferably after a trip to the liquor store.

I use the back of my hand to blot away wetness and the softened face putty before I say goodbye to Troy and Patti one more time. They are a beautiful couple, inside and out, and I hope we'll continue our friendship long after this competition is over. St. Louis isn't that far from Chicago. I could definitely make a weekend out of it and travel south for a visit. Besides, I realize as they walk away and head over to chat with Ben that I'd love to introduce Eli to him. Troy is the most unique person I've met in a long time with his big warm heart and his caring demeanor. He's someone who makes me feel like a better person just by being around him.

As I make my way towards the backstage area, I'm headed off by a tall cowboy wearing a concerned look on his face. "You okay?" he asks, those all-knowing eyes searching my face as if looking for the answer.

"Yeah," I reply, offering a hint of a small smile.

"You were cryin'," he retorts and takes a step closer. Not too close, but close enough that I catch a whiff of his cologne. It's spicy with a hint of the outdoors, and I'm instantly hyperaware of his presence.

"It was nothing, really."

"Layne, I -" he starts but is cut off by the camera that's practically shoved in our faces. It's amazing how you can be followed 24/7 by a camera, your entire life filmed for the world to see, yet you don't even know they're there anymore. I think I'm just so used to them lurking in the corners that you become completely oblivious to their presence. Crazy, right?

"I'll see you at rehearsal in the morning. Thanks, Beau," I say as casually as possible as I head back behind the stage to gather my stuff.

Right now I need to be alone. I need a moment to wallow in my own solitude and just process. First off, there's the weight of my loneliness sitting on my chest. Not loneliness from people per se, because I definitely have friends here–even if Troy went home tonight. No, my loneliness stems from my home life that I miss terribly. What I wouldn't give to help Eli with his bath or sit next to him while I sip coffee and he devours pancakes at the breakfast table. Then there's my mom. I never would have thought I'd miss her as much as I do, but I really do miss her. She's as much a part of my daily life and routine as he is.

And then there's the competition. I'm learning really quickly that everyone has their own agenda, and if you don't fit into it, well back the fuck up. Women are catty creatures who are manipulative and conniving, and while I can't blame them for looking out for number one, throwing me under the bus with vicious rumors and lies isn't the way to go about it.

Note to self: Keep your friends close and your enemies closer.

Since we're discussing rumors, that brings me to my next dilemma. Beau. Gorgeous, sexy, sweet, caring, and completely unobtainable Beau. He's my coach. A show representative. And he's forbidden.

How am I going to stay away from him when my entire being is telling me to run and leap into his arms? I've worked too hard, endured weeks of Shawna's crap, to throw it all away for…for what? We aren't anything. He says he's attracted to me, so what? What happens after this show? I live in Chicago and he's a Nashville recording artist with a current tour schedule taking him from one end of the country to the other. I'm sure he doesn't have the time or the energy to deal with a long distance relationship with a woman who has a kid.

So where does that leave me?

Nowhere.

As I slip under the bedspread after talking to Mom for the night and washing the show off me with a quick shower, my mind returns to Beau. Why I keep torturing myself by continually bringing up the topic is beyond me. Apparently, I'm a glutton for punishment.

Note to self: Work harder on finding a hobby.

My mind keeps replaying the kiss. Kisses. I think that if I didn't feel the electricity in those kisses, then I could move on, knowing that a relationship with him wouldn't work out. But the fact still remains that there was something more–something deep and meaningful–in those kisses. I felt it, and I know he felt it. Those intoxicating words he said to me only cement that little sliver of hope that we could really have a chance if we were allowed to.

But we're not allowed to.

Not now.

Maybe not ever.

I'm nowhere closer to the answers I'm looking for an hour later. As I toss and turn and look for that comfortable position to fall asleep in, I conclude that I'm going to do whatever it takes to make it until the end. Well, everything within reason. I'm not about to take lessons in manipulation from Cold-Hearted Barbie. But that does mean that I have to stay away from Beau. No more flirting. No more kisses. No more closet rendezvous. Focus. Focus on the competition. Be professional, be courteous, and for the love of God, behave!

I just hope my heart actually listens to my head this time.

Chapter Fifteen

Note to self: Practice Hard. Play Harder.

"Are you going to tell me what happened last night?" Beau asks from his stool across from me.

"Nothing happened. I just had to say goodbye to a friend. That's all," I reply, studying the music sheet in front of me.

"I'm sure that was difficult, but those kinda tears? That was something else. I could feel it. I could see it all over your face. Talk to me, darlin'," he says, gently prodding me into submission. I look up and am instantly pulled into those amazing eyes with his sincerity and compassion.

I stare at him for several heartbeats trying to decide how much of my life I want to give up. I want to share everything with Beau the man, but I'm scared to dive into it all with Beau my coach, the country superstar. Before I can open my mouth, he jumps up and moves his stool around the music stands and sits right next to me.

"What is it?"

I sigh deeply knowing that he won't let me go without spilling the reason for my emotional breakdown last night. "Tell me why you picked this song."

"What?" he asks, confused about how we jumped from my personal problems to the song I'm singing this week. "Joan Jett? Because she rocks. Even a small town cowboy like me can respect her ability to rock out better than most men from the eighties. This song is classic. Sassy. Take no shit from a man. He did her wrong and she's lettin' him have it. Besides lovin' the song, I think you'd kill it on stage and it suits you well. Why?"

I take another deep breath before I continue. "I have a son. His name is Eli and he's three-years-old."

"You have a kid? What's he like?" he asks, his surprise instantly transforming into genuine interest.

"He's perfect. He has dark brown hair and matching eyes. His smile lights up the entire room, and his heart is bigger than anyone's I know. He's at home with my mom while I'm here and it's slowly killing me inside every day. I miss him a lot," I say, my words dropping down to just above a whisper. Beau reaches over and wipes at the tear on my cheek. The tear I didn't even realize I was shedding.

"He sounds like an awesome kid," he replies with a sideways smile.

"He's the best."

"So, he's at home with your mom? Where's his dad?"

Colton. There's a subject I don't like to talk about, and especially with someone like Beau Tanner. The last thing I want is the reminder of my stupidity or the fact that it's possible to give one person so much control over you–over your heart–that they leave it in devastated, shattered pieces when they give it back.

"That's a long story, and I think you have a plane to catch shortly," I reply trying to buy a little more time.

"I have time, and you're my last rehearsal this morning. So? Tell me about his dad."

"His dad. Well, Eli never met him. Colton was my high school sweetheart. We started dating our senior year, and were inseparable. You know, all that sweet and sappy young love stuff where you think you'll be together forever and live happily ever after. When we graduated high school, Colton went off to the Air Force and was stationed at a base in Missouri. We did the whole long distance relationship thing for as long as we could. He came home as often as possible, but it wasn't as much as I thought it would be."

I look up, gauging Beau's reaction to my story thus far. His face is tight like he doesn't like the direction that it's heading. I haven't even gotten to the good parts yet. "He had just been home for a weekend, celebrating my twenty-first birthday. It was a little late since he was at the mercy of the Air Force, but we were able to spend time together nonetheless. That next week, he was involved in a training accident. The helicopter he was in went down. Mechanical failure. There were six men onboard. All gone."

"God, Layne, I'm so sorry," Beau says as he places his big, warm hand over mine. Warmth and comfort spread through me like a summer breeze, instantly settling my racing heart. I still haven't even gotten to the really good part yet.

"Yeah, well, that was a horrible time in my life. Even worse when his fiancée showed up at the funeral."

The words hang in the air like an anvil, ready to slice and dice the first person who moves. I've always kept my past with Colton to myself because I never wanted anyone to know the shame I carry. The embarrassment. I don't want to see the looks of pity. I don't want to see the looks of astonishment. I don't want to see it written all over their faces when they start to wonder what I did wrong to drive my boyfriend into the arms of another woman. I don't want to see it because I live with it every day.

"Jesus. This song. Wow, I'd say it suddenly takes on a whole new meanin'," he mumbles.

After several seconds of silence, I finally look up at his face, but I don't see pity. I don't see shock or even disappointment. I see rage. I see anger. I see a fierceness I've never experienced from another man before. Like he's upset *for* me, not *at* me.

"That man was a coward. I'm sorry he's gone and I'm sorry you had to endure what ya did, darlin', but that man isn't a man. Anyone who can lead two different lives without so much as battin' an eye isn't worth it."

"Oh, trust me, I know. It took me awhile, but eventually I was able to see that. At that moment, though? All I saw was what I was lacking. All I saw was how I failed. I failed myself. I failed him. I failed my son."

"When did Eli come into play?"

"About a month after the funeral, I was ill all the time. At first, my mom chalked it up to the emotions of the situation and depression that I was diagnosed with. It was nearly impossible to get out of bed half the time, and when I did, I didn't make it past the living room sofa. Mom convinced me to go back to the doctor and get checked out. He had put me on an antidepressant a few weeks before that, but she felt like I needed to get checked again.

When the doc checked me more thoroughly, it was quite the surprise to all of us."

"I bet. You might be the strongest person I've ever met. Not everyone can go through that kind of drama and come out on the other side."

"It was a long road, that's for sure. But I wanted to be the best person–the best parent I could possibly be for my son. He's the best part of me and the one person that makes me feel whole again. Holding him in my arms gave me a sense of purpose for the first time in so long. It's the hardest thing in the world to be halfway around the country and only be able to see his face on a small phone or computer screen," I confess as my emotions lodge themselves in my throat again.

I look up when Beau doesn't respond. I find his eyes searching my face, so many emotions parading through his crystal clear eyes. Neither of us says anything more as we continue to have a conversation without words. The way we communicate without speaking is a heady feeling, like we've connected on some deeper, much more meaningful level than ever before.

"Beau, your car is waiting," Gabby says from the doorway, pulling us out of the quietness we were bathed in.

"Oh, right," he answers before clearing his throat. "I guess I need to head out. We'll pick back up on rehearsals Sunday night. I'll be back around three and Gabby has your schedule for the next few days."

"Sounds good," I respond.

Returning our conversation back towards the competition and away from my personal train wreck of a life is for the best. Because when this is all said and done, I'll be heading back to Chicago, and Beau will be heading back to Nashville.

He gathers up his stuff while I do the same, trying with everything I have not to glance back up at him. "Hey," he whispers, stepping close to me. My questioning eyes lock with intense gray ones. "Are you okay with this song choice? I can switch it if ya need me to. Somethin' that doesn't quite strike ya straight in the chest like a knife."

"No, I'm okay," I reply adamantly. Besides not wanting to be difficult, I truly do love this song, with or without the reflection of my past in part of the lyrics.

"Well, if you're sure, then we'll keep it. At least something rockin' for this week. I'm workin' on something great for ya for next week."

"Sounds good, boss," I tease, though I don't miss the reference to me still being here another week.

"Hey," he says, locking eyes with me again as he steps closer and drops his voice. "I want to talk with ya this weekend. Is it okay if I text ya?" he asks with a smidge of uneasy in his voice.

"Yeah, um, sure. About the competition?"

"No. About anything other than the show. I just want to get to know ya better, and I feel like we just barely grazed the surface. Besides, I didn't even get to tell ya about how I charmed my teacher in the third grade into givin' me an extra recess with the older kids," he says with a crooked smile and a wink.

I don't answer; I just offer a small, friendly smile back at the gorgeous cowboy next to me. Beau exits the room, leaving me in solitude once again. He wants to get to know me? That's the impression I just got. Maybe Beau and I have more similarities than I originally thought. Maybe Beau could use a friend outside of the industry, outside of the show. Lord knows I enjoy spending what little time we've had together, conversing and sharing. Even if what was shared was some of my darkest secrets and insecurities. The simple fact that I *want* to share that part of my life with him is something in and of itself. And those kisses…don't get me started on the kisses.

I gather up the rest of my stuff and head towards the door. I have sessions tomorrow with wardrobe and the show vocal coaches to practice my next song "I Hate Myself For Loving You." Nobody rocks like Joan Jett and I can't wait to sink my teeth into this song. The fact that he picked it before I shared my past doesn't go unnoticed by me. As cheesy and childish as it sounds, it's like it was fate or destiny. He picked a song for me without knowing my past, yet it describes me, and my relationship with my ex, better than most could possibly understand.

Whatever you call it, it appears that Mr. Beau Tanner and I have a connection unlike anything I've ever experienced. I just wish I knew what to do about it.

*****

"Come on, we're heading out tonight," Corie says from my hotel room doorway.

"Uh, *we* are?" I ask, eyebrows raised sky high.

"Yes, we are. You, me, Ben, and a few others. We're going to a club down the street. It won't be a late night since we have early morning fittings," she says. "Change your clothes. You look like a mom in those sweats," she adds with a wrinkled up nose as she takes in my gray sweats and my Chicago Blackhawks t-shirt.

"I am a mom," I mumble as I move to let her in.

"I know, but that doesn't mean you have to dress like it," she sasses with a pointed look.

"I wasn't planning on going anywhere so I'm in my comfy clothes," I defend, mirroring her stance with my arms crossed firmly over my chest.

"We'll we're going dancing and to have a few drinks. Come on," she says as she pulls open my closet.

Thirty minutes later, our small group is making their way to Club Vogue, within a short walking distance of the hotel. After paying the ten-dollar entrance fee, we make our way to the bar. They're two deep the entire length of the bar which reminds me of home. Chaser's usually has them wrapped around, two, sometimes, three deep. Nights like this are the nights I love; live for. They keep you hopping and pouring. I'd take a busy night over a dead night anytime.

"What are ya havin'?" Ben asks, pressed firmly against my shoulder as we all are jostled towards the bar.

"Just water tonight," I holler over the heavy dance music pumping through the speakers.

"No way. One drink."

"No, I really shouldn't. I have an early morning fitting before a whole slew of rehearsals."

"One drink. I'll get you in bed safely tonight. I promise," he adds with a little smirk and wink.

God, why can't I be attracted to Ben? He's obtainable, for starters. Yet, I feel nothing for him. It's sad, really.

"Okay, one drink. Jack and Coke, please." I try to dig money out of my pocket, but Ben waves me off.

With drinks in hand, we make our way to the far end of the club where we spot a vacant table. Maxwell agrees to watch our drinks at the table as the rest of us head out to the dance floor to get lost in a song or two. It feels great to laugh and let loose for a bit. With the sadness that has surrounded me these last few days as I struggle to deal with homesickness, and the soap opera drama with Beau and the show, it feels unbelievable to smile and shake my ass. Even Ben's continuous wandering hand doesn't seem to bother me as much as it usually does.

"Drink," Corie says as she fans her flush face.

As I sit down in an empty chair at our table, my phone vibrates from my back pocket. At first glance of the initials on my screen, my heart gives a little flutter. Beau.

BT: *What ya doin?*

A simple text message, but one that makes me smile none the less.

Me: *Club Vogue with gang.*

It doesn't take but a few moments before his reply is waiting for me.

BT: *Sounds like fun. Who's the gang?*

Me: *Corie, Ben, Maxwell, Jess*

BT: *Ben as in the Ben who is always lookin' at you like you hang the moon?*

His reply catches me off guard. I know that Ben has a little crush on me, but is it that apparent to everyone else, too? What's more alarming is the fact that Beau's reply seems to have a little underlying jealousy in it.

Me: *Jealous?*

BT: *Of Ben being there with ya right now n not me? Hell yes!*

Okay, now that response I wasn't expecting. Beau is jealous of someone he has no need to worry about. As much as Ben might be interested in something more than friendship, I am not, and I've made that clear to Ben. But before I reply, another message appears from Beau.

BT: *I want to be there right now with your body pressed against mine as we dance. I want to be there to watch you let yourself go and enjoy the nite. It kills me that I'm in Atlanta and you're there. With Ben.*

Me: *I'm not with Ben. He's not the one I want to dance with and let go with.*

BT: *Who do you want to let go with, darlin?*

Me: *You*

There. Sent. Without even batting an eyelash, I told him exactly what I wanted. Of course, he's miles and miles away and not staring at me with those intense eyes, so it's easier to say the things I'd probably never say if we were face to face.

BT: *If I were there right now, I'd be kissin you.*

"Hey, what are you doing over there? You've been so engrossed in your phone that you missed your shot," Corie says firmly. I glance down and see the full shot glass sitting in front of me while everyone else's is empty.

"Oh, sorry," I reply as I place my phone back in my pocket without replying. As much as I'd prefer to talk to him right now, Beau is going to have to wait.

I quickly down the shot, which I discover is Fireball, and allow Corie and Jess to lead me back to the dance floor. We laugh and dance, moving our bodies in rhythm of the upbeat music. Every few songs, we slip back over to the table to enjoy our drinks or take a shot. Ben and Maxwell sit around the table, talking sports and girls.

Well after midnight, we head out of the club and towards the hotel. My phone vibrates in my pocket, which instantly makes me think of Beau. I never replied to his earlier text.

BT: *Did I lose you?*

Such a simple text, yet so full of underlining meaning.

Me: *Nope. Got distracted at the club. Heading home now.*

BT: *Did you have fun?*

Me: *Yep. Probably more to drink than I should have. ;)*

BT: *That's ok. As long as you're going home by yourself.*

Me: *Definitely. There's only one cowboy I'd be heading home with.*

BT: *God, I so fucking wish I were with ya right now.*

And because I can't seem to help myself, I ask the burning question.

Me: *What would you do with me?*

His reply is instantaneous.

BT: *Whatever the fuck I wanted.*

It vibrates again in my hand before I can even process his words.

BT: *I'd start with that sweet mouth of yours and work my way down your entire body.*

Holy shit! My entire body spasms with excitement. His words are like an elixir, a drug that I crave.

Me: *Aren't you at a concert? Shouldn't you be working, not hitting on me?*

BT: *I just finished my show and waiting to pull out to head to the next stop.*

Me: *I'm almost back to hotel.*

BT: *Will you keep me company?*

Me: *Sure.*

When we reach the hotel, I have barely pulled my nose out of my phone. He tells me all about his first gig when he was a green rookie straight out of high school, playing at a dive bar with a cage around the stage. His cocky attitude was quickly given a gut-check as he realized that breaking into the music scene wasn't as easy as just showing up and getting a record deal. Beau's story is fascinating, to say the least. Nothing came easy to the award winning country powerhouse that we all know today. Back then, Beau struggled and considered giving it all up on many occasions.

BT: *That's when James Rollins walked into the club I was playin. He offered me a shot and I'll forever be grateful to him.*

Me: *Sounds amazing.*

BT: *Can I call you?*

I'm throwing on my pajamas as his latest text message arrives. I quickly scrub off the remnants of my makeup and type out a quick reply.

Me: *Aren't we talking?*

BT: *Yes, but I need to hear your voice.*

Well, then…

Before I can reply, the phone sitting next to the bathroom sink is ringing. Sharing my life with Beau has been easy all night, but now to hear his voice? My heart rate kicks up a few hundred beats per minute before I even pick up the phone.

"I didn't say yes," I tease in way of greeting.

"True, but this way, ya don't have the chance to say no."

"I would never say no," I tell him, knowing that I mean so much more than just referring to his offer to call me.

"That's good to know. So, what are ya doin' now?"

"Getting ready for bed," I tell him as I take my phone and plop down on the mattress.

"Well, I should probably let ya go," he quips with a yawn.

"Sounds like you could use a bed yourself," I reply, yawning myself since yawning is always contagious.

"I could. I'll be back on Sunday afternoon, and I'm thinkin' I might need a few moments of your time. In private." The underlying meaning is so obvious that a deaf man could hear it.

"Aren't we supposed to be staying away from each other in private?"

"Yep, but sometimes I just need a quick little fix. You know, like a hit. A shot. Somethin' to tide me over 'til I can get my next fix of you, which won't be too far off since I can't seem to control myself around ya." The honesty in his statement is like a gut-check. My stomach flops around like a fish out of water, and it's good to know that he's feeling the same things I feel.

"Your words are making it so hard to stay away," I whisper honestly.

"Darlin', you have no idea what *hard* is."

I gasp loudly at his statement. Never before have I been so seduced by a few simple words. Even for someone who is affected by song lyrics on a daily basis, I've never been so intoxicated by words before in my life.

"I dream about you," he confesses softly into the phone.

"You do?" I whisper as if concerned who might overhear.

"Yeah. Almost every night," he adds after a pause. His confession rocks my very foundation.

"I dream about you, too."

"Really? What do you dream about?" he encourages, a hint of a smile laced in his words.

"Stuff," I reply vaguely.

"I dream about stuff too. Stuff like your lips and your mouth and the things I want to do to them. And then there's your hands. I dream a lot about how your hands feel against my body. I wake up so fuckin' hard, I have to jack off in the shower to images of your beautiful face."

I gasp at his confession.

"I'm sorry. That was probably too much information," he says.

"No," I say quickly. "Actually, you're not alone on the dreams."

"Do you touch yourself, Layne? What do you picture when you close your eyes and touch your body?"

His words ignite something deep inside me. My body yearns for his. "I think about you. I picture you when I touch myself." My confession takes me by surprise, but feels freeing to say the words aloud.

"Fuck, that is the hottest thing ever. Every time I see you now I'm going to picture you with your hands all over your beautiful body."

"You have to stop that. I have a hard enough time concentrating when you're in the room. The last thing I need is to think about *other* things in your presence. I'll never be able to sing without blushing."

"I promised that I would try to control myself when I'm around ya, and I will. But sometimes, I'm going to fall off the wagon. Especially when I imagine you lying on your bed in sexy lil' pj's and touching yourself."

"But I'm wearing sweats," I counter with a smile.

"A guy can dream, sweetheart, and right now, my mind is working overtime. Just let me have my thoughts. It's all I have right now."

"Okay."

"Okay."

There's silence as we both absorb our conversation. I want him. He wants me. Yet, neither of us is able to do anything about it. So, we'll dream. Until this show is over, our dreams are all we'll have.

"Go to sleep, beautiful."

"You can't say that, Beau."

"Why? You are the most beautiful woman I've ever known," he tells me. His honesty courses through the phone, zapping me straight to the core.

"Because I can't be distracted by your words. I need to focus on this show so I can provide Eli with a better life."

"Eli has a better life just by *you* being a part of it, Layne. *You* are the reason he has an amazing life. *You* are the reason he is loved beyond his ability to even recognize it. And *you* are the reason I can't stop thinkin' about returning to Los Angeles. Not the show, Layne. You."

I have no idea how to respond to that. If I was able to produce sounds at this moment, I'm not ever sure they'd be actual words.

"Go to sleep. Have sweet dreams. Dream of me, and know that I will be dreamin' of you. Even though I'm not supposed to, my dreams are all I have right now," he adds before telling me good night.

I mumble something incoherent and sign off. My head is a mess right now, his words affecting me in more ways than I ever could have imagined. Mostly because for the first time since I've been here, the competition is placing a distant second to what I'm feeling for Beau. He makes me want to throw caution to the wind and say forget it to this entire thing.

But I owe it to Eli and my mom to finish this out. I owe it to myself, and I even owe it to Beau. He has worked hard to prepare me week after week for the cutthroat competition that is *Rising Star*. I owe it to him to give it my all. And, unfortunately, giving it my all means no distractions.

Beau is a distraction.

So, for the thousandth time in the past week, I tell myself to forget about our attraction and concentrate on the prize at the end of the road. The record contract. The cash. It's all there, just waiting for me to grab ahold of it.

I just pray that I don't trip and fall on my ass on the way to the top.

Chapter Sixteen

Note to self: When your world starts to crumble around you, just keep smiling! And make mental note of names to add to the hit list.

I arrive at the studio at nine o'clock on Wednesday morning for my scheduled final stage rehearsal. Tonight is another live performance for votes before tomorrow night's elimination round. I've been working with Beau and the show vocal coaches to perfect my song for this evening, and feel confident and ready for the performance. Since our team performed as a group last week, the other two teams are performing group performances tomorrow night. Beau has hinted that next week's shows will start contestant duets, and I can't wait to see what that's all about.

"Layne, they're looking for you in conference room A," Gabby says moments before I step out onto the stage to run through my song one final time with Mallory, the choreographer.

"Who's looking for me?" I ask, confused about who would pull me away from my final practice.

"Everyone. The network," she says with a pointed 'I told you so' look.

The network? Oh my God, this can't be good, can it?

My legs are numb as they carry me towards the network executives. Gabby doesn't say anything else as she leads me through a series of hallways, past offices that I didn't even know were here. After a quick knock on the closed door, she opens it and allows me to enter.

Inside the room sit about six men and women all dressed in professional suits and dresses. Sitting at the end of the conference room table is the man with the starring role in my dreams. Beau Tanner. I swallow the golf ball that's suddenly lodged in my throat and return my focus to the man standing at the opposite end of the table.

"Layne, it's good to finally meet you. I am Jackson Zimmerman, President of the network. Please have a seat," he says, motioning to the empty seat next to Beau.

I feel all eyes on me as I make my way to my seat. I was just about to step on the stage for my final dress rehearsal so my attire isn't exactly "executive" appropriate. The tight leather dress and blood-red pumps don't do much for my confidence as I stare down the faces of the handful of people who could decide my fate on this show. The *real* people who decide if I even perform tonight.

"Miss Carter, I'm going to be frank with you. We've had concerns from other contestants as to the extent of your relationship with your coach, Beau Tanner. This is something that we take very seriously. Contracts were signed by all parties at this table–namely you and Mr. Tanner. Now, while we encourage you all to continue to live your lives, we can't have relationships between the coaches and the contestants. You recall signing the agreement, is that correct?"

"Yes, sir," I reply through my dry throat.

"You don't need us to produce the document you signed? Margaret from Legal is here and would be happy to show you the document with your signature," he states, indicating towards the woman to his left.

"No, sir. I recall the document."

"Good. Now. We have a slight dilemma with this entire situation. We've had a lengthy conversation with Beau and he ensures us that your relationship is purely friendship and in no way breaks the contracts that you've both signed. Is that how you'd describe it?"

"Yes, sir. Beau and I are friends, nothing more." I don't dare risk a glance over at him. I don't know what would be worse: seeing him so casual at this moment or him seeing straight through the lies.

"That's good. But, here's the dilemma. Apparently, America loves the thought of you two together."

I'm startled by his words, looking up at him with big, shocked eyes. Now, I look over at Beau for the first time since I've sat down. He's staring at me with those intense eyes that hold a hint of laughter.

"The website, which hosts the Behind the Scenes videos, has increased traffic ten-fold. Social media is abuzz with speculation about your relationship. The network has done extensive polls on the topic in recent days and it seems that America wants to see more of you and Beau, Layne."

"Sir?"

"So, while we're in no way condoning the breach of your contract with us, we are maybe encouraging you to…*tease* the audience a little more."

"What do ya mean by that?" Beau asks, speaking up for the first time since I walked into the room.

"Oh, you know, little touches here or extended glances there," the woman on the right of Mr. Zimmerman says.

"So you want us to flirt?" Beau asks.

"Yes," she confirms.

"It's all about giving the viewers what they want, and right now...they want more of you two." Six sets of eyes bounce between Beau and me. "We want you to tease the audience. Leave them speculating. Make them want to come back for more. That's where tonight's special performance comes into play," he says with a big wolfish grin.

Oh, shit. I look around the room at the brightly smiling faces and twinkling eyes. Something tells me I'm not going to like this. Not one bit.

*****

"Ladies and Gentlemen, welcome to *Rising Star*. Tonight, we have an exciting night of performances lined up for you as each contestant performs for your votes. All twelve contestants are ready to go this week, but at the end of the night tomorrow, only ten will stay. That's right, this week the *two* contestants with the lowest number of votes will be sent home, missing out of their chance to be the next *Rising Star*. Are you ready?" Becker asks the audience who is on their feet, cheering.

"Tonight, we're going to kick off our show with a special performance. Social media has been abuzz lately with speculation about a certain contestant and her coach. To set the record straight, let's hear it for Layne Carter," Becker says as the spotlight shines brightly, illuminating my position on the far corner of the stage.

After this morning's meeting, I wasn't a fan of their master plan. In fact, I hated it. I don't want to be treated like a chess piece, strategically moved from place to place for the benefit of the network, for the show. But, here I am. About to perform a song that can only be labeled as "a cock tease." There is no way that this song performance will set the record straight. In fact, it'll probably only confirm everyone's assumptions. Right or wrong, they're going to be led to believe one thing after this song.

Beau met me in the hallway after the meeting. His attitude towards the entire situation appeared too casual. It was like he was happy to be a performing monkey for these yahoos. But then he looked at me and said, "Now, I get to touch ya and I don't have to worry about what they'll say."

Everything inside of me melted at that moment. Being able to touch Beau or stare at him without worry of who's watching is the only silver lining to this cluster-fuck idea. But the powers that be have spoken. The idea was planted and now they're all sitting back, watching it grow like mold on cheese, ready to reap the benefits. Ratings gold.

The familiar beat to the song Beau and I just worked on all day starts up. I look out and see him sitting at the coach's table in front of the stage. I bring the mic up to my mouth and start to sing the words that I reviewed in a crash course earlier.

"People are talkin', talkin' 'bout people. I hear them whisper, you won't believe it. They think we're lovers, kept under cover. I just ignore it, but they keep sayin' we laugh just a little too loud..."

I sing the rest of my part as the audience feeds off my every word, whispering to each other as if confirmation was just declared on live television. And I don't blame them. If I were watching from the outside looking in, I'd believe that I was confirming a secret love affair to the world. Hell, isn't that what the song practically screams? And it doesn't help when Beau grabs the microphone he was secretly hiding underneath the table and stands up.

"I feel so foolish, I've never noticed. You'd act so nervous, could you be fallin' for me? It took a rumor to make me wonder. Now I'm convinced, I'm goin' under. Thinkin' 'bout you every day..."

Beau walks up the stairs at the end of the stage, joining me front and center. We sing Bonnie Raitt's, "Something To Talk About" together for the entire world to see. I didn't even get the opportunity to call my mom before tonight's performance. A quick text message telling her that I had so much to talk about was all I could get in. I'm sure she's practically foaming at the mouth to get to me after this little publicity stunt. Hell, she's probably already picking out wedding reception venues.

The thing that no one will know is that even though this is for the good of publicity, the looks we steal are real. Singing with Beau is as natural as the conversations we've shared and the kisses we've stolen.

"Layne, Beau. We've heard the rumors about something going on between you two. What can you tell us about that performance? What does it mean?" Becker asks when the song is complete.

"Nothin' to tell. I'm Layne's coach and her friend. Everyone's gonna think what everyone's gonna think, ya know?" Beau remains cool and collected like always.

"Layne, anything to add?" Becker asks and holds the mic in front of my face.

"Just that I'm here to compete like everyone else and rumors aren't going to keep me from this competition," I add.

"Well, I didn't hear a confirmation or a denial so you decide, America," Becker says. He's basically holding his big wooden spoon, stirring the pot of drama that has become my life. Good times.

*****

"Layne, you're up next," Gabby says from the doorway of the green room. Corie was first up tonight and did an excellent rendition of Colbie Calliat's "Try." I hope it's enough to keep her here another week. Just the thought of dealing with these catty people without my friend and ally is terrifying.

With the exception of Ben and sometimes Maxwell, no one really speaks to me. Yet I hear plenty from them as they stand on the outskirts of the room, discussing my "relationship" with Beau. Everyone is so certain that I've slept my way to this point that it's almost laughable. It doesn't help that Shawna is running her mouth like a freight train with nothing in the way but wide-open spaces. She keeps everyone talking with her "insider knowledge." I mean she was rooming with me for a short time, right? Apparently, that makes her the resident expert of everything in my life. Throw in a few first-hand encounters and you have all the makings for a healthy dose of the dramatics. Hell, maybe if I engaged in just a little piece of the crap they're saying about me, I'd be much more relaxed and better equipped to deal with it all.

Note to self: If you're going to pretend to sleep with a judge, maybe it's time to sample the goods.

I've become accustomed to the talking. When I found out that Colton had a fiancée, I couldn't escape the whispers. Even in a city like Chicago, they followed me everywhere I went. No one messed with me at Chaser's, though. Whether because I was considered old news by then or because Tiffany put the fear of God in anyone who even thought about mentioning it, I'm not sure. But, I know that since I started at the bar, I haven't had too much trouble with gossip.

Until now.

I wait for my cue before stepping out on the stage. Three weeks in and this has become like second nature now. I reach my starting position and smile brightly, waiting for the band to strike up my music. When the familiar beat washes through me and I'm bathed in bright lights, I forget everything. I forget everyone backstage, sitting in the audience, and even those sitting at the table in front of me. I let go and sing because that's what I do–all I can do. When the going gets tough, I get lost in my music. When all else fails, I submerge my mind in the one thing to bring me comfort, besides my son. Because when it's all said and done, these people will be gone, but the music will still be there. Deep inside me, wrapped around me like a blanket, embedded in my soul like a familiar tattoo.

I stand in the heat of the spotlight wearing my sky-high red heels, tight leather tank top and matching black leather pants. Add in a little bit of teasing from a big bottle of expensive hairspray, some dark, heavy eyeliner, and I look like I stepped out of a 1980's Joan Jett video.

"Midnight, gettin' uptight, where are you? You said you'd meet me, now it's quarter to two. I know I'm hangin' but I'm still wantin' you..."

This is my favorite part of performing. The moment where I work the stage, engage the crowd, and just feel the beat, the rhythm. This song speaks to me better than any song I've sang so far, so when I feel my spirits soar for the first time in I don't even know how long, I know it's as a result of this song. I feel playful. Energetic. Unstoppable.

When the song is finally over, I take in everything around me. If I go home after tonight, it's not because I didn't give it everything I have. It's not because I did something I wasn't supposed to do...even though I was pretty damn close. Multiple times. It wasn't because I couldn't do it at all. It was because now just isn't my time. This show, this opportunity wasn't right for my life at this moment. And that's okay.

I look over at the coaches who all wear matching smiles. When I lock eyes with Beau, I feel it clear down to my painted toenails. They actually curl a little in the tip of my heels as I recall the forbidden kisses we've shared. Though those kisses can't happen anymore, that doesn't mean I can't fantasize about them. Lord knows I dream about them all night and think about them all day.

If I go home tomorrow night, I'll miss out on those stolen glances, illicit kisses, and the smoldering looks–just like the look I'm getting right now. If I go home, I'll deal. Without Beau.

I hope that the fans will spare me for at least one more night.

Chapter Seventeen

Note to self: Elevator music isn't so bad.

When I warily step onto the elevator at the hotel on Thursday night, luck is not on my side. I'm the only occupant with Drama Llama Barbie. She looks pristine in her black and white dress and her peep-toe pumps, hints of bright red nail polish from her daily pedicure poking through. Her hair is still up from tonight's reveal show, but hers appears more natural. Like she was born with style and elegance. Her entire appearance makes her look like she stepped off the runway and decided to grace us mere mortals with her presence. Too bad she's the Devil in disguise.

Note to self: Take the stairs. Your ass and your self-esteem will thank you.

"I don't know how you did it again this week, but the fact that you're still here is a poor reflection on this show. It's supposed to be about finding the next big star. You shouldn't even have made it out of the first round," she says while examining her perfect French manicure.

This evening when they called my name, as the first contestant saved, was a shock–to me and a few of the other contestants. Audible gasps were heard, and while I didn't turn around, I'm pretty sure I know where those came from. The look on Beau's face as he looked on from his position at the table was one of pure excitement and joy. He seemed genuinely happy that I was safe for another week. Whether it's because of my ability to perform on stage or our budding attraction towards each other, I don't know. Though, I'm hoping it's the former, and that the latter is just an added perk to me still being here.

"You don't have to be jealous of me, Shawna." I look her square in the eye and can see the moment her anger reaches boiling point. Smoke practically billows out of her ears.

"Jealous? Puh-lease! I'm not jealous of someone who's sleeping with a coach. Not to overlook the fact that you're sleeping with a male contestant too. I'm here fair and square because I'm the best, not because I'm a slut," she says just before the elevator doors open, depositing us on the third floor.

"You don't know what you're talking about. I'm not sleeping with a coach or anyone else. And as I recall, I beat you *fair and square* in the first round of eliminations. Which means *I'm* here because I'm the best. You're here because you're lucky." And with that, I turn and walk towards my room.

If the daggers she's shooting at me through her eyes could have actually killed me, I would have dropped before I even finished my little victory speech. The moment is short lived, though, as I make my way to my room. I hear the loud clank of a door behind me and finally breathe my first real deep breath since I stepped onto that elevator. When I slip inside my own room, her accusations hit me square in the chest.

Sleeping with a contestant? You've got to be kidding me!

If I were enjoying half the sex everyone around here thinks I'm having, I'd be in pretty good shape! Much better than the reality. Reality is that I don't even own a BOB. When you have a toddler who sleeps in the same bedroom as you, battery operated toys aren't exactly something you indulge in. No, when I need to scratch that itch, that's when I find someone who isn't looking for a relationship. The thing I've learned about working at Chaser's is that there are plenty of men out there looking for a little no-strings-attached sex. Though, I rarely leave with someone from the bar. I prefer to visit an establishment a few miles away that I'm not employed by. There's less risk of them making surprise visits while I'm on the clock.

Maybe the fact that I can't even remember the last time I engaged in said activities is the real reason for my hostility. When I sit down and think about it–really, really think about it–I can't even remember my last fling. Brad? Or was it Jax? Either had the same result. I met them at the uppity bar, a frequent hangout for after work executives or blue collared society, where I let them buy me a drink. That's how it always starts, right? One drink that leads to another which leads to a few grazes with your hand or resting it on a leg. Then, you add in batted eyelashes and a few more casual touches. Finally, it's out the door and towards the agreed upon meeting location. Most of the time, it's at their house or apartment. Never at mine. A few have even taken me to a hotel–not the seedy kind that you pay by the hour, but definitely not the kind where the bellhop escorts you up to your room with your luggage.

Sex is fun. I've always enjoyed it; especially with someone I consider "my type." Brown or dark blond hair with green eyes. A physique that doesn't scream Curls for the Girls or Gym Selfie Taker, but does scream Gym Membership. Someone who dresses for their job and wears it comfortably whether it be at an office or out in the field somewhere. That's why my attraction to Beau is so confusing. He's *nothing* like my usual type. Except his body. His body is all hard muscle and bold lines. He screams sexuality. Sex that would be, no doubt, off the chart. Nuclear. Mind-altering. The kind that leaves destruction and a little devastation in its wake.

It's too late to call Mom tonight, though I fire off a few text messages before heading to bed. We talked in great lengths last night after my performance with Beau. She understood my dilemma, caught between what the network wants and what I want. Ultimately, if I'm going to have a real chance at winning this thing, I know I have to play nice with the network holding the purse strings. I can't deny them when they hold my future in their greedy little palms. All I can do is play along. And maybe enjoy the ride.

Lord knows stealing glances and touches with Beau Tanner isn't going to be a hardship. Not one damn bit!

*****

"Two things," Beau says from underneath that black Stetson hat. "First, I have a surprise for you, but I'll get to that in just a few. I want to tell you what song you're singing this week."

"Bring it," I tell him, bouncing in my seat. Last week, he told me he was working on something different for me.

"I know you're not a fan of country, but I want you to give it a shot this week. I want to slow it down this week and touch on something softer for you. Have ya heard of Faith Hill?" he asks.

"Yeah, I've heard of her, but I don't know much that she sings. Wait, she's married to the hot cowboy, right?"

Beau's eyebrow shoots upward, disappearing completely underneath that hat. "Really?"

"Yeah, well, I may not know a lot about country music, but everyone knows Tim whatever-his-name-is."

"Whatever-his-name-is. Oh my God," he mumbles, eyes cast downward as he shakes his head in disbelief. "*Tim McGraw* is the definition of country music. I grew up listenin' to him, singin' his songs. He's one of the main reasons why I chose country music."

"Well, I don't know about all of that, but he's one of my favorite cowboys," I tease.

"One of your favorites?" he asks with a big smile.

"Yeah, he's number two," I reply without releasing the smile I'm holding in.

"Number two. Who's number one?" he asks, inching just a little bit closer on his stool.

"Luke somebody," I reply as straight-faced as humanly possible. Seriously, I should get an award for this performance. *I'd like to thank the Academy...* Never mind the fact that I don't even really know who this Luke guy is, but everyone is always talking about him. Something about his amazing pelvic thrusts and ass wiggles.

"I quit," Beau says dramatically as he throws his hands up in the air.

"You quit because I don't know who Luke is or because you're not my favorite cowboy?"

Beau walks around until he's standing directly in front of me. When he leans forward, his scent invades my senses, teasing me in the best possible way. When he squeezes his hands on the edges of my stool, the outsides brushing against my ass, I almost melt into a warm pile of goo.

"I think you're lying," he whispers, his lips a breath away from my own. My breathing comes out in short little pants as I gaze into his smoldering eyes. They're ablaze with something deep, something dark, and something very dirty.

"About what?" I finally manger to get out through the little pants I can breathe.

"About who your number one cowboy is. I don't think Luke somebody gets you all worked up like you are right now. I think *this* cowboy is the only one who gets this kinda reaction from ya. And I think that I want to test that theory," he whispers, his breath kissing my ear.

But he doesn't test it.

Instead he pulls back and out of my personal space. I feel the void of his heat instantly and crave to plaster myself against him. Then the reality of the situation sets in. The camera hovers nearby recording our every move, our every word. Understanding sets in as to why Beau was whispering practically against my ear just moments ago.

"So, do you want to know what song?" he asks, standing his full six foot, two inch frame blocking half the light reflecting behind him.

"Yeah."

"'Breathe'."

"I am breathing," I retort.

Beau just closes his eyes and shakes his head before the laughter erupts from his gut. "No, the name of the song is 'Breathe.' Jesus, you are so difficult."

"I am not. It's not my fault I don't know every country song sung by every country artist out there."

"Fine, I'll concede that point. Before we run through this, I wanted to tell ya that we're starting duets this week. You're paired up with Ben."

"Ben? What are we singing?"

"I'm still working on it. You guys are scheduled for a practice tomorrow morning. I'll have it narrowed down by then," he says as he steps back around his music stand.

"Wait. Tomorrow? Don't you have shows?"

"Not for a couple of weeks. I had a short break planned from the tour so I can focus on the show for a bit. I do it for each season. It helps with my concentration. If I could take the entire season of the show off from touring and give it my full attention, I would. But that don't pay the bills or the crew and my band. So, the song. Let's run through it a few times right now. We have a bit left before ya have to go to wardrobe."

After listening to the music, giving me a feel for the song, Beau and I run through my latest song several times. It's a beautiful song. To think that you can have that kind of passion and love, feel that kind of all-consuming desire for someone is a heady feeling. Not only is it a little bit of a wake-up call, but it also plants a little seed deep within my soul.

For the first time in a very long time, I start to entertain the idea of wanting that. I start to picture the something more that might be out there for me. Something for Eli and me, together. And that doesn't scare me as much as I thought it would.

As I head back to the hotel after a long day at the studio, I run through the lyrics of the song several more times. The more I sing it, the more I can't fight the image that accompanies it. The image of a certain tall, gorgeous cowboy. He twists me up inside and leaves me longing for more. Beau is dangerous with a capital D, and now he's all I think about. I run through our entire morning together so many times I could play it backwards in my sleep. The song reveal. The hidden touches. The teasing. Everything he said. Then, I remember…

I didn't even get to ask him about his surprise.

*****

"Mom, you sound like you're in a tunnel. Why don't you call me back?" I ask just as a knock sounds at the door. I climb off my bed and step over to the door, phone still pressed firmly against my head. When I look out, I don't see anyone through the peephole.

"Mom, I gotta go. Someone's knocking," I say as I fling open the door.

To say I'm surprised is an understatement. Standing on the other side of my door is my mom and my son. I don't even realize I'm crying as I throw my arms around them, pulling them so tightly against my chest, I wonder if I'll ever be able to suck in air. But the reality is that I'm finally able to breathe. For the first time in weeks, I can feel like I can truly take a deep breath of sweet oxygen.

"Are you surprised?" she asks through her own tears.

"Are you kidding me? What are you doing here?"

"It's part of your surprise," she says as she releases her hold on Eli and leaves him tucked solely in my arms.

"What surprise?" I ask, confused.

"Beau. He had Eli and me flown in this morning," she says with a knowing smile.

Beau did this? I can't even believe it, yet I can completely see it. The man I've gotten to know these past few weeks is caring and considerate. He's also spontaneous, apparently.

"Beau did this?" I ask, vocalizing the words in my head.

"Yep, arranged it earlier in the week. He said he knew you'd still be here after Thursday," she says as she sets her purse down on the bed.

"He can't do this. Everyone will read into this whole stunt, too," I reply, sitting down on the edge of the bed.

"He brought in Ben's sister, too, Layne. We're going with you to rehearsal today so we can see how this whole thing works. He said something about you and Ben rehearsing for your duet."

"Wait. You talked to Beau?" I ask.

"Well, duh. Of course I talked to him."

Eli shimmies down my lap and reaches for the remote control. After finding a channel with cartoons, I help him climb up on my bed next to me and settles in for *Paw Patrol*.

"That man is crazy for you, Layne. He called to find out about coming out here for a bit. He offered to pay my missed salary and all the travel expenses. I wasn't about to let him pay for my missed time from work, but he negotiated well enough and ended up covering all of our travel expenses. He's even upgrading our room to a suite so that you can stay with us while we're here," she says.

"Wow, that's so nice of him. And he brought in Ben's sister too?" I ask in way of seeking confirmation.

"Yep. We rode from the airport together. She's a sweetheart. You'll meet her shortly when we get to the studio."

I glance down at the clock on the nightstand, absently stroking Eli's head. Just to feel his little body against mine again leaves me settled. "We need to head out soon."

"Yeah, he was going to surprise you at the studio, but I didn't think this moment should have been in public and recorded. I guess they're going to fake another reveal when we get there for the cameras."

Great. More acting.

I gather up my bags and my son and head for the door. With Maxwell being in the bottom two on Thursday night, he was sent home from the competition, leaving Ben and myself the sole two contestants on Team Beau. It worries me a little that they're dropping like flies on our team. Hopefully that's a trend that doesn't continue in the upcoming week.

When we get to the studio, I happily show Mom and Eli around. We finish our tour at our small rehearsal studio where I find a smiling Beau. He's standing in the corner with Ben and his sister. The way her hand is casually resting on his forearm sends prickles of something through my body. Could it be jealousy? God knows that it feels like it.

"There they are," Ben says with a huge smile. He walks over pulls me into an unexpected tight hug.

I stand so straight it's like someone attached a rod from the back of my neck to my ankles. It doesn't help when my shocked eyes slam into the equally shocked ones of Beau. Except there's something more in his eyes. Anger. Jealousy. Like he wants to pull Ben off of me, rip off his arms, and beat him to death with them.

I pull myself out of Ben's arms while Beau hovers over his shoulder looking like a bear with a thorn in his paw. "This is my mother, Grace," I say to the three people in front of me. "And this little man is my son, Eli."

"You have a son?" Ben asks with pure shock…and maybe horror written on his face.

I pay no attention to him because it's Beau that I'm drawn to. He crouches down in front of Eli and offers him a warm smile. "Hey, lil' man. My name is Beau."

"Hi," Eli whispers shyly as he hides most of his face behind my right leg.

"Did you like the big airplane?" he asks, still crouching and having the conversation completely with Eli.

"I got these," he whispers quietly as he pulls a little pair of plastic wings from his shorts pocket.

"Those are cool. That means you're an honorary pilot. Maybe someday you'll fly planes just like that one, huh?"

Eli nods vigorously as he steps out from behind my leg.

"Do ya want to come up front with me and watch your mom?" Beau asks. Eli stares up at him with big, wide, trusting eyes before he places his small hand inside of Beau's much bigger one.

Before they can make their way up front, Eli points to Beau's hat. "I like your hat."

"This ol' thing?" Beau reaches up and removes his hat, placing it on my son's head. It's huge and swallows Eli's head whole, but the smile he gives me when he turns around is enough to melt the glaciers in Antarctica. Instantly a lump the size of a tennis ball lodges in my throat causing me to choke on unspoken emotions. "Come on, Eli. I have a special spot up front for ya."

I watch helplessly as Beau leads my son by the hand up to the front of the room. He picks him up and places him on his stool, tipping the hat back so that he can see his eyes. The smile that Eli gives him mirrors the one I see on Beau's handsome face. The entire exchange pulls at my heartstrings, exposing my heart piece by agonizing piece. Something unravels in my chest. Something that resembles longing.

"This is my sister, Sara," Ben says, breaking the Beau spell I'm under.

"Oh, hi, Sara. I'm Layne," I reply, expending my hand to the petite brunette.

"Oh, I've heard all about you," she replies with a meaningful smile. Something tells me that it has something to do with Ben's crush.

"Let's go ahead and get started," Beau says.

Mom and Sara walk over to the stools along the far wall and get comfortable to view today's rehearsals. Their eyes continually connect with the camera floating around the room. I've become so used to their tag-alongs that I don't even know they're there anymore. For someone on the outside who's not used to the invasion, I can see where it can be distracting and uncomfortable.

"You guys are the last duet of Wednesday night's show. I've considered several different songs and finally settled on one that I think will balance both of your ranges and your styles. So, for this week, you guys are singin' Lady Antibellum's 'Just A Kiss'," Beau says, staring straight at me–hell, straight to my soul–as he speaks.

Memories of our shared kisses flood my mind. The images flash on repeat and I can practically feel his lips touching mine all over again. I try to shake off the images, but looking up at Beau doesn't help. The look in his eyes tells me all I need to know. I touch my tingling lips and know that he's reliving the same moments I am. From several feet away, I can feel his touch.

"This is the perfect song for me and Layne," Ben says cheerfully next to me.

And just like that…moment shattered.

"Let's run through it a few times before I add the music. Layne, I know you're probably not familiar with this song, so don't hesitate to ask any questions ya may have," Beau says.

Over the next hour, we run through the song several times. The words are beautiful. It's a song about longing for that one perfect kiss. Nothing more. Just a kiss to signify the start of a budding relationship. The underlying meaning behind this song doesn't go unnoticed by me. Neither do the smoldering looks Beau throws my way when everyone else's eyes are elsewhere.

Eli was superb during rehearsal. Beau let him push the buttons on the mp3 player when we added the music. I can tell by the bright smile on his face that he felt like such a big helper and part of the rehearsal. Of course, wearing Beau's hat the entire rehearsal only helped cement the fact that he was top dog for the day.

"So, we're all goin' to dinner tonight," Beau says at the end of practice. "There's an excellent hibachi grill not too far from the hotel that I thought would be great. They have a kids menu," he says and looks directly at me. "I checked."

My knees turn to jelly and my heart does this crazy schoolgirl flutter. This man is making it impossible to continue to resist him day in and day out. It's getting harder not to lean in and kiss him. Contract and show be damned.

"I'll meet y'all at the hotel. Say six o'clock?"

We all agree and head towards the waiting van. Ben and Sara chat animatedly the entire trip, making us laugh with their sibling banter. Yet, I can't stop thinking about Beau. I know. Nothing new, right?

I just hope I can keep it together long enough to get through this show. Hell, I'd be happy to just get through this night.

*****

"You look beautiful," Beau whispers in my ear as we're led towards a grill at the far end of the restaurant. The entire place is buzzing with energy. I've only ever been to a hibachi grill one other time and I left with my cheeks hurting from laughter and stuffed to the gills.

"Thank you," I whisper back as I let Eli pull me towards our spot.

"I'm in da middle," he exclaims as he reaches for Beau for help onto his chair.

Fortunately, I'm saved from having to sit by Ben, who was hovering closely, when my mom grabs the empty seat next to me.

Beau sits on the other side of Eli leaving Sara to his left and Ben on the other side of her.

Sara instantly strikes up a conversation with Beau, which haggles my annoyance. I try not to let it show, but when Beau catches my eye and raises his eyebrow in question, a faint blush creeps up my neck.

We each place our order with the waiter. Mom and I chose the chicken and shrimp with fried vegetables and rice while I ordered chicken and lo mein noodles for Eli. Beau chose the steak and shrimp with veggies and rice, and Sara and Ben each stuck with the salmon and shrimp.

The mood is light as we enjoy our pre-dinner cocktails. I catch Ben watching me over the shoulders of Sara and Beau, but try not to let it get to me. Beau casually rests his arm on the back of Eli's chair, which leaves his arm hanging right by my shoulder. Occasionally, I feel the slightest touch of his finger against my bare skin. Each graze is like a bolt of lightning straight to the apex of my legs. God, what I wouldn't give to feel those hands on me in *other* places.

When our chef comes out, he instantly makes sure the grill is clean. He starts to set out his supplies, spreads the oil down on the grill top, and grabs his spatulas.

"Watch this, buddy," Beau says to Eli who is watching wide-eyed for the show to start.

"Lean back, Eli," I tell him as I pull his chair back a little from the table. When they light the oil on fire, flames shoot up, dancing high above the top of the grill. It's amazing to watch, but could definitely sear the hair off your arms or eyebrows if you're not careful.

Note to self: Eyebrow-less is NOT the look I'm going for tonight.

There's not much opportunity to visit while the chef is cooking. He flips his spatulas around, spinning them and catching them like some oriental version of the movie "Cocktail." He even tries tossing cooked pieces of chicken from his utensils into Beau and Ben's mouths. It takes several tries, but Beau finally catches a piece of meat in his mouth. Eli cheers loudly and seems pleased when Beau offers him a friendly, happy smile.

"So, Beau, did I hear you're dating Penelope Shaw?" Sara asks, resting her hand on his forearm again.

"Um, no. I'm not," he replies with that country drawl so prominent.

"Oh, I thought I read somewhere that you were. My mistake," she says, batting her eyelashes just a little bit more.

"Nope. I was seen in public with her a few weeks ago at a meeting of mutual friends, and ya know how the media is. Seen in public means ya must be gettin' hitched," he says with the shake of his head.

He's hatless tonight, which is a completely different way to view Beau. I've seen him take off his hat several times and run his long, lean fingers through those dark locks, but tonight the only indication of the cowboy underneath is the boots on his feet. His hair is styled nicely with no sign of hat-head, which tells me he must have showered before tonight's dinner. Beau in the shower: God, talk about a mental image I'll happily carry with me for the rest of the night!

"So you're not seeing anyone?" she asks with a blindingly bright eager smile.

"Nope, but I'm not really lookin' either."

"Yeah, but sometimes those are the best relationships. The ones you weren't looking for when they find you," my mom adds to the conversation, drawing everyone's attention to the woman over my shoulder.

"That's absolutely true," Beau says. When I look back at him, those gray eyes are focused exclusively on me. My heart rate spikes and my palms start to feel a little damp. I'm sure my breathing looks similar to that of a poodle in heat.

The moment we share is broken when Sara grabs his arm and pulls him closer. Beau's a great sport, not wanting to be rude to the overzealous woman, but doesn't exactly respond to her advances either. Not that I blame her at all! If I was single (which I am) and not under contractual obligations (we all know the answer to that one), then I'd probably throw myself at the hottie in the seat next to me too!

"I'd love to see LA while I'm here. Are you familiar with it, Beau?" Sara asks not-so-subtly. Again, touching his arm.

"Only a handful of places and landmarks. When I'm here, I just don't have time to sightsee," Beau says. "But they have tours, I'm told, that you can take and see all the Stars' homes and stuff. You should check into one," he adds politely. Denied. Something about that makes me smile internally.

"Yes, well, maybe I will," she replies with a small smile.

After dinner, we head back to the hotel. Beau is still with us, riding shotgun in the network van that we're using for this evening. I'm not sure how he arrived at the restaurant, but apparently it wasn't in his own vehicle. Knowing the network, he either has his own driver or his own car to use.

"Beau, wanna see my Legos?" Eli asks with wide, innocent eyes.

"I'd love to, buddy," he replies, throwing him an award-winning smile that makes my belly flip-flop.

"You can help me build a house. I wike to build houses," Eli adds.

The air crackles as we make our way to the bank of elevators. Eli has Beau's full attention as they discuss different things you can make with Legos. Eli has those larger blocks that he loves to build things with. He's too little for the tiny Legos right now, but if his love for building things continues, I can see many Lego purchases in my future.

As we step off the elevator on the top floor, I follow my mom towards our suite. We had moved all of my belongings up here earlier in the day before rehearsal. Eli and I are set up in the larger of the two rooms while Mom happily chose the smaller room. The view from the main seating area is stunning. You can see the mountains majestically rising in the background, dotted with million dollar mountainside homes that all look like they could tumble down the mountain if someone so much as sneezes.

"Beau, can I get you something to drink?" my mom offers from the small kitchen.

"I'm good, thank you."

I grab a bottle of water from the fridge as Beau sits in the middle of the floor and prepares to build a house with building blocks with my three-year-old. The sound of their laughter echoes off the walls in the kitchen, but it's the unsaid words from my mom that are the loudest.

"What?" I ask.

"Are you going to tell him?"

"Tell him what?"

"That you have feelings for him," she says matter-of-factly.

"Mom, don't go there. You know that I can't afford to develop feelings for him. Nothing can happen between us right now. Even after the show, it's not likely that anything will develop."

"What if something has already developed? I know you, Layne. I know how you guard your heart. I know how you protect yourself from men for fear that they'll hurt and disappoint you. Well, not all men are like Colton. Some are actually good, decent men. Your father was a great man who loved fiercely and loyally. He was taken from us too soon and I live with that loss every day. But, you can't be afraid to try, Layne. You can't be afraid to give your heart to someone. Because someday, someone isn't going to give it back. Someday, they're going to keep it and give you theirs in return. Someday, all of the tears and the hurt will just go away because someone takes it all away. They will make you forget because they love you so fiercely that you have no other choice but to love them back. Live for that moment, Layne. When you find it, hang onto it."

I blink rapidly to keep the tears at bay. I can't cry now. Beau is not twenty feet away, playing with my son in the other room. Yet, her words strike me so deeply that I can't help but to let one fall.

I've watched my mom mourn the loss of my dad every day. She gets by, coping in her own way, but she has never been the same since the day we laid him in the ground.

"What about you?" I choke out.

"What about me? I had the perfect life for a while with your father and you. I miss him every day. But lately I've been trying to enjoy life again. I realized not that long ago that I can enjoy life, the company of a man, and still always love your father. He'll always be in my heart, even if my heart is leading me towards someone else. That's the circle of life, Layne."

"Wait. Towards another man? What are you talking about?"

"Well," she says, shifting uncomfortably. "What if I told you I had a date not that long ago and that I've been meeting a new friend for lunch over the past several weeks?"

"I would be happy for you. Who is it?"

"Umm…Lee."

"Lee!? From Chaser's, Lee?" Suddenly things start to click into place.

"Yes, Lee from Chaser's. He's been divorced for a while now and we've been enjoying each other's company."

"I'm happy for you, Mom," I tell her honestly as I walk across the room and pull her into a hug.

"Yes, well, it's still new. I don't know if anything will come of it, but I enjoy spending time with him nonetheless."

"He has always seemed like a nice man. Though, if he hurts you, I'm going to have to maim him," I tell her resulting in a laugh.

"Excuse me, ladies, but I'm supposed to grab ya and show ya our newest creation," Beau says uncomfortably from the doorway.

I quickly step away from my mom, wipe away the rogue tear, and follow him into the living room where Eli has their tower proudly on display.

"It's awesome, Eli," I tell my son.

"Thanks, Mommy. Beau helped make it tall! It's the tallest tower ever!"

"It sure is," I tell him, bending down and kissing him on the crown of the head.

"Eli, why don't you come with me? It's time to take a bath, and Mommy can visit with Beau before he heads out," my mom says.

"I can do it, Mom," I retort.

"I know you can, but I don't mind doing it tonight," she says with a wink before scooting Eli off to the guest bedroom.

We stand in awkward silence for a few moments before Beau says, "Wanna step out onto the balcony?"

"Sure," I reply, following him towards the sliding glass door.

Outside, the air is cool, but not enough to require a jacket. Night is falling and the roadways are littered with headlights. The sound of traffic is constant. That's something I've noticed about LA. Even in the dead of night, you can always hear traffic. It's like the city is always in motion.

A chill settles over me as we both look out over the city. I can feel his body heat next to me, and it warms me clear down to my toes.

"Are you cold?" Beau asks, taking note of my goose bumps.

"Not really," I reply honestly. I just leave out the part about my goose bumps being caused by his mere presence.

Before I even know what's happening, Beau pulls me against his warmth, wrapping his arms securely around me. "I had a good time tonight," he mumbles against the top of my head.

"Me too." Honestly, I did.

"So, I take it ya liked my surprise?"

"Yours was the best I've had in a long time," I tell him.

"Are we still talkin' about the surprise?" he asks with just hint of that cockiness that I've become accustomed to.

I laugh before replying, "Yes. What did you think I was talking about?"

Beau looks down at me, causing my neck to crane upward to meet his eyes. "This," he says moments before his warm, lush lips meet mine. I shiver as heat floods my body, sending waves of anticipation coursing through my blood stream.

The kiss starts out slow, but it doesn't take long before our need for each other starts to rear its head. With one swift swipe of his tongue against the seam of my lips, I'm opening up and granting him access. His tongue is everywhere. The way it strokes my own sends my entire world spinning. I grab tightly to the back of his black t-shirt, holding on for dear life. God, can this man kiss.

I barely register movement until his hands dip underneath the back of my shirt. His touch almost burns me as his hot, calloused fingers graze the sensitive skin of my lower back. My moan is swallowed by his mouth and by the night.

Suddenly, there are too many clothes. The barriers between us are too great, restricting and confining. I snake my leg up and around his strong leg. I can feel his hardened length pressed against my stomach, begging to be released, to be touched. I grind myself against him, rubbing and trying to relieve the pressure between my legs. Pressure that Beau created. Pressure that only Beau can release.

But before it can go any further, Beau starts to pull away. I whimper as I try to pull him snugly against me, but he resists. He stands directly in front of me, my leg still wrapped firmly around his waist with our hands locked on each other's bodies. But the distance is there. It takes everything I have to not attack those lips again as I attempt to wrangle in my breathing.

"I can't let this happen, Layne. Fuck, as much as I want it to, I can't do this here. I can't risk someone findin' out. They'd send you home and your time on the show would be over. Besides the fact that you deserve to be here, deserve a shot at winnin' this whole thing, I can't risk sendin' ya home early. You not being here every day would kill me. Not seeing you, not stealin' touches and glances, it would slowly kill me inside. You've become the very air that I need." His hands make their way up to my face. His eyes are full of lust and desire, but something else, too. Affection. Suddenly, I feel like I'm the most cherished person in the world.

His confession does so much to my already overheated body. Happiness that he cares enough for me to not risk my future, not risk my chance on this show. Joy that he feels something for me that seems to be so much more than a quick roll in the sack. Excitement that I can bring this man to his knees. The feelings I've warned myself against are already there. They're alive, deep and true. I care more for this man than I've allowed myself to care for any other in four years. In fact, he's quickly becoming the only man I've ever truly cared for. Everyone before him fades away in comparison.

"I know you're right, but I can't seem to make myself pull away from you," I whisper.

The light in his eyes is enough to brighten up the darkest nights. "I feel the same way," he says before placing another gentle kiss on my sensitive lips. "For tonight, I need to walk away. But please know that even through I'm walking away, it isn't for lack of want. I want to stay here with you so damn bad I'm afraid I might explode," he says, giving a little head nod to his southern region.

I chuckle. "I want you to stay, too."

"I promise, sweetheart, that very, very soon, I will finish this kiss. I will make you scream my name so many times that it'll be the only name you ever remember. I will be inside of you so long that you won't be able to remember what it feels like without me there."

Good God, if that doesn't make me almost orgasm right then and there.

"That song you're singing next week with Ben? That song is for me. Not him. Me. When ya sing those words, know that it's my kiss on your lips. Remember that it's my kiss that longs to taste ya," he whispers before placing another soft kiss on my lips.

Later that night, I struggle to sleep. I toss and turn for hours on end, praying for the quiet to swallow me whole. As much as I try, though, I can't sleep. I can't stop remembering that kiss. I can't stop replaying his words. For the first time in years, I don't want to stop. I want to explore this attraction. I want to follow it wherever it may lead. I want to finish what we started. Sleep may never come tonight. Instead, I'll let the silence surround me, lost in my own thoughts and desires.

And wonder if maybe, somewhere out there, he's lying awake and thinking of me too.

Chapter Eighteen

Note to self: Give it everything you've got, and then dig a little deeper for more.

"And for another great duet, please help me welcome back to the stage Ben Atwood and Layne Carter," Becker says to the camera, followed by a round of applause from the live audience.

Mallory positioned Ben and I on opposite sides of the stage for this performance. Throughout the song, we'll slowly work our way around and towards each other before we meet in the middle for the last chorus. It represents the dramatic nature of the song, the dancing around each other while looking for that kiss.

The live band begins the music, a piano melody soft and slow. My back is to Ben as I raise the mic, but that doesn't matter. I could be staring directly at him and it wouldn't be his lips I was thinking about. When it's time, I start to sing Lady Antibellum's words. *"Lying here with you so close to me, it's hard to fight these feelings when it feels so hard to breathe. Caught up in this moment, caught up in your smile."*

Even when Ben starts to sing his part, it's not his voice I hear. He's not the one singing those passionate words to me. I imagine

Beau standing directly in front of me: his smile, his eyes, his hunger. It's Beau.

I never look over at the man sitting at the table in front of the stage. I know that if I look, I'll never be able to concentrate on the song, yet as Ben and I make our way through the song, I can't resist the pull that Beau has. I'm drawn to him like a moth to a flame. Finally, as I make my way to center stage, I can't fight his gravitational pull any longer. I want to be looking at him when I sing these words.

His eyes are fire. Bright, hot, and full of intensity. Hypnotized, I see it. I see our kiss replayed through them. He's remembering, too. *"You'll be in my dreams…tonight…tonight…tonight."* Truer words have never been spoken.

We finally make it to the end of the song. Ben and I are standing directly in front of each other, center stage, singing, *"With a kiss goodnight…kiss goodnight."*

And then suddenly, Ben kisses me. I'm so shocked that I stand there, paralyzed, for what feels like minutes. Hours. Forever. The kiss could in reality only last three seconds, but they are the longest three seconds of my life. When he pulls away, a smile crosses his face, but it does nothing to ease the shocked look on mine.

Note to Self: Shit! Ben just kissed me! On National television. Screw the note! I'm freaking the hell out right now!

Ben turns and waves to the audience as they applaud our song, but my eyes are instantly seeking the only pair that matters right now. Beau.

And his eyes are furious.

*****

"Layne, you're up next," Gabby says from the doorway of the green room.

I swear I'm having an out of body experience right now. No way did Ben just kiss me in front of God, Beau, and the entire viewing audience. In the world of instant rewind, TiVo, YouTube, and cell phone cameras, I was just kissed by a man on National television in front of the man I've been secretly stealing kisses from. All. On. Camera.

No way did that just happen. But it did. If the deadly look in Beau's eyes were any indication, I'd say that Ben Atwood is lucky to still be alive right now. It's probably a good thing Ben is nowhere to be found at this moment.

I have no idea how I changed into my white dress; I don't remember any of it. I don't remember having my hair and makeup freshened up. Yet, here I am, standing behind the stage, getting ready to perform my song that'll determine my fate this week. How in the hell am I supposed to concentrate on this beautiful song when all I can think about is Ben. Beau. The kiss. That other kiss.

Wardrobe chose a long, white gown with an A-line waist. The strapless dress is whimsical and flowing and has a slight train that trails behind me as I walk. It's gorgeous. My makeup is subtle, hair swept up in an elegant up-do, and my heels are tall, strappy, and hurt like hell.

Yet, I feel nothing but confused as I wait for my next turn to perform. Scared.

"Hey," I hear from behind me in that deep southern drawl that I've come to crave.

I whip around quickly, almost throwing myself off balance. Beau reaches out and grabs a hold, keeping me upright. The smile he gives me is tight, until his eyes travel down the length of me. He takes in my dress and his entire demeanor changes. When his eyes return to mine, they're softer. Appreciative.

"I didn't know he was going to do that," I defend instantly.

"I know," he says, stepping in a little closer. "That was the hardest thing I've ever done; sittin' there without showin' any emotion or reaction when all I wanted to do was run up on that stage and punch him square in the fuckin' face."

"You did?" I choke out.

"Are you kidding? He touched you, your lips. Do you realize what kind of damage control I'm going to have to do later tonight when I can steal you away and get you alone?"

I'm saved from having to reply–which is good because I don't know if I could answer anyway–when Gabby comes up and tells me it's time to get out on stage and for Beau to get out at the coach's table before we go live.

"Deep breaths, Layne. Just remember to…breathe," he says as he squeezes my hand and walks through the heavy curtain and towards his post.

Note to self: Just remember to breathe. Easy, right?

Beau was right. I need this performance. As an artist, I need to demonstrate my softer side, even though I rarely let it show. In fact, I've never felt the need or desire to let it loose. I've always found my solace in rock music; classic hits from the 70's and 80's.

But tonight, as I take the stage in a stunning dress, I find that I suddenly can't wait to show the world the softer Layne.

"I can feel the magic floating in the air, being with you gets me that way..."

I sing the classic Faith Hill song as I work the stage, the crowd. My movements are slow and deliberate, just like the song. I don't risk a glance at Beau this time around. I'm very much aware of his presence within the massive room, but I avoid eye contact. Instead I focus on the hundreds of eyes staring back at me from the crowd. I sing the song as if I could be singing it to them. For them.

When it's all said and done, the comments I receive from the coaches are humbling.

"You were born for this," Felix says with a huge grin.

"Yeah, I agree. This softer Layne is just as outstanding as the hard rocker Layne," JoJo chimed in.

But it's Beau's that hold the most meaning. "I feel like we've all just witnessed a phoenix risin' up out of the ashes. Ya took your passion, your heart and soul for music, and put it into that song. Ya made me feel things, moved me in ways no one ever has just by hearin' those words drip off your lips. That was, without a doubt, the performance of the night. Hell, of the show," he says as the crowd erupts into overwhelming applause.

The smile on my face must be blinding. I couldn't control it if I tried. I don't even know what words I reply to Becker before he says, "If you'd like to see Layne Carter return next week, then she needs your votes. Call 1-800-555-7006 or log on and vote at risingstar.com. For our final performance of the evening, please welcome Corie Brooks."

And just like that, my night is done.

*****

"What are ya doin'?" Beau's drawl asks over the phone.

"Trying to sleep," I whisper so I don't wake Eli next to me in the king sized bed.

"Tryin'?"

"Yeah," I reply.

"Can ya talk?"

"Give me a minute," I reply as I slip out of bed and out of the room, though I leave the door cracked so that I can hear Eli in case he wakes up. I step through the common room and slip out the sliding glass door leading to the balcony. "Okay."

"Where did ya go? It sounds like you're outside."

"I'm on the balcony. I didn't want to wake Mom or Eli."

"Ya did great tonight," he says with the hint of a smile in his voice.

"Thanks. You pick great songs," I tell him, smiling back.

"Yeah, well, I'm suddenly not so fond of the Lady A song."

"Me neither," I reply, shuddering at the thought of Ben kissing me again.

"Have you talked to him?"

"Surprisingly no. The only time I saw him after the performance was when we were all on stage at the end of the show. I have no idea what he was thinking," I say.

"I know exactly what he was thinkin'. He wants you, has for weeks. You can see it in his eyes, Layne."

"Yeah, Troy said that much to me a few weeks ago, so I made it clear to Ben that we were only friends. That kiss was completely unwelcome."

"You don't hafta tell me that, sweetheart. I saw it all over your face. You weren't exactly happy that it happened."

"Of course not. And you didn't look very happy yourself."

"Are you kiddin'? I was ready to beat the shit out of him. The only thing that held me back from assault charges was the fact that we were on TV. Any other situation and I woulda killed him."

"What does this mean, Beau? I mean, we're not exactly in a relationship."

"Yet. We're not in a relationship yet, sweetheart. I have every intention of findin' out more about you and why I have these crazy, uncontrollable feelings whenever you're near. I'm makin' no bones about my intentions towards you after we finish this show, so you tell me. What do ya want?"

You. Us. Together. So many intense feelings swirl around inside me like a typhoon. I can't even get my center of gravity, but maybe that's okay. Maybe that's what this is all about. Love? Maybe that's what real love is.

Of course, I'm not about to start sputtering off things like the L word, so I just stick with, "I want to see where this goes, Beau." That's the truth.

"Don't be scared, Layne. Don't be scared of us. I promise ya that things will fall into place. Everything has a way of workin' out. Just trust me."

He leaves the proverbial door wide open. That's just it. Can I trust Beau? I trusted Colton and look where that got me. Can I trust him to not take my heart and leave it battered and bruised when he walks away? Because let's face it, Beau is probably going to walk away at some point. It could be a month; it could be a year.

But what if he doesn't? My mom's words from last night replay through my mind. I'm ready to move on, right? Will I finally be able to let go of the past and set out to discover my future?

Only one thing's for sure: I want to find out.

Note to self: Breathe.

Chapter Nineteen

Note to self: Kick ass and take names.

At the end of that fourth week, the voters saved me for once again. Speculation about the budding relationship between Beau and me has remained front and center everywhere I go, in everything I do. Throw in speculation about Ben's kiss on the show that fateful Wednesday night, and collectively, we've remained a hot topic around water coolers. We're holding strong on all of the entertainment news shows and over social media. The reality show threesome. Shawna still holds the big spoon, stirring the pot and keeping the drama-train rolling full steam ahead.

Slowly over the last three weeks, we've continued to dwindle down until only four contestants. Four contestants and two weeks. It's hard to believe I'm still in this competition, fighting every week for my position on this show. And it hasn't been easy.

Two weeks ago, I said goodbye to my Mom and my son. It was the hardest thing I've ever done, watching them walk through the airport, leaving me on one side of that velvet rope. I don't know when the last time was that I cried that hard. My entire chest was gutted when I watched them walk around the corner and out of sight. Even the warm hand on my back didn't seem to bring me much comfort. Beau held me the entire way back from LAX and even walked me up to my old hotel room. The room felt hollow, as if my extended week with my mom and son didn't exist. He steered me towards my bed and laid next to me while I cried big fat crocodile tears. We fell asleep together on the top of the bedspread, fully clothed and holding hands.

When I woke in the morning, he was gone.

Today, we're practicing for our coach's duet. Yep, I get to sing with Beau this week. With only two weeks left, we're down to the best of the best. Weird to consider myself in a class like that, but I've come to realize that I must really have something if I've endured six other vote-offs and am still here.

Three other contestants remain: Ben, Jamal, and Shawna. I said goodbye to Corie last week after an emotional performance with her before the vote-off. It was the first time we sang together, but had felt like we'd done it a million times over. Again, with the tears.

Note to self: Kleenex. How much is it to buy stock?

"Well, what did you pick?" I ask the cowboy on the stool across from me.

"Don't you wanna know," he sasses back.

"Yes, actually, I do."

My solo performance this week is a hit straight from the nineties. I'll be performing No Doubt's "Spiderwebs," and I'm stoked. I haven't heard this song since I was younger and just the name brought a huge smile to my face. Who doesn't love Gwen Stefani? This song is energetic and fun. It's perfect for this week's performance.

"Don't You Wanna Stay?" he asks with a clever little smile.

251

"Are you trying to confuse me?"

"Jason somebody and Kelly Clarkson," he replies, finally letting that smile fly.

"Ahh, gotcha. Do I get to sing Kelly?"

"No, you're singin' Jason somebody. I'll be singin' Kelly."

"Good thinking. It'll keep everyone on their toes. Plus, when you hit those high notes, it's sure to put us right back into the spotlight. Page two just isn't the same as front page entertainment news coverage," I reply.

"True. I hate sharing pages with not-as-worthy celebrities."

"So, let's hear the song, I haven't heard it in a few years," I tell him as he pulls out his mp3 player.

I close my eyes as the words sung by Jason Aldean and Kelly Clarkson fill the room. The song is about a couple lost in a single moment together and not wanting to let it go. It's a romantic ballad filled with that big romantic gesture, and honestly, it doesn't surprise me that Beau would pick this song to sing together. In a way, this song represents us. Our journey. Even behind the scenes, we've embarked on a romantic journey filled with potholes and roadblocks. The biggest, of course, being the one thing that technically brought us together: the show.

We run through the song together several times, working on my runs of the high notes multiple times. Kelly Clarkson has an amazing range, and it's one that you have to nail, because if you don't, it'll kill the song. And the last thing I want to do is be the reason we sound like crap.

"There. That time was better. Take a big breath before ya go into it and you'll be fine. I'm not worried about ya," he says confidently.

"Okay. I'll run them tonight until they're all I know," I say.

Beau doesn't say anything, which draws my attention towards him. He's staring at me, the small lift of the corner of his mouth the only indication that he's smiling. The intensity in his face makes me squirm on my stool. There's something brewing dark and dirty behind those eyes.

"Just so ya know, I'm going to touch you during our performance." Air lodges in my throat as my eyes widen in surprise. He keeps those hypnotizing orbs focused solely on me as he gets up and stops directly in front of me. "This song makes me wanna touch you so don't be surprised when I touch your face like this," he says as he reaches forward and gently strokes my cheek. "Or if I touch your arm like this," he says moments before he runs his warm fingers up my arms from my wrist to my elbow. My reaction to his words, his touches, is undeniable.

Every ounce of oxygen is sucked from the room like some lust-filled vacuum. Even if I could speak, I wouldn't know what to say. We're at an impasse right now. We both want something more, but something more isn't an option at this moment. Instead, we indulge in those little touches, a few shared kisses, and a whole bunch of phone conversations. Especially when he's on the road for appearances, we steal as much free time as we can spare over the phone and without prying cameras.

Of course, the rumors are still swirling. Well, I guess you can say that they aren't technically "rumors" anymore. With the exception of us actually sleeping together, we have definitely formed a bond. A relationship. We just aren't able to take it to the next level yet.

Damn it.

But in another way, that's good. We're learning so much about each other without involving sex. He's shared his background with me, the troubles he's dealt with in past relationships, and his dreams for the future. Funny, that some of those dreams are the same as mine. I try not to get too excited about that part, though. Once a cynic, always a cynic.

But I'm trying.

Later today, Ben is traveling with Beau to Salt Lake City for a concert. The whole thing concerns me a little since things between Ben and Beau have appeared a little tense since that on-stage kiss a few weeks ago. Ben will get to experience firsthand the excitement of the industry and performing on stage. Tomorrow, I fly out to Denver and do the same. Sunday, we'll fly back to LA and jump right back into rehearsals for this next week. The other two contestants are all doing the same with their coach at some point this weekend, and the entire experience will be caught on camera and part of next week's shows.

"So, you're meetin' me in Denver tomorrow afternoon. Ya already got the schedule, right?"

"Yes, Gabby gave it to me last night after the show," I say as I gather up my sheet music.

"Good. Here, you need to learn this," he says as he hands me another sheet of music.

"What's this?" I ask, looking it over.

"That's the song we're gonna sing on stage tomorrow night," he says.

"I'm singing on stage with you?" I ask astonished.

"Yep. Ben's joinin' me on stage tonight to sing 'Whiskey Bottle,'" Beau says, referring to his first number one hit, a tidbit of information I learned only a few weeks ago. "We're singing that."

"You can't be serious," I say deadpanned.

"As a heart attack. Study up. We'll only have a short amount of time to run it for sound check."

I continue to look over the music sheet as Beau leans in. "I'll call you later," he whispers against my ear, sending little sparks of fire coursing through my body.

Long after Beau is gone, I sit on that stool and read the music. It's a beautiful song, but I can't think of where I've heard it before. Nothing sounds familiar to me. I'm sure it's a country song, and Lord knows my knowledge of country music isn't very extensive. I guess I'm going to have to fire up the laptop and do a little research.

Note to self: Grab some ice cream. A night of internet stalking is about to commence.

*****

I didn't find the song and it's driving me crazy. I searched all night in just about every lyrics website I could find. Even Wikipedia produced a big ol' goose egg. Which brings me to the now where I'm following my driver at Denver International Airport as he weaves through the crowd and heads towards his waiting town car. Next stop: Pepsi Arena. And that much closer to Beau Tanner where I can hopefully get some answers.

When I arrive at the arena–and when I say *I* arrive, that means me and a camera crew–we are instantly escorted to the backstage area. I'm introduced to a handful of crew members, band members, and some of the management team for Beau's label. I feel it instantly the moment Beau walks into the large room. It's as if everyone else just fades away leaving only him and me.

Oh, how I wish…

"You're here," he says with a big smile. I take in his appearance. Still ruggedly handsome but gone is the cowboy hat and boots. Beau Tanner is walking around in a ball cap and running shoes. His usual Wrangler-wearing ass is covered by a pair of mesh running shorts and a loose fitting tank top is the only thing between me and the corded muscles of his tan chest.

And oh, what a chest it is. It's the first time I've ever gotten to ogle him. He's broad and muscular with ripples in all the right places. Plus, he has a tattoo. A big, dark tattoo with hard lines and dramatic shading. However, I can only see the top of it since it disappears below the neck of his shirt.

I feel eyes on me and realize that someone is talking, probably to me. I look up and my eyes immediately slam into the smiling ones and cocky grin. The damn cowboy just caught me ogling his body as I commit it to memory. Mother in heaven!

Note to self: When ogling, make sure the person you're staring at doesn't catch you! You'll never hear the end of it.

I try to shake off my Tiffany-approved eye-fucking moment, but his gaze won't let me go. I'm sucked in like one of those alien invasion movies.

"Did ya review the song?" he asks, that cocky smile not wavering from his too-handsome face.

"Yes, but what song is it?" I ask.

"Andrew here is going to give ya a backstage tour and show ya our set up. I'm going to take a quick shower, and then we'll run the song on stage. Sound good?"

Andrew gently places his hand on my lower back and leads me down a long hallway, away from Beau. Which reminds me that he never answered my question about the song.

Andrew shows me several different areas of the backstage including a makeup and wardrobe area, warm-up room, and a meet and greet room. But the massive stage is what holds my attention right now. I feel so small, so minute while standing in the middle of the hard platform. It's shaped like a W which gives Beau the opportunity to engage several sections of the arena, allowing the fans on the floor an up close and personal experience.

Someday...

Note to self: You're allowed to dream. So dream big.

I walk up to a mic in the middle of the stage and can't help but touch it. I don't know if I'll ever sing at a platform like this, but the fantasy is real. The desire to achieve that dream exists. When I hear the familiar clicking of cowboy boots, I turn around without dropping my hand from the microphone. Beau is there, watching me as if I'm the most fascinating person in the world.

"You look good up here. Natural."

"I don't know about that. Give it a few hours when these seats are all filled and I'll be ready to pee down my leg," I say with a chuckle.

Beau smiles before saying, "You ready to run the song?"

"Yes."

Over the next hour, I work with Beau on the music and with a woman named Angela, who works as a stage choreographer for the crew. She tells me when I'll enter the stage and from what angle. She shows me which mic I use and tells me at what part during the song I'm to move. She basically gives me a crash course on my positioning during the performance.

I watch from the side of the stage as Beau runs through his mic check. Each member of his band joins him and makes sure their instruments are tuned up and ready to go. The entire experience is a fascinating process. When I go to concerts, I just show up. I never knew all the different elements that went into the actual concert. It's an eye-opener.

Shadowing Beau is easy. He's a natural with his fans and does whatever it takes to make them comfortable and give them the best show possible. My first Meet and Greet is definitely interesting. Women have no qualms about throwing themselves at a country music superstar–not that I blame them. At first, it made me a little uneasy. Hugs aren't just hugs when they involve groping hands. Kisses aren't just kisses when they are placed on his lips. It is a hard pill to swallow. That is until I looked at him, and the look he gives me is for my eyes only. Like I need to hang a 'Private' sign on the doorknob. His eyes roam over my body, only straying long enough to take a quick photo or sign a t-shirt. Then, those amazing gray eyes are right back on me.

I've never had my own pre-show ritual. I haven't needed one. So while the guys run through some warm-ups, I pull out my trusty mp3 player and find something to calm my racing heart. The song? Poison's "Talk Dirty To Me." I don't know why exactly, but this song distracts me from what's about to happen. Sitting on an old, lumpy sofa in the backstage area, I can finally feel my heart rate slowing.

I'm lost in the lyrics when I sense Beau's presence. His shadow falls over me, but I don't look. I'm too busy trying to keep calm. Beau pulls one of the ear buds from my ear and lifts it to his own. Glancing at him for the first time, the look on his face is priceless when he discovers what I'm listening to. His eyebrows shoot upward, completely hidden beneath the bill of his hat.

Plopping down beside me on the couch, Beau and I get lost in the hair band music pumping through the ear buds. When the song finally ends, I realize I'm as relaxed as I'll ever be. I truly don't know if it's from the music or the man, but serenity has finally settled in, and I'm suddenly energized and ready for tonight's performance.

Neither Beau nor I have yet to speak as the next song on my random playlist starts. Instantly, I recognize the intro since it's one of my favorite songs. Poison's "Lay Your Body Down" is cranked up in one ear, since the other bud is currently attached to Beau's head. I hum along with the first few lines, closing my eyes, as I get lost in the familiar words. What happens next catches me completely by surprise. Beau starts to sing the lyrics. Keeping my eyes training on a chair in front of us, I listen to the smooth timbers of his voice as he sings the song about watching your love push you away.

After a few lines, I jump in and sing with him. We keep our volume low as the rest of the band mingles and preps for the show around us, paying us no attention.

Suddenly we're at my favorite part of the song. Where he tries to convince her to stay. *"So let's draw the blinds, forget wasted time, and let them old demons die. Take ahold of my hand, then you'd understand, why love's worth one more try."*

Beau reaches over and grabs ahold of my left hand that's resting on the couch. When he links our fingers together, I feel so much more than his hand. I feel something so shocking and direct, straight to the heart of me. My entire world is rocked on its foundation, but then righted again. Almost like he's the balm to heal my ache. And it's right here and now that I realize that I want Beau to help me. I want him to mend my broken heart and help piece back together the tattered pieces. I want him to kiss away any doubt and uncertainty. I want him to hold my hand and show me that love *is* worth another try, just like the lyrics state.

I don't even realize that a tear has escaped until he reaches over and wipes it away. I'm lost in a sea of steel gray eyes with more tenderness and softness in them that I've ever known. So much goes unsaid in this moment, yet I can see his feelings reflected in his eyes.

Our private moment is broken when movement catches my attention. The camera zooms in as close as possible, I'm sure, as the cameraman films our exchange. As if sensing my immediate uneasiness, Beau lets go of my hand, removes the ear bud, and stands up. He gives me his trademark cocky smile before slipping over to his band mates for the remaining few minutes before they go on stage.

What the hell was that? I have no clue. I do know that Beau knows the words to one of my all-time favorite songs–a rock song. And not even a popular one, at that. Beau definitely keeps me guessing. Just when I think I have him all figured out, he goes and does something like this. Knows my song *and* holds my hand through my favorite part. If this man isn't perfect for me, then I don't know who is. But then again, skepticism steps in, and I can't help but wonder when the proverbial shoe is going to drop.

While Beau starts the show, I'm led to a dressing room in the backstage area where I find a short black dress with a big silver belt and black cowboy boots. The detail in the boots is exquisite. Silver and hot pink stitching in the form of angel wings on the sides. The entire ensemble puts a smile on my face as I realize that I'm about to wear my first pair of cowboy boots. On stage. With Beau.

A woman quickly styles my hair so that it's pulled back and away from my face while still leaving it down with big curls. My eyes have that smoky, sultry look and are a tad darker than I would have liked. She assured me that they always go darker for the lighting.

I watch most of the concert from the side of the stage. Beau is electric when he performs, guitar in hand, as he works the stage. I can see why all the girls ages two through ninety-two love him. He's drop dead gorgeous with a southern drawl that I never knew was so damn sexy, and he has moves that are all that and a bag of chips.

Suddenly, my time is upon us. Beau talks to the crowd for a few moments, getting them all riled up before his band starts the now familiar melody. The song is slow and packed with meaning. The whole thing screams sexual tension. While I wait for my cue to step out on stage, Beau starts to sing.

"From that first moment, I knew there was somethin'

Somethin' bout you that speaks to me so true.

Every moment with you makes me alive,

Every beat of my heart for only you.

Your skin against my skin, your lips against my lips,

Your touch is my undoin', I crave you underneath my fingertips.

Stay with me tonight, Stay with me tomorrow.

Stay with me forever, until the end of time.

Just stay with me

Stay with me."

And that's my cue to step out onto the stage. The lights are blindingly hot and remind me of the ones on the show. The crowd is there, yelling and cheering, yet I don't see them. I only see the man in front of me at the front of the stage. I bring the microphone up to my mouth as I reply to his words.

I've been hurt so many times before,

And I'm afraid to move too fast.

Letting go is never easy,

But when I'm with you I forget the past.

You make the fear disappear and my smile feel brand new,

I want your arms wrapped around me, a touch from only you.

Stay with me tonight, Stay with me tomorrow.

Stay with me forever, until the end of time.

Just stay with me

Stay with me."

We sing together, our eyes locked in the middle of that stage, as if no one else in the world exists. This song feels eerily familiar, yet the words are so new. Beau touches my face as he sings; the intimate gesture that he warned me was coming. Even with thousands of fans watching, along with a camera crew documenting this entire experience, I don't mind. His hand on me feels right. Just like the words I sing.

"It's you and me against the world,

But it doesn't matter as long as you stay.

Right by my side, just stay beside me.

Stay with me.

Yeah, stay with me."

Before I know it, my time on stage is done. The song is over, yet I can't seem to walk away. Our eyes are locked as I register the screaming fans surrounding us. My breath catches in my throat, and I wonder if he's going to kiss me. The look in his eyes is fierce and primal. I lick my lips in anticipation, but the moment is severed when the band starts the intro for the next song.

"Ladies and gentleman, Layne Carter," Beau says into the microphone without taking his eyes off of me.

And just like that, with the super-human strength I didn't even know I possessed, I walk away.

*****

"You're already checked in. Here's your room key," Andrew says as he escorts me into the hotel in downtown Denver.

"Thank you," I reply as I wheel my overnight bag towards the elevator.

"If you need anything, just buzz the front desk. A car will be here at ten in the morning to take you and Beau to the airport for your flight back to LA."

The elevator deposits me on the top floor of the posh hotel. Inside, the suite is massive. It's quite probably twice the size as the suite I stayed in with my mom and son while they were in LA. This one has a full kitchen, an office, a massive sitting room with more gadgets than an electronics store, and two huge bedrooms. Two bedrooms? Why in the world am I staying in such as large suite? It's the kind of suite that's reserved for presidents and millionaires. Not bartenders with musical aspirations.

Just as I get ready to phone the front desk, the door opens. The sight before me steals my breath and unravels every brain cell I possess. Beau walks in. When our eyes meet–mine filled with shock, I'm sure–he gives me a small smile.

"You're here?"

"I am," he says as he drops his duffle bag on the floor at his feet. "But just so you know, Ben and I shared a suite last night, too. It was the hardest thing I've ever done to not punch him in the face every time he opened his mouth."

"He's not so bad, you know. If you got to know him, you'd probably like him a bit," I say, feeling the need to defend one of my friends. Even if that friend likes to cross the line a little.

"He had his hands and his lips on you. I hate his fucking guts," Beau replies seriously.

Well, then…

"Which room is mine?" I ask, steering the conversation towards a safer topic. Sleep. Yet, something feels so intimate about that too.

"Either one. I'll take the small one if ya'd like," he says and starts to walk towards the door behind me.

"No, I'll take that one. You're the star here, not me."

Beau stops directly in front of me. His eyes search my face before he replies, "There is no star here tonight. Just a man and a woman. Sharing a hotel suite."

The underlying meaning slams into me with so much force, it almost knocks me on my ass. Tonight, Beau and I are sharing a hotel suite. Albeit different rooms, but we'll be sleeping in close proximity. His head resting on his pillow mere rooms away. His body wearing nothing but a sheet or maybe a pair of silk boxers. Yeah, there'll be no sleeping tonight.

"Go get ready for bed and then come back out and we'll discuss the show," he says as he heads towards the smaller of the two rooms which is still twice the size of my bedroom back at home in Chicago.

I'm left alone in the main seating area so I quickly gather up my luggage and head into the master suite. Gasping when I step inside the room, I didn't even know they made beds that big. What's bigger than a king size bed? The bedspread is white and satin with huge, fluffy, luxurious pillows. There's a beautifully delicate dresser and a matching wardrobe along the back wall, but the best feature is definitely the massive French doors that lead to a private deck. When I slide open the door, I'm shocked to find a hot tub, cover off and lights shining as if it's ready to go.

Okay, I'm definitely using that before bed.

As I run my fingers through the water, I'm startled when I hear Beau's boots behind me. "There's another door," he says, pointing to the doorway that leads to the sitting area with his hand holding a tumbler of something dark.

"Oh," I reply. It's all I've got.

"Why don't you get in?" he asks before taking a sip of the amber liquid.

"I didn't bring a suit," I tell him.

"Who said anything 'bout a suit?" he asks, that dark eyebrow disappearing underneath the brim of his hat.

Tingles of anticipation skitter through my body. I've never been skinny dipping, and the thought both excites and terrifies me. Do I want to take this step with Beau? The line is drawn in the sand, and I fear that once I step over it, I'll never be able to turn back. Can I risk my entire future, a recording contract with a major record label, for Beau? It doesn't even take me a nanosecond to know without a doubt that the answer is yes. I was fine before the show without a recording contract, and I'll be fine afterwards without one as well.

I kick off the tennis shoes that I chose to wear for travel. They're comfy and familiar, and make it easy to maneuver in a crowded airport. Beau's eyes darken even more, if that's even possible. I don't say a word as I grab the hem of my sweatshirt and pull it up and over my head. The cooler night air kisses my already heated body, resulting in immediate goose bumps. I stand before Beau wearing a blue lace bra and my jeans, arching my eyebrow at him as in challenge.

Beau answers immediately by removing his Stetson. He throws it down on the chaise lounge and bends down to remove his boots. When he pulls his tucked shirt out of the top of his jeans, my entire body ignites with awareness. We're really about to do this.

Standing before me, bare-chested with that tattoo on full display, Beau waits for me to make my next move. I reach down and unsnap my jeans. I slowly–seductively–shimmy out of the tight material until they're piled around my feet. I rip off my socks next, leaving me standing before him in a blue lace bra and matching boy cut panties.

Beau's eyes flare with passion as he drinks me in. They roam over me several times as if committing to memory every curve, every stitch of fabric. My heart rate beats so fast in my chest that I'm sure he can see it from his position in front of me.

I watch, helplessly, as Beau reaches down and unsnaps the button on his worn Wranglers. My mouth goes dry as he slowly lowers the zipper and starts to push them down his strong legs. Dark hair sprinkles his powerful thighs, extending down his well-defined calves.

Here it is. This is the moment we both decide if we're going to cross the line.

I can head back to my room, pull the covers up to my chin, and try to forget about everything. We can go back to being coach and student. No lines have been crossed, and no contracts have been broken.

Or I can forget the show, forget everything, and just *be*. Be with the man I've wanted since I first laid eyes on him. Be with the man who wants me so fiercely in return that he's willing to risk everything–his reputation, his contractual obligations–for me.

Do I stay or do I go?

Readers,

If you were in Layne's shoes, what would you do? Would you risk everything for the one person that makes you feel alive and wanted? Or would you choose the safe route to ensure that your dreams can come true?

You decide.

Choose which way the story ends.

If you want to see Layne walk away and finish the show she was so destined to perform on, then choose The Safe Door.

If you think Layne should follow her heart and choose Beau, then choose The Dangerous Door.

And maybe when you've read your first choice, go back and read the other too. You can't go wrong with either ending!

The Safe Door

Beau stands before me wearing nothing but a pair of black boxer briefs molded to his powerful thighs and lean waist. He's beautiful. The man is pure sex, and I long to wrap my body around him and purr like a cat. Beau steps closer until I can feel the heat of his body through the Colorado chill. His need is evident if you take into consideration the massive Boy Scout approved tent pitched on the front of his undies, but I can also see it in his eyes. Unfortunately, that's not all I see. There's hesitancy mixed with desire. Indecision. Uncertainty because of contracts, television producers, cameras, and imaginary lines in the sand. Even though he wants me–as much as I want him, I'm sure–he knows that by crossing this line, we are letting them win. Letting the headlines proclaiming us a couple, the gossips like Shawna Reece running their mouths and spreading rumors, they all become the victors in this game if we succumb to our desires and let go.

I know it. And Beau knows it.

"Layne?" he whispers, his voice hoarse with desire and claim. "I want you so bad. I want to be with you more than I want my next fuckin' breath, but I can't. I can't strip this away from ya.

You are doing this show for your son, to give him a better life. If we sleep together, then I ruin that for the both of ya."

"Beau, if we sleep together, it would be a mutual decision. I would be a part of the destructive end results as much as you would. That decision wouldn't solely be on you," I tell him as he steps forward again, encompassing my nearly naked body in the warmth of his arms. Suddenly I feel more exposed than ever before, and I'm not talking about my lack of clothing.

The night is silent as I wrap my arms around his chest. He smells clean and woodsy from his earlier post-show shower and his warm breath feathers lightly across my forehead. His embrace is fierce and consuming, his skin against mine hot, as if he's trying to hold on to some relevance of control by holding me tightly. God, what I wouldn't give to strip the remainder of clothes away and have my wicked way with him, but I know he's right.

We shouldn't.

"I think you're right. We need to stay focused on the last two weeks of the show. Then, we'll see what happens."

Beau's light southern chuckle sends little flutters of butterflies soaring in my stomach. "Oh, don't take my hesitancy as anything noble, darlin'. As soon as they sign off-air on the final show, I'm carryin' ya off the stage and into the first storage closet I can find. I plan to show ya just how *bad* I want you," he whispers in the night. The decisiveness of his words and the hard erection in his underwear both fortify his statement as certainty and genuine.

Beau's kiss consumes me, pulling me under the water. But I don't fear the drowning or suffocation. As long as Beau is the one sinking under with me, I know I'll be okay.

After the world's most delicious kiss that takes me higher than the clouds above the Colorado mountains, Beau pulls back ever so slightly and gazes down into my eyes. The hunger is still very much there, but he manages to reel it in. "Over and over and over again. We may be in that storage closet for days," he adds with that cocky half grin I've come to adore. "Come on. I want to snuggle up with ya, but I can't risk takin' this into one of the bedrooms. I'm only human, and the very male part of me is already protestin'."

Leading me towards an oversized chaise lounge on the deck, Beau indicates for me to take a seat. I watch as he slips inside and returns moments later wearing a pair of loose sweatpants and a faded t-shirt and carrying another shirt and a big, fuzzy blanket. He slips the large, worn t-shirt over my head before slipping behind me on the chaise, pulling my body snuggly into the apex of his legs and covering us both with warmth. The combination of his body heat and the blanket keeps the cooler night at bay.

There's something almost magical about the moment. The cool breeze, the stars twinkling brightly through the calm night sky, and Beau's body wrapped around mine like a fine mink shawl. He continually runs his rough hand up the outside of my thigh and back down to my knee, while the other hand is enveloped around mine. His kisses and the power of his words still consume my thoughts and dominate my desires.

But it's Beau's steady heartbeat that slowly lulls me into the best night of sleep ever.

Chapter Twenty

Note to self: Cross Brazilian wax off the list. Cross it off with black permanent marker.

"Ladies and gentlemen, tonight on *Rising Star*, you're going to hear an individual performance from each of our remaining four contestants, as well as a duet with their coach. When we open the voting lines at the end of the show, it's up to you to determine who moves on to the final round next week. Will it be Ben, Jamal, Shawna, or Layne who is crowned the next *Rising Star*? Your votes will help determine their fate. We'll get to our first performance of the night after this..." The camera pans to cover the four of us, front and center, on stage. My nerves have kicked into high gear, and listening to Becker state so matter-of-factly that for one contestant, the road ends this week isn't helping.

While the show takes the necessary commercial break, the four of us slip backstage to prepare for our individual performances. I'm wearing a black dress with an intricate silver design weaved through it, representing the spider webs that I'll be singing about this evening. Before the show's prep work, I visited a salon and indulged in a little personal primping. While I was plucked, waxed, massaged, and exfoliated by a team of foreign women, I was able to relax and enjoy a bit of calm before the storm. Well, that was until they whipped out the wax. Apparently, a Brazilian wax isn't what I thought it was. Leaving practically no hair and barely any skin in the nether region, I left the salon sore and slightly sticky from wax residue. Did you know Brazilian waxes are the equivalent of modern day torture devices?

Note to self: Contact the CIA and see about adding Brazilian wax to their list of techniques to make a man speak. Slap a little wax across their balls and I bet any man would sing like a canary.

As I wait to go back on stage, I'm not as nervous about my individual performance as much as I am my duet with Beau. I can belt out No Doubt with the best of them. It's the romantic country-rock crossover ballad that I'll be singing with my superstar coach this evening that has me all sorts of flustered.

I'm up first tonight for individual performance. As I wait for my cue beside the stage, I hear the clicking of heels behind me. I ignore her presence as much as I can. I refuse to let Shawna instigate me into a verbal sparring match right before I hit the stage.

Evidently, my ignoring doesn't seem to faze Bitchy Barbie. "Break a leg," she says sweetly, yet dripping with as much sarcasm as she can muster.

"Thanks," I reply sweetly.

"Oh no, I mean really break a leg." Blond Barbie struts away in her sky riser stilettos as I receive my cue to take the stage.

The lights are still low as I wait for my introduction. Even though I can't see Beau sitting at the coach's table, I can feel his presence. I know his eyes are glued to me, running up the length of my body from my black heels to my wildly teased hair. Goose bumps pepper my skin at the thought of him watching me, but not being able to see him in return. It's exhilarating and intoxicating all at the same time.

Finally, Becker speaks the words I've been waiting for. The house band begins the opening notes of No Doubt's "Spiderwebs" as I bring the microphone up to my mouth. *"You think that we connect, that the chemistry's correct, your words walk right through my ears, presuming I like what I hear…"*

The beat is up-tempo, the words quick off my tongue, and the stage calls me as I move with each line I hastily deliver.

"Sorry I'm not home right now, I'm walking into spiderwebs, so leave a message and I'll call you back. A likely story, but leave a message and I'll call you back."

Two minutes later, my performance is ending. As I have for each week before, I wait for Becker to join me center stage. The applause is almost deafening, the smiles on the faces of the coaches–especially Beau–beaming. "Layne, let's hear from some coaches. JoJo?"

"Wow, Layne. We've seen you rock the house. We've seen you cross over to the dark side and step into some country music." JoJo gives Beau a bright smile. "We've even seen you tackle something a bit on the bluesy side. And tonight, you showed just how versatile you are as a singer and as a performer, by leading with that song. You nailed it, sister. " The audience applauds again as her words soak in. What an amazing compliment from such an acclaimed artist.

"Felix?"

"Girl, you are the *Rising Star*." His words steal my ability to breathe. I try to suck in air, but for some foreign reason, I'm unsuccessful. "Gwen Stefani is an icon. She has one of the most unique voices in music. It's edgy and rocker-chick, and you stepped up to the plate and knocked it out of the freaking park. Hell, out of the state," he adds.

After the applause dies back down, Becker turns to Beau. "Beau, she's your girl. What did you think of tonights performance?" The way Becker said "your girl" didn't go unnoticed by me or by Beau if the way his eyebrow raised and that half cocky grin strikes beneath his Stetson, is any indication.

"Ya know," Beau starts, but seems to stumble on his words. "I thank my lucky stars every day that she picked me. I feel like I'm on the ride of my life right now, and the best part is, I know this is only the beginning for her."

As Beau speaks those words, I get the distinct feeling that he isn't entirely talking about my performance on the show. Tingles of awareness and exhilaration ripple through me at his implication. This is only the beginning of my music career, sure, but it's also the beginning of something more. Something deeper. Something real. And *that* is the greatest praise I could ever receive.

"Layne, this has been a busy week for Team Beau. Last weekend you went to Denver with your coach and performed on stage. How was the experience?" Becker asks.

"Eye opening, to say the least. To feel that energy, that excitement was like nothing I've ever experienced before. I am honored to share the stage with such a dynamic performer." The massive room erupts into applause at my mention of their beloved cowboy.

"Layne, since I have you here, the rumors are flying rampant this past week following your performance and stay with Beau. What would you say in response to those rumors?"

"That they're just that–rumors. Any relationship made on this show has been professional and moral."

"Thank you, Layne Carter. If you'd like to see Layne in the final three, be sure to cast your vote when the polling period begins. Up next, a duet between Ben Atwood and Beau Tanner." And when the spotlights fade, I'm finally free to step off stage.

Later in the show, I walk out onto the riser on the stage and await my cue. After performing my song earlier in the show for votes, this piece is purely for entertainment. No votes will be cast. No comments will be made. Just Beau and I performing together on stage. Again.

The familiar melody of Jason Aldean and Kelly Clarkson's "Don't You Wanna Stay" fills the auditorium. I'm positioned above Beau on a riser on the opposite side of the stage. The choreography has us singing apart, yet slowly working our way towards each other until we meet in the middle of the stage.

"I really hate to let this moment go, touching your skin and your hair fallin' slow. When a goodbye kiss feels like this..."

My mind is flooded with memories of kisses shared with Beau. The janitor closet, the hotel room, backstage in his dressing room. All of those kisses come flooding back in bright, Technicolor. Each one better than the last.

"Let's take it slow, I don't wanna move too fast. I don't wanna just make love, I wanna make love last. When you're up this high, it's a sad goodbye..."

My feet are moving down the steps of the riser on their own accord. It's as if they know, that with each step they take, they're heading towards Beau. Like some invisible, cosmic pull, we move in unison towards one another. Our eyes locked and unable to look away, we get closer and closer to the other as we sing the song we've rehearsed only a handful of times.

"Don't you wanna stay here a little while? Don't you wanna hold each other tight? Don't you wanna fall asleep with me tonight? Don't you wanna stay here a little while? We could make forever feel this way. Don't you wanna stay?"

As if I didn't feel those words reaching into my soul, I sure feel their power when Beau reaches out with his left hand and caresses my cheek. It's a sweet, seductive, and possessive gesture that leaves me breathless and slightly off-kilter. Thank God we're reaching the end of the song, because I'm not sure how much more of his touch I'd be able to handle in front of millions. There's no way to appear unaffected when my entire world is spinning out of control. I long to throw caution to the wind, step into his arms, and kiss his lips. Television show be damned.

But before I can act on the desire, the song ends and the spotlights fade. When the main lighting comes back up, Beau and I are still staring at one another, transfixed on the person standing mere inches away. His hand drops and shifts possessively onto my lower back as we turn and wave to the crowd. My smile feels forced as I politely acknowledge the throng of people, wishing they would all just disappear and transport Beau and I back into our own little cocoon of togetherness. Where cameras, stages, and fans screaming our names don't exist.

Beau and I head backstage as Becker introduces the final performance of the night. Shawna takes the stage, but my attention is anywhere but on her. In fact, the only place my attention is focused is on the man holding my hand, leading me towards one of the back hallways. As soon as we round the corner, I'm engulfed in his arms and pulled tightly against his chest. His cologne mixes with a hint of sweat as he runs his hands down my back to rest at the place where my back meets my ass.

When he shifts and looks at me with those needy gray eyes, he whispers, "Not kissing you out there was the hardest thing I've ever done."

I start to lean into his body to claim the kiss he was insinuating, when a shadow falls on the hallway floor. Instantly, my mind remembers where we are. I jump back, disentangling our bodies from one another, a fraction of a second before the camera turns the corner and is positioned right in front of us. I can only pray that my guilt and embarrassment isn't written all over my heavily make-upped face.

Beau seems to recover quickly as well. "Great job tonight, Layne. I hope the votes come through in your favor." He offers me a wide, friendly smile and heads back the way we came, the camera hot on his heels.

I wait a few seconds before following in his black-leathered boot wake. I catch Beau chatting with the other contestant remaining on his team: Ben.

Last Sunday night, I had to slide on my big girl panties and have the painfully awkward conversation with Ben that has been needed for several weeks. Telling him that there was absolutely no chance for anything to happen between us seemed to dim the light in his eyes. I needed him to understand that I wasn't interested in anything more than friendship from him. He said he understood but the look of hurt in his eyes still ripped at my guts. We parted with an awkward hug, and haven't had anymore exchanges since.

Even though Beau looks calm and friendly as he chats with Ben, I know the storm is brewing within him. Not only is he *not* a fan of Ben's, but if the way his back is ramrod straight is any indication, I'd say Beau is annoyed. Frustrated, maybe.

Huh. Maybe he's sexually frustrated like me.

A girl could only hope, right?

Note to self: See what's left in the liquor cabinet to help relieve this sexual frustration.

*****

"Mine."

That one word threads through my mind in a flood of raw need and hunger. His hands lift my shirt, exposing the lace bra underneath. His fingers are calloused and warm against my oversensitive nipples, pushing against the coarse material.

Desire pools deep in my belly, consuming me like a raging wildfire.

His mouth sucks greedily at one of my nipples through my bra. With each swipe of his masterful tongue, I'm pushed closer and closer to the edge of nirvana. As he slowly moves the restraining material aside, steel gray eyes lock on me, devouring me as if I were a Thanksgiving Day feast.

The feel of his tongue against bare flesh causes a deep moan to rip from my body. He laps and sucks at one, then my second exposed breast. I wriggle against his engorged cock, my body seemingly completely out of my own control.

Slowly, his hand slides down my stomach. His eyes remain locked on mine as his hand pushes past the waist of my pants and finds damn wet lace. He closes his eyes and groans a possessive, strangled cry. His fingers move past the thin material of my hopeless panties and meet smooth, bare skin.

His eyes slam into mine once more as his fingers flex against my wet, swollen flesh.

"Mine."

I startle awake once more with my fingers pressed firmly against my core. My body calls to Beau as I reach orgasm without even fully waking. And that's okay. I long for my dreams. Dreams where it's okay to be with Beau.

Dreams where he can be mine.

Chapter Twenty-One

Note to self: Sometimes justice is best served cold.

"Ladies and gentlemen, tonight we have our final elimination before next week's big finale show. Four contestants stand beside me on this stage, but at the end of the show, only three will remain. Who will move on? Ben Atwood from Team Beau? Shawna Reece from Team Sophia? Layne Carter from Team Beau? Or Jamal Jefferson from Team Felix? Tonight we find out which three move on and which one goes home brokenhearted." Becker smiles a blindingly white grin at the camera before the light on the camera turns off, signaling we're off air.

The four remaining contestants are ushered backstage and into the green room. This place has practically become our second home, after the studio in which we practice day in and day out. However, steadily over the last several weeks, the quantity of room occupants has shrunk considerably.

Tonight's show is a star-studded affair. Blake Shelton, One Direction, and last season's big winner, Shay Douglas, will all light up the *Rising Star* stage throughout the course of the show. I'm secretly hoping to catch a few minutes with Shay so that I can tell her how much I enjoy her music. She doesn't sing my usual style, but I can appreciate her pop music. I'd be lying if I said I haven't danced around the bar after it closes to her latest single, "Just You Wait." Doc MZ has a thing for the leggy brunette, and feels the need to blare her music as much as he can.

The hour long reveal show actually flies by. Before I know it, I'm standing on the stage next to Shawna. Jamal and Ben were both declared safe for next week's finale earlier in the show. It's seems like some sort of cosmic déjà vu that I'm standing beside the one woman I went against in the very first week, and won.

Now as I stand beside Shawna in her beautiful red and gold dress with her red cowboy boots and perfect blond hair, I realize I'm just as nervous now as I was that very first week. Except now I feel like there's more riding on this announcement. I've vested weeks of time, sweat, and even tears into this show, and I'm so close. So very close to the end.

So close to winning.

"It's time to find out who moves on and who goes home. Layne, Shawna. Only one of you will be moving to the finale next week to compete to be the next *Rising Star*. And it's time to find out who."

Becker has the dramatic pause down pat as he takes his sweet-ass time removing an envelope from his suit pocket. I want to throw my arms in the air and scream at him to get on with it. You know, fling myself down on the ground and flail my arms around like one of Eli's temper tantrums. I'm sure America would love to witness that moment of glory.

Becker makes a big show of tearing it open and pulling out the enclosed card. I don't watch what he does from this point on because my eyes move on their own accord and focus on the steel pair across the stage. Beau's eyes are fixed on me, gazing intently and offering me every bit of confidence and encouragement that he can. Shy of standing up, walking up on the stage, and taking me in his arms, I feel his comfort and support as we wait for my fate to be revealed.

"Layne, Shawna. It was an epic battle in the first round where Layne emerged the victor, as chosen by Beau Tanner." I hear Shawna growl beside me, but I keep my eyes fixed on the pair that is grounding and calming me. "Tonight, the decision is based upon fan votes. The woman moving on to the final round is…"

I suck in a deep breath, my eyes glued to my favorite cowboy, and wait.

"Layne Carter."

*****

I have no clue what time it is when I finally make it back to my hotel room. Following the show, Ben, Jamal, and I had to pose for dozens of promotional photos that will be used over the next several days. After several group shots on stage, we then each posed with our respective coaches. Having Beau stand so close to me and not be able to touch him the way I wanted to, was torture. It didn't help that during one round of photos, Beau wrapped his hand around my side and pulled me snuggly into his hard chest. I just pray that the pictures don't show the primal reaction with which my body responded to him.

I wish I could say Shawna left respectfully and with dignity. But if I know anything about Shawna Reece, it's that she lacks the ability to think rationally and behave appropriately. Lord knows she's shown her ass more times than I'd like to have seen over the course of this show. Fire practically shot from her ears when my name was announced as victor. She glared at me with such intensity, I should have dropped dead right there in the middle of the stage from the voodoo eye-death she dealt me.

Of course, it didn't help that she was practically shooed to the corner so that the crowd could get their first glimpse of the final three. The cameras were thrust in my face and the questions from Becker flew, all to catch my initial reaction to his big announcement. It was almost completely overwhelming. I started to feel panicky until I looked up and caught Beau's reaction. He was standing up and clapping his hands, all while gazing hungrily up at me from beneath that sexy Stetson. When I caught sight of his excited look, laced with concern for me, I started to calm down. The cameras and the voices all faded away until I was able to focus on one thing at a time: namely Becker's questions.

Following the show, everyone within a two-block radius of the studio heard Shawna's dramatic exit. She threw profanity-laced insults and bogus accusations at me, claiming once again that I was sleeping my way through the show. But this time, she started throwing around network names including Jackson Zimmerman. Her allegations included terms like "lawsuit" and "lawyers" and "daddy" throughout her rage-induced eruption. But when the powers that be themselves arrived at the stage, she quickly shut her mouth. Even Shawna must have realized that running her mouth was going to get her nothing but the door against her ass on her way out.

After the necessary photos and a handful of television and radio network interviews, we were finally ushered towards an awaiting car. Adrenaline had run its course as we slowly made our way towards the hotel. Exhaustion had set in and the excitement of the live reveal had left us each wrung out and drained.

I don't even remember the elevator ride to my room. Ben practically carried me from the car to my doorway, helping dig my keycard from my small purse and inserting it into the door. Ben takes my bag and deposits it on the second bed while I sit down on my own bed, dropping my purse on the mattress beside me. My eyes are closed and I hear him moving about my room. He removes my black boots and throws the corner of the bedspread over me. I know I should get up and undress. I should remove the quarter-inch of stage makeup I'm wearing. I should see Ben out of my room and thank him for his assistance. But I don't. I can't move.

The last thing I hear before succumbing to sleep is the loud clicking of the shutting door as he exits my room.

*****

What feels like five minutes later, the distant ringing of my cell phone awakens me. Fumbling in the dark, I find my small purse that still houses my phone. I don't even open my eyes to see who is calling when I answer.

"Lo?"

"Layne? Are ya alright, darlin'?" Beau asks, his deep southern drawl so predominant in the dead of night.

"Yeah, just exhausted."

"I've been textin' and callin' ya. I was startin' to get a little freaked out that something had happened to you."

Despite myself, I smile knowing that Beau was concerned for me. "I'm fine. I was so dog-tired by the time they let us leave the studio," I tell him, sitting up and opening my eyes for the first time since arriving back to my hotel room. I'm bathed in dull light from the lamp across the room. I'm assuming Ben left it on for me.

"I know ya were, that's why I was tryin' to get ahold of ya. To make sure ya made it back safely." Oh. I think my heart just melted into a big pile of mushy goo. I can hear the faint rustling of material in the background, and my mind instantly thinks of Beau lying naked in bed within those covers.

"I did. Ben helped me up to my room."

There's a long pregnant pause before he asks, "Ben?" There's no missing the fact that his voice is laced with annoyance and something else. Jealousy.

"Yeah, Ben. I practically fell asleep in the car ride back to the hotel and he helped carry me inside."

"Ben carried you? Into your hotel room?"

"Yes," I say, trying to figure out a way to defuse the situation I see brewing. "He helped get me inside my hotel room. And then he left."

Silence greets me on the other side of the line. I debate on what to say next. Even though nothing happened, I find myself caught between defending Ben against whatever accusations Beau is about to hurl at him, and letting Beau know that it's ultimately my decision if something were to ever happen between Ben and myself. I'm technically still single, and I have a right to have whoever I want in my hotel room with me.

He must sense my irritation as much as I feel his through the phone. "I'm sorry, Layne. That guy just makes me see red whenever I think about him around you. I know I don't have a claim on ya…yet, but that doesn't mean I have to like him hangin' around you. Even if his intentions are pure, I just don't trust him."

"All he did was help me in my room and turn on a light. I heard the door close before I even fell asleep."

Beau sighs heavily in the phone. "Forgive me, sweetheart. For some crazy reason, I turn all jealous and possessive when it comes to you. I'm not used to dealin' with this green-eyed reaction. Congratulations, again," he adds, his voice changing to a more cheerful one.

"Thank you. Do you know what I'm singing for the finale?" I ask, yawning and lying back down on the bed.

"I do. But I can't tell ya yet. We'll have to do the big reveal tomorrow for the cameras. Or should I say tonight, since it's after three a.m."

It's quiet for several minutes. I relax into my pillow and close my eyes. Listening to Beau's slow and steady breathing, I'm lulled back towards sleep. "I should let ya go," Beau whispers. "You've had a long night."

"What if I just wanted you to stay on the line? I like listening to you breathe. It makes me feel like you're right here beside me," I mumble in a sleepy voice.

"Then I'm not going anywhere. I'll stay right here for as long as you want me to. Anytime you need me, I'm right here, Layne." His voice, even laced with his own exhaustion, is strong and steady. I can hear the conviction in his words and it makes my heart race just a little bit faster.

Music starts softly in the background. Within a few seconds, Beau is singing along to a country song I'm not familiar with. Of course, that doesn't surprise me since most of the country songs I've learned have been newly acquired since meeting Beau Tanner.

One song quickly becomes two, which then turns into three. Lying in bed, I'm completely mesmerized by his deep voice, all sweet and sexy and intoxicating. I've heard him sing plenty, but never like this. Never have the words been so intimate and raw. It's as if the words he's singing are for me and me alone, and as I lie in bed, I know that they are. I feel the emotions he feels for me pouring through the phone. It's as if no one else exists in the world. It's just Beau and me. Together.

His soft, seductive words about finding love and holding on to it forever are the last thing I recall before slowly drifting back to sleep.

*****

Between practices with Beau, the choreographer, and a vocal coach, dress fittings and sleep, I have little room for anything else come the weekend–and that includes eating. It's the final weekend before the big live two-day finale, and I'm running on fumes. Saturday nights before would involve some sort of physical torture with Corie, followed by drinks and dancing at a local club. Now, I'm more homesick than ever, and just want to curl up in bed and sleep until Tuesday.

Of course, we all know that'll never happen.

After an hour-long Skype chat with Eli and my mom, I take a quick shower and settle in to watch *Friends* reruns. My phone rings before Rachel hops on the plane for London to disrupt Ross' wedding to Emily. I smile at the name on the screen.

"What are you doing?"

"Talkin' to you," Beau says with a smile.

"You're kidding me. I never would have guessed," I retort with a chuckle.

"I have an idea," he says, all signs of humor gone.

"What's up?" I ask, sitting up straight in bed.

"A car is going to be pullin' up in front of the hotel in about ten minutes. Get in the car. No need to dress up or change. We're goin' somewhere without cameras or pryin' eyes. No questions asked." Of course, the first thing I want to do is ask a question: namely, where am I going? But I refrain from doing the one thing he told me not to do.

Besides, I trust him.

Note to self: Never get into cars with strangers. Unless that stranger is a gorgeous cowboy with the sexiest southern drawl. Then, don't walk. Run to the car!

"Deal?" he asks.

"I have to go. I have to be downstairs in ten minutes," I say with one of those big, cheeky grins on my face.

Beau's laughter is the last thing I hear before signing off the phone.

After brushing out my hair, I throw back on my bra and change my t-shirt because no one wants to be caught with a country hottie without a bra and wearing an oversized shirt with sleeping puppies. I found a vintage seventies rock tee at a local thrift shop last weekend and I have yet to wear it. While Beau said there was no need to change my clothes, I still feel the need to exchange my holey sweatpants for something different. Throwing on the first pair of shorts I find in the drawer, I quickly slip into the bathroom to freshen up before heading downstairs.

A black town car is waiting beneath the awning as I slip outside. A friendly looking, older gentleman in a black suit opens the back door for me. I'm disappointed when I realize the backseat is empty. Once inside, he closes the door, engulfing me in cool air conditioning and silence.

"Good evening, Miss Carter. Mr. Tanner asks that you relax for a few moments. We'll be at our destination within fifteen minutes or so," the man says, smiling at me in the rearview mirror.

"And where exactly is our destination, sir?" I ask.

He chuckles but never takes his eyes off of me in the mirror. "You can call me Al, ma'am. And as far as our destination goes, I've been instructed to remind you that there are to be no questions asked."

"Cheeky bastard, isn't he? Are all cowboys this damn stubborn?" I mumble, not realizing I said it loud enough for Al to hear.

His laughter fills the car. "He is indeed, Miss Carter. He also said that you might try to persuade me into giving up the location. In that case, I am to remind you that all good things come to those who wait." With one more smile in the rearview mirror, Al winks at me before turning his attention to the road before him.

Fifteen minutes later, we pull in front of a large, non-descriptive brick building with very few lights on. Before Al can exit the car, my door opens, revealing one handsome cowboy. The smile he gives me could melt the polar icecaps in December; maybe even strip the panties off a nun in church on Sunday morning. Either way, that gorgeous smile is aimed directly at me.

Beau extends his hand, assisting me from the vehicle. "Did ya have a nice trip?"

"Yes," I tell him breathlessly as he leads me towards the front doors.

"Did you ask Al where you were going?"

"Of course not," I tell him, fretting innocence.

Beau's laughter is better than any music. "I bet you didn't," he says with a firm shake of his head. "This way," he adds as we step inside and head towards a bank of elevators. I don't ask any questions as Beau presses the button for the tenth floor.

Inside the elevator, I can feel his eyes blazing a trail of fire up and down my body. I fight my desire to look at him for as long as I can, but in the end, it's fruitless. When my eyes connect with his, I feel the effects of their burn all the way to my toes. This man has the uncanny ability to touch every part of my body with only his eyes, leaving me yearning for more and rendering me speechless.

When we reach our floor and the door opens, I walk alongside Beau, his hand warming the base of my spine, until we reach the second door on the left. Inside, the room is set up like a small rehearsal studio, similar to the one we use for the studio.

"What is this place?" I ask, taking in the wall of instruments and the comfortable seating.

"This is my rehearsal studio while I'm in Los Angeles. The band and I practice here from time to time while I'm stuck here with show commitments. It's also the place I escape to when I need to get away from all of the show people and the cameras."

"This is a nice place," I tell him, looking around the large room a second time.

"This is the one place I don't allow the studio to film. It's like my own private sanctuary, ya know? No cameras. No lights.

No production assistants telling me where to stand. Just me, my instruments, and a little free time."

I don't really know what to say, so I opt to remain quiet. I'm not sure why he brought me here, but his "no questions" statement comes to mind again, so I don't ask. Instead, I walk over to a drum set in the corner of the room. I've never really played an instrument before unless you count chopsticks on the old piano in the backroom of Chaser's. But even though I don't play, doesn't mean I haven't always wanted to.

"Have you ever played?" he asks, startling me with his closeness.

"No."

"Come on," Beau says, grabbing my hand and pulling me towards the drums.

Beau takes a seat on the stool and slaps his left leg. His eyes are alive as if a challenge has been made. Of course, I'm not one to back down from any challenge, so I straddle his leg–careful not to kick the drum set in front of me–and have a seat on Beau's leg. The position is incredibly erotic and makes me want to start rubbing my crotch against him like a dog in heat. *Down, girl.*

"Alright, pick a song," Beau says, suddenly pulling a pair of drumsticks from a bucket next to the drums.

"Just pick a song? Any song I want and you'll play it?"

"No, we'll play it. Pick."

So I throw out the first song I think of. "'Barracuda' by Heart."

"Excellent choice, darlin'. The Wilson sisters have recently become a personal favorite of mine."

And with that, he begins to drum the opening beat of the song. I quickly find myself tapping along with my foot, and feel the song taking shape. Of course, it's not as good as it probably could be considering his movements are restricted somewhat by the woman sitting on his lap.

When he gets to the part where the lyrics come into play, he stops and hands me the sticks. "Your turn."

"But, I don't know how to play," I defend, staring at the sticks like they're a snake that might try to bite me.

"Sure you do. Just feel the music and the beat. Even if ya don't hit the right drums, you still could tap out the beat with your eyes closed. So do it. Close your eyes and just feel the music."

Hesitantly taking the warm drumsticks in my hands, I get ready to make a fool of myself on the drums. But I know this music like the back of my hand, so I take a few deep breaths and close my eyes. Then I begin to play.

Note to self: Next time you're going to pick up a foreign instrument, select a slower song.

Surprisingly, I think I do all right by the time I make it somewhere in the middle of the song. Oh, it's not anything near performance ready, but you can tell there's a song deep down. Way, way down. But the important thing is that I feel the beat, feel the music. It pulls me in and holds me captive.

Just like the man I'm sitting on.

Taking my hands in his, Beau slows down the noise and helps drum a steady beat. Suddenly we've gone from hard and rockin' to slow and seductive. His hands are hot wrapped around mine, and I feel his warm breath tickling my ear as he slowly hypnotizes me with each inhale and exhale. An uncontrollable shiver rips through my body, but it has nothing to do with the coolness of the room and everything to do with this man and the way he touches me.

We play in unison for several minutes, playing a song that I'm not familiar with. Hell, for all I know, Beau is making it up as we go. All I know is that I'm entranced with the music, the steady tapping of the drums, and the one-hundred percent all-man hottie with his arms wrapped around me.

Shivers rip through my body like a tornado and goose bumps pepper my skin when Beau gently brushes his lips against the back of my neck. "You smell like heaven. It's a little bit of something floral wrapped in sweetness. Like tulips dipped in sugar. It makes me want to lick this part of your neck," he says as he runs his tongue down my neck and toward my collarbone. "And suck on ya. Right. Here," Beau says, punctuating each word by gently sucking open-mouthed on my tingly skin.

"You can't say that to me," I whisper without conviction, finding it difficult to speak with my suddenly too thick tongue.

"Why not?" he whispers against my flushed skin.

"Because it makes me want more. And I can't have more," I reply with a groan. My body is fully charged, a live wire of electricity, with no relief in sight.

"*Yet,* Layne. We can't have more *yet.* I promise you that as soon as this show is finished, I will know what the rest of your skin tastes like. I am going to savor every inch of your delectable body. I am going to kiss every part of you as I strip you naked, and then I am going to do things to you–every single one of the wicked things I've fantasized about–until you are screaming my name and left satisfied and boneless. And then I'm going to do them all over again. Why? Because one time isn't going to be nearly enough with you. I might need days. Weeks. Fuck, I might need to spend the rest of my life consumed by you. Only you."

As potent as Beau's touch is, it doesn't hold a candle to the power of his words. My brain completely short circuits, my entire body erupting into flames, and my breath practically non-existent. And the crazy part is that if I were to die right now, in this exact moment, I would go happy. Wrapped in Beau's arms with his lips against my skin is heaven.

"Come on," he finally says, detangling our limbs from one another. It takes self-control I didn't realize I possessed to release my hold on Beau, but I somehow manage.

"Stand here," he says, turning me so that I'm facing a wall of mirrors. I watch as he walks over to a line of instruments, plucking a vintage white Gibson guitar from a stand. When he returns to where he left me standing, he swings the intsrument over my shoulder and helps secure the strap.

"Ever play this one?" he asks as he wraps his arms around me and helps place my fingers on the instrument.

"A few times. Never anything that constitutes actual playing. A friend who works at the same bar as me likes to play and tried to teach me a few things," I tell him, my voice a breathy mix of anxiety and anticipation.

"I'm going to try not to visualize some guy with his arms wrapped around you. It makes me insane with jealousy, Layne. And I've never been a jealous man before," he states honestly, his eyes locked on mine as we gaze at each other through the mirror.

After several heartbeats, he clears his throat and looks down at our hands. "Tuck it under your arm like so, and place your fingers here and here. Curl your thumb underneath the neck of the guitar like this. It should be fairly comfortable. Your index finger is fret one. That's B," says as he moves me fingers. "Fret two is your middle finger and that's D, and put your ring finger here. That's A. Now, gently with the pick, strum downward like so," he says, demonstrating the movement.

The sounds vibrate through my fingers and a faint tickle ripples through my arms. After a few demonstrations, he lets me try a few times on my own. Beau never steps away though, just keeps his front plastered to my back. His voice is soft as he instructs me on which positions to move my fingers.

Before long, I'm playing something that resembles actual music. Beau is patient and gentle as he teaches me to play one of his songs. Whoever thought that someday I'd learn to play guitar–a country song to boot–was clearly slightly delusional. What's even more amazing is the fact that I'm actually able to concentrate on playing. Beau steals little nibbles of my neck and tenderly strokes the outsides of my arms as he hums along with the tune I'm attempting to play.

After about an hour of messing around, Beau unsnaps the strap and returns the guitar to the empty stand amongst the mass of instruments. A quick check of the clock on my phone tells me that it's late. I spoke with Eli and Mom this afternoon between my wardrobe fitting and a vocal lesson, but it's moments like these–late at night–where I miss my son.

"I don't want to just assume, but will ya stay with me tonight?" Beau asks.

"Yes."

"Good," he says with a smile. "Because I wasn't goin' to let ya leave anyway. Saves me from havin' to kidnap ya," he adds as he leads me towards the couch along the outside wall.

"Glad we can avoid the felony charges," I say through a giggle.

My laugh quickly dies in my throat as Beau strips his ever-present cowboy hat from his head and drops it on the chair. Waves of dark hair are both matted to his head and askew from the hat, making my fingers twitch to touch those enticing locks. Then he pulls his black t-shirt out from the waist of his jeans, grabs the back of the neck, and quickly pulls his shirt over his head in one fluid motion. You know, that sexy way that only guys can do? Not only was the shirt removal exquisite, but the tight, ripped abs and hard pecs that were hiding underneath are a pretty freaking spectacular sight. Never have I forgotten how unbelievable Beau's body is, but that doesn't mean it still doesn't stop me in my tracks and make me want to sing to the angels a Hallelujah chorus when he stands before me, naked from the waistline up.

"Stop staring at me like that. Otherwise, I'll forget all about being a gentleman and take you ten ways to Sunday on that couch." The look in his eyes tells the story of how serious he is. Dead serious. Beau's need and desire for me hasn't wavered or diminished in the least bit since our first real encounter in the closet at the studio.

I don't respond as I reach down and pull off my ankle boots. Beau walks over and confirms that the lock is thrown on the door and flips off the overhead florescent lights. The only light in the room now is the City of Los Angeles' lights that bleed through the windows in the massive room. But even with little light, Beau has no problems finding me in the dark. It's as if his body is attuned to mine. Like a homing beacon, I know he would find me in a sea of thousands of other people.

Removing his jeans, Beau finally stands before me in only gray boxer briefs. His thick length is standing proud against his underwear, and I struggle not to focus all of my attention on the newest arrival in the room. But Beau doesn't draw attention to his erection. Instead, he lies down on the couch. Even through the dark room, I can see his feet hanging off the end of the standard-size couch.

Without giving it another thought, I remove my socks and shorts before grabbing the hem of my shirt and pulling it up and over my head. The cool room kisses my flushed skin as I reach around and unsnap my bra. I feel Beau's eyes on me as the material slips down my arms and falls to the floor. His hiss is the only sound in the room as I stand there–naked except for a red satin thong–and let him drink his fill. Before joining him on the couch, I reach down and grab Beau's discarded t-shirt and slip it over my head. I'm instantly assaulted with the scent of Beau. If he weren't staring at me like a Thanksgiving feast, I'd take a moment to sniff the soft material of the shirt.

Instead, I make my way to the couch and slip onto the thin sliver of real estate not occupied by the big cowboy. My head rests on his bicep while my back is pressed snuggly against the entire length of his body–from shoulders to ankles. Even through the shirt, I feel the heat of his skin against me. Not to mention the throbbing erection he has pressed firmly between my ass cheeks. The cotton of his boxer briefs does nothing to lessen the contact. No, it's not skin on skin, but it's damn close, and my body is alive and hungry. The throb between my legs shows no sign of subsiding, especially with Beau pressed against me.

"Don't move, sweetheart," Beau whispers against my ear. "If ya wiggle anymore, I'm not going to be held accountable for my actions. Seein' you in nothing but my t-shirt was torture enough, but having your sweet body pressed against mine is taking every bit of restraint I have. You are killin' me," he groans hoarsely, his words laced with his pain. It makes my heart swell that much more knowing that I can bring an award-winning country superstar to his knees. Me. Little ol' me with her imperfect body and inability to cook real meals. My response lodges in my throat and refuses to surface so I nuzzle his arm a bit with my cheek and snuggle a little deeper into his embrace.

After several minutes of silently listening to Beau's steady breath against my head, I finally say, "Thank you for bringing me here this evening. I had a great time."

"You're welcome, sweetheart. Go to sleep. We'll have to sneak out of here early in the morning to beat some of the people coming into this building. Some work with my record label which isn't a problem, but there's some that I don't trust. One look at you coming out of my studio with bedhead and wrinkled clothes will fuel the tabloids for days," he says as he kisses the back of my head and pulls me closer. Even though I'd kill to explore the impressive hard-on pressed against my backside with my tongue, I know he's right.

The last thing I recall is how comfortable and so very right this feels. Falling asleep in his arms, as if my body was made to fit against his, laughing and teasing each other while he taught me to play some of his instruments, and even those stolen kisses and soft caresses in the privacy of Beau's studio, it's as if we're the only two people who exist in the world. And for just a little while, we are.

He was made for me.

Chapter Twenty-Two

Note to self: If you don't believe in yourself, what do you have?

"Last song reveal. Are you ready for this?" Beau asks from his stool across from me. I'm a mixture of nerves and excitement as I wait to hear what Beau has in mind for my final performance for fan votes.

"Bring it." My voice is cool and calm, though on the inside, I'm anything but. My stomach is knotted so tight, I fear I might never eat right again.

"Are you sure? You might not be happy with my selection," he says, that sexy eyebrow arching and disappearing beneath his Stetson.

"You haven't steered me wrong yet. What have you got?" I ask, all but bouncing on my stool. Nervous energy flows through me like a tidal wave.

"Miranda."

I stare at him and blink once. Twice. Fine, I blink about a dozen times before I find my voice. "Country?" I ask, unsure why he would pick a song that doesn't fall within my preferred genre. My comfort zone.

"Yep. I think this song was made for you. It's sassy, aggressive, and even though it's country, I think your rock background would complement it nicely." Beau stares intently at me from the other side of his music stand. "In other words, I think you'll fucking rock the shit out of this song." Beau doesn't even flinch at the use of his f-bomb as the cameras zoomed in on our faces to catch both sides of the conversation.

His eyes are hard. Intense. But mixed in flows pride and adoration. And that's the bottom line: Beau has unwavering faith in me as a performer. He believes I can tackle this song because he believes in me. Even though this song isn't what I'd pick, I know I can do this because Beau feels that this song is the right fit for my final performance. And I trust him.

"Okay," I tell him confidently.

"Do ya want to know what song?" he asks, smirking beneath the wide brim of his trademark cowboy hat.

"It doesn't matter," I tell him.

"No?" he asks, that eyebrow disappearing once again beneath the hat.

"No. Because I trust you."

Beau watches me for several moments–moments that extend into a lifetime. A conversation is carried between us, without even saying a word. It's a mutual acceptance of trust by both parties, as well as an understanding of something more. Something that feels a lot like love. It's scary and freeing all at the same time. It's dangerous and exciting. It's real.

Suddenly, he's on his feet and moving. He pulls me into his chest, wrapping his protective arms around me. I slide my hands up his back, gripping at the dark material of his shirt. Resting my cheek on his chest, our grip remains tight and our breathing synchronized. I'm hypnotized by his heartbeat thumping steadily against my ear. We stand there, locked in each other's embrace, for a while. Even the movement of the camera crew doesn't pull us from our embrace.

Relaxing his hold, Beau eases back and looks down at me, that cocky smirk firmly in place. "You ready to win this thing?"

"I'm ready," I tell him confidently, my smile matching his.

"Then let's do this."

*****

Do you know what's more nerve-wracking than getting ready to perform the finale of a live reality show and duet with the likes of Grammy winning icons Nancy and Ann Wilson of Heart before a studio audience of thousands, with millions watching at home?

Nothing. Nothing's more nerve-wracking than that.

Note to self: If you're going to throw up, just make sure it's not on Nancy or Ann's shoes.

We just received the ten-minute cue. Ten minutes before we go live. Ten minutes before I sing with the other remaining contestants to start the show. Ten minutes before I prepare for my final performance for viewer votes.

Ten minutes left to freak out!

"You've got this," Beau says behind me, that southern drawl like a sweet caress.

"I've got this," I confirm, turning around to face the man behind me.

"Why do you look like you're goin' to be sick?" he asks, fighting the urge to crack a smile.

"Because I might just need to throw up."

"You'll be fine. Nothing to worry about, sweetheart. You've done this a dozen times before."

"Yes, but this is different. This is for everything I've wanted; for myself *and* for Eli."

"Darlin', you've been fighting for that this entire time. From the first day you stepped into auditions, it's been for everything. You're just a whole lot closer now than ya were a few months back. And ya know what? Whatever happens today, you've already won. You know that you can do anything you put your mind to even if the results are a loss. You're teachin' your son one of the most important life lessons there are. You've taught him to reach for the stars and fight for his dreams. Even if your name isn't called on that stage tomorrow, you've won so much more than a record contract and some money. You've won self-discovery. You know who ya are and what you're worth. And, darlin', what you're worth is the world."

Suddenly, there's no air left in this massive building. I'm unable to breathe around the golf ball sized lump firmly taking up residency in my throat. I fight the tears, blinking several times, so that I don't ruin my dark, dramatic makeup. Beau takes his rough thumb and catches the tear that slips from the corner of my eye.

"Don't cry, babe," he whispers. "You're worth everything to me." His words slice through every ounce of pain I've carried for the last four years. Colton cheating on me. Colton dying before I had a chance to maim him for his deception. Working my ass off for tips that I use to raise my son. It all washes away with the tenderness of his words and the touch of his hand.

"Places everyone!"

Everyone rushes to get in place. Final checks of hair and makeup are given by backstage crew. It's time.

Last call for throwing up!

I turn and look at Beau's bright eyes, shining with something we've yet to specify. I see it as clearly as I feel it in my own heart. My heart has been telling me that I love him for a while now. I've just chosen to ignore that pesky organ because I didn't think I was worthy of such a strong emotion. Not when the last time I loved a man, it was thrown back in my face, tainted and brimming with laughter.

"Your son is here. I've spent the last thirty minutes with him in the audience. He's so fuckin' excited to see ya tonight, sweetheart. I made sure Eli and your mom are sitting in the best place possible. They'll be right behind me. So know that when you go on stage. Look at them or not, it's up to you. I just didn't want you to be blindsided and freeze."

My heart stops beating. My son is here. Beau made sure Eli was here for the biggest two nights of my life. It takes every ounce of control I have not to blurt out my feelings for him right now, in front of the cast and crew. Instead, I give him a watery smile and pray that my love reflects in my eyes.

And when my eyes meet his, I see nothing but his love reflecting in the warm pools of his eyes too. I feel his strength and hear the magnitude of the words left unspoken. Apart, we were two people, lonely and searching for something more. Together, we are greatness. Together, we are one.

Note to self: Win or lose, as soon as this show ends, tell Beau how you feel!

Beau gives my hands one final squeeze before turning and heading towards the stage. I slowly make my way over to stage right and wait for my cue. Standing next to Ben and Jamal, I take a few deep breaths and wait for the show to begin.

*****

"Welcome to the final week of *Rising Star*. In just over twenty-four hours, we will be crowning a brand new *Rising Star*. We have three amazing hopefuls ready to perform for your votes one last time. We also have a star-studded show in store for you tonight and tomorrow. Without further ado, I present your four *Rising Star* coaches, Felix, JoJo, Sophia, and Beau!"

You can feel the rumble of the applause behind the massive curtain. Ben, Jamal, and I are positioned in a Jeep Wrangler, ready to perform choreography we've gruelingly worked on for the past forty-eight hours. It's the first time a vehicle is being driven onto the stage during a performance on this network. Rumor has it that they pulled the plug on the idea before it even got off the ground, but after a few meetings and negotiations, the powers that be agreed to the large production. So now I sit in the back of the topless red Jeep Wrangler and wait for the cue to begin singing "Cruise" by Florida Georgia Line.

As soon as we get the cue that the stage is cleared, Ben starts the Jeep and puts it in drive. We wait for the signal, microphones already poised at our mouths and wait. And then the light appears. Five, Four, Three, Two...

"Baby, you a song, you make me wanna roll my windows down and cruise..."

And with that, Ben drives us onto the stage. The crowd erupts and is immediately on their feet as Jamal sings from the passenger seat lines made famous by Nelly in the remix version of the hit song. I'm standing up in the back of the Jeep, hanging on to the roll bar as if my life depends on it. It has nothing to do with Ben's driving–in reality he's only driving about 20 feet onto the middle of the stage at five miles per hour–but has everything to do with my nerves. As I get ready to sing my next line and Ben comes around to help me down, after shutting off and exiting the vehicle, I finally feel the music pulse through me. It relaxes me in a strange way.

"It'd look a hell of a lot better with me up in it..." I sing, the lyrics edited just a bit to fit me and the fact that I'm a woman singing as opposed to a man singing of a woman.

Together, our trio makes our way across the stage, each of us acknowledging the fans in the audience in our own way. For me, it's zeroing in on the three-year-old little boy standing proudly in the audience behind Beau Tanner. I offer him the biggest smile I can manage while still singing the lyrics. Beau doesn't miss the exchange either, turns around and makes a silly face at my son. If I wasn't already head over heels in love with the goof, I would have completely fallen right then and there.

As I move and dance–yes, dance. Thank you choreographers–I can't help but reminisce on the last eight weeks.

The lights. The music. The stage. The judges. The other contestants. All of the hard work and commitment to the show comes down to this. It's all about to end. Win or lose, there is no next week.

"Come on, girl. Get those windows down and cruise…"

"Ladies and gentlemen, your final three: Layne, Jamal, and Ben. We'll be back with our first performer singing for your votes after this." Becker smiles until he receives the signal that we're off-air, and then we're ushered off stage.

And now the real competition begins.

*****

I'm about to go on as the second performer of the night. The song Beau chose for me as my final number is perfect. Yep. I'll be the first to admit, it's the ideal selection for me. The black and blue dress I'm wearing is bulky and heavy against my body, primarily because I'm technically wearing two of them. My long brown hair is swept up in a tight French twist and my makeup flawless. I look exquisite in my black Jimmy Choo pumps. Every bit the pristine, perfect housewife I'm trying to resemble.

But that's where the resemblance ends. I'm anything but perfect. There isn't a flawless bone in my body. And if you don't count my son, my greatest accomplishment is learning how to make homemade French toast without burning the house down.

"Layne, you're up in one minute," I hear from a young woman positioned by the stage and wearing a headset and a scowl.

Running through a few lines of the lyrics in my head, I prepare myself to take the stage. The whole world is about to see me perform for the last time for their votes. Knowing that Eli is in the audience, watching and waiting for me to perform, is enough cause to make me give this more than one hundred percent.

And then they're cuing me to step up to stage left. Becker is on the stage giving a glowing introduction and showing highlights of my previous weeks on the competitive show. I can't see the massive screen above the stage, but I can hear the laughter and the awes from the audience.

The lighting is subtle, but only for a moment. When I'm positioned center stage, the blinding lights flash and the familiar melody of Miranda Lambert's "Mama's Broken Heart" starts. I smile brightly at the first few rows of the audience since that's as far as I can see and bring the mic to my mouth.

"I cut my bangs with some rusty kitchen scissors. I screamed his name 'til the neighbors called the cops. I numbed the pain at the expense of my liver. Don't know what I did next, all I know I couldn't stop."

I love this song. I love the lyrics, the sass, the drama. I especially love what is coming up. Part of being a performer, I've learned, is acting; being someone else for a short period of time. And this is the performance of a lifetime. I'm moving, I'm singing, I'm entertaining the audience to the best of my ability.

And here comes my favorite part…

"Powder your nose, paint your toes, line your lips and keep 'em closed. Cross your legs, dot your I's, don't ever let them see you cry."

The music drops off completely along with the lights. The massive room is bathed in pure darkness with the exception of minimal lighting at the stairs for safety. I spring into action, ripping off the top dress which was designed to breakaway easily. The second dress underneath is the exact same dress, yet this one is torn and tattered. I release the clip at the back of my head and my hair falls in a crazy mess of hairsprayed chaos. I kick off a single shoe, and toss it to the woman waiting just off to my left.

When the lights return–just a few short seconds later–I'm left unruly and disheveled on stage, just as the song reflects. My movements are choppy and hurried as I walk towards the edge of the stage, mic poised at my mouth to continue the song.

"Go and fix your makeup, well it's just a break up. Run and hide your crazy and start actin' like a lady. 'Cause I raised you better, gotta keep it together. Even when you fall apart, but this ain't my mama's broken heart."

I stick the ending like a damn Olympic gymnast. The crowd doesn't even wait for the music to fade. They are on their feet, cheering for me. Excitement and relief washes over me like a spring rain. I glance over and see Beau. There he is: the man I love. He's standing at his chair with his arms raised high above his head in victory. My beaming smile surely matches the one I see on his gorgeous face.

Becker asks me questions, and I'll be damned if I know what answers I give. I could have told him aliens invaded my body and I wouldn't have realized it. My eyes remain locked on gray orbs of radiating excitement and pure love. I can feel it from twenty yards away.

And it's the best feeling in the world.

Chapter Twenty-Three

Note to self: Sometimes you just have to let go and be free.

After spending last night following the broadcast with my mom and Eli, waking up with his little body next to mine was like a dream. When we go home to Chicago, I'm not sure I'll be able to let him sleep in his own bed again. For now–or at least the next three nights–Eli will be snuggled securely against my body in my hotel room while mom sleeps in the second full-size bed in the room.

Today is the day.

The *Rising Star* Finale.

One show to determine my fate. The voting period is almost closed. The stage is almost set. One last performance–just for the fun of it.

I'm sitting down in the makeup chair, the tiny black spandex piece of material that they call a dress hidden beneath the cape. My leg is bouncing which only causes looks of annoyance to be thrown my way from Mary, my favorite makeup artist. The other artist, Sasha, preps her station beside me. I always cringe when I get the busty redhead with long manicured talons. Not only is her attitude snippy and she treats you like you're a bother from the moment you sit in her chair, but she tends to go heavier on the black eyeliner than anyone without a streetwalker position listed on their resume wants to wear.

"Are you excited?" Mary asks as she brushes loose powder on my forehead.

"Are you kidding? I'm so excited, and I just can't hide it," I smart off, knowing that the petite blond will get a chuckle out of it. Mary is the queen of one-liners.

"You've got this in the bag, girl. I've been voting for you since week one on my smartphone," Mary whispers and offers a wink through the mirror.

I'm just about the reply when the chair next to me moves and a new face appears in my peripheral vision. Holy. Shit. Nancy Wilson just sat down in the chair next to me.

"Hey! You must be Layne," she says with a big smile.

Holy. Shit. Nancy Wilson just spoke to me. And she knows my name.

Note to self: Uhhhh...I got nothing. Holy! Shit!

"You are Layne, right?" Nancy says with a knowing smile. All the while I just gape at her like a freaking moron.

"Uh huh," I finally choke out. *Smooth, Layne.*

"Well, Ann and I are super stoked to sing with you tonight. We've been rooting for you since the beginning," she says casually as Eagle Talons starts working on her makeup.

"You have?"

"Sure have. We're big fans of the show. We both actually cheered when you knocked Shawna out of the first round. I could tell right away that she was a crazy diva. But you? You're more my style. You've got a natural talent that is pure and edgy. Your light will shine brightly if you let it, Layne. You need to just let go and be free. Let the music guide you and you can't go wrong."

Seriously, I have no words. All I can do is stare at Nancy freaking Wilson–my musical muse–and blink. My brain officially shuts down. I'm fangirling so hard right now, I'm afraid I won't ever be able to speak again.

"Thank you," I finally get past my dry throat.

"No, thank you for sending that girl packing not once, but twice," she says with a wink before turning her attention back to the mirror. "Sorry we weren't able to make it here sooner so we could practice for tonight. I know we'll be rushed to run the song a few times before the broadcast starts, but I'm not worried. After you performed 'Crazy On You' a few weeks back, I knew that if anyone could pull off a quick rehearsal right before going on stage, it was you. And Beau says that 'Barracuda' is the perfect song for us to sing. I'm excited," she adds.

"I can't believe I'm going to share the stage with you. That right there is a dream come true."

"Well, we're honored to share the stage with you," Nancy says as Mary removes my cape and prepares to send me to hair. "And we'll meet you in the green room as soon as we're camera ready," she adds.

"Thank you," I whisper for the second time before standing. My legs feel boneless and I'm afraid they won't hold my body upright. I'm going to freaking fall flat on my ass right in front of Nancy Wilson. And Sasha will probably have her cell phone out quicker than a drunk takes that first sip of whiskey and broadcast that shit all over social media.

Heading towards the room where hair is done, I turn back and face a beaming Mary. "You're the best, Mary."

"Yep. Working in front of this mirror all day is something I can totally see myself doing," she quips, causing Nancy and myself to bust up laughing. Sasha, on the other hand, looks as if she just sucked on a lemon.

"You've got this, Layne. Go win this damn show," she says with a bright smile.

"Thanks. Well, I'm off like a prom dress," I say with a wink before slipping away.

*****

Standing mid-stage with the Wilson sisters is the culmination of my time on this reality show. Performing one of my favorite songs with them is beyond epic. Sharing this stage, mere feet away from my musical inspirations is a surreal feeling. It's like an out of body experience where you're dreaming of standing naked in Times Square, but no one really sees you and keeps walking by. Except now, everyone and their little brother sees me. And, thankfully, I'm not naked.

Note to self: Get their autograph before they leave.

The distinctive voice of Nancy Wilson starts to sing the lyrics I could sing backwards in my sleep. I watch starstruck as Nancy sings the first lines of the song. Her smile is wide as she looks at me expectantly to sing the next part.

"Smile like the sun, kisses for everyone. And tales, it never fails."

Working the stage, I let go of everything: the stress, the drama, the show, the long nights in a claustrophobic hotel room, the coming and going until I'm dead on my feet. I feel the words and live the beat. It consumes me like a raging wildfire, nomadic and gaining in intensity as it devours everything in its path. I do what Nancy said and let go. I'm free.

"If the real thing don't do the trick, no, you better make up something quick. You gonna burn, burn, burn, burn, burn it to the wick. Ooooo, Barra-Barracuda."

Next thing I know, I'm standing at the back of the stage next to the drummer. He winks at me, my cue to dramatically give him a little shove. He steps away from the stool and hands me the drumsticks. Beau and I practiced this part endlessly over the past twenty-four hours, and I'm ready. Positioning the sticks in my hand, I take over where he left off. Nancy and Ann are each just off to the side of the drum set, bouncing their heads along with the beat while Ann plays along with me on her guitar. It's an easy line of music to drum. I'm basically just repeating the same thing over and over. But I'm doing it. I'm playing the drums on the stage with the Wilson sisters.

Best. Moment. Ever.

The applause at the end of the song is eardrum-shattering. My ears ring, my breathing is labored, and my heart pumps feverishly in my chest, and you couldn't scrape the smile off my face with a putty knife.

Of course, instantly, my eyes seek out Eli. He's standing on his seat, cheering endlessly, next to my mom. I don't even attempt to fight the tears that threaten to spill from my eyes. To have my family with me as I stand on this stage for the final time is humbling and heartwarming. To see the man I've come to love watching on is surreal and breathtaking.

Standing up from the stool, I join Nancy and Ann center stage and give the audience a bow. Beau's sexy smirk is so bright you could probably see it from an airliner flying at thirty-thousand feet. With another quick bow, Becker says something to the crowd before the lights dim and the cameras are put on standby.

There it is. Done. My final performance on *Rising Star*.

*****

"Ladies and gentlemen, it all comes down to this. Your votes have been tallied and the results are in. Every single vote counted in what is probably the closest vote we've seen yet on the show. Three contestants remain, but only one will become the next *Rising Star*." Becker beams at the camera as Ben, Jamal, and I stand just off to his right with our hands linked.

I can feel the nervous energy coursing from their hands into my sweaty palms, and vice versa. I'm barely breathing as I stand there on shaky legs and await the decision of the voting public. My stomach is a mess of nerves and excitement. If this is what a politician goes through before the votes are in–and continually go through it election after election–then I think I'll pass. This nauseatingly stressful situation is for the damn birds.

Note to self: Never run for office.

"And now, it's the moment we've all been waiting for. Who will be your *Rising Star*? Ben Atwood of Team Beau? Layne Carter of Team Beau? Or Jamal Jefferson of Team Felix? Let's find out. Right. Now."

The silence in the massive studio is deafening. It's as if the entire world is waiting with bated breath to find out who the winner is. As Becker draws out the suspense, a few fans give in to the silence and shout a name. "Ben!" "Go Jamal!" "It's Layne!" My grip on the hands I'm holding tightens as the answer is revealed to the host from within the confines of the white envelope.

"Your next *Rising Star* is…" I suck in a deep breath and hold it. Praying that my legs keep me upright, I lock eyes with Beau's gray ones. "Layne Carter!"

I feel weightless, as I'm shaken, hugged, and lifted from the ground. I have no idea who is holding me, but I'm thankful to not have to stand at this moment. This surreal, incredible moment.

I'm swept from person to person on the stage before I eventually make my way to Becker. I can't see through the sea of confetti raining down on the stage. My tears are real and my smile genuine as I try to soak up this incredible moment.

"Layne, tell me what it's like to be the next *Rising Star*?" Becker asks, his arm firmly around my shoulder in support, which I'm incredibly thankful for. It's probably the only thing keeping me from kissing hardwood right now.

"Becker, I have no words. I don't even know what to say. This moment is unlike anything I've ever experienced."

"Tell me who is here with you today?" he asks.

"My mom, Grace, and my son, Eli, are here for me tonight, and I just wanted to tell them that I love them more than anything. And thank you to my friends back home in Chicago. Tiffany and the rest of the Chaser's crew, thank you guys for your continued support."

"Layne, let's talk about your coach, Beau Tanner. What was it like working with Beau?"

"Incredible. When I entered this competition, Beau was the one coach that I really couldn't see myself working with," I say honestly, rewarding me with chuckles from the audience. "But that last split-second decision was probably the greatest of my life. Beau is amazing. Not only as a person, but as a coach, a vocalist, a mentor, and a friend. His advice was invaluable and indispensable for me as I advanced through the show."

"Of course, no one can forget the rumors you and Beau were plagued with throughout the show. Anything to say to that?"

Before I can answer, I feel his presence. Without setting my eyes on him, I know Beau is there. And he's close. His voice skims over my skin like smooth, soft cashmere, as his breath tickles the shell of my ear. Warmth in the form of Beau's hand caresses along my hip as I slowly turn around. Without even thinking, I launch myself into his arms. The first thing I notice–besides the fact that I'm wrapped in Beau's strong arms–is his smell. It's intoxicating and comforting all at the same time. It's familiar. It's home.

"I knew you'd win," he whispers against my ear.

"I couldn't have done it without you," I tell him honestly.

"That's not true," he says as he sets me back down on my feet. "You had it in you all along, babe. *You* did this. You. I just helped everyone see what was there all along."

Without thinking, without caring who is watching, I kiss him. Right there in the middle of the stage on live television, I kiss Beau Tanner with everything I have, and everything I am. I pay no attention to the noise around us; the whispers and the giggles and the gasps are all but nonexistent. I kiss the man I love in celebration and in acknowledgement. With his hands weaved in my hair, Beau claims my lips, my heart, and my life right there in the middle of the stage.

A smile spreads across his lips as we slowly pull away. A small hand tugs on the hem of my skirt, causing me to release the man before me and turn my attention to the other man in my life– a much smaller man. Eli's excitement is contagious as I pick him up, giving him the hardest squeeze I can manage without crushing his little body.

"Mommy! You did it!" he exclaims. The only response I can give him is a teary smile and gently rain kisses down on his adorable little face.

"I'm so proud of you, honey," my mom says behind me. Without setting Eli down, I turn and throw my arms around my mom. She believed in me way before I believed in myself.

"I love you, Mom. Thank you for the nudge," I tell her.

"Oh, you're welcome, sweetie. I knew you could do it all along." She gives me another fierce hug, wrapping her arms around both Eli and me. It's so natural, so right. It's been the three of us against the world for a few years now, but as I feel Beau place his warm hand possessively on my lower back, I know that we're a trio no longer. Now, we're a quartet.

Eli jumps from my arms straight into Beau's. As I wave to the crowd through the raining confetti and smile brightly for the cameras, I know that not many things in life will top this moment. With my son in one arm, Beau wraps his free hand around my waist and pulls me in tight.

"Well, ladies and gentlemen, I guess we have our answer. I'm Becker James for *Rising Star*. Have a good night."

Chapter Twenty-Four

Note to self: Closets are a pretty great place to hangout.

I've smiled and grinned my way through dozens of interviews and hundreds of photos. Through the whole thing, one person has remained by my side or just off to the side, never out of view. Even after he sent my mom and Eli back to the hotel to get some sleep, Beau's presence hasn't wavered. He's my constant, my calm, in a moment of pure chaos.

When the madness starts to ebb, I finally find myself alone in the interview room with Beau. We both stare at each other through tired, glassy eyes. Before either of us speaks, Beau gives me a knowing smirk. That look, combined with that sexy lift of the corner of his lips, does crazy things to my lady parts. I find myself crossing and uncrossing my legs several times to try to alleviate the ache. When his eyebrow arches and disappears beneath the brim of his Stetson, I almost orgasm right there in the chair.

Beau is laughing at my evident discomfort when Gabby, who has been stationed outside the door running interference and organizing the plethora of interviews, pokes her head inside the room. "Hey, guys, you're all done for the night."

"Thank God," I mumble as I take a drink from the bottle of water she brought me earlier in the evening.

"You've been awesome as always, Gabby," Beau says as he stands up and stretches. The muscles in his arms flex while his shirt pulls from the waist of those sexy Wranglers. A sliver of tan skin is exposed and it takes every ounce of restraint I possess to not lean over and run my tongue along the bare flesh.

"You guys are free to go. There's a car out front for you, Layne, when you're ready to head back to the hotel," Gabby says through a yawn, offering a wave as she turns and exits. Without either of us replying, Beau and I watch her leave the room, the exhaustion of the day clearly weighing on the young production assistant.

When Beau's steel gray eyes return to me, it's with longing front and center. He casually strolls over to where I stand just a few feet away, and gently grips my shoulders, running his hands down the outsides of my bare arms. It's meant as a soothing motion, but does little to soothe the want and ache between my legs.

"Some of those reporters wouldn't let go of the secret relationship angle," I mumble, concentrating on the fluid, upward motion of his hands as they stroke my arms and upper back.

Everyone asked what the status of our relationship was, and each one received the same answer: there wasn't a relationship.

Until now.

Now, the show is technically over. With the exception of a few contractual obligations in the coming weeks for appearances, all of the reasons for us to not be together are behind us. I'm not even looking for them in the rearview mirror because as far as I'm concerned, there's no reason to look back. Not when the man I want is standing directly before me. Why look back when my eyes are firmly focused forward.

"And do you know what I kept thinking the entire time I was sitting in that chair beside you?"

"What?" I ask in a breathless voice I barely recognize as my own.

"You. What it would be like to finally be with you. Inside you. Mine."

His lips claim me, possessively and with little question as to the level of desire he's feeling. Beau swipes his tongue across the seam of my lips causing a shudder to race through my body. That tongue. That magical tongue that could surely do wonders on a woman with little to no recent sexual activity. In fact, when Beau kisses me, I can't remember at all the last time I ever felt this loved, worshipped. Lord knows my body has never responded like this with anyone before. Was there anyone else even close to Beau Tanner? Hell no.

This is so much better than in the dreams. This is real.

Moaning allows Beau to plunge his tongue into my mouth. He tastes like heaven as our mouths slide and caress, our hands gripping and grasping, until we're both driven so stark raving mad that I fear there's no end in sight. Nothing but eternal longing and all-consuming lust. That's how Beau makes me feel. Unwavering to the love I have for this man.

"Come with me?" he asks, running his lips down the column of my neck.

"Okay," I mumble moments before I'm practically dragged from the room. And by dragged, I mean wrapped up in Beau's strong arms and carried from the room. Of course, I go willingly, wrapping my legs around his waist and threading my arms around his neck. The position also gives me a perfect angle on those swollen, lush lips of his, which I happily devour until we bump into a wall. Fortunately, the hallway is empty as Beau walks us towards a door at the end of the corridor.

STORAGE

I smirk at the man holding me up greedily by my ass, rubbing the hard length of his impressive bulge against the apex of my legs. "I told you that as soon as this show was over, I was throwing you over my shoulder and finding a storage closet somewhere." Without even testing the knob, Beau throws it open and walks inside the dimly lit room. Something tells me the availability of this room wasn't a coincidence.

Beau throws the lock on the knob and walks over to an abandoned wooden desk that's clearly seen better days. "Our first time should be in a bed with room service and champagne on a tray beside the bed. But, I can't wait for that, darlin'. I need you more than I need air. I need to touch you and feel your body against mine. I need to be inside you so fuckin' bad, I could care less where it actually happens. But if you want the whole bed and wine and roses thing, I'll gladly carry you out of here right now. As bad as I want you right now, I'll wait. For you."

I don't even have to give it another thought. There's no way I want to wait. I don't need a bed or flowers or even fancy wine. I just need this man. "I'm not leaving this room until I've had my fill of you," I tell him. "And that might be a very, very long time."

"Oh, don't go a thinkin' I'm goin' to let you go anytime soon." And then his mouth makes a declaration once more. His kiss is bruising, as if everything leading up to this moment has completely pushed him over the edge of control. Gone is my measured Beau. In its place is a hungry, feral man who is hell-bent on claiming his woman. His need as pure and driven as freshly fallen Chicago snow.

With steady hands, Beau begins to unzip the side of my black top. The thick material pulls away easily, and with the help of his hands, it's pushed up and over my head quickly. The black strapless bra isn't anything sexy, but if the way he's devouring my girls with his eyes was any indication, I'd say he's happy with the simple black satin undergarment.

"You are so fuckin' beautiful," he whispers, his breath coming out a little choppy.

Gripping his shirt at the sides, I give him a knowing look. Beau extends his hands to the ceiling as I remove the shirt completely. Even in the faint light of the room, I can see his glorious chest on full display. "You're not so bad yourself, cowboy," I say, running my hands up the hard plains of his chest. I could seriously gape at this man's chest for hours on end it's so perfectly sculpted. The tattoos he has adorning his chest and upper arms do nothing to hinder the level of this man's hotness. He is sex appeal, plain and simple.

With hands that hold a slight tremble, Beau reaches to the back of my leather skirt and gives the zipper a tug. His eyes follow the descent of the skirt, devouring every inch of my legs, as he slowly drags the material downward. Cool air greets my feverish skin, leaving me completely exposed and vulnerable in a little black thong. When the skirt is pooled at my feet, Beau's eyes finally slam back into mine with the force of a hammer. They're ravenous and almost angry with desire.

As much as we both want to savor this moment, our desire is getting the best of us. Beau picks me up under the armpits and sets me down in the middle of the old wooden desk. He works feverishly at removing first one black ankle boot, and then the next. Throwing the thin little socks somewhere over his shoulder, I'm left wearing nothing but my black lace thong and strapless pushup bra.

Beau's groan fills the small storage space. His eyes rake over my body once, then again, as if he can't seem to look his fill. No part of my body is left untouched by his gray eyes, and with each passing moment, I'm left wanting him more and more.

Finally, I can't take anymore. "Touch me, Beau. Please." Even to my own ears, my voice sounds raw and pained.

"If I touch you right now, I won't be able to slow down. I don't want to rush this, but I'm afraid I won't be able to stop myself from slammin' into you hard and fast. I don't want that for our first time," he says, his voice hoarse and wounded.

"I don't want you to go slow, Beau. I want you to take me, claim me as yours. I want to feel everything with you because you're everything to me. I want all of you," I tell him honestly. His eyes, filled with liquid fire from my words, bore into me. "We can go slow the next time."

As my words sink in, it's like flipping a switch. Beau reaches around and removes my bra. His tongue is warm against my overly sensitive nipples as he licks and nips at each puckered peak. I groan as he gently cups my breasts, licking and tasting each one equally before sliding his hands down to the remaining material covering my body.

Hooking his thumbs beneath the panties, Beau pulls. But he doesn't pull down the way I expect him to. Instead, he pulls out and rips the thin threads from my body. I gape down at him, surprised by his boldness, yet turned on more than I thought humanly possible.

"Holy shit, you're so wet. I can see it from here," he groans before running his finger along the seam of my legs. "God, I want to taste you," he whispers as he slides a finger inside of my body. The invasion causes me to buck up off the desk, seeking out more of his contact.

Sliding a second finger inside my body, Beau's mouth drops to my breasts. The sensation of his tongue licking my nipples, along with his fingers inside of my body, pushes me closer to the orgasm I crave. When his teeth latch down on one bud and his thumb slides across my clit, while his fingers slam into me, I fall headfirst into a brightly lit sea of euphoria. Blood swooshes in my ears as Beau continues to tease and prolong my release as much as he can. When I finally finish, I'm left spent and boneless, just the way he wanted me.

I barely even hear the sound of the condom being ripped open. The fact that I didn't get to see Beau strip the rest of the way saddens me, but I can't seem to force my heavy eyes open.

"Look at me, Layne," he says, his voice rough with need.

His words break through my post-orgasmic bliss, and I open my eyes to see a very naked Beau standing between my legs. His erection is long and hard and poised at my entrance as if silently begging for the cue.

Suddenly, I need to touch him. Sitting up, I reach forward, wrapping my arms around his neck and my legs around his waist. The movement pushes the tip of his cock inside me. I hear him suck in a deep breath as he closes his eyes to savor this moment.

"Look at me," I tell him. Beau's eyes open quickly and slam into mine. I see desire plainly in those smoky eyes, and I see the moment they soften into something more.

Beau gently starts to push forward, my body gripping his large erection. When he's completely seated within me, the tightness starts to subside, but the fullness remains. I've never felt anything like this before. As if there's no room for even air within my body. I'm consumed completely by Beau. Body, mind, and soul.

With my arms still wrapped around his neck, I pull him in for a kiss. It's slow and tantalizing as I convey my feelings for him through this one simple act. Still seated completely inside of me, Beau grabs my face with both of his hands and tenderly runs his fingers down my cheeks. "I love you, Layne. I'm so fuckin' in love with you," he whispers.

My heart stops beating as I absorb those sweet words. Only Beau could take a profanity laced declaration of love and turn it erotic, as if it were foreplay. "I love you, too," I confess, freeing the words and the feelings I've carried locked inside of me for weeks now.

Beau momentarily closes his eyes as if to savor those words. A smile plays on his lips as he brushes them across mine. "Fuck, you feel so good," he says as he slowly starts to pull out.

I quiver against his touch and revel in his words as Beau starts to move. His pace quickly turns from slow and seductive to fast and hard. Lying back on the desk, Beau takes me to places I've never imagined with each thrust of his hips.

My core starts to tighten once more as Beau's body drives it right back to the edge of oblivion. Keeping my eyes glued to his, I watch as Beau pushes me over, quickly followed by his own release. "Mine," he groans, deep and loud. My body convulses with each powerful thrust of his body into mine, fueled by the potency of that one word. Eventually, we still, both gasping for air and blinded by the bright lights of our releases.

Taking me in his arms, Beau nuzzles against my neck. Our sweaty bodies stick together in a tangled mess of trembling limbs. "That was better than I dreamed of. I knew our first time would be amazin' but that was out of this world."

"It was unbelievable," I confirm. After several minutes of lying there, catching our breath, I finally speak again. "I can't feel my legs," I tell him with a giggle.

Beau chuckles a southern drawl before rising up to his elbows. His eyes are much softer, but still shine with adoration. "I love you, Layne Carter," he confirms once more.

"I love you, Beau Tanner." The words have never felt so right. Saying them to Beau is as natural as breathing.

I may not know what comes next, but I'm not afraid to find out. I'm taking another chance on love–a chance I swore I wouldn't take again–and I'm a better person for doing it. I won't let the fear of the unknown keep me from living the life I want for myself and for my son. Beau is that life. No, I may not know what's around the corner, but with Beau by my side, I'm ready to find out.

Him and I.

The cowboy and the rocker making beautiful music, note by note, line by line.

It may not be like the average fairy tales written, but this one's ours.

This is only the beginning…

If you originally chose The Safe Door, you can continue to the next page to read The Dangerous Door.

The Dangerous Door

Here it is. This is the moment we both decide if we're going to cross that line.

I can head back to my room, pull the covers up to my chin, and forget about everything. We can go back to being coach and student. No lines have been crossed, and no contracts have been broken.

Or I can forget the show, forget everything, and just *be*. Be with the man I've wanted since I first laid eyes on him. Be with the man who wants me so fiercely in return that he's willing to risk everything–his reputation, his contractual obligations–for me.

Do I stay or do I go?

Without any hesitation, I reach back and unsnap the clasp of my bra. My eyes remain locked on his as I let the material fall from my chest and down my trembling arms. His eyes are pulled downward and there's an audible hiss as he takes in my almost naked body. I go for broke as I gently push my panties from my hips and down my legs. Standing before him, naked, is exhilarating. Better than I ever could have imagined this moment. And this moment has only just begun.

I watch helplessly as Beau mimics my actions. He pushes those tight boxer briefs that leave absolutely nothing to the imagination down his long legs. His actions seem so much more exact as his large erection bounces free. There are no words as we both stand before each other, completely naked, and looking our fill.

Ten seconds or ten minutes later, I slowly make my way over to the hot tub. The water almost scalds me as I slowly lower my body into the welcoming warmth. Bubbles tickle my overly sensitive skin as I glance up and wait. Will he join me?

I don't have to wait too long for my answer because seconds later, Beau is slipping into the hot tub with me. He remains on the opposite side, though, directly across from me. We continue to stare at each other as if having an entire conversation without even speaking. I can see his desire, his wants, his needs. Even if I didn't just see the evidence of it when he removed his boxers, I can see it written clearly in his dark eyes.

Without speaking, Beau offers me a wet hand. I take it without hesitation and he pulls me through the water and into his lap. I straddle him, truly feeling the softness of his skin for the first time. The hot water only seems to magnify the heat of the moment. His erection presses against my core as he runs his wet hands up my neck and threads them into my hair.

I shiver from the mixture of his touch and the cool air as his lips finally meet mine. The kiss starts hesitant as if testing the waters or waiting for me to change my mind, but that isn't happening. And it doesn't take long until this kiss turns raw. Unadulterated need and lust. The dam breaks, and we're all hands and lips and teeth. I grind my center against him as his tongue plunges deep into my mouth. He tastes like alcohol and something

I can only associate with Beau. It's a taste I'll never forget. And never get enough of.

Beau runs his left hand down my neck and touches my chest. Lightning strikes my slick core as he plays with my nipples, pulling and massaging them with his calloused fingers. The moan that escapes my mouth is swallowed up by the night as I close my eyes, absorbed and lost in the feel of his hands on me.

After showering each breast with plenty of attention, his hand finally glides downward. When he touches my center, I almost come completely undone. I whimper as his fingers stroke and tease the very essence of me. When I open my eyes, they collide with black, dilated pupils. I'm just about to lean forward and kiss those delicious lips when I feel the first finger enter me. The sensation is out of this world, like nothing I've ever felt before. I uncontrollably roll against his hand, intensifying the feel of his hand against my clit. When he adds the second finger, I'm lost. His lips attack mine with ferocious hunger as he glides his fingers through the wetness inside of me, bringing me towards the edge of release. My entire body is flying high as my internal muscles lock around his fingers, pulling him deeper than I ever thought possible. His thumb grazes the little bundle of nerves and I soar over the edge. I shatter into a million tiny pieces as I come violently on his hand.

Beau slows down as I start to float down from the clouds. "I will never get the image of you coming like that out of my head. When I'm old and gray, I will still imagine this moment and remember it with such precision, such detail. But right now, I need to be inside you." His words fuel the fire I didn't know was still smoldering. My body rages back to life, ready for another round.

"But not here. Not in a hot tub. I want to take you for the first time in a bed," he adds as he places open-mouthed kisses on my lips, cheeks, and chin.

"Okay," I reply, not about to deny us this moment.

Beau stands up with me still locked around his waist. He steps out of the hot tub, careful not to slip and fall on the now wet deck. The air is cold and sends chills through my body as Beau walks through the French door leading to my suite. Gently, he sets me down on the edge of the bed, but I don't let go. I pull him down on top of me as I lie back on the bedspread.

I kiss his lips with such intensity that it steals my breath, not that I could really breathe right now anyway. Beau's weight deliciously presses down on my entire body as his hands begin to explore me once again. When he reaches my center, he finds that I'm still wet with want.

"God, you're so wet," he whispers against my lips.

"You. You do this to me," I reply as his lips caress mine and my legs tighten around his hips.

"Are you sure?" he asks, his eyes searching my own.

"More than I've ever been sure about anything in my life," I tell him honestly.

And now we both step over the line–together. So far over that line that I can't even see it anymore.

"I need to go get protection," he says as he runs his hands up my sides and caresses my chest.

"I don't want you to leave. I'm clean, I promise. And I'm on birth control," I confess.

"I'm clean, too. I swear. I get tested every six months and I was tested before this season started."

"Then make love to me without it," I whisper as his eyes widen.

"Yes, m'am," he answers as he slides us both up the bed. He lays me out and takes in my wet, naked body. I don't feel the cold air anymore. No, it's replaced by the raging inferno of desire that can only be associated with Beau Tanner.

With gentle precision, Beau lines up his pulsating erection at my entrance. Our eyes are locked as he slowly starts to push forward.

"Mine," he whispers the moment he's completely seated inside of me. From root to tip, he fills me so wholly and perfectly. My mind blanks from the intense sensations of our intimate connection. We continue to stare deeply into each other's eyes as we become one for the first time.

After several silent moments, which allow me to adjust to the size of him, a fine sheen of sweat breaks out over his brow. "I have to move, baby," he confesses as his face tightens.

"Then move, Beau," I direct.

He starts out slow and easy as my insides loosen up to accommodate him. His lips are tender and soft as he slowly slides in and out of me. I can see the moment that his fragile control starts to slip. His face becomes tighter and his breathing more labored. As if completely on its own, his body starts to pick up the pace. He takes me for the ride of my life as our bodies slap and grind towards a shared release. I keep my legs firmly locked around his narrow hips as he slams his body into me with enough force to rattle the bedframe.

The sound of our bodies connecting and our moans of pleasure are the only sounds in the room. Beau pushes me higher and higher towards orgasm. His hands grip and slide along my skin as if he can't get enough of my body, pushing me to the point of no return. When I can't hang on any longer, I let myself slide over the edge of oblivion. Beau joins me moments later, our bodies as one while our mutual releases throw us orbiting into another world. A world where only we exist. Us. Together.

When we both start to gain control of our breathing, Beau slides his body from within mine. He curls up against me, pulling me tightly so that not even air can slip between our connected bodies. His warmth wraps around me, heating me better than the blanket we lie on ever could.

"I care for you, Layne. More than I've ever cared for anyone before," Beau whispers into the dark. The meaning is evident, but doesn't send me into the panic attack that I expected to come with that sort of revelation. Maybe because I care for him more than I ever have before too.

So when I reply, the words are honest and easy. "Me, too."

We lie in silence for several minutes as the implications hang over us. There's no going back. Hell, I wouldn't even if I could.

"Tell me about the song. I couldn't find it online when I looked it up."

"I wrote it," he answers, confirming what I deep down probably already knew.

"It's a beautiful song. I really like it."

"It's for you. I wrote it for you."

The air is expelled from my lungs as I feel his arms strengthen around me like he's afraid I'm going to bolt. But what he doesn't know is that I won't. I can't. Even as the fear of being hurt, being betrayed, niggles in the back of my mind, I force it back and won't let it take root. Beau isn't Colton.

"Thank you. It's the greatest gift anyone has ever given me, except for Eli," I say.

"We've got a big decision to make, Layne. Tonight was so much more than sex. At least it was for me," he says.

"It was for me, too."

"Good. We have a choice to make about the show. We can go on, pretending this night didn't happen and finish out the last two weeks. Or we go to the network and pull out."

I've already thought about this choice. We can go about our lives and finish out the show, but then I have to live with the fact that I broke the contract and didn't tell anyone. Can I live with that decision? Or we tell the network and risk lawsuits. It's not an easy decision, but a necessary one.

Whatever we decide, we will do it together. Because when it's all said and done, we both made the decision to sleep together. We both broke the agreement within the documents we signed. We both destroyed our futures on *Rising Star*.

And now we have to deal with the consequences.

Chapter Twenty

Note to self: Even when your world shatters around you, smile.

I knock on the door and wait for the answer. I'm practically shaking in my black dress slacks and stylish pink top. I should have worn flats for this moment, but there's something about a great pair of heels that seems to raise your confidence. So, heels it is.

"Come in," I hear from the other side of the door.

I step through the entryway and come face to face with the six faces I met with several weeks ago. Could it really have been that long since I was advised to flirt with Beau? So much has happened since that day.

"Thank you for seeing me," I say as confidently as I can muster as I step forward and sit in the swivel office chair facing the room.

"I have to admit, your request for this meeting was a bit of a surprise and has piqued our interest," Jackson Zimmerman says from his post at the head of the table.

"The reason I'm here is simple. I have broken the contract in which I signed before coming on this show."

"Which part of the contract did you break?" he asks with his eyebrows arched, his chin casually resting on his right fist as if he has not a care in the world.

"The part about not engaging in a sexual relationship with a show coach," I tell him confidently, not breaking eye contact.

That makes him sit up straighter. "I see. And I take it you broke the agreement with Beau Tanner?"

"Yes, sir."

"I see. You are aware that the document you signed states that you can be sued within full reach of this network and the record label for breach of contract, correct?"

"Sir, I am aware of that clause. It wasn't my intention to deceive the network or the label, but I couldn't live with myself if I didn't come clean."

"Your honesty is appreciated, Miss Carter. I'm afraid that we're going to have to consult with Legal and discuss the terms of the agreement."

"I understand, sir. Thank you for your time," I say as I stand up.

"We'll be in touch shortly, Miss Carter."

"Of course, sir." As I step towards the door, I hesitate and turn back to the room. "May I ask as to what will happen to Beau, sir?"

"Well, I can't say exactly without speaking with Legal, but I imagine he'll be let go from the show. How it will be handled is yet to be seen," he answers.

"Okay. Thank you for your time," I say as I slip out the door.

It's done. I've told the network and ultimately sealed my fate. As I walk down the long empty hallway, I head straight for the door leading to the street. I walk out that door for probably the last time. Away from the studio and the show. Headed home with my head held high.

And with that, my time on *Rising Star* has come to an end.

*****

"I knew your relationship would eventually come out," I hear from behind me as I wait for the elevator.

I do everything I can to ignore the woman standing behind me. If I can just get on this elevator and out of this hotel, I'll never have to see her again. I pull my luggage onto the elevator and pray that the door closes before she can get on. No luck.

"What, nothing to say?"

"Nothing I care to say to you," I reply as we start our descent.

"I'd been telling them for weeks that you were screwing him. It's the only reason you made it past the first round. It's the only way you ever would have beat me," she snipes.

"You know what, Shawna? I did beat you. Fair and square. I didn't have a relationship with Beau until Saturday night. That first showdown on the show? I won. Not you. And do you want to know why? Because I was better than you. Period. And while I might not be on this show any longer, just remember that the only reason you still are is because someone else picked you up *AFTER* you were let go. So, while you may still win this whole thing, remember that at one time, you actually came in last." And with that, I exit the opening elevator doors and step out with my head held high.

The van is waiting to take me to the studio. I have a meeting with the network executives before I head to the airport to catch my flight home. Beau called me last night and told me that they were meeting and we'd know our fate today. Though, deep down, I already know it's all over.

We talked for hours last night about the what-if's and the what-could-have-been's. He wouldn't let me sulk as the reality of our situation weighed down on me. I don't have anything to my name so if the network decides to sue me for breach of contract, I'm up a creek without a paddle.

Note to self: Stock up on paddles. Looks like I'm going to need them.

We never discussed a future, though. While we may have thought to ourselves about what will happen to us after the show, neither of us voiced those concerns. Instead, we focused on making each other laugh and getting to know each other further. I've spent weeks in the presence of this man and I feel like I'm getting to know the real him–not the one he shows to the prying eyes of the world. The real Beau who loves Fruity Pebbles cereal and riding his Harley Davidson whenever he can.

The van pulls up in front of the studio and I head inside. Gabby is waiting for me and offers me a tight smile. I return her greeting with a hello, but for the most part, follow quietly behind her as she leads me back down the long, familiar hallway towards the conference room. She knocks and waits for the cue to open the door.

When I step inside, I see several more gentlemen around the table. They are dressed impeccably in designer suits and groomed to perfection. Mr. Zimmerman is seated at the head of the table with his five minions around him. The one face that I'm surprised to see belongs to the man I've gotten myself into this mess with. I lock eyes with Beau for the first time since we returned Sunday afternoon. Just the sight of him releases wild little flutters in my stomach.

"Miss Carter, will you please have a seat?" Mr. Zimmerman directs. I nod at him before taking the vacant seat next to Beau.

"Layne, Beau, we're here today to discuss the breach of contract that you've both admitted to. I've brought in Roland to make sure that everything is discussed and decided upon collectively so that no lawsuits can be made in the future by any party."

I take a deep breath before he continues. "Last evening, we met and were prepared to hold you both accountable to the terms of the contractual breach. Layne, for you those terms would be to terminate your participation of the show, along with a substantial financial lawsuit." I gulp hard at the words and their implications. Any lawsuit would be substantial to my family and me.

"You are also prohibited to ever participate on any show on this network or any other network. Additionally, you are not allowed to sell your story for profit in any way."

Mr. Zimmerman looks over at Beau. "Beau, your contract is similar to that signed by Miss Carter. Your participation of this network and that of any other network will include award shows and other appearances for a period of three years. You understand those terms, correct?"

Beau nods his head without so much as a word. Can they do that? Can they forbid him for performing or attending award shows that are to be televised on the network? Apparently, they can.

"But, here's the dilemma. America loves you. Last night, word got out that you were both being released from the show and the outpour is overwhelming. They want more Layne and Beau."

Shock must be evident on my face. "It's true," the woman next to Mr. Zimmerman states. "Social media is buzzing. They started petitions and are flooding the network with calls, emails, and contacts through social media outlets. Hell, you even have a trending hashtag," she adds with a chuckle.

"So, you see the dilemma we face? We can't exactly let you go for fear that we'll be crucified by the viewers who are so adamant in their support of you."

I blink several times as I try to absorb his words and their meaning. I feel a warm hand on my leg and reach down and link my fingers through his. I feel stronger suddenly knowing that I'm not alone at this table; that no matter what the outcome of this meeting, I have his support and his affection.

And in return, he has my love. I can deny it until I'm blue in the face, but the fact still remains that I'm in love with him. I knew it Saturday night as we made love. I knew it the next morning while we ate breakfast wrapped only in plush robes on the deck of the hotel room. And I sure as hell knew it when I sat down at this very table yesterday and confessed my sins to the people that hold all of the cards.

The only thing left now is to tell Beau. Because no matter the outcome of this meeting–no matter the fines, lawsuits, and rules they throw at me–my love for him will still be there, bright and shining like the North Star; pulling me in and gripping my soul like the music notes I sing. Guiding me home.

"After an early meeting today to renegotiate our deal, we've come up with terms that we all hope you'll find more than sufficient. Layne, you'll still be removed from the show as a contestant. You will not participate in the final two weeks of shows and have no chance at winning the record contract or the prize money."

I nod my head in acknowledgement knowing that that was always the least of my worries. "You are forbidden to participate in any other shows on any other network for a period of ten years. You are also forbidden from selling your story for any financial gain for a period of ten years. We will *not* hold you financially responsible to the dollar amount listed on your contract with the understanding that you agree to all of the new terms."

I can do that, right?

"Beau, you are also removed from the remainder of this season and we'll find a replacement coach to finish out the final two weeks of the show. However, we will not hold your position on the show over your head. We want you. The fans of the show want you. You will be able to return as a coach next season. You are forbidden from performing or profiting from any other network show with the exception of pre-approved award shows," he says to Beau. I feel Beau's hand tighten around mine.

"Now, here's the catalyst. The *other* term to our deal. You both will participate in the final show, performing a duet together that the network chooses. You will also agree to participate in a future network special that is still in the works. It will detail your relationship through the show *Rising Star*, as well as continue to follow you up until the point of the airing and producing of the special. This would happen sooner, rather than later. The network also has the right to add any sequential specials for a period of three years. Think Nick and Jessica, Tori and Dean. You know, a reality show," he adds with a smile.

"If there should ever be a wedding or major life event within the next five years, the network has first rights to a special. These are the terms. Take them or leave them. If you leave them, know that the original terms of the contract will be enforced."

"What do you mean by a special?" Beau asks.

"A special program with a minimum of one hour in duration. Not a full-fledged show, but more of a single documentary to allow the viewers a glimpse of your lives together. You two are ratings gold. America loves you and we want to keep that love alive."

"Can I have a few minutes to speak with Layne?" Beau asks from his seat next to me.

"Sure. You can step into the hallway and come back when you are finished."

I follow Beau into the hallway and am instantly engulfed in a warm, comforting hug. "I'm not worried about the terms of my contract, I'm worried about yours. I can't imagine you have the finances to cover the dollar amount attached to it, right?" he asks as he keeps his hold on me.

"Yeah, I don't exactly have that kind of disposable cash."

"I would cover it for ya. I would do anything to make this go away for ya," he replies. But I could never let him do that, and I think he knows it.

"I can't let you to do that, Beau. I'm just as responsible for this mess as you."

"Then, let's talk about the new contract. I don't give a shit about the show. I will walk away from it right now if I have to. The money means nothing to me. I don't give a shit about appearances and show performances. I'll be just fine without all that extra crap.

The new contract has some perks, but I don't exactly like the idea of those specials."

"It's one special with the possibility of more if we should ever, you know, get married or something," I reply, dropping my eyes as the faint blush creeps up my neck. We haven't even talked about a future and here we were discussing the possibility of a televised wedding. Kill me now.

"Hey," he says as he raises my chin up so that our eyes are locked. "I feel like the network has us by the balls here. Though I don't like the idea of the network turnin' us into a circus show, it doesn't seem so bad if you're there with me."

"I kind of agree," I smile. "But Eli. I have to protect him. I won't subject him to the show."

"I agree. I'll make sure that's included in the terms."

"So, we're going to do this?"

"Yeah, we're gonna do this. Together."

And with that, he places a tender kiss on my lips as if sealing our fate. Before we can let the kiss get too carried away, Beau pulls back. "We should head back in there," he says with a smile.

"Yes," I confirm and link my fingers through his.

"Let's get this over with then," he adds as he leads me back through the door.

Chapter Twenty-One

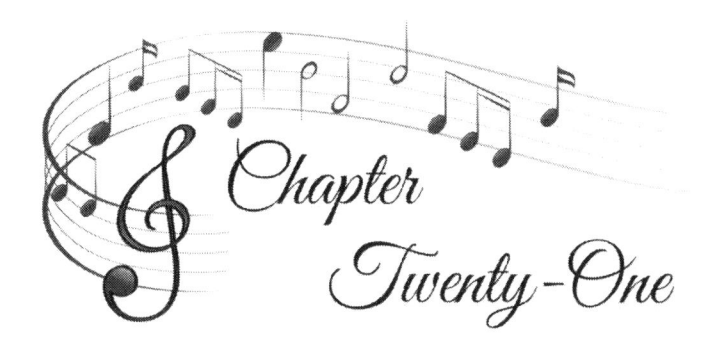

Note to self: Sometimes, out of the fire births a phoenix. Beautiful. Freeing. And that's when your life takes flight.

"And now, returning for the first time to *Rising Star* since they were ousted a little over a week ago, performing a brand new song, I give to you Beau Tanner and Layne Carter," Becker says as the crowd stands on their feet.

Beau is already out on stage looking smashing in his standard black boots, tight Wranglers, delicious black t-shirt that grips his muscular arms, and Stetson hat. The music starts as I watch from stage right.

"From that first moment, I knew there was somethin'

Somethin' bout you that speaks to me so true.

Every moment with you makes me alive,

Every beat of my heart for only you.

Your skin against my skin, your lips against my lips,

Your touch is my undoin', I crave you underneath my fingertips.

Stay with me tonight, Stay with me tomorrow.

Stay with me forever, until the end of time.

Just stay with me

Stay with me."

I walk out onto the stage I haven't sung on in a day shy of two weeks. Familiarity washes over me as I take in the stage and the lights.

"I've been hurt so many times before,

And I'm afraid to move too fast.

Letting go is never easy,

But when I'm with you I forget the past.

You make the fear disappear and my smile feel brand new,

I want your arms wrapped around me, a touch from only you.

Stay with me tonight, Stay with me tomorrow.

Stay with me forever, until the end of time.

Just stay with me

Stay with me."

For only the second time, Beau and I perform together as a duet. But this time, there's no hesitation. There's no hiding. There's only him and me on the stage singing the sweet words he wrote for us. Those music notes, imbedded so deeply into my heart, into my soul. A place that only Beau Tanner can touch.

"It's you and me against the world,

But it doesn't matter as long as you stay.

Right by my side, just stay beside me.

Stay with me.

Yeah, stay with me."

Without being scripted, Beau moves his microphone and touches his lips to mine. The screaming crowd suddenly doesn't exist as I revel in the feel of this man's lips against my own.

"I love you," I whisper for the first time.

"I love you, too, babe," he whispers back with a smile that could light up a stadium. And then he deepens the kiss, threading his fingers through my hair and holding on for dear life.

"Layne, Beau, remember this is a family show," Becker chastises with a laugh. "Can I ask how it's been since you both left the show?"

"It has been perfect, Becker," Beau says with a smile, his hand firmly around mine.

"So I take it you two are together now?" he asks.

"I've always been a private guy, Becker, and I'm going to continue to do so for those I love. Just know that you haven't seen the last of Beau and Layne. Together."

The smile I offer him practically splits my face in half. Together. I arrived in Los Angeles months ago, not knowing what to expect. Even then, I couldn't imagine that this road would take me to where I am now.

No, I may not have won the record contract from *Rising Star*. I may not have the prize money that would help set Eli and I up for a better life. But I think what I'm walking away with is so much better. I discovered a better self on this journey. I've learned about letting go of the past in order to move forward. And I've learned to put my faith and trust into another man, which is something I wasn't sure I would ever be able to do again.

Hand in hand, I walk away with Beau.

The man I love.

Epilogue

3 months later

Note to self: I will never look at a music video the same. Ever.

I feel like I've held the same pose, done the same things over and over and over again. And that's probably because I have. We arrived at the studio at six a.m. and are finishing up the last scene as the sky is cast into a beautiful dusk of yellow and orange. We've recorded the ending at least six times already, each time from a slightly different angle to capture the setting sun. Who knew making a music video was so damn draining?

I follow Beau towards the Mercedes SUV parked in the small lot behind the studio. He's practically dragging me along in my black cowboy boots, my knees throbbing and my legs weak. The man that means more than any other–Eli excluded–opens the passenger door and waits until I slide into our vehicle. As soon as I'm securely in the seat, he leans through the open door and places another kiss on my lips. You'd think that it would get old, but it doesn't. His desire to kiss me mirrors my desire to let him. I can't imagine a day where kissing him wouldn't hold the same appeal. His lips are my drug.

The backdoor opens and the reminder of what is happening slides into the backseat. The large black camera is poised directly at us, catching every moment of our shared kiss for the world to soon see.

It has been three months since the conclusion of *Rising Star*. Beau and I stayed to watch as the new champion was crowned. When they announced Ben Atwood as the winner, I was elated for my friend. He was hesitant to hug me at first, I'm pretty sure that had something to do with the fact that Beau growled at him when he approached and refused to let go of my hand. But I still hugged my former teammate and congratulated him on his victory. Beau even shook his hand and offered congratulations. When Ben returned his attention to me, he placed a gentle kiss on my cheek, turned back to Beau, and said, "Take care of her." I held my breath as Beau extended his hand again and shook, silently confirming his promise to do just that.

After the show, I went back home to Chicago. The outpour I received when returning to my old life was amazing. Tiffany was there to put an instant smile on my face while I returned to my old job at Chaser's. Evenings were spent on the phone with Beau. Even though the show didn't monopolize his time, his commitment to his own record label and tour did. He finished out the last few weeks of his tour before flying to Chicago and knocking on my door.

Beau stayed in Chicago for a month while we determined where our future led. Ultimately, it was Eli who made the decision for us the day he came home from preschool and told us he wanted to move with Beau. How the little guy even knew we were discussing that very possibility still chokes me up. My son is enamored with the handsome cowboy, following him everywhere he goes. It's a sight I never thought I'd see, but am so eternally grateful that it happened.

And Beau is just as caught up in Eli. My son is front and center in every decision he makes from where he's taking me to dinner to where we're going afterwards. It's as if Eli is permanently attached to Beau's hip; the father figure my son has never had.

It took me only a few weeks to get all of my affairs in order and plan the move. Mom had decided to stay in Chicago, but for how long is still unknown. Mom and Lee have been dating since she returned home from her visit to LA. We've enjoyed several dinners all together: Mom, Lee, Beau, Eli, and me. Lee loves to engage Beau in debates over the merit of new country vs. classic country. One big happy family.

The day we finished packing up the U-Haul will forever be one of the hardest days of my life. Tears streamed unchecked down my face as I clung tightly to the woman who has loved and supported me my entire life. She's more than just my mother; she's my best friend, and I miss her every day.

Nashville is so completely different than Chicago. While still a fast-paced city, it has a slightly laid back feel to it. Plus, there are cowboy hats and boots everywhere you turn, at least in the part of the city that we now live in. Eli took to the new style like a fish to water. He begged Beau to find him his own cowboy boots and a hat, which of course, Beau readily obliged. Even though he may wear his own small cowboy hat in public, his favorite hat to wear at home is Beau's ol' worn black one. Even if it's still on his head, Beau will take it off and drop it down on my son's head. He swims in it, but the picture is so adorable, you can't help but smile every time you see it.

Today we're leaving the downtown music studio where Beau records his albums. The first video for his new single was filmed today at different locations within the studio. The entire experience was an eye-opener, to say the least.

As Beau slides into the driver's seat of our SUV, another black vehicle pulls up behind us. Now we can go. We make our way through the streets of Nashville, winding our way towards the home we now share. It's bigger than any house I've ever seen. Together over the past month, we've been slowly making the house our home. Beau gave me free reign to make any changes that I wanted. The house was beautifully, professionally decorated so the only changes I made were to a guest room, which is now Eli's room, and the family room, which is warm and inviting with toys strewn everywhere.

The buzz surrounding our time on the show still hasn't died down completely, and now it's even worse with all the hype of the special program the network is planning. Beau and I continue to be extremely private, and that makes the invasion that much more difficult to deal with. Every time someone asks about our relationship, we always answer with a polite "no comment." The only problem with that statement is that it neither denies nor confirms the rumors hemorrhaging from the media, giving the viewers and readers the opportunity to draw their own conclusion. And that's fine. Our story will be told soon enough.

One more night in the presence of the film crew before we can return to our normal lives. Well, as normal as can be expected when your significant other is a musical genius. Beau's fourth album is produced and getting ready for distribution. Most of it was planned in what little down time he was allotted while we were on the show, but he added one song to the track list before he would approve the final edition.

"Ready?" Beau asks, snapping me out of my thoughts.

"Of course," I reply as we both slide out of the vehicle.

Hand in hand, we walk up the steps leading towards our front door. We've slightly altered our routine to accommodate the camera crew that is shadowing us. It's more difficult for them to make their way out of the vehicle in the garage and get through the interior door that leads to the mudroom. Plus, something about lighting, yada, yada, yada.

Laughter floats from the family room that instantly warms my heart. I'll never tire of hearing my son's sweet voice or his happy laughter. And lately, since Beau has entered our lives, I hear that sweet sound nonstop.

"We're home," I holler from the front entry.

I hear his little feet on the hardwood floor as he runs to greet us.

"Mommy!" Eli yells, followed closely behind by his newest friend, a six-month-old rescue pup named Waylon. I never imagined having a dog, but all it took was Eli mentioning it one time, and suddenly Beau is buying dog treats and chew toys.

"Hi, sweetheart," I tell my son as he plasters a big hug around my neck. "Were you a good boy for Grandma?" I ask, looking over his shoulder for confirmation.

"Yep!" he exclaims as he shimmies down my lap and launches himself at Beau.

"Hey, buddy."

"Guess what, Beau. Grandma and Lee are going to move here with us!"

I look up at my mom who isn't even trying to hide her smile. Beau and I had invited her to stay a week ago when we planned their visit to Nashville, but I didn't push the issue. She had promised to think about relocating here and that was good enough for me.

"Really?" I ask as tears fill my eyes.

"Yeah, really. I know you really only invited me temporarily, but I talked with Lee and we both thought we'd like the change," she starts.

"Are you kidding me? Of course, you're both welcome," I say as I pull her into a fierce hug. Just the thought of having my mom close again brings me much joy and happiness.

"Well, Beau offered us the guest house out back, so we won't be moving in here with you. I'll still be close enough to help with Eli while you're at the studio and stuff," she adds with a smile.

The studio. Our studio. There's a small studio behind the house that Beau had built when he purchased this place. It's the perfect location to record music or write songs. That's what I've been doing these past few weeks. I've been writing music. It's something I've never tried nor ever realized I'd wanted to try. When we settled in, Beau took me out back and showed me his private little oasis. He started working with me further on playing the guitar, just a few basic notes, but suddenly, words started to flow. Beau started to write the more I started to say. By the end of a very late night, we had written a song. Together.

While Eli attends his new school, I spend my time in the studio. I've written several songs or even more snippets of lyrics or pieces of melodies. I'm not sure if they're any good, but Beau seems to get excited with each piece of music I show him.

Over dinner, we discuss plans to move Mom and Lee to Nashville. Beau is a planner and executer so when he gets an idea in his head, he's going to sit down and figure it out until it's set in stone and right. He can't seem to move on until the problem is solved or the dilemma taken care of. Which works well for us because I'm a little more laid back.

The camera crew follows us around like Waylon, trailing and circling at our feet everywhere we go. To the store. To the park. To the studio. We've spent hours in the studio writing and playing around, and I'm starting to question the network's vision on this so-called reality show. Because in reality, we're boring as hell.

That night, we finally fall into the one place the cameras aren't allowed to go: our bedroom. It's our escape away from the demands, the noises, and the realities of life. Here, we're just Beau and Layne, and we're usually naked.

"Here ya are," Beau says from the doorway of my little sitting area that I use for reading.

"Here I am," I say with a small smile. As Beau steps closer, I shut my book and set it down on the small table sitting right next to his favorite guitar.

"I was thinkin', we should fire up the jets tonight," he says as he squats down in front of me. I run my hands through his dark hair, savoring the rare moment of Beau without a hat on.

"Fill it up," I tell him, referring to our large jetted garden tub in the master bathroom. Every time we're in it, I'm reminded of the hot tub in Denver, and especially what followed.

Once we're both inside, me nestled comfortably within his strong legs, I finally start to shake off the stress of the day. Beau runs his rough hands along the outside of my arms, up to my shoulders, and then down my back. Everything seems to float away as I let the soothing pressure of his hands lull my mind into nothingness.

"So what did ya think of your first music video?" he asks, that deep, twangy southern drawl tickling the shell of my ear.

"It was exhausting."

Beau's soft chuckle fills our bathroom. "That they are, darlin'. Are ya ready for the world to see it? Not only is it your big video debut, but the way we're ending it is like openin' the proverbial door and allowin' the world to step inside our private lives."

"They're already here. Even if we weren't doing this special, they'd be there because of your career."

"And yours…"

"Well, I think I have to achieve a career in order to endorse one," I tell him.

"Don't sell yourself short. You've already sold two songs in the last few weeks. Keep that shit up and you'll be the bread winner in this household and not me." I know that isn't even remotely possible, but I appreciate him trying to boost my ego a bit.

He's correct, though. I have sold two songs in the last couple of weeks. One is being pitched to Little Big Town and the other to Chris Young, respectfully, by their labels. Who would have guessed I'd be writing music that was primarily country? Definitely not me. I still don't even know who half of the stars I meet on the street are. Beau has to point them out to me every dang time. It's embarrassing, actually. I live in freaking Nashville, could be standing next to George Strait, and I probably wouldn't realize it.

Note to self: See if they have a Country Legends for Dummies book.

"Only two more days," Beau whispers as he softly caresses my back.

"Only two more days, but then the show will air in a month or so and our quiet will turn right back to crazy."

"Sweetheart, our life is always crazy. The only quiet I get is when I'm in here with you."

"In the bathtub?" I sass.

"Not exactly what I meant," he chuckles. "When I'm behind these closed doors where no one is permitted, I'm finally allowed to breathe. The stress of the business, making music, the demands, cameras and fans, it all fades away. I can finally be me when I'm with you." His statement is punctuated with his lips caressing my shoulder.

An uncontrollable shiver tears through my body. My skin is flush from the water, but starts to burn under each graze of those long fingers. His hands glide smoothly over my wet body, stroking and seducing me with each touch.

Suddenly, Beau stands, water cascading over his perfect body. His erection is tall and proud, silently begging for a little attention. My fingers twitch to give it all the care it needs.

Beau doesn't speak as he steps out, wraps a towel around his waist and releases the drain. With water dripping from his arms, he reaches down and picks me up from the tub. Not even bothering to grab a second towel, he cradles my wet body in his arms and heads towards our bedroom.

"Where are we going?"

"I'm takin' the woman I love to bed."

*****

Two Months Later

Holy crap, I'm about to see myself on television. Again. The network special airs tonight–*Beau & Layne: In Love*. After four days of following us around at home like a new puppy, as well as covering the first stop on Beau's tour that kicked off a little over a month ago, I was glad to see three cameramen, one producer, and four production assistants take off at the end of filming. It was exhausting and invasive.

Eli will make minimal appearances in the special that airs tonight. Before I could even voice my motherly overture about him not being affected by filming and keeping his air time to a bare minimum, Beau had already stepped in and laid down the law. There's something about that cowboy when he gets all bossy and uses that low, no-nonsense, this-is-how-it's-gonna-be voice. That voice does crazy things to my lady parts. Especially when he takes an authoritative stance regarding Eli.

Beau has never overstepped when it comes to Eli. In fact, it's quite the opposite. I find myself easily sharing the parenting responsibilities with him, allowing him to discipline or teach him important life skills like cooking eggs and picking up your socks off the bathroom floor. Sharing the parenting load comes easy when I'm sharing it with Beau. He's going to make an amazing father. Someday.

"Mommy! There you are!" Eli shouts over the sound of the television. We're sitting all together on the worn leather couch that Beau refuses to get rid of for sentimental reasons. This couch was the first thing he purchased when he moved to Nashville from Oklahoma in search of a musical career. Even though the thing is old and well-worn, it's more comfortable than any piece of furniture I've ever owned so I'm in no hurry to get rid of it. I just like to get him all riled up by threatening to toss it in the trash. *Shhhhh.*

I turn my attention to the massive television centered on the wall in the rustic family room at the rear of the house. Sure enough, there I am with Beau as the intro to our special plays out. You can't hear words over the love song the network purchased the rights to use–the song I'm now very familiar with.

Eventually, the brief intro ends with that full-on, steamy kiss from our final episode. Becker stands before the camera, positioned in the center of the *Rising Star* stage. "Good evening, ladies and gentlemen. I'm Becker James, host of *Rising Star*. Over the next hour, we're going to have a special look at the relationship of Beau Tanner and Layne Carter. As you may recall, Beau and Layne took social media by storm towards the end of last season's show. Let's take a look back at how it all started."

Highlights of the show fill the screen. From my audition for the judges and first glimpse of Beau to the accusations by contestants over our speculated relationship. It's all there in high definition color. The producers focused on the smoldering looks and extra-long glances when we thought the cameras weren't rolling. But, as always, the cameras caught everything!

Eventually, we get a glimpse at Beau and Layne now. The first shot is of us walking hand-in-hand out the front door of the home we share, each of us carrying a travel mug of coffee. The first thing I notice is the extra poundage I apparently have put on in the ass and hips region. I guess when they say the camera adds ten pounds, they aren't shitting...

Note to self: Lay off the midnight snack-sized Snickers.

On the couch next to me, Beau picks up Eli and sets him on his lap. Eli sits transfixed on the television screen, watching our every move with a subtle little smile. Beau takes his free hand and links his fingers with mine. The gesture is soothing and reassuring.

"You look hot in those pants," he whispers.

"I look like I've eaten nothing but Oreos since I left the show."

"You speak nonsense, woman. You're hotter than a crawfish boil on the Fourth of July."

I stare at the man I love for several seconds before bursting into fits of laughter. "Did you just speak Southernese to me? Is it considered a compliment in Oklahoma to compare me to crawfish?"

"Naw, I just wanted to make ya laugh. What I wanted to say wasn't exactly appropriate for small ears." Beau's eyes turn to smoldering ash right before my very eyes. He goes from casual to turned-on in point two seconds flat. The sudden desire to cross my legs is strong, but I know it's futile against the ache that only Beau can create.

Beau seems to read me like a book and leans over to kiss my shoulder. The soft caress of his lips against my skin promises things to come with each swipe of those very talented lips. "Behave, you."

The sound of singing draws my attention back to the television. Over the next thirty minutes, we watch with America as our lives are broadcast for the world to see. My time in the little studio behind the house, Beau picking Eli up from preschool, a grocery store run, and, of course, backstage access from his show at the Ryman Auditorium–the show that kicked off his latest tour. The producers do a great job at showing how hectic, yet incredibly normal our lives are. There's no fighting. No drama. No unnecessary stage acting to boost ratings or create more hype. Just Beau and me and what works for us.

At the very end of the program, Becker thanks us for participating in the network's special. *As if we had a choice...*

"I leave you tonight with the exclusive first look at Beau Tanner's new video for "Stay With Me," off his forthcoming album, *Cross The Line,* releasing later this year. Beau and Layne sang this song on their very last episode together. I hope you enjoy."

The familiar opening melody to the song I sang on stage with Beau in Denver–the one he wrote for me–starts to play. While I was a major part of the process of making this music video, I have yet to see the finished product. Beau viewed it a week ago, but I wouldn't let him give me the details. I opted to be surprised tonight with the rest of America.

The beginning shows Beau walking into the recording studio, down the long hall with photos of famous smiling faces hanging from the walls, and into the control room. He looks hot in a pair of tight Wranglers, a western style black button-up shirt, worn boots, and his trademark Stetson cowboy hat. I understand instantly that the video is depicting the process of making a video. Quickly, Beau is standing in the middle of the recording studio singing into the mic.

His voice is low and seductive as he sings the opening lines of our song. The video bounces between Beau standing in the recording booth and master producer, JP Sanders, in the control room. JP is the cream of the crop when it comes to record producers, and Beau was extremely excited to secure him for his new album.

When Beau gets to the refrain, he sings strongly and confidently into the mic. It's a euphoric experience watching him sing, even if it's on screen. He holds so much passion for what he does that it's truly hypnotizing to witness.

Suddenly, Beau reaches the end of the refrain and pulls back from the mic. I step slowly into the shot, moving to a second microphone that wasn't visible until this moment. The producer was going for a casual, yet chic look for the video so I'm wearing a black smock-style top that hangs off my right shoulder, a jean skirt that borders on too short, and pair of black cowboy boots. Yep. Beau convinced me to buy my first pair of boots, swearing that they're more comfortable than anything I've ever worn. And after you get past the initial "breaking in" period, I concede that they are pretty dang comfy.

The hairs on my arms stand on end when I start to sing. Even though the video took two days and was shot from so many different angles that it left my head spinning, the finished product is amazing. It really doesn't look as if it's a compilation of dozens of cut and pasted takes. It looks like one fluid take from start to finish.

When I finish the second refrain, it cuts to Beau and I sitting in the control room, smiling and cutting up with JP. We both bob our head to whatever it is he's playing from the board. Looking relaxed, Beau and I smile at each other between cuts of Beau playing the guitar in the studio.

Finally, Beau and I step up to our microphone. Instead of using two mics, we're shown sharing a singular microphone. We each hold the mic stand, his hand wrapped protectively around mine. This is the first real indication that whatever started at the end of the reality show has continued. Oh, sure there has been speculation. Paparazzi have stalked us religiously since our time on the show ended, but we made sure to never give them what they really wanted. What they received instead was photos of us walking together or riding in the car. Touching or anything intimate was rarely displayed for the world to see, which is what led to the most recent rumors–break-up gossip.

Together, we sing the remainder of the song. It's about love and a future. About asking the other to spend the rest of their life together. It speaks of hope and commitment. Everything Beau and I stand for, but have never allowed everyone else to see.

Until now.

As the song winds down, the video cuts to the production room where you see hands moving slides on a soundboard, each one having such a key part in the audio quality coming from the adjacent room. Reaching the end of the song, JP moves all of the slides downward, fading all of the elements of the music.

And there we are. Exiting the studio and heading out to the street. Beau isn't alone like he was when he entered the studio. This time, his hand is wrapped firmly around mine as I walk beside him. Stepping onto the sidewalk outside, the glass door closes, separating us from the camera that was following us.

But the camera doesn't cut. Instead it captures the moment that the world has been waiting for. Beau dips me in the middle of the sidewalk, in full view of the cameras recording our every movement. When he kisses me, it's fierce. Passionate. Absolute.

When he brings my left hand up to his face, Beau essentially flashes the camera the big piece of juicy story they've been waiting for. What America has been waiting for.

Confirmation.

Adorning my left ring finger is a glimpse of the breathtaking diamond and sapphire engagement ring Beau and Eli presented to me the night before we started making this video. This was never part of the original plan, but when JP told us of his vision on that first day of filming, we went with it. Knowing that the network was striving for that big bang factor, I'd say they definitely got their money's worth.

The video fades to black.

I finally pull my eyes away from the television and glance at my fiancé. His soft eyes match his smile as he gazes at me with more love than I ever expected to receive in this life. The video may be over, but our lives have only just begun. I have no idea where we're headed, but as long as we're together, we'll weather any storm.

He is the music notes that complete my life and make my heart sing.

My song begins and ends with him.

~ THE END ~

If you originally chose The Dangerous Door, you can go back and read The Safe Door here.

Also by Lacey Black

Rivers Edge series

Trust Me, Rivers Edge book 1 (Maddox and Avery) – FREE at all retailers http://amzn.com/B00MV4DHAS

~ *#1 Bestseller in Contemporary Romance & #3 in overall free e-books on Amazon*

~ *#2 Bestseller in overall free e-books on iBooks*

Fight Me, Rivers Edge book 2 (Jake and Erin) http://amzn.com/B00P89GD2M

Expect Me, Rivers Edge book 3 (Travis and Josselyn) http://amzn.com/B00S5H69DM

Promise Me: A Novella, Rivers Edge book 3.5 (Jase and Holly) http://amzn.com/B00VC70G0Y

Protect Me, Rivers Edge book 4 (Nate and Lia) http://amzn.com/B00Y9CS3YA

Boss Me, Rivers Edge book 5 (Will and Carmen) http://amzn.com/B015BS3LWE

Trust Us: A Rivers Edge Christmas Novella (Maddox and Avery) http://amzn.com/B01BFMSNPK

~ *This novella was a part of the Christmas Miracles Anthology and will be releasing as an individual e-book soon!*

Bound Together series

Lacey Black

Submerged, book 1 (Blake & Carly)
http://amzn.com/B0190P5EPQ

Coming Soon

Profited, Bound Together series book 2

Acknowledgements

A huge thank you to everyone who had their hand in this release! Sara Eirew for another beautiful cover. Nazarea and the InkSlinger PR team. My amazing editor, Kara Hildebrand. Joanne Thompson for your masterful line edits. Sandra Shipman and Lisa McGuire for beta reading. Holly Collins for reading the pieces of this book as I created it. Brenda Wright for working your formatting genius on a difficult project. Lacey's Ladies for helping spread the word and making me smile. My husband Jason and our two little ones, thank you for your forgiveness on the nights I get lost behind a computer screen. And to all the readers for sticking by me as I discover different styles of romance that speak to me.

This book was a long time in the making. When I first brainstormed, Layne wasn't supposed to sleep with Beau. As I was writing and got to the hotel room scene, she went and did it anyway–completely on her own. She rewrote the entire ending. Then I got to the end and I couldn't stop thinking about it. The book continued to speak to me, and I realized that maybe two endings was okay. So, I went back and wrote the original ending that this book was supposed to have (the Safe Door).

I hope you enjoyed this book and will consider leaving a review when you're finished!

Lacey

About the Author

Lacey Black is a Midwestern girl with a passion for reading, writing, and shopping. She carries her e-reader with her everywhere she goes so she never misses an opportunity to read a few pages. Always looking for a happily ever after, Lacey is passionate about contemporary romance novels and enjoys it further when you mix in a little suspense. She resides in a small town in Illinois with her husband, two children, and a chocolate lab. Lacey loves watching NASCAR races, shooting guns, and should only consume one mixed drink because she's a lightweight.

Email: laceyblackwrites@gmail.com

Facebook: https://www.facebook.com/authorlaceyblack

Twitter: https://twitter.com/AuthLaceyBlack

Blog: https://laceyblack.wordpress.com